W9-BMO-549

JUMP UP AND SAY!

[A Collection of Black Storytelling]

LINDA GOSS
and CLAY GOSS

A TOUCHSTONE BOOK
Published by Simon & Schuster
NEW YORK   LONDON   TORONTO   SYDNEY   TOKYO   SINGAPORE

TOUCHSTONE
Rockefeller Center
1230 Avenue of the Americas
New York, NY 10020

Copyright © 1995 by Linda Goss and Clay Goss
All rights reserved,
including the right of reproduction
in whole or in part in any form.

TOUCHSTONE and colophon are registered trademarks
of Simon & Schuster Inc.

Designed by Irving Perkins Associates, Inc.

Manufactured in the United States of America

1   3   5   7   9   10   8   6   4   2

Library of Congress Cataloging-in-Publication Data
Jump up and say! : a collection of Black storytelling / [edited by] Linda Goss and
Clay Goss.
p.   cm.
"A Touchstone book."
Includes bibliographical references and index.
1. Short stories, American—Afro-American authors.
2. Afro-Americans—Fiction.   I. Goss, Linda.   II. Goss, Clay.
PS647.A35J85   1995
813'.0108896073—dc20   95-22008
CIP
ISBN 0-684-81001-8

I. TITLE

*Grateful acknowledgment is made to the following sources for permission to
reprint material in their control:*

Cover painting by Jacob Lawrence: *Harriet Tubman Series No. 4.* Casein tem-
pera on gessoed hardboard, 12 by 17⅞ inches. "On a hot summer day about
1820, a group of slave children were tumbling in the sandy soil in the state of
Maryland—and among them was one, Harriet Tubman," Dorchester County,
Maryland. © 1991 Hampton University.

(continued at back of book)

Acknowledgments

—◦◦◦—

There is nothing like storytelling to bring folks closer together. Working with Clay, my husband, on this anthology has been quite an experience. After twenty-five years of marriage, we still have a lot to talk about. Storytelling does that to you. We had fun discussing and fussing, sharing and swearing over WHAT was going into the book. We wanted to put in so much more. Perhaps next time. In storytelling you always want to leave your listener wanting to hear more.

Special thanks to Sheila M. Curry, our editor, who is a jewel. And to Carla Glasser, our agent, who is another precious being. And Dan Lane.

Special thanks to Aisha Goss, Rhonda White, Carole Weathers, Mary Carter Smith, David A. Anderson/Sankofa, The National Association of Black Storytellers, Njeri and My Solitude, The Charles Blockson Library at Temple University, Berry & Culp, Willie McNear, Sharon Wellons Bonsu, Joe Bonsu, and their son Kyle Bonsu, Paul Carter Harrison, the kind folks at Upattinas, and Uhuru Goss.

Dedication and Libation

Aláfia! (Yoruba, greeting of peace)

Bop! A-Goong, GOOng!
Bop! A-Goong, GOOng!

A Lú Bembé! A lú Bembé!
We're playing the drums! We're playing the drums!

To the all-being, all-knowing maker and shaper of all things, we give thanks

To the winds, the oceans, the planets, the sun and stars, we give respect.

To our ancestors and elders, and the ones in our families who ignited the fire in our imaginations, our grandfathers, Murphy McNear and Carl Ivey, we give honor.

To our mothers, Willie Louise McNear and Alfreda Jackson, and our children, Aisha, Uhuru, and Jamaal, and to the memory of our fathers, Willie Murphy McNear and Douglass P. Jackson, we give our love.

To the National Association of Black Storytellers, In the Tradition . . . National Festival of Black Storytelling, and the Zeta Phi Beta Sorority, Inc., and the Beta Delta Zeta Chapter, we give praise.

To Aesop, Solomon, Anansi, Scheherazade, Pushkin, Dumas, Harriet Powers, Langston Hughes, Zora Neale Hurston, Jacob Lawrence, Katherine Dunham, Romare Bearden, Augusta Baker, Mary Carter Smith (Mother Griot), Hugh Morgan Hill (Brother Blue), Faith Ringgold, Beverly Buchanan, Carrie Mae Weems, John Biggers, Bessie Harvey, Monita and Ed Love, Louise Bennett (Miss Lou), Paul Keens-Douglas (Tim-Tim), Alex Haley, and unknown bards, gewels, griots, and storytellers, we give praise.

A-Goonnnnnnnnnnnnng, bop! A-Goong, Goong!

Contents

—∞∞∞—

PART I

THE BREAKING DAY HAS WISDOM,
THE FALLING DAY EXPERIENCE: MORAL TALES

PART II

I WILL NEVER BE ANY SERVICE TO ANYONE AS A SLAVE: STORIES ABOUT FREEDOM

PART III

WHEN THE HEART OVERFLOWS, IT COMES OUT THROUGH THE MOUTH: MEMORIES AND STORIES ABOUT FAMILY AND FRIENDS

PART IV

WHAT'S THE 411? YOU GOT IT GOIN' ON: RHYTHM TALK

PART V

IF I'M LYING, I'M FLYING: HUMOROUS TALES

PART VI

As Restless as the Tempestuous Billow on the Boundless Sea: Stories, Songs, and Poems of Protest and Change

PART VII

If You Holler Too Loud, You'll Wake Up the Ghosts: Ghost Tales and Superstitions

PART VIII

NOW THAT TAKES THE CAKE:
SOUL FOOD AND FOOD MEMORIES

Narrative has never been merely entertainment for me. It is, I believe, one of the principal ways in which we absorb knowledge. I hope you will understand, then, why I begin these remarks with the opening phrase of what must be the oldest sentence in the world, and the earliest one we remember from childhood: "Once upon a time . . ."

—TONI MORRISON

Preface

Kric? Krac![1]

Once upon a time
And far across the sea
Some people set some ships a-sail
And came back here with me.

And when they got me here
They sold me to someone
Who would not let me speak my language
So I lost my Native Tongue.

They worked me long and hard
They paid me no money
They said I wasn't a human being
That is known as Slavery.

Indeed I was a slave
No rights to call my own
But still I had a Memory
Of a Place I once called HOME.

This place stayed in my mind
It would not leave my dreams
The homeland of my Ancestors
Where we had Kings and Queens.

Where we had our own land
Where we had families and clans
Where we were free like we were meant to be
A Free Woman. A Free Child. A Free Man.

---

[1] "Kric? Krac!" is a popular saying in the French West Indies, especially Haiti and Martinique. The storyteller calls out "Kric?" to signal the audience that he or she has a story to tell. The response is "Krac," indicating that the audience wants to hear the story.

Where we could sing and dance
Where Anansi talked
We told our own stories
And monkeys camelwalked

And spirits hitched a ride
Way up on a breeze
And Sungura the trickster
Jumped over palm trees.

So while we were still slaves
We kept our old stories alive
And passed them on to our children
So they would remember the jive.

We took the tales out of Africa
And placed them in the Deep South.
We cradled the words from the Bush
And put them in Buh Rabbit's mouth.

The oldest way in which people gather to share the dance and tell the story is to form a circle. Each year at the National Festival of Black Storytelling, "In The Tradition . . . ," the call is given, "Story! Story telling time!" In response the audience rises up and dances to the beat of the drums. The people join hands and form the circle of love. This moving ritual has occurred since 1983 and is comprised of those who love to tell stories and those who love to listen to them. *Talk that Talk: An Anthology of African-American Storytelling*, edited by Linda Goss and Marian Barnes (Simon & Schuster, 1989) came from that circle. That anthology included stories told by preachers, healers, teachers, comedians, blues singers, poets, dancers, rappers, liars, painters, and historians. *Jump Up and Say!: A Collection of Black Storytelling* widens the circle. This anthology includes praise songs, letters, story songs, protest stories, riddles, recipes, superstitions, quotes, proverbs, poetry, animal fables, ghost tales, humorous tales, family stories, jazz stories, and examples of storytelling in African-American theater and film.

The storytelling circle of love lifts up the spirits. The circle is a renewal, a rebirth, and a rejoicing. *Jump Up and Say!* embraces and expresses those same feelings. Read the stories aloud, dance to them, sing to them, shout to them, and above all "pass them on down, hand them on around."

A story, a story
Take what you like
And save some for me.
Spread the Word!

Introduction

—⁂—

Herein is a feast, a dazzling display of narrative art at its most personal and its most profound. A strange thing happens to me when I pick up this book: I become a child again in search of a good story hidden here somewhere, which I can hardly wait to find. A rollicking festival of words and images affects me in ways that, even as a boy, I had learned to depend on. The true definition of who I truly was—not a nigger boy whose life was of little more consequence than that of a mule, or a pig, or a goat—but someone worthy, and loved, and beautiful, composed entirely of magic. A magic that could come to life only in the world—my world—created for me by these stories.

I knew of history, too, and that was filled with honor, struggle, and pain. History was always a warning and an example. I turned to history for refuge and for instruction, and to walk at my side through treacherous and perilous landscapes, reminding me to watch myself every step of the way on pain of being trapped and punished by a cruel white world that was always out to get me. History was the rope that kept trying to rescue little boys from quicksand. How to avoid confrontation with the Ku Klux Klan and not be lynched, that's what history could tell me, so I kept an eye open and an ear open for history at all times.

But it was to storytelling that I ran, as fast as I could, laughing in advance at the thought of the pleasure and surprise that was surely waiting for me. And here it is again in *Jump Up and Say!* after all these years. I pick up this book and start to salivate. I know what is coming, waiting for me in these pages, and my soul is satisfied!

—Ossie Davis
March 1995

Praise Song

A praise song or praise poem is a tribute to someone or something of value. Sometimes it is a chant with words and phrases fitted together like pieces of fabric sewn together to make a patchwork quilt. The first paragraph is transcribed from the Twi language, which is spoken in Ghana.

SPIDER

Who gave word? Who gave word? Who gave word?
Who gave word to Hearing
For Hearing to have told Anansi
For Anansi to have told the Creator
For Creator to have made the Things?

A TELL-A-TALE

Anansi spun a web to the Sky God
Sky God had all the stories
Anansi performed three great tasks
Sky God gave the stories to Anansi
Anansi gave them to the People
The people passed them on

STORYTELLERS

Gatekeepers of History
Dreamweavers of Fantasy

STORYTELLING

Medicine for the Spirit
Healing for the Soul

Praise Song: Challenge

Roy Farrar

The genre and process of storytelling, the tradition of orality, is one character-ized by the conjuring of image, by stylistic rhythm and thematic poignancy. This, too, is the essence of poetry. "Challenge" embodies the collective voice and experience of a people, journeying, revealing themselves through time. It is the griot's song, retelling the story of those who have come before and reinvigorating the essential wisdoms for the life of the human community and its future.

When we used to come together
when we used to build pyramids and points of light
   above the desert's scorching sand,
traversing a continent with salt and gold
and charting the anatomy and universe
and honor the ancestors
we were a strong people—

when we used to come together
stuffed and stacked beneath deck
rocking to the rhythms of the sea and misery
and belly-wrenched upon the shores to turn the land and tow
   barges, mine the under-earth and sow and reap
and wait another hungry night
with empty hands clasped to an unfamiliar god . . . and endure
we were a strong people—

when we used to come together
and bleed our sweat and tears and prayers and songs
through Sunday-starched white shirts and neckties and
hats full of fancy and attitude and "Mah God!"
and everybody filled cups and spirits soared and say "Amen"
we were a strong people

when we used to come together
and come north and west and urban

following a star, moss, the breeze and promise
our instinctual lead
by wagon, car, boxcar, foot, and faith, movin'
with the scent of freedom on our tongues
we were a strong people

when we used to come together
and sit silent righteous at the dining stools and stores and
strongholds of injustice and march to the doorsteps of oppression
into the face of fear, hatred, hose, and dog and absorb-deflect
the force with justice pangs and conscience
and call racism by its name
we were a strong people

when we used to come together
when we used to rise like a black tide of bitter frustration
exhausted with the patient promise of better days ahead
and assassinated efforts and heroes and cry "burn, baby, burn"
and conjure "Black Power" and "It's Nation-Time"
and arm each other with "brother" and "sister" and our smiles
and infiltrate every American aspect with blackness
we were a strong people

now . . . when we come together
in the classroom and corridor, park/playground, and poolroom
    streetcorner, campus, church, kitchen, and conference
we can invoke our ancestors' singing
and revisit and define ourselves and dreams
and stir the wind blowing scents of freedom, burning
afresh in our children's nostrils
and the taste of struggle on their tongues
and see that we need not kill each other nor ourselves
through the barrel of pipe or pistol or neglect or at all
nor watch us die and forget
that what we need is to care for each other, nurture who we are,
and remember when we come together
we are a strong people—

PART I

The Breaking Day Has Wisdom, the Falling Day Experience

Moral Tales

To acknowledge our ancestors means we are aware that we did not make ourselves, that the line stretches all the way back, perhaps, to God; or to gods. We remember them because it is an easy thing to forget that we are not the first to suffer, rebel, fight, love, and die; the grace with which we embrace life, in spite of the pain, the sorrows, is always a measure of what has gone before.

—ALICE WALKER,
"In these Dissenting Times"

The fool's heart is in his mouth, the wise one's mouth is in his heart. (West Africa)

Eggs shouldn't dance with rocks. (Haiti)

Wisdom enclosed in the heart is like a light in a jug. (East Africa)

When the mouth stumbles, it is worse than the foot. (West Africa)

Nana

Julie Dash (from the film, Daughters of the Dust)

This film is about the tensions between tradition and assimilation. It tells the story of the Peazants, an African-American family who lived on the Gullah sea islands off the coast of Georgia and South Carolina during the turn of the century (1890s). Most of the family members prepare to go to the mainland in search of a "better way of life." But Nana Peazant, eighty-eight years old and matriarch of the family, will remain on the islands. Therefore, she makes a "Hand" which is a charm bag as a symbol of her undying love, good luck, and African pride. She wants the family to kiss the Hand before they leave.

The following text is an excerpt from the screenplay.

Nana removes a lock of hair from her tin can.

NANA (TO THE WOMEN AROUND HER)

When I was a child, my mother cut
this from her hair before she
was sold away from us.

Nana adds some of her own hair to what she has saved of her mother's hair. She kisses the hair and inserts both of them into the "Hand" that she is creating.

NANA

Now, I'm adding my own hair.
There must be a bond . . . a
connection, between those that
go up North, and those who across
the sea. A connection!
We are as two people in one body.
The last of the old, and the
first of the new. We will always
live this double life, you know,
because we're from the sea. We
came here in chains, and we must
survive. We must survive.
There's salt-water in our
blood. . . .

The Young Lion

Teju the Storyteller (Tejumola F. Ologboni)

Teju was the name of my great-great-grandfather, a young African stolen from Nigeria and sold as a slave in 1859. Records show that he eventually landed in Tennessee where my great-grandfather was born. From there the family traveled to Arkansas, Kansas (where I was born), and Milwaukee, where the family moved in 1956 when I was eleven. The big turning point in my life came in 1968 when I attended graduate school at Indiana University in Bloomington, Indiana, and heard Alex Haley speak about his research leading up to the book *Roots.* I was inspired enough to search out my own roots. I knew that my mother's great-grandfather was from South Africa, but I didn't know much about my father's side and I wanted to know. I was lucky and found the right people at the right time. When I got to Nigeria in 1972, they knew the whole story of my great-great-grandfather. I call myself Teju the Storyteller in honor of his memory.

On my fourteenth birthday I made a real important discovery. That discovery was simply this: that I was fourteen. I was in the bathroom, and I stepped on the scale to see how much I weighed. Now, my mother kept this scale because she wanted to see if she was gaining weight. She weighed about 107 pounds, and she was always trying to get bigger. You know, she was taking "Weight-On" and all these extra calorie kinds of things to help you gain weight. Well, when I looked at the scale, I realized that I weighed 112 pounds. Check this out: My momma weighed only 107 pounds. *And* I was two inches taller than her. And something occurred to me: Hey, I'm fourteen, I'm bigger than her, taller than her. I knew I was stronger than her. Hey, I don't have to take no more *whupping.*

Around that time in my life one of the things that I used to like to do was torment my little sister, and of course she went crying to Momma and Momma told me to stop. I messed with my sister again. Then my mother said if I didn't stop she was going to whip me. Well, I made a face at my sister, and my sister hollered, "Momma!" Momma called me into the kitchen. She said, "Didn't I tell you to stop! I told you I was going to give you a whipping, boy."

I said, "Hey, Momma, look, I'm fourteen. I'm just about a man, and like, hey, I don't have to take no more whippings."

Well! I never, ever got hit in the chest with a pot before, but I'm glad it wasn't a skillet. The second time she hit me with the broom, the handle broke. When my eyes came back in focus, Momma said, "Sit down! Shut up! And listen. . . . Don't never think I don't love you. And because I do, I'm telling you this. Now look here, boy. In the beginning when God was creating everything, she had a plan. She gave everybody a job, a responsibility to do, boy. Now I know that you noticed that I said that God was a *she*. Yes, God was a woman. And I know everybody thinks that God was a man. But a long time ago, African people—and we are Africans, boy—thought of God as a woman. 'Cause after all, God gave birth to the earth. Who gives birth? Men or women?"

I didn't say nothing.

She said, "Who creates more beauty? Men or women? Well, you know that's women. And not only that, God is loving and nurturing. And you know women are the ones that are loving and nurturing. God is merciful and forgiving. Right, boy? And you know whenever you get in trouble, who do you run to? Huh . . . huh?"

Well, I didn't run to my father, that's for sure. Another thing I was thinking of while I was sitting there is that God is a jealous God, and you know who's the most jealous?

My momma went on: "So God gave every animal, everything she created, a purpose. Told the flowers to look good and smell good. Told the trees and the grass to make air. And told the butterflies, 'You gon be the ones that's gon bring beauty to the world. Just everybody gon think you beautiful, butterflies. Birds, you gon sing and bring everybody a happy song. Hyena, you gon show everybody how to laugh and be happy. And donkey, you gon be the jokers, you know, the comedians, but you also gon show everybody how to do gymnastics. Now, owl, you gon be the wise one. Okay, lion, you gon be the king. Cheetah, you gon be Mr Speedy, okay? You gon teach everybody how to run. Ants, y'all gon show everybody how to work together.' Etcetera, etcetera, etcetera. She gave all the animals a job.

"The lion said, 'Wow! God made me king.' The lion went over to the fox and said, 'Hey, fox, God made me king, man.'

"The fox said, 'Man, I ain't got no time for that. Can't you see I'm trying to scheme up on a deal, and you over here talking about this "king" stuff. I ain't got time for that jive.'

"The lion said, 'Man, he don't want to treat me like a king.' So then the lion went over to the hyena and said, 'Hey, hyena, check it out, man. God made me king.'

"The hyena said, 'Ha, ha, ha, ha, ha, ha . . .'

"The lion said, 'Dog, man. That's cold.'

"He went over to the zebra and said, 'Hey, zebra, you know, when God was givin' everybody everything, you know, the jobs to do, God made me the king.'

"The zebra said, 'Man, I'm trying to get a drink of water. There's crocodiles in this water. I gotta stay on the lookout. Will you just let me get my drink of water, all right?'

"The lion thought, Aw, man, don't nobody want to treat me like a king. Oh, I know what to do. I'll go to the owl. The owl is wise. 'Hey, owl?'

"The owl said, 'Hooooo.'

" 'It's me, lion.'

" 'Who?'

" 'It's me, lion. I want you to help me.'

" 'Whooooooo?'

"The lion said, 'Why do you keep saying who?'

" ' 'Cause that's what God told me to say. Well, anyway, okay, I'll help you.'

" 'God said I was the king. But the problem is don't nobody want to treat me like a king. How can I get people to treat me like a king?'

"The owl said, 'Hmmm . . . well, it seems to me that if you want them to treat you like a king, then you gotta get their attention. You know, like a king gets attention.'

"The lion said, 'How am I going to do that?'

"The owl said, 'Man, look, one question at a time. I got a whole bunch of other stuff to figure out. I ain't got time for that, all right?'

"So the lion thought, Get their attention like a king. Hmmm. I'll go see the monkey. He's a real showman. So the lion went over to the monkey's tree.

" 'Hey, monkey! Come down here for a minute. Now listen, God made me the king, but nobody wants to treat me like a king. The owl said that I should get everybody's attention. Tell me, monkey, how can I get their attention?'

"The monkey said, 'Well, I don't know nothing about no kings, but I do know how to get attention. The way I see it is this: If you pop them upside the head, you'll get their attention. Once you get their attention, you can ask them if they know you're the king.'

" 'Well, I don't know . . . But I guess it's worth a try.' So the lion walked up to the fox and said, 'Hey, fox.'

"The fox looked around, like he had a attitude, and said, 'What do you wan—'

"*Kapow!* The lion slapped the fox. 'Who's the king?'

" 'You!' the fox said quickly. 'You the king, man! Dag, what did you do that for? You the king, okay?'

"The lion said, *'Wow!* He said I was the king. Hey, hyena, get over here!' *Splat!* 'Who's the king?'

" 'Ha, ha, ha, ha, you the king, ha, ha, ha.' The hyena ran away laughing, 'You the king, ha, ha, ha, you the king, ha, ha, ha.'

"The lion said, 'Oh, boy. Yeah. King Lion! . . . Hey, zebra, wait up! I want a word with you.'

"The zebra stopped walking. 'What?'

"*Slaaappp!* 'Who's the king,' said the lion.

"The zebra neighed, 'You. You. You the one, man. You the baddest king I ever saw.'

"The lion saw the antelope by the water hole. 'Hey, antelope!'

"The antelope jumped back all scared and said, 'Hey, man. I saw the whole thing, and lion, man, you the king. Straight up! Hey, King Lion, what's up? You the *king.*'

"The lion puffed up his chest and started walking cool. 'Yeah, awww right!' He stuck his head up and strutted. He was walking through the grasslands. Everybody was looking at him. He walked past the giraffe. The giraffe said, 'Hey, King Lion, what's happnin'!' The lion shook his mane and said, real cool, 'Hey, what's up?' and thought to himself, I'm the king. Yeahhhh!

"The lion walked down by the water hole. He just knew he had it altogether. When the other animals spoke, he would just nod his head, all tough. Standing over by the side was Ms. Elephant with her baby, eating grass. The lion walked past her, and she didn't say nothin'. He looked at her. She looked at him. She still didn't say nothin'. The lion thought, I'm gonna give you another chance. The lion backed up and walked past her again. She still didn't say nothin'. He said, 'Well?'

" 'What is it that you want, lion? Can't you see I'm busy, pulling this grass, feedin' my child here?'

"The lion walked up to Ms. Elephant, hauled off, and slapped her. *Blap!* 'Who's the king!'

"She looked at him, squinted her eyes, and said, 'Boy is you done lost your mind?'

"*Kapayow!* 'Groooowl! I said who's the king?'

"Ms. Elephant reared up, bellowed, 'Ahhhrrrghhhh! Ahrrghh!' She reached down and grabbed him around the neck with her trunk and *baaaaam!* slammed him into a tree, *bam!* slammed him into another tree, *bam!* slammed him into another tree, and then *blam!* slammed him on the ground. She was fixin' to slam him again. She dangled him in the air.

" 'Wait a minute! Wait a minute,' squealed the lion. 'You don't have to get so mad, just 'cause you don't know the answer.' "

Then my mother said, "Now, boy, I know that you think you a young lion. But I'm an old elephant. So before you think about jumping up in my face, you better think again. You got that, boy?"

"Yes, ma'am," I managed to mumble.

"Now to this very day, lions, as bad as they are, don't mess with elephants."

Then she told me what her daddy always told his kids. It was what she always said when she was through talking to me. She said, "A word to the wise is sufficient. Go now and govern yourself accordingly."

Don't Pay Bad for Bad

Amos Tutuola

Amos Tutuola draws his characters from Yoruba legend and culture in Nigeria, his homeland. The title suggests a moral and requires our observation, comment, and attention. Amos Tutuola is a master storyteller.

Dola and Babi were good friends in their days. Both were young ladies, and they had loved each other heartily from when they were children. They always wore the same kind of dress, and they went together everywhere in their village, and to other villages as well. They did everything together, so much so that anyone who did not know their parents believed they were twins.

So Dola and Babi went about together until when they grew to be the age for marriage. Because they loved each other so much, they decided within themselves to marry two men who were born of the same mother and father, and who lived together in the same house, so that they might be with each other always.

Luckily, a few days after Dola and Babi decided to do so, they heard of two young men who were born of the same mother and father, and who lived together in the same house. So Babi married one of the young men while Dola married the second one, who was older than the first one. So Dola and Babi were very happy now, living together as they had before they had been married in their husbands' house.

A few days after their marriage, Dola cleared a part of the front of the house very neatly. She sowed one kola-nut on the spot. After some weeks the kola-nut shot up. Then she filled up one earthen jar with water and she put it before her new kola-nut tree. Then every early morning, Dola would go and kneel down before the tree and jar. She would pray to the tree to help her to get a baby very soon, and after the prayer, she would drink some of the water which was inside the earthen jar. After that, she would go back to her room before the other people in the house woke. Dola did this early every morning, because she believed that there was a certain spirit who came and blessed the kola-nut tree and the water in the night.

After some months, the kola-nut tree grew to the height of about one meter. But now the domestic animals of the village began to eat the leaves of the tree, and this hindered its growth.

One morning, Babi met Dola abruptly as she knelt down before the kola-nut tree and jar and prayed. After she had prayed and then stood up, Babi asked in surprise, "Dola, what were you telling your kola-nut tree?"

"Oh, this kola-nut tree is my god, and I ask it every morning to help me get a baby soon," Dola explained calmly, pointing a finger at the tree and jar.

When Babi noticed that the animals of the village had eaten nearly all the leaves of the tree, she went back to her room. She took the top part of her large water pot, the bottom of which had broken away. She gave it to Dola, and she told her to shield her kola-nut tree with it so that the animals wouldn't be able to eat its leaves again.

Dola took the large pot from her and thanked her fervently. Then she shielded her tree with it, and as from that morning the animals were unable to eat the leaves of the tree. And so it was growing steadily in the center of the large pot.

A few years later, the tree yielded the first kola-nuts. The first kola-nuts that the tree yielded were of the best quality in the village, and because the nuts were the best quality, the kola-nut buyers hastily bought all the nuts, paying a considerable amount of money. Similarly, when the tree yielded the second and third kola-nuts, the buyers bought them with large amounts of money as before.

In selling the kola-nuts, Dola became a wealthy woman within a short period. Having seen this, Babi became jealous of Dola's wealth.

Jealously, Babi demanded back the water pot: "Dola, will you please return my large water pot to me this morning?"

Dola was greatly shocked. She asked, "What? The broken water pot without a bottom?"

"Yes, my broken water pot. I want to take it back this morning," Babi replied with a jealous voice.

"Well, the water pot cannot be returned to you at this time unless I break it into pieces before it can come from around my kola-nut tree," Dola replied with a dead voice.

"You must not break it or split the head of my water pot before you return it to me!" Babi shouted angrily.

"I say it cannot be taken away from the tree without breaking it or cutting the tree down," Dola explained angrily.

Babi boomed on Dola: "Yes, you may cut your tree down if you wish to do so. But all I want from you is my water pot!"

Dola reminded Babi with a calm voice, "Please, Babi, I remind you now that both of us started our friendship when we were children. Because of that, don't try to take your water pot back at this time."

"Yes, of course, I don't forget at any time that we are friends. But at all costs, I want the water pot now," Babi insisted with a great noise.

That revealed to Dola at last that Babi simply wanted to destroy her kola-nut tree so that she might not get the nuts from it to sell anymore. She went to the chief of the village. She begged him to help her persuade Babi not to take the head of her water pot back.

However, when the chief of the village failed to persuade Babi not to take the water pot back from Dola, he judged the case in favor of Babi and said that Dola must return the water pot to her.

Then to her sorrow, Dola's kola-nut tree was cut down, and the water pot was taken away from the tree without breaking, and Dola returned it to Babi. Now, Babi was very happy and she burst out laughing not because of the water pot but because Dola's kola-nut tree had been cut down, as she believed that Dola would not get kola-nuts to sell again.

As soon as the water pot was returned to Babi, she and Dola entered the house and they continued their friendship, for Dola did not show in her behavior toward Babi that her tree which had been cut down was a great sorrow for her.

A few months after the tree was cut down, Babi was delivered of a female baby. And on the morning that the baby was named, Dola gave her a fine brass ring as a present. Dola told Babi to put the ring on the baby's neck, brass being one of the most precious metals in those days.

Babi, with laughter, took the brass ring from Dola, and with great admiration she put it on the baby's neck immediately. And this brass ring so much beautified the baby that, from her beautiful look, now it seemed as if she was created with it. The brass ring was carefully molded without any joint.

Then ten years passed away like one day. One fine morning, as the baby —who was by then a daughter—was celebrating her tenth birthday, Dola walked gently into Babi's sitting room and said, "Babi, my good friend. I shall be very glad if you will return my brass ring this morning." Dola smiled to see that Babi's guests were silent with shock.

Babi stood up suddenly, scowling, and shouted, "Which brass ring?"

"My brass ring which is on your daughter's neck now." Dola pointed a finger at Babi's daughter's neck, explaining as if she were simply joking.

"This very brass ring which is on my daughter's neck now?" Babi, after clearing her throat, shouted to show disapproval of Dola's demand: "Dola! You are joking!"

Dola scowled and replied softly, "I am not joking in any way, and I want you to return my brass ring now."

Babi grunted like a pig, "Hmm!" and begged with extreme misery and with tears rolling down her cheeks, "Please, my good friend, don't try to take your brass ring back now. As you know, before the ring can be taken away from my daughter's neck, her head will be cut off first because it is already bigger than the ring!"

"I don't tell you to cut off the head of your daughter, but all I want is my brass ring, and I want it without cutting it."

At last, when Dola still insisted on taking her brass ring back, Babi went to the same chief of the village. She told him that Dola was attempting to kill her daughter.

Fortunately, the chief judged the case in favor of Dola when she explained to him how her kola-nut tree was cut down when Babi insisted on taking her water pot back ten years ago.

And in the judgment the chief added that the head of Babi's daughter would be cut off on the assembly ground which was in front of his palace, and also in the presence of all the people of the village, so that everyone might learn that jealousy was bad. Then a special day was fixed for beheading the daughter.

When the day was reached, and after all the people of the village had gathered on the assembly ground, and the chief and his prominent people had been seated, then the chief called Babi loudly. He told her to put her ten-year-old daughter in the middle of the circle, and she obeyed. She and her daughter stood wobbling with fear while the swordsman, who was ready to behead the daughter, stood fiercely behind the daughter with a long dazzling sword in his hand.

The crowd of people, prominent people, and the chief were so overwhelmed by mercy that all were quiet suddenly while looking at the poor innocent daughter and her mother Babi, who looked thin and gaunt.

It was some minutes before the chief could reluctantly announce to Babi loudly, "Now, Babi, today is Dola's day. Just as Dola's kola-nut tree was cut down ten years ago when you insisted and took back the head of your water pot from her, it is so that the head of your daughter will be cut off now, when Dola's brass ring will be taken away from the neck of your daughter and then it will be given back to Dola!" The gathering mumbled with grief, and then all became quiet at once.

Then as the chief closed his eyes with grief, he gave the order to the swordsman to behead Babi's daughter. But, just as the swordsman raised his sword up to cut the head off, Dola hastily stopped him by pulling his arm down, and then she announced loudly, "It will be a great pity if this daughter of mine is killed, because she has not offended me. No! It was her jealous mother.

"And I believe, if we continue to pay 'bad' for 'bad,' bad will never finish on earth. Therefore, I forgive Babi all that she has done to my kola-nut tree of which she was jealous!"

The chief and the rest of the people clapped and shouted loudly with happiness when they heard this announcement from Dola. Then everyone went back to his or her house. And Dola and Babi were still good friends throughout the rest of their lives.

How the Leopard Got His Claws

Chinua Achebe and John Iroaganachi

If you look at the world in terms of storytelling, you have, first of all, the man who agitates, the man who drums up the people—I call him the drummer. Then you have the warrior, who goes forward and fights. But you also have the storyteller who recounts the event, and this is the one who survives, who outlives all the others. It is the storyteller who makes us what we are, who creates history. The storyteller creates the memory that the survivors must have; otherwise, their surviving would have no meaning.

—CHINUA ACHEBE

In the beginning . . . all the animals in the forest lived as friends. Their king was the leopard. He was strong, but gentle and wise. He ruled the animals well, and they all liked him.

At that time the animals did not fight one another. Most of them had no sharp teeth or claws. They did not need them. Even King Leopard had only small teeth. He had no claws at all.

Only the dog had big, sharp teeth. The other animals said he was ugly, and they laughed at him.

"It is foolish to carry sharp things in the mouth," said the tortoise.

"I think so, too," said the goat.

The monkey jumped in and began to tease the dog.

"Don't worry, my dear friend," said the monkey. "You need your teeth to clear your farm."

The animals laughed at the monkey's joke.

When the farming season came round, King Leopard led the animals to their farmland. They all worked hard to prepare their plots. At the end of the day they returned home tired. They sat on log benches in the village square. As they rested they told stories and drank palm wine.

But soon it would be the rainy season, and the animals would have no shelter from the rain.

The deer took this problem to King Leopard. They talked about it for a long time. King Leopard decided to call the animals together to discuss it.

One bright morning . . . King Leopard beat his royal drum. When the animals heard the drum, they gathered at the village square. The tortoise was there. The goat was there, too. The sheep, the grass-cutter, the monkey, the hedgehog, the baboon, the dog and many others were there.

King Leopard greeted them and said, "I have called you together to plan how we can make ourselves a common shelter."

"This is a good idea," said the giraffe.

"Yes, a very good idea," said many other animals.

"But why do we need a common house?" said the dog. He had never liked King Leopard.

"The dog has asked a good question," said the duck. "Why do we need a common shelter?"

"We do need somewhere to rest when we return from our farms," replied King Leopard.

"And besides," said the goat, "we need a shelter from the rain."

"I don't mind being wet," said the duck. "In fact, I like it. I know that the goat does not like water on his body. Let him go and build a shelter."

"We need a shelter," said the monkey, jumping up and down in excitement.

"Perhaps we need one, perhaps we don't," said the lazy baboon sitting on the low fence of the square.

The dog spoke again. "We are wasting our time. Those who need a shelter should build it. I live in a cave, and it is enough for me." Then he walked away. The duck followed him out.

"Does anyone else want to leave?" asked King Leopard. No one answered or made a move to go.

"Very well," said King Leopard. "Let the rest of us build the village hall."

The animals soon scattered about to find building materials. The tortoise copied the pattern on his back and made the plan of the roof. The giant rat and mouse dug the foundations. Some animals brought sticks, some ropes, others made roof-mats.

As they built the house, they sang many happy songs. They also told many jokes. Although they worked very hard, everyone was merry.

After many weeks they finished the building.

It was a fine building. The animals were pleased with it. They agreed to open it with a very special meeting.

On the opening day the animals, their wives and children gathered in the hall. King Leopard then made a short speech. He said: "This hall is yours to enjoy. You worked very hard together to build it. I am proud of you."

The animals clapped their hands and gave three cheers to their king.

From that day they rested in their new hall whenever they returned from their farm.

But the dog and the duck kept away from the hall.

One morning the animals went to their farms as usual. King Leopard went to visit a chief in another village.

At first the sun was shining. Then strong winds began to blow. Dark clouds hid the sun. The first rain was coming. The songbirds stopped their singing. The humming insects became quiet. Lightning flashed across the dark clouds. Claps of thunder sounded. The rain poured and poured.

The animals in their farms saw the rain coming and began to hurry to the village hall.

The dog also saw the rain coming and returned to his cave. But it was a very, very heavy rain. Water began to enter the cave. Soon it was flooded.

The dog ran from one end of his cave to the other. But the water followed him everywhere. At last he ran out of the cave altogether and made straight for the hall of the animals.

The deer was already there. He was surprised to see the dog enter the hall.

"What do you want here?" said the deer to the dog.

"It is none of your business," replied the dog.

"It is my business," said the deer. "Please go out, this hall is for those who built it."

Then the dog attacked the deer and bit him with his big, sharp teeth. The deer cried with pain. The dog seized him by the neck and threw him out into the rain.

The other animals came in one after the other.

The dog barked and threw each of them out. They stood together shivering and crying in the rain. The dog kept barking and showing his teeth.

Then the deer cried out:

> O Leopard our noble king,
> Where are you?
> Spotted king of the forest,
> Where are you?
> Even if you are far away
> Come, hurry home:
> The worst has happened to us
> The worst has happened to us . . .
> The house the animals built
> The cruel dog keeps us from it,
> The common shelter we built
> The cruel dog keeps us from it,
> The worst has happened to us
> The worst has happened to us . . .

The cry of the deer rang out loud and clear. It was carried by the wind. King Leopard heard it on his way back from his journey and began to run toward the village hall.

As he got near, he saw the animals, wet and sheltering under a tree. They were all crying. As he got nearer still, he could see the dog walking up and down inside the hall.

King Leopard was very angry. "Come out of the hall at once," he said to the dog. The dog barked and rushed at him. They began to fight. The dog bit the leopard and tore his skin with his claws. King Leopard was covered with blood. The dog went back to the hall. He stood at the door barking and barking. "Who is next? Who! Who!" he barked.

King Leopard turned to the animals and said: "Let us go in together and drive out the enemy. He is strong, but he is alone. We are many. Together we can drive him out of our house."

But the goat said: "We cannot face him. Look at his strong teeth! He will only tear us to pieces!"

"The goat is right," said the animals. "He is too strong for us."

The tortoise stood up and said: "I am sure we are all sorry about what has happened to the leopard. But he was foolish to talk to the dog the way he did. It is foolish to annoy such a powerful person as the dog. Let us make peace with him. I don't know what you others think. But I think he should have been our king all along. He is strong; he is handsome. Let us go on our knees and salute him."

"Hear! Hear!" said all the animals. "Hail the dog!"

Tears began to roll down the face of the leopard. His heart was heavy. He loved the animals greatly. But they had turned their backs on him. Now he knew they were cowards. So he turned his back on them and went away. Because of his many wounds he was weak and tired. So he lay down after a while to rest under a tree, far from the village.

The animals saw him go. But they did not care. They were too busy praising their new king, the dog. The tortoise carved a new staff for him. The toad made a new song in his praise:

> The dog is great
> The dog is good
> The dog gives us our daily food.
> We love his head, we love his jaws
> We love his feet and all his claws.

The dog looked round the circle of animals and asked, "Where is the leopard?"

"We think he has gone away, O King," said the goat.

"Why? He has no right to go away," said the dog. "Nobody has a right to leave our village and its beautiful hall. We must all stay together."

"Indeed," shouted the animals. "We must stay together! The leopard must return to the village! Our wise king has spoken! It is good to have a wise king!"

The dog then called out the names of six strong animals and said to them: "Go at once and bring back the leopard. If he should refuse to follow you, you must drag him along. If we let him go, others may soon follow his wicked example until there is no one left in our village. That would be a very bad thing indeed. It is my duty as your king to make sure that we all live together. The leopard is a wicked animal. That is why he wants to go away and live by himself. It is our duty to stop him. Nobody has a right to go away from our village and our beautiful hall."

"Nobody has a right to go away from the village," sang all the animals as the six messengers went to look for the leopard.

They found him resting under the tree beyond the village. Although he was wounded and weak he still looked like a king. So the six messengers stood at a little distance and spoke to him.

"Our new king, the dog, has ordered you to return to the village," they said.

"He says that no one has a right to leave the village," said the pig.

"Yes, no one has a right to leave our village and its beautiful hall," said the others.

The leopard looked at them with contempt. Then he got up slowly. The six animals fell back. But the leopard did not go toward them. He turned his back on them and began to go away—slowly and painfully. One of the animals picked up a stone and threw it at him. Then all the others immediately picked up stones and began to throw. As they threw they chanted: "No one has a right to leave our village! No one has a right to leave our village!"

Although some of the stones hit the leopard and hurt him, he did not turn round even once. He continued walking until he no longer heard the noise of the animals.

The leopard traveled seven days and seven nights. Then he came to the house of the blacksmith. The old man was sitting at his forge. The leopard said to him: "I want the strongest teeth you can make from iron. And I want the most deadly claws you can make from bronze."

The blacksmith said: "Why do you need such terrible things?" The leopard told his story. Then the blacksmith said: "I do not blame you."

The blacksmith worked a whole day on the teeth, and another full day on the claws. The leopard was pleased with them. He put them on and thanked the blacksmith. Then he left and went to the house of Thunder.

The leopard knocked at the door and Thunder roared across the sky.

"I want some of your sound in my voice," said the leopard. "Even a little bit."

"Why do you want my sound in your voice?" asked Thunder. "And why have you got those terrible teeth and claws?"

The leopard told his story. "I do not blame you," said Thunder. He gave the sound to the leopard. "Thank you for the gift," said the leopard. And he began his journey home.

The leopard journeyed for seven days and seven nights and returned to the village of the animals. There he found the animals dancing in a circle round the dog. He stood for a while watching them with contempt and great anger. They were too busy to notice his presence. He made a deep, terrifying roar. At the same time he sprang into the center of the circle. The animals stopped their song. The dog dropped his staff. The leopard seized him and bit and clawed him without mercy. Then he threw him out of the circle.

All the animals *trembled*.

But they were too afraid to run. The leopard turned to them and said:

"You miserable worms. You shameless cowards. I was a kind and gentle king, but you turned against me. From today I shall rule the forest with terror. The life of our village is ended."

"What about our hall?" asked the tortoise with a trembling voice.

"Let everyone take from the hall what he put into it," said the leopard.

The animals began to weep as they had wept long ago in the rain. "Please forgive us, O Leopard," they cried.

"Let everyone take from the hall what he put into it," repeated the leopard. "And hurry up!" he thundered.

So the animals pulled their hall apart. Some carried away the wood, and some took the roof-mats. Others took away doors and windows. The toad brought his talking drum and began to beat it to the leopard and to sing:

> Alive or dead the leopard is king.
> Beware my friend, don't twist his tail.

But the leopard roared like thunder and the toad dropped his drum and the animals scattered in the forest.

The dog had already run a long way when the leopard roared. Now he ran faster and faster. His body was covered with blood, and he was very, very weak. He wanted to stop and rest a little. But the fear of the leopard was greater than his weakness. So he staggered and fell and got up and staggered on and on and on. . . .

After many days the dog came to the house of the hunter.

"Please protect me from the leopard," he cried.

"What will you do for me in return?" asked the hunter.

"I will be your slave," said the dog. "Any day you are hungry for meat I shall show you the way to the forest. There we can hunt together and kill my fellow animals."

"All right, come in," said the hunter.

Today the animals are no longer friends, but enemies. The strong among them attack and kill the weak. The leopard, full of anger, eats up anyone he can lay his hands on. The hunter, led by the dog, goes to the forest from time to time and shoots any animals he can find. Perhaps the animals will make peace among themselves someday and live together again. Then they can keep away the hunter who is their common enemy.

Frozen in Time

Darlene Sterling

"Frozen in Time" is the first story I ever wrote. It was also the first story I ever told as a storyteller. I was in the Zora Neale Hurston Storytelling Contest and really wanted to be one of the winners. Ideas and words just started coming in my head, so I wrote them down. I made up the characters' names because I wanted them to sound like African names. I chose Senegal as the place where everything happens because I had read about the Griots in Senegal and then looked at a map and noticed that Senegal was right on the edge of Africa. The main thing I'm trying to say in the story is that parents should never abandon their children. From the time a child is a newborn on through adulthood, parents should always stand by their child.

In an African village in Senegal there lived the Tubu family, a mother, a father, and their twin children, Khalifh and Omika. Each year during harvest time, a festival was held to honor their late great king, Kanbu Hama. He had been the most respected in all of Africa.

A few days before the festival, everyone in the village was busy. Momma and Poppa Tubu wanted to keep the twins out of trouble and sent them to gather wood and fruit. On the day before the festival, the Tubus needed an important message delivered to another village.

"Khalifh! Omika!" Momma Tubu called.

"Coming, Momma," answered the twins.

"Your father and I want you to take a message to the village of Malaya," said Momma Tubu.

"Do you know how to get there?" asked Father Tubu.

"Yes, Father. We'll go through the forest, over the mountain, and into the country," replied the twins.

"Listen to me very closely," said Father Tubu. "Do not speak to or listen to anyone on your way there or back."

"Be back before the sun leaves the mountain," said Mother Tubu.

Off went the twins, skipping and humming through the forest. When the twins reached the mountain, they discovered two paths, one going left and the other going right. Before they could decide what to do, they heard a mysterious voice. "Take the left path," it said. The startled twins turned around and saw a tall man wearing an orange-striped gown. He was taller than anyone they had ever seen. The twins looked at each other with amazement.

Khalifh said, "O-O-Omika, did you see a g-g-giant man?"

Before his sister could answer, they noticed that the mysterious man had vanished. For a couple of seconds the twins did not move.

Finally Omika came out of shock and nudged Khalifh. "Come on, we have to go to Malaya."

"What about the giant?" asked Khalifh.

Omika said, "I'd rather face the giant again than face our parents if we don't deliver the message." She grabbed Khalifh's hand and pulled him onto the left path. High cold winds blew. The twins walked slower and slower and slower until they could walk no more. They became frozen in place. The twins looked like two white statues.

The sun left the mountain. There was no sight of the twins. A massive search began for them. Their parents screamed along with other villagers, "Khalifh, Omika!" "My children, where are you?" "Please come back!" "Omika!" "Khalifh!" They went to the village where the twins were supposed to deliver the message. "I'm very sorry," said the chief, "but your children never arrived." After several months the search ended.

It was now spring, and still no sign of the twins. Then one night one of the young children in the village had a nightmare about Omika and Khalifh. She dreamed about their being hidden somewhere on the left side of the mountain. The next day she told Mother and Father Tubu about her dream. Quickly the Tubus and all the people from the village rushed to the mountain. They noticed that the left side was covered with snow. They tried to push through the snow but couldn't get through. Mother and Father Tubu broke through the crowd. "We will try to get through," said Father Tubu. The parents pushed and groaned. "Uh! Eeek!" They became caught up in a blizzard. *Woosh! Woosh!* The wind blew and pushed the parents toward an icy figure until they were in front of it. "Oh, my goodness," they screamed. "It's the twins!"

They tried to break the icy figure open with their bare hands, but their hands stung when they touched the icy figure that trapped the twins. They knew if they touched the frozen figure again, it would hurt them badly. "The only thing we can do now," said Mother Tubu, "is pray: Please, Lord, forgive us for what we have done. We take full responsibility for what has happened to our children. Never again will we let our children travel outside of the village alone. We respect our ancestor, King Khanbu Hama. Please free our twins from their icy prison."

A rumble came upon the mountain, and a tall African man appeared. "Let this be a lesson to all people. Never abandon your children to the world."

All at once a bright light appeared. The light was so strong, it destroyed the blizzard and melted the icy prison that trapped the twins. They were unharmed and happy to be united with their parents once again. Joyous and happy, the Tubus vowed never to abandon their twins to the world again.

Buttermilk

Adora L. Dupree

"Buttermilk" is one of the first family stories I told. When the idea came to me to tell stories about my family, I thought it would be best if I told on myself first before I started telling on my siblings. The events are all true.

There are nine children in my family, and since we were born in the forties, fifties, and sixties, we are a part of the baby boom generation. We grew up when television was just getting started as the great American pastime, during the years of the civil rights movement and increased government focus on and spending for domestic social problems. It was that increased government spending for something called "commodities" that facilitated my learning a big lesson.

When I was ten years old, there were seven of us Dupree children on the scene. In addition to my parents, my mother's father also lived with us. Granddaddy had heart trouble and could no longer live by himself. That was ten people in a two-bedroom, one-bathroom house. We were poor, but I didn't know it. I recall overhearing my father say at one point that he made $400 a month. I thought we were rich. That sounded like a lot of money to me. Even in 1960, however, $400 didn't go very far in caring for ten people.

Naturally, my parents did what they could to insulate us from the horrors of poverty. One of my mother's major concerns was making sure we each had a bed of our own to sleep in. (And since I'm the oldest girl, I was very grateful for that.) So we had two sets of bunk beds, a baby crib, and a roll-away bed all in one bedroom. On the enclosed back porch, my older brother had his bed, and my grandfather slept in the shed out back which my dad had fixed up so it could be used. Sleeping was then taken care of.

The bathroom presented a bigger problem. Once we got it in the house, it seemed that there was always a line. I can recall just getting settled in the bathroom with my book when someone would come knocking on the door: "I gotta go, I gotta go."

My mother proved to be an efficient manager of the logistics of getting six children up, washed, fed, and ready for school between the hours of 5 and 7 A.M. The bad part was she would usually get me up first. I don't know why she never got my older brother up first. Then I had to wait for two hours until everyone else was ready for school when all I wanted to do was go back to sleep.

Fortunately, my father worked at night and did not require the bathroom in the morning. My mother worked at home (with that many children, what else would she do?), and so she did her toiletries after we left. My grandfather had a slop jar that he kept by his bed and used during the night, and brought to the house to empty in the morning after we left.

The funny times were coming back home from an outing. During those years, African Americans could not just stop anywhere to use the bathroom. Especially in the South there were signs above public toilets designating "white" or "colored." If there was no "colored" sign, then we wouldn't be able to use the facilities. Consequently, we were often arriving home from visiting our grandmother in South Carolina, or even from a shopping trip, with full bladders. As the car turned the corner to our street, a chorus of "Me first, me first" was heard from the backseat of the Buick. Everyone wanted dibs on the bathroom. As we streamed out of the car a line of kids went to neighbors' houses on the right and left, and the remainder danced up and down on the front porch until the door was opened and we could race to the bathroom.

As challenging as the sleeping and bathroom problems proved to be, the major problem we faced was feeding everyone. My mother was a real whiz in the kitchen. She *knew* how to cook. She could even make beans and cornbread taste good when you had to eat them every day, which sometimes we did. But her first line of action was a rule that none of the children could get any food from the kitchen without asking first. I mean, not even a peanut butter sandwich or cheese and crackers. We thought it was terribly unfair since all of our friends could get anything they wanted when they wanted. Of course I know now that if Mother had turned seven hungry children loose in her kitchen, there would have been no food left when she got ready to cook.

And Mother was a genius with a chicken. She could take a chicken and cut it up—she always bought the whole chicken because they were cheaper—so that each one of us could get a piece. That's right, we each got one piece of chicken. My father and grandfather each got a half of the breast (but Mother had to broil Granddaddy's because of his heart); my mother ate a chicken wing because she said it was her favorite part; my older brother and I each got a thigh; the drumsticks went to the twin girls; the twin boys—one got the other wing, his twin got the back. My baby brother complains to this day that all he ever ate was the chicken neck— until, that is, the older children started leaving home, and he could graduate up to the next larger piece of chicken.

Often we wanted to bring a friend home from church for dinner on

Sunday. Chicken was just Sunday dinner, you know. My mother would say, "Sure they can come, but you know you have to share your piece of chicken." You would really have to love that friend to give up the only piece of chicken you were going to have all week. Sometimes we brought a friend home, and sometimes we didn't.

My father would also do things to make the food stretch. And this is where the government comes in. During those years the government passed out commodities to people who were receiving public assistance. Commodities were food the farmers sold to the government, which in turn gave it to poor people. Our family was not on public assistance, my daddy made too much money—remember, $400 a month. But many people in our neighborhood were. When they had extra bags of flour or cornmeal or rice, they would often give them to my father, and he would bring them home. And commodities always came in brown paper packaging. I remember the powdered egg mix he brought home. It came in a brown paper envelope.

To prepare it, the powder was mixed with a couple of real eggs and some water, and when the mixture was scrambled, it was supposed to taste like real eggs. But as soon as I would get it under my nose, I knew this was not real eggs. It tasted awful!

One day Daddy brought home another brown paper envelope. I thought, Oh, no, more powdered eggs. But Daddy took milk from the icebox, poured it into a glass pitcher, and dumped in the contents of the envelope. I picked up the package. It was buttermilk powder. I was watching him as he put the powder in the regular milk and stirred it to turn the regular milk into buttermilk. I wasn't sure how this was making the food stretch since I didn't even like regular milk. But I must have been really hungry that day. That buttermilk started looking good to me, and then it smelled good. You know, it even sounded good, the clinking of the spoon on the sides of the glass pitcher as the milk was being stirred.

So I said, "Daddy, can I have some buttermilk?"

After correcting me—"It's 'may I,' not 'can,' "—Daddy said a strange thing to me. He said, "Your eyes are too big for your stomach."

Well, I didn't know what that had to do with my having buttermilk, so I just shrugged and said, "Yes, sir, but can—I mean may I—have some buttermilk, please?"

Daddy said, "Sure." So I happily jumped up and got a glass, a nice tall glass, and poured it full of buttermilk. I took a big swallow, and eeewwwwggggghhhh! It tasted horrible. I went to the sink with the glass, and Daddy said, "What are you doing?"

"I'm going to pour this out. It tastes awful."

Daddy said, "No, you're not. We don't waste food here. You asked for it, you got it, and now you're going to drink it."

"But Daddy," I started, and he gave me *that look* that shut me up immediately, 'cause you didn't argue with my daddy. And I said, "Yes, sir."

I sat back down with the buttermilk. It didn't look so good anymore, didn't smell good, and every time I tried to drink it, I thought I was going to throw up. Well, I sat there and played with the condensation on the glass, turned it around and around in my hands, until finally the buttermilk was warm. I said, "Daddy, this buttermilk is warm. Can . . . may I put it in the icebox to cool off?"

"Sure," Daddy said.

So I put the buttermilk in the icebox and headed for the back door. I was stopped by Daddy's voice, "Where are you going?"

"Outside to play, sir."

"No, you're going to stay in here until that buttermilk is finished."

Again I started, "But Daddy," and immediately switched to "Yes, sir," when I got *the look.*

I figured that soon Daddy would go outside and mow the lawn or work on the car or something. He was always doing something around the house. And when he left, then I would be able to dump the buttermilk. But remember, I told you I had six brothers and sisters then, plus my mother and grandfather. It is very difficult to be alone in the kitchen of a house that small with that many people. And do you know that brothers and sisters will snitch on you? Of course they all had heard about me and the buttermilk by that time, and every time I started to pour it out, they would say, "I'ma tell Mama. I'ma tell Daddy. Oooooweee. I'ma tell on you."

I never did get a chance to pour it out. Then Mama came into the kitchen to cook dinner. It was the middle of the week, and would you believe we were having fried chicken and biscuits. You haven't tasted biscuits until you've tasted my mother's. Ummmmmuh! I sat there and watched her cutting the chicken and then washing it. She dropped each piece into a paper bag into which she had put flour, salt, and pepper. After she shook the bag vigorously, she placed the chicken in the hot grease. Next she mixed the biscuits and rolled out the dough. My favorite part was when she cut them out with the biscuit cutter. When she placed them on the baking sheet and put them in the oven, that kitchen was smelling good. My stomach was growling. I could hardly wait to sink my teeth into that chicken.

Soon all the food was ready, and everyone came into the kitchen to eat. I pulled up to the table with the rest. My daddy looked at me and said, "What do you think you're doing?"

"Getting ready to eat, sir."

"Did you finish that buttermilk?"

"No, sir," and I hung my head because I knew what was coming next.

"Well, you don't get any food until that buttermilk is finished."

"But Daddy," I started, and as I got that buttermilk from the icebox, the tears started down my face. My daddy was being mean to me, and he didn't even care that I was hungry, and he was going to make me drink that old nasty buttermilk, and all my brothers and sisters were going to eat up all the chicken and biscuits, and I wouldn't get anything to eat, and nobody loved me . . . I had a real pity party. Through my tears I watched my siblings putting butter and jelly on their biscuits, taking big bites; and eating their chicken.

Soon everyone was finished, and I still had that dumb old buttermilk. But I got an idea. Perhaps if I held my nose while I drank it, I wouldn't be able to taste it. So I held my nose, took several big gulps, and the buttermilk was gone! I didn't even throw up! Mama had saved me a piece of chicken and two biscuits. It wasn't even my regular piece, and two biscuits when I could have eaten ten all by myself. But I was really grateful that she had saved me anything because I didn't think I was going to eat that night.

Well, I learned a big lesson that day. No, I did not learn to like buttermilk —but I did learn what Daddy meant when he said, "Your eyes are too big for your stomach."

All That Glitters

Munah Mayo

Every morning I begin my day by doing the Buddhist practice, and every evening I end my day by doing the Buddhist practice, which includes the chanting of *Nam-myoho-renge-kyo*.

I was born to indigenous Liberians in Greenville Sinoe County, Liberia, a country in West Africa. The president of our country sent me to the United States during the 1970s to attend college at Saint Mary's of the Springs, which later became Ohio Dominican College. I was known by one of those Americo-Liberian names.

Some of my friends would say, "You come from Africa, and you don't have an African name."

"I do have an African name," I would reply. "My name is Munah."

"What does your name mean?" they would ask.

"I don't know," I would say. No one had asked me what my name meant before I came to America.

"That's a nice name. Why don't you use it?"

So when I returned to Liberia during my first vacation break, I asked my mother what my name meant. The word *munah* means jump, but as a name that is from Kru (the language and name of my people) folklore, it means "the heart jumps." This name was usually given to babies who were so charismatic that your heart would jump (that is, skip a beat) when you saw them. Munah was not my original name, however. I can't remember what it was except that it was my father's mother's name, which was given to me because it is our tradition to name the first girl child after the father's mother.

I was told that when I was three months old, I was very sick. My family thought I was going to die. They took me to medical doctors, but none of them could find out what was wrong with me. So they took me to a "medicine man" who called the baby's spirit. The baby's spirit told the medicine man, "I am not my father's mother. I am my mother's mother. I am Munah. I'll leave and come back when it is time for you to recognize me as Munah."

My family changed my name to Munah, and I became well.

I am happy to be in America, yet I am saddened about the current war and conditions in Liberia. The situation is horrible. For months I didn't know the whereabouts of my family. I have since been told that my father is dead. He died in October 1993, but I did not hear about it until January 1994. I learned in March 1994 that my mother and her six grandchildren are alive, but she is not in good health. My son had to walk from Liberia to the Ivory Coast. It took him a month to get there. Now he is living in Atlanta, Georgia.

I received a letter from a dear friend of mine. She sent me this letter with no return address. She said in the letter that she has no food and no clothing. She eats grass to stay alive. I send money to my family, and I will help my friend also. But how can I with no return address? I will help her. I will find a way. In 1993 I became an American citizen, but I will always be a Liberian.

I remember that when I was a child, we would gather every evening for storytelling after dinner. Everyone told a story. Even the children were encouraged to tell stories to the best of their ability. One of my favorites, which I still remember, is one of the Kru stories.

A man left his home and traveled far away. He came to a village. There he met a woman and fell madly in love with her. He wanted to marry her and take her back to his home, but her people tried to discourage her from going away with him. But she would not listen because she loved him. So they were married in her village. The day after the wedding they began the long journey to his home. When they came to the next village, the man said, "Dear wife, I borrowed something from this village, and I must return it."

"Very well," said his wife.

So the man returned his shirt. They set off again, and when they entered the next village, the man said, "Dear wife, I borrowed something from this village, and I must return it."

"Very well," said his wife.

So the man returned his pants. They set off again, and when they entered the next village, the man said, "Dear wife, I borrowed something from this village, and I must return it."

"Very well," said his wife.

So the man returned his shoes. Every time they would enter the next village, the man would return something.

At the next village, he returned his hat.
At the next village, he returned his teeth.
At the next village, he returned his eyes.
"Eeeeeek!" the wife screamed. "I married the devil."
"All that glitters is not gold."

Nzambi and the Earth Connection

David A. Anderson/Sankofa

Nzambi Mpungu is the name assigned to the supreme god by several of the African groups residing along the Zaire River. His daughter Nzambi is given dominion over the earth. I have assigned her the name "Mother Earth." In this role she activates the elements that bring human beings into existence. The story is loosely based on the Igbo (Nigeria) story in which the stomach, not satisfied with the honorable place it had been given, pleaded to be placed in front where it could see (and catch) everything.

Long before there were people, the brand-new Earth was nothing much to look at. Hot and dry, it was, and not so much as a roach to kick up dust. It was . . . boring. Nzambi, who had given birth to Earth, decided she would give her child some life. She fenced off forty acres or so, chipped up some cocoa beans, right fine, and worked that into the soil. Then, for every twenty-nine and a half inches, Nzambi dropped a yam seed. She called for Rain, and Rain sprinkled the soil with sweet, lemony raindrops. She called for Sun, and he gave the soil warm hugs.

The soil was so divine that nearly everything Nzambi planted took root and grew great, green, and gorgeous. But it still wasn't right. That little patch down in the back twenty wasn't doing a thing. It was determined to be bored. Nzambi put her hands on her hips and said, "You got your nerve. Got a mind to slap a cotton plant crost your behind."

Nzambi, ever clever, decided to do something different. She put on some music, and when the beat got good, she got down, turned around in the rhythm, and planted a few ahdz and enzz in that little patch that didn't even have a weed growing in it. The ahdz and the enzz sent out roots and shoots, and they just eased themselves out into that rich, yammy, chocolaty soil: "Aa-a-a-h-h," sighed the ahdz. "O-o-oo-h-h," cooed the enzz. It felt so good that they kept on easing out and stretching out and growing! Like . . . there was wiggling toaz and pointing feengurz. Throatz La la, la-lahed. I-lashes blinkety-blink, blink bla-blinked. Hedzz, hipbz and the pitz-of-armz were doing their own things, and ell-bow laughed 'cause it was funny. Tung was already hanging out with the sweet potato pie and chocolate chips.

Nzambi was so pleased, she decided to check out the rest of her Baby Earth. She called all the ahdz, and every last one of the enzz together: "I see that you are happy, and I'm happy, too; you make this place so-o-o-o beautiful." All of them just cooed and sighed, and wiggled and tickled, and blew big, sweet bubbles in the soil.

All this made Nzambi very, very happy. "I'm going to leave ya'll for a while," Nzambi said. "But you will be fine because the warm sunlight and the sweet, lemony raindrops will be here for you. They will help you keep your home clean. All ya'll have to do is work together and respect each other."

All the enzz and ahdz ooh-aahed and promised Nzambi that they would keep their home beautiful. She waved to them, then stepped onto the first wave that came by, and finger-popped till she was out of sight. But as soon as she was out of sight, I-eeze saw something hands said belonged to them. Hands lost control and scratched hedzz so bad, they ached. Mouthz ran behind baxx, and tungs tattled to the noazez butting in. Eerz got full of what wasn't even said to them. Before nee could bend, all those parts were fighting: biting, booting; slapping, zapping, ca-bapping; clipping and whipping; jabbing and stabbing. And what they didn't say about each other woulda made you puke. It was so loud and lewd, Nzambi lost the beat.

Across the waves and over the breakers she boogied, back to that place. It was in ruins: gummed up with grungy, greasy, gloppy garbage; water so foul, stinking like old sneakers; air so nasty, burning Nzambi's eyes. Grotesque grunts and groans grated against her ear. Nzambi was angry. She was steaming! Mostly, she was sad. She ordered all the ahdz, and all the enzz to clean up the mess.

They limped around, tried to straighten what they had made crooked, repair what they had broken. Nzambi made them dump all the beyond-repair ahdz at the left gate, and all the never-will-be clean-again enzz at the right gate. Sun came and burned off most of the pollution, and Rain downpoured until everything washed clean.

Things looked better, though not as beautiful as before. Nzambi thought about what had happened. She got an idea. "We'll make a new start. I'm going to fix it so that ahdz and enzz will have to cooperate."

She chose some of this and some of that; a bushel of those and a pinch of them. She probed, pulled, plucked, pasted, packed, pruned, and pretty soon there it was. She stood it up and turned it around. "Hmmm. Look like you been put together from . . . from . . . Oh, well. I made you. You are mine, and I love you."

Compared to today's bodies, what Nzambi had made looked okay. "But," she said, "you need something that will make you want to cooperate each day."

She thought about it for a whole day before declaring, "Umm, hmm."

She picked through the leftover parts piled up at the left dump, and she dipped into the damaged discards dumped to the right. She snipped and sewed and stitched those scraps into a . . . stomach. She stuck it right behind the wribpz. Right off, the stomach started complaining: "How come I got to be behind all them skinny wribpz?" Nzambi sighed and dropped the stomach down to where it was just above the hipbz and right out in front.

"That's what I call a body," she said. She told that body: "Things can never again taste as good as sweet potato pie with chocolate chips on the side, but you will be able to live well. All you have to do is cooperate. All the parts will *have to* cooperate, because your stomach can get hurt by what goes into it. You got to take care of *your* stomach."

Because it sets right out front where it can get hurt, stomach to this day is often nervous. But the body parts worked together to take care of the stomach and the human being growing around that stomach. Nzambi was so pleased that she gave the whole assembly the name Human Being and tossed in a little ole serpent and a mule as bonuses.

Nzambi recycled most of the leftovers and fashioned a whole bunch of bodies. Made them stomachs, too. She made stomachs unreal. Some were neat; some were just plain old bellies. But each stomach had a body, and all parts of each body were connected. It was so groovy that one upset stomach talked its body into being very quiet until it burped—and felt better?

Nzambi gathered all the human beings together: "Before I take off on my world tour, I want to tell you that everything you need is right here. You must take care of your forty acres and mule. It won't be easy: You are made up of different shapes, shades, and sizes of scrap, and what there is of your brains is also made of scrap. But just like all parts of your bodies work together in order to survive, I want you to cooperate with each other. Respect each other as you would your stomach."

There was agreement. All the funny little humans said, "Yes." All the big goofy humans said, "Yes." All the blah, in-between humans said, "Maybe?" Nzambi didn't hear that. She was busy thrusting her hands down into a now clean pool of water. From that crystal-clear water she pulled a rainbow. Nzambi climbed on the arch of the rainbow, and as she rode across the sky, she could hear the humans singing, ". . . foot bone connected to the ankle bone, and the . . ."

The Rain Came

Grace Ogot

Grace Ogot is one of the best-known African women writers, yet she is still being discovered in the United States. She grew up in Kenya's Central Nyanza

District, and her experiences as a nurse, midwifery tutor, broadcaster, script writer, and community development officer have put her in touch with the cultural beliefs of her people and the continued conflicts within modern East African society. Well known as a short story writer, Grace Ogot is interested in the woman in society. "The Rain Came" is her most popular story.

The chief was still far from the gate when his daughter Oganda saw him. She ran to meet him. Breathlessly she asked her father, "What is the news, great Chief? Everyone in the village is anxiously waiting to hear when it will rain." Labong'o held out his hands for his daughter, but he did not say a word. Puzzled by her father's cold attitude Oganda ran back to the village to warn the others that the chief was back.

The atmosphere in the village was tense and confused. Everyone moved aimlessly and fussed in the yard without actually doing any work. A young woman whispered to her co-wife, "If they have not solved this rain business today, the chief will crack." They had watched him getting thinner and thinner as the people kept on pestering him. "Our cattle lie dying in the fields," they reported. "Soon it will be our children and then ourselves. Tell us what to do to save our lives, oh great Chief." So the chief had daily prayed with the Almighty through the ancestors to deliver them from their distress.

Instead of calling the family together and giving them the news immediately, Labong'o went to his own hut, a sign that he was not to be disturbed. Having replaced the shutter, he sat in the dimly lit hut to contemplate.

It was no longer a question of being the chief of hunger-stricken people that weighed Labong'o's heart. It was the life of his only daughter that was at stake. At the time when Oganda came to meet him, he saw the glittering chain shining around her waist. The prophecy was complete. "It is Oganda, Oganda, my only daughter, who must die so young." Labong'o burst into tears before finishing the sentence. The chief must not weep. Society had declared him the bravest of men. But Labong'o did not care anymore. He assumed the position of a simple father and wept bitterly. He loved his people, the Luo, but what were the Luo for him without Oganda? Her life had brought a new life in Labong'o's world and he ruled better than he could remember. How would the spirit of the village survive his beautiful daughter? "There are so many homes and so many parents who have daughters. Why choose this one? She is all I have." Labong'o spoke as if the ancestors were there in the hut and he could see them face to face. Perhaps they were there, warning him to remember his promise on the day he was enthroned when he said aloud, before the elders, "I will lay down life, if necessary, and the life of my household to save this tribe from the hands of the enemy." "Deny! Deny!" he could hear the voice of his forefathers mocking him.

When Labong'o was consecrated chief, he was only a young man. Unlike his father, he ruled for many years with only one wife. But people rebuked him because his only wife did not bear him a daughter. He married a second, a third, and a fourth wife. But they all gave birth to male children. When Labong'o married a fifth wife, she bore him a daughter. They called her Oganda, meaning "beans," because her skin was very fair. Out of Labong'o's twenty children, Oganda was the only girl. Though she was the chief's favorite, her mother's co-wives swallowed their jealous feelings and showered her with love. After all, they said, Oganda was a female child whose days in the royal family were numbered. She would soon marry at a tender age and leave the enviable position to someone else.

Never in his life had he been faced with such an impossible decision. Refusing to yield to the rainmaker's request would mean sacrificing the whole tribe, putting the interests of the individual above those of the society. More than that, it would mean disobeying the ancestors, and most probably wiping the Luo people from the surface of the earth. On the other hand, to let Oganda die as a ransom for the people would permanently cripple Labong'o spiritually. He knew he would never be the same chief again.

The words of Ndithi, the medicine man, still echoed in his ears. "Podho, the ancestor of the Luo, appeared to me in a dream last night, and he asked me to speak to the chief and the people," Ndithi had said to the gathering of tribesmen. "A young woman who has not known a man must die so that the country may have rain. While Podho was still talking to me, I saw a young woman standing at the lakeside, her hands raised above her head. Her skin was as fair as the skin of young deer in the wilderness. Her tall slender figure stood like a lonely reed at the riverbank. Her sleepy eyes wore a sad look like that of a bereaved mother. She wore a gold ring on her left ear and a glittering brass chain around her waist. As I still marveled at the beauty of this young woman, Podho told me, 'Out of all the women in this land, we have chosen this one. Let her offer herself a sacrifice to the lake monster! And on that day the rain will come down in torrents. Let everyone stay at home on that day, lest he be carried away by the floods.' "

Outside there was a strange stillness, except for the thirsty birds that sang lazily on the dying trees. The blinding midday heat had forced the people to retire to their huts. Not far away from the chief's hut, two guards were snoring away quietly. Labong'o removed his crown and the large eagle head that hung loosely on his shoulders. He left the hut, and instead of asking Nyabog'o the messenger to beat the drum, he went straight and beat it himself. In no time the whole household had assembled under the siala tree where he usually addressed them. He told Oganda to wait a while in her grandmother's hut.

When Labong'o stood to address his household, his voice was hoarse and the tears choked him. He started to speak, but words refused to leave his lips. His wives and sons knew there was great danger. Perhaps their enemies had declared war on them. Labong'o's eyes were red, and they could see he had been weeping. At last he told them. "One whom we love and treasure must be taken away from us. Oganda is to die." Labong'o's voice was so faint that he could not hear it himself. But he continued. "The ancestors have chosen her to be offered as a sacrifice to the lake monster in order that we may have rain."

They were completely stunned. As a confused murmur broke out, Oganda's mother fainted and was carried off to her own hut. But the other people rejoiced. They danced around singing and chanting, "Oganda is the lucky one to die for the people. If it is to save the people, let Oganda go."

In her grandmother's hut Oganda wondered what the whole family was discussing about her that she could not hear. Her grandmother's hut was well away from the chief's court, and, much as she strained her ears, she could not hear what was said. "It must be marriage," she concluded. It was an accepted custom for the family to discuss their daughter's future marriage behind her back. A faint smile played on Oganda's lips as she thought of the several young men who swallowed saliva at the mere mention of her name.

There was Kech, the son of a neighboring clan elder. Kech was very handsome. He had sweet, meek eyes and a roaring laughter. He would make a wonderful father, Oganda thought. But they would not be a good match. Kech was a bit too short to be her husband. It would humiliate her to have to look down at Kech each time she spoke to him. Then she thought of Dimo, the tall young man who had already distinguished himself as a brave warrior and an outstanding wrestler. Dimo adored Oganda, but Oganda thought he would make a cruel husband, always quarreling and ready to fight. No, she did not like him. Oganda fingered the glittering chain on her waist as she thought of Osinda. A long time ago when she was quite young Osinda had given her that chain, and instead of wearing it around her neck several times, she wore it round her waist where it could stay permanently. She heard her heart pounding so loudly as she thought of him. She whispered, "Let it be you they are discussing, Osinda, the lovely one. Come now and take me away . . ."

The lean figure in the doorway startled Oganda who was rapt in thought about the man she loved. "You have frightened me, Grandma," said Oganda, laughing. "Tell me, is it my marriage you were discussing? You can take it from me that I won't marry any of them." A smile played on her lips again. She was coaxing the old lady to tell her quickly, to tell her they were pleased with Osinda.

In the open space outside, the excited relatives were dancing and singing. They were coming to the hut now, each carrying a gift to put at

Oganda's feet. As their singing got nearer, Oganda was able to hear what they were saying: "If it is to save the people, if it is to give us rain, let Oganda go. Let Oganda die for her people and for her ancestors." Was she mad to think that they were singing about her? How could she die? She found the lean figure of her grandmother barring the door. She could not get out. The look on her grandmother's face warned her that there was danger around the corner. "Grandma, it is not marriage then?" Oganda asked urgently. She suddenly felt panicky, like a mouse cornered by a hungry cat. Forgetting that there was only one door in the hut, Oganda fought desperately to find another exit. She must fight for her life. But there was none.

She closed her eyes and leapt like a wild tiger through the door, knocking her grandmother flat to the ground. There outside in mourning garments Labong'o stood motionless, his hands folded at the back. He held his daughter's hand and led her away from the excited crowd to the little red-painted hut where her mother was resting. Here he broke the news officially to his daughter.

For a long time the three souls who loved one another dearly sat in darkness. It was no good speaking. And even if they tried, the words could not have come out. In the past they had been like three cooking stones, sharing their burdens. Taking Oganda away from them would leave two useless stones which would not hold a cooking pot.

News that the beautiful daughter of the chief was to be sacrificed to give the people rain spread across the country like wind. At sunset the chief's village was full of relatives and friends who had come to congratulate Oganda. Many more were on their way coming, carrying their gifts. They would dance till morning to keep her company. And in the morning they would prepare her a big farewell feast. All these relatives thought it a great honor to be selected by the spirits to die in order that the society may live. "Oganda's name will always remain a living name among us," they boasted.

But was it maternal love that prevented Minya from rejoicing with the other women? Was it the memory of the agony and pain of childbirth that made her feel so sorrowful? Or was it the deep warmth and understanding that passes between a suckling babe and her mother that made Oganda part of her life, her flesh? Of course it was an honor, a great honor, for her daughter to be chosen to die for the country. But what could she gain once her only daughter was blown away by the wind? There were so many other women in the land, why choose her daughter, her only child! Had human life any meaning at all—other women had houses full of children while she, Minya, had to lose her only child!

In the cloudless sky the moon shone brightly, and the numerous stars glittered with a bewitching beauty. The dancers of all age groups assembled to dance before Oganda, who sat close to her mother, sobbing quietly. All these years she had been with her people she thought she understood them. But now she discovered that she was a stranger among them. If they loved her as they had always professed, why were they not making any attempt to save her? Did her people really understand what it felt like to die young? Unable to restrain her emotions any longer, she sobbed loudly as her age group got up to dance. They were young and beautiful, and very soon they would marry and have their own children. They would have husbands to love and little huts for themselves. They would have reached maturity. Oganda touched the chain around her waist as she thought of Osinda. She wished Osinda was there, too, among her friends. "Perhaps he is ill," she thought gravely. The chain comforted Oganda—she would die with it around her waist and wear it in the underground world.

In the morning a big feast was prepared for Oganda. The women prepared many different tasty dishes so that she could pick and choose. "People don't eat after death," they said. Delicious though the food looked, Oganda touched none of it. Let the happy people eat. She contented herself with sips of water from a little calabash.

The time for her departure was drawing near, and each minute was precious. It was a day's journey to the lake. She was to walk all night, passing through the great forest. But nothing could touch her, not even the denizens of the forest. She was already anointed with sacred oil. From the time Oganda received the sad news, she had expected Osinda to appear any moment. But he was not there. A relative told her that Osinda was away on a private visit. Oganda realized that she would never see her beloved again.

In the late afternoon the whole village stood at the gate to say good-bye and to see her for the last time. Her mother wept on her neck for a long time. The great chief in a mourning skin came to the gate barefooted, and mingled with the people—a simple father in grief. He took off his wrist bracelet and put it on his daughter's wrist, saying, "You will always live among us. The spirit of our forefathers is with you."

Tongue-tied and unbelieving, Oganda stood there before the people. She had nothing to say. She looked at her home once more. She could hear her heart beating so painfully within her. All her childhood plans were coming to an end. She felt like a flower nipped in the bud, never to enjoy the morning dew again. She looked at her weeping mother and whispered. "Whenever you want to see me, always look at the sunset. I will be there."

Oganda turned southward to start her trek to the lake. Her parents, relatives, friends, and admirers stood at the gate and watched her go.

Her beautiful slender figure grew smaller and smaller till she mingled with the thin dry trees in the forest. As Oganda walked the lonely path that wound its way in the wilderness, she sang a song, and her own voice kept her company.

The ancestors have said Oganda must die
The daughter of the chief must be sacrificed.
When the lake monster feeds on my flesh,
The people will have rain.
Yes, the rain will come down in torrents,
And the floods will wash away the sandy beaches
When the daughter of the chief dies in the lake.
My age group has consented
My parents have consented
So have my friends and relatives.
Let Oganda die to give us rain.
My age group are young and ripe,
Ripe for womanhood and motherhood
But Oganda must die young,
Oganda must sleep with the ancestors.
Yes, rain will come down in torrents.

The red rays of the setting sun embraced Oganda, and she looked like a burning candle in the wilderness.

The people who came to hear her sad song were touched by her beauty. But they all said the same thing. "If it is to save the people, if it is to give us rain, then be not afraid. Your name will forever live among us."

At midnight Oganda was tired and weary. She could walk no more. She sat under a big tree, and having sipped water from her calabash, she rested her head on the tree trunk and slept.

When Oganda woke up in the morning, the sun was high in the sky. After walking for many hours, she reached the *tong'*, a strip of land that separated the inhabited part of the country from the sacred place *(kar lamo)*. No layman could enter this place and come out alive—only those who had direct contact with the spirits and the Almighty were allowed to enter this holy of holies. But Oganda had to pass through this sacred land on her way to the lake, which she had to reach at sunset.

A large crowd gathered to see her for the last time. Her voice was now hoarse and painful, but there was no need to worry anymore. Soon she would not have to sing. The crowd looked at Oganda sympathetically, mumbling words she could not hear. But none of them pleaded for life. As Oganda opened the gate, a child, a young child, broke loose from the crowd and ran toward her. The child took a small earring from her sweaty hands and gave it to Oganda, saying, "When you reach the world of the dead, give this earring to my sister. She died last week. She forgot this ring." Oganda, taken aback by the strange request, took the little ring and handed her precious water and food to the child. She did not need them now. Oganda did not know whether to laugh or cry. She had heard mourners sending their love to their sweethearts, long dead, but this idea of sending gifts was new to her.

Oganda held her breath as she crossed the barrier to enter the sacred land. She looked appealingly at the crowd, but there was no response. Their minds were too preoccupied with their own survival. Rain was the precious medicine they were longing for, and the sooner Oganda could get to her destination the better.

A strange feeling possessed Oganda as she picked her way in the sacred land. There were strange noises that often startled her, and her first reaction was to take to her heels. But she remembered that she had to fulfill the wish of her people. She was exhausted, but the path was still winding. Then suddenly the path ended on sandy land. The water had retreated miles away from the shore, leaving a wide stretch of sand. Beyond this was the vast expanse of water.

Oganda felt afraid. She wanted to picture the size and shape of the monster, but fear would not let her. The society did not talk about it, nor did the crying children who were silenced by the mention of its name. The sun was still up, but it was no longer hot. For a long time Oganda walked ankle-deep in the sand. She was exhausted and longed desperately for her calabash of water. As she moved on, she had a strange feeling that something was following her. Was it the monster? Her hair stood erect, and a cold paralyzing feeling ran along her spine. She looked behind, sideways and in front, but there was nothing except a cloud of dust.

Oganda pulled up and hurried, but the feeling did not leave her and her whole body became saturated with perspiration.

The sun was going down fast, and the lake shore seemed to move along with it.

Oganda started to run. She must be at the lake before sunset. As she ran she heard a noise coming from behind. She looked back sharply, and something resembling a moving bush was frantically running after her. It was about to catch up with her.

Oganda ran with all her strength. She was now determined to throw herself into the water even before sunset. She did not look back, but the creature was upon her. She made an effort to cry out, as in a nightmare, but she could not hear her own voice. The creature caught up with Oganda. In the utter confusion, as Oganda came face to face with the unidentified creature, a strong hand grabbed her. But she fell flat on the sand and fainted.

When the lake breeze brought her back to consciousness, a man was bending over her. ". . . !!" Oganda opened her mouth to speak, but she had lost her voice. She swallowed a mouthful of water poured into her mouth by the stranger.

"Osinda, Osinda! Please let me die. Let me run, the sun is going down. Let me die, let them have rain." Osinda fondled the glittering chain around Oganda's waist and wiped the tears from her face.

"We must escape quickly to the unknown land," Osinda said urgently. "We must run away from the wrath of the ancestors and the retaliation of the monster."

"But the curse is upon me, Osinda. I am no good to you anymore. And moreover the eyes of the ancestors will follow us everywhere and bad luck will befall us. Nor can we escape from the monster."

Oganda broke loose, afraid to escape, but Osinda grabbed her hands again.

"Listen to me, Oganda! Listen! Here are two coats!" He then covered the whole of Oganda's body, except her eyes, with a leafy attire made from the twigs of Bwombwe. "These will protect us from the eyes of the ancestors and the wrath of the monster. Now let us run out of here." He held Oganda's hand, and they ran from the sacred land, avoiding the path that Oganda had followed.

The bush was thick, and the long grass entangled their feet as they ran. Halfway through the sacred land they stopped and looked back. The sun was almost touching the surface of the water. They were frightened. They continued to run, now faster, to avoid the sinking sun.

"Have faith, Oganda—that thing will not reach us."

When they reached the barrier and looked behind them, trembling, only a tip of the sun could be seen above the water's surface.

"It is gone! It is gone!" Oganda wept, hiding her face in her hands.

"Weep not, daughter of the chief. Let us run, let us escape."

There was a bright lightning. They looked up, frightened. Above them black furious clouds started to gather. They began to run. Then the thunder roared, and the rain came down in torrents.

A Village of Women

Shanta

"A Village of Women" is part of a collection called *Light Worker*, a culmination of many years of exploring storytelling, music, meditation, and channeling. It is a collection of stories and music that reflect my intent to synthesize art and spirituality. I am a storyteller because telling stories is a way to share the joy I derive from stories.

Meditation has helped me to become balanced and centered in the light of my own higher self. And channeling, being open to the wisdom and guidance and even the creativity the universe has to share with all of us, is for me simply a way of listening. I hear the Creator's plan for my life, and I hear the angels, or spirits, or the special messengers who help to guide us on this earth walk.

But whatever name they are called, I experience them as loving friends and beings of light. I feel honored to be their vehicle for sharing these special stories that urge us toward being our best selves.

There was once a village full of women, beautiful women, strong, intelligent women, powerful women. This village had an attractiveness that caused other women from many different places to go and stay there for a while. Some would then go home. Others decided to live there.

One day a message was received in that place, and all of the women gathered to hear its contents. The message said that the women had a specific period of time in which to discover all that they were and all that they had come to the earth to do. If by the end of that period (and no one remembers now how long it was) they had not come into the full knowledge of who they were and why they were here, they would all forget everything that they knew.

The women received this challenge joyfully: "Yes! An opportunity to come into fuller knowledge!"

So they went about this task lovingly, creatively.

But then it got to the point when there were only five days left before their time was up. Anxiety started stirring up in these women. There was not a single woman in that place who felt she had completed her task.

So the women came together, and, as they discussed it, each woman expressed a feeling that there was something missing, that there was something she did not yet know. But after coming so far, the thought of having to forget everything was too horrible to even imagine.

So they put their minds together, literally. Each woman projected a portion of her mind into the center of their living space. And that collective mind (which of course was connected to The Great Mind) percolated there. It mixed around. And it came up with a plan.

The plan was that for the remaining five days the women were to live in total silence. No words would be spoken. No entertainment would be sought. Certainly they could still smile and share hugs and hold hands. And, all the while, each woman would continue to contribute a portion of her mind to that collective mind.

And that is how it was.

By the evening of the third day, some of the older women were smiling. By the evening of the fourth day, some of the other women were smiling, too. And by the afternoon of the fifth day, all the women were smiling, dancing, singing, rejoicing. For at the very same moment all the women knew exactly who they were and what they had come here to do.

While they were in the silence, that collective mind absorbed and became absorbed by The Great Mind. The moment this merger was complete was the moment each woman felt her knowledge was complete. And she rejoiced that she would be able to remember.

The women continued to live in that place. They were very happy, very creative, very wise.

Some of the women left that village, then came back. Some of them left and never returned. One of them might have been your grandmother or your next-door neighbor. Some of them might be walking around today.

If you recognize one of these women, grab her hand. Ask her if you can put your mind together with hers so that you, too, can live a wonderful life, a creative life, an incredible life.

Full Circle

Walter Dallas

Story theater in African societies exists primarily on three planes:

The first plane is the actual event in real time. In days long gone but not forgotten, Ga hunters, for example, used to leave the coastal areas of Ghana and go up-country to hunt for food, At the end of the hunting season, the entire town would welcome the men back with a joyous homecoming celebration. Food and palm wine flowed as every home opened its doors for the biggest party of the season. The streets were full of people, and one would be welcomed into any house to eat, dance, drink, and make new friends. The Ga Festival is an annual celebration in Ghana although the men no longer leave en masse for the hunt in exactly the same way. But the yearly reenactment of the homecoming is pure theater and exists on the second plane. The entire town transforms itself and retells the story of the Ga homecoming. The men represent the hunters, of course, and some even wear colorful traditional dress and body paintings whose motives are not only aesthetic but also status indicators. Everyone is acting, improvising, and stepping in and out of the story as needed, transforming to move the story to its climax.

If this Ga Festival were to be created on a stage in a theater as part of a scripted production, we would witness the Ga Festival on the third plane, that of theatrical production. Actors would play specific roles. This event could be exciting, visually and emotionally powerful, if transformation and improvisation occurs.

Story theater means theater in which storytelling technique involves an intricate layering of character, ritual, improvisation, time, place, transformation, imagination, motivations, and so forth, a kind of stacking that resembles the stacking of one story on another to create, for example, a ten-story building. The cement that holds the stories together is the power in the ability to transform time, place, object, and character: the ability to become one with the event, to transform, to construct, destruct, and, at any given moment, to step outside of the action like a griot who bears witness because he remembers with his feelings and touches with his voice—like a fetish priestess who becomes one with her mission or the ritualistic Ashanti Asafo-hene, the king who at once recreates the past, transforms the present, points toward the future, and is, by the way, the consummate actor and storyteller existing on the stage of the second plane.

As a director I'm fascinated by circles, the power of the circle and the transformation of time, space, and character in theater. My earliest recollections of storytelling include events sitting in circles, around campfires. Coming full circle, going around in circles, storytelling in circle represents power and the ability to transform.

PART II

—⁓—

I Will Never Be Any Service to Anyone as a Slave

Stories About Freedom

Where are your monuments, your battles, martyrs?
Where is your tribal memory? Sirs
in that grey vault. The Sea. The Sea
has locked them up. The Sea is History.

—DEREK WALCOTT, "The Sea is History"

"Once upon a time there was an old woman. Blind but wise." Or was it an old man? A guru, perhaps. Or a *griot* soothing restless children. I have heard this story, or one exactly like it, in the lore of several cultures.

"Once upon a time there was an old woman. Blind Wise."

In the version I know the woman is the daughter of slaves, black, American, and lives alone in a small house outside of town. Her reputation for wisdom is without peer and without question.

—TONI MORRISON, accepting the Nobel
Prize for Literature

Not to know is bad, not to want to know is worse. (West Africa)

A people without a knowledge of their history is like a tree without roots. (West Africa)

If you ask no questions, you will gain no knowledge. (Central Africa.)

You better mind what you talk, you better mind what you talk about. (African American)

A Riddle for Freedom

William J. Faulkner

My fondest memories of Dad telling the folktales would be after dinner on Sunday afternoons as we sat around the round dining table in our sunny, informal dining area, almost always with company present. The most remembered stories, Dad's favorites, I think, were "The Magic Gate" (entitled "Brer Wolf's Magic Gate" in his collection of folktales), "Brer Tiger and the Big Wind," and "The Riddle for Freedom," for which he never seemed to give us the answer until he wrote the book. Whenever he told the stories, however, we were always spellbound and fascinated as he brought to life the "tales of olden days, when the animals used to walk and talk like menfolk."

—Marie Faulkner Brown

Having heard about Big Tom's escape to freedom, I wanted to know about other slaves who had managed to flee their masters. Simon Brown had stores of such tales to tell, and one of the best was about a smart plow-hand named Jim, who "riddled his way to freedom." This is his story, as Simon told it to me.

Now, when I was a slave in old Virginia, I met this plow-hand named Jim. He was the smartest slave on the whole plantation—and on any plantation around. Well, one Christmas morning, Jim knocked on the Big House step, and old Master John Brown came out on the piazza.

"Good morning, Master," said Jim.

"Good morning, Jim," answered Master John.

"Christmas gift, Master," called out Jim, practicing an old plantation tradition.

"Oh, you caught me!" said Master John. "You said 'Christmas gift' first. So, what do you want me to give you?"

"I want my freedom, Master. Now, if I can tell you a riddle you can't answer, will you give me my freedom?"

Master John studied for a minute, and then he said, "Yes, Jim, I'll do it." He must have figured that no slave was smart enough to fool his master.

A whole year passed by, and Christmas came again. Then Jim rode a young colt up to the Big House, and he knocked on the steps. Old Master came out.

"Good morning, Master," said Jim.

"Good morning, Jim."

"Master, would you please call your family and all the house servants out on the piazza, and take down the horn and blow up the field hands—

all for to hear the riddle I promised last Christmas to tell you for my freedom."

Well, Master John called the family and the servants out of the house, and he took the horn down from the wall on the piazza, and he blew for the field hands to come from the quarters to hear Jim's riddle. When everyone was gathered, Jim mounted the colt and began to tell his riddle. And this is what Jim said:

> "Sambo, lingo, lang tang,
> Chicken, he flutters the do lang tang.
> Old eighteen hundred and fifty-one,
> As I went in and out again,
> Out the dead the living came.

> "Under the gravel I do travel;
> On the cold iron I do stand.
> I ride the filly never foaled,
> And hold the damsel in my hand.

> "Water knee-deep in the clan,
> And not a wiggle-tail to be seen.
> Seven there were, but six there be;
> As I'm a virgin, set me free!"

Master John Brown's face turned red. He walked up and down the piazza. Jim was his best plow-hand, and he didn't want to give him up. Old Master threw his hat on the floor, but he just couldn't answer Jim's riddle.

Finally Jim said, "I'll tell you one more time, Master, and if you can't answer me then, I know you'll give me my freedom, because your word is as good as your bond. Now, here I come again with the riddle." And Jim told the riddle once more, real fast.

But Master John couldn't give the answer, and at last he said to Jim, "All right, Jim, you got your freedom—and the colt, too, as a Christmas gift."

So, after telling the answer to the riddle, Jim rode off across the field with his freedom papers in his hand. And from that day to this, he was never a slave anymore.

After the story, Simon and I sat in silence for a moment. Then he said, "Now, Willie, you've been off to school. What was the answer to the riddle? You don't know?"

It wasn't until I became fourteen years old that the old man told me the answer. Here it is.

> *Sambo, lingo, lang tang,*
> *Chicken, he flutters the do lang tang.*

"That was just the introduction," said Simon.

> *Old eighteen hundred and fifty-one*

was the year it happened.

> *As I went in and out again,*
> *Out the dead the living came.*

As Jim went in and out of his cabin, he had seen the skeleton of a horse on the edge of the woods, and out of it had come Sis Partridge and her drove of young ones.

> *Under the gravel I do travel.*

Jim had put gravel in the top of his hat, and of course his master couldn't see it.

> *On the cold iron I do stand.*

Jim had his feet in the iron stirrups of the saddle.

> *I ride the filly never foaled,*
> *And hold the damsel in my hand.*

Jim was riding a colt that never was foaled, or born, because its mother had died in the birthing. Jim had delivered the colt alive, and then had made a whip out of the hide of the mother, the dam. Of course Master John didn't know anything about that.

> *Water knee-deep in the clan,*
> *And not a wiggle-tail to be seen.*

Jim had his boots full of water, but there was no way for his master to see the wiggle-tails.

> *Seven there were, but six there be;*
> *As I'm a virgin, set me free.*

Sis Patridge had seven eggs in her nest, but one had spoiled, so only six hatched out. And since Jim was an innocent man, he asked to be set free.

"Ah, yes," said Simon. "A lot of people think the slaves liked to be in bondage. But I want to tell you, every one of them that was worth his salt wanted to be free. And, like Big Tom and Jim, they did most anything to get that way. Yes, siree, freedom came hard and slow to us black folks, and now we've got it, we mustn't ever let it go. You remember that, Willie. You hear me? You remember that."

ANCIENT RIDDLE

Anamonkwan etwa asuo mu.   The footpath crosses the river.
Asuo etwa anamonkwan mu.   The river crosses the footpath.
Hwan ne panyin?   Which one is older?
Onipa na oboo okwan.   People made the path.
Asuo de Yebe tooye.   We came to meet the river.
Asuo wo ho firi tete.   The river is from long ago.
Obo Adee Tete Odomankoma, na   The Creator, Almighty God, created
   oyoo ye.   it.

from the Atumpan, talking drums of Ghana
(Twi)

HERITAGE

It has never been easy being of two cultures.
I am Blackfoot and Crow.
I am Black. I am African American.
I hear the African and the Indian drums.

Candece Tarpley

EVEN THE CLOTH CAN TALK

Eti kro nko agyina. It takes more than one head to form a committee.

—Proverb woven on Kente cloth, royal
fabric made by the Ashanti weavers of
Ghana.

The Odyssey of Peter Still: A Man Who Bought Himself

Gloria Tuggle Still

Before I met my husband, Kenneth Still, I knew nothing of the Still family and their celebrated family reunion. I have embarked upon a wonderful journey through history, and I am glad that my seven children and fourteen grandchildren are a part of that history.

The family journey began in West Africa and continued across the ocean to

South Jersey in the United States where, in the 1600s, a young Guinea prince "in the direct line" bestowed on his clan the precious gift that has allowed them to follow their roots through three hundred years of American History. He gave them a last name: Still.

I collected the Still family stories from Clarence "Clem" Still, the official patriarch and historian for the Still family. The family has been celebrating their reunion for over 125 years. The reunion is held in Lawnside, New Jersey, known for its great-tasting barbecue.

A journey of a thousand miles began on a sweltering hot afternoon in 1804 on the Eastern Shore of Maryland. Kincaid, a tall, hollow-cheeked man with stringy hair and eyes set deep in the sockets, tossed two terrified little boys into the hold of a flat-bottomed boat.

Kincaid was a small-time player in the terrible trade of human suffering. He bought and sold human beings. The boys were eight-year-old Levin Still and his six-year-old brother Peter. They were sold to Kincaid by Saunders Griffin.

But the life story of little Levin and especially the accomplishments of Peter would come to hold a significant place in history. He would grow up to become a man undaunted by adversity. In the end he would become known in the United States, Canada, and Europe as "The Man Who Bought Himself."

Earlier, Peter's father, Levin Still, Sr., had vowed he would die rather than "bear the yoke" of slavery. Afraid that Still might kill himself, Griffin allowed him to buy his freedom for a small price. But Griffin refused to release his family. Keeping Peter and Levin, Peter's sisters Mahalah and Keturah, and Peter's mother Sidney was Griffin's revenge against his father.

Undaunted, Peter's mother and father made a plan. As soon as Still was free and settled up north with a place for his family, word of mouth came back to the slave quarters. Peter's mother gathered her little band together and ran away to be with her husband.

The brave family reunited, at a place near Greenwich, New Jersey. Their joy did not last, however. Within weeks the slave hunters found them. Chained and shackled, mother and children were taken back to Maryland.

Within months Peter's mother had "resolved to again make a bold strike for freedom" and reunite her family. This time she would take only the girls with her—girls were most vulnerable in slave quarters. She would travel farther into New Jersey, to a place called Burlington County. She would change her name from Sidney to Charity. She would disappear with her husband into an isolated section of the county called the Pine Barrens. When the family was settled, her husband would slip back under the cover of darkness and steal away Peter and Levin. Meanwhile, the boys would be relatively safe under the watchful eye of their grandmother.

But the parents had not anticipated the rage of Saunders Griffin when he found Peter and Levin's mother had run away again. Griffin had thought she was "cured" of her desire to run. She went about her chores, seemingly tranquil, singing some of the good old Methodist tunes, and baking all his favorites, especially those golden brown biscuits. She did his every bidding and never grumbled. As a result he had concluded she was better contented than ever, and allowed her garret door to remain unlocked at night.

When her escape was discovered, Griffin went on a rampage and sold Peter and his brother down the river. That was how Peter and Levin were headed down south to Kentucky.

Among the mass of human chattel in the hold of the boat was an old woman. She took frightened little Peter into her arms and comforted him.

"Mmmm, mmmm," she cooed, "Mmmm, po' li'l man. Don' you cry."

"Want my mama," the little boy cried.

"I don't think you gon' find yo' mama, li'l man." The old woman gently rocked the little boy against her bosom to quiet the new spasm of tears brought on by her announcement.

"But I am gonna find my mama. I *gotta* find my mama," the small boy wailed.

"What your name li'l man?"

"Peter . . . my name Peter, and dis my brother Levin."

"Now Peter—you, too, Levin—y'all got one chance, *maybe.*" She lowered her voice to a whisper. "What you gotta do is tell people at that plantation where they takin' you that you been stole from a place called Philadelphia. I hear tell dat colored folks is free in Philadelphia, and if you can fin' a white man you can trus' and tell how you been stole from there and sold away from your mama, maybe you can git free and find your folks. Can you 'member dat, Peter? 'Member dat now, an den say Fee-lee-del-fee-a for Granny Mose. Say it now."

"I can say it, Granny. I can say Fee-lee-del-fee-a." He continued to sob, but the uncontrolled bawling had stopped.

For almost half a century Peter held on to the old woman's words. At the time of his mother's escape, he and Levin were too young to know that they were slaves. He believed then and he continued to believe he had been stolen from his mother. He believed in and longed for a home he thought he knew, Philadelphia.

Levin was never able to reconcile Peter's everlasting optimism, however. Eventually Kincaid sold the boys to John Fisher, the owner of a brickyard in Lexington, Kentucky. The boys were bought to be "offbearers." They were beaten and worked like a team of mules. Bearers worked in pairs, each pair having to cart off three thousand bricks a day. In the beginning, because of Peter's size, he was put to work inside the Fisher home, in the garden, and around the farm. It was there that little Peter told his story to Fisher's son and his young friend from a neighboring farm. The friend said his daddy could help anyone who had been unduly wronged.

"Well, we was stole from our mama," Peter told Ted Clay. "And we be free 'cause we was stole from Fee-lee-del-fee-a. An' Granny Mose say colored people be free dere."

After meeting the boy's father and telling him his story, Peter waited. Peter believed Senator Henry Clay when he told him, "First we must find out where you were stolen from so we can send you back there. It would be foolish to raise the issue with Fisher otherwise."

But at the end of three years, Peter and Levin still belonged to John Fisher, the mason, who lived on Main Street in Lexington, Kentucky. Young Ted Clay had been so certain that a great man like his father would help the boys find their way home, even Levin had dared to hope, "jus' a little."

Time dragged by until one day the boys learned that Fisher planned to sell his brickyard. The boys were fearful of separation. The yard was finally sold, and for an extra $450 the boys were included as part of the deal. The buyer, Nat Gist, was known for his drunken stupors. It was in one of his stupors that Gist ordered Peter to "take off your shirt and cross your hands." Peter and Levin had been warned that Master Nattie's favorite form of punishment was "bucking." Gist lashed Peter's hands together and threw them down over his knees. He then took a long broom handle and thrust it under Peter's knees, locking him into a whipping position.

Over and over the whip lashed through the air. Peter saw his own blood leaking through the rough wooden floor. Finally Gist removed the stick from behind Peter's knees and unbound his hands.

"Next time I'll leave you in the buck all day!" Gist declared.

But Peter vowed there would be no next time. In a low, quiet voice he would sing, "Got one mind for the boss to see. Got another mind for what I know is me."

Peter and Levin left Kentucky because Nattie Gist died. They were willed to Gist's nephew Levi, along with a cherry bedstead with bedding, a bowl and pitcher, a sorrel horse, Aunt Mary, ten sacks of coffee, and a barrel of sperm oil.

Levi Gist lived in Bainbridge, Alabama, and by the time Peter and Levin reached Bainbridge, a feeling of dread had settled over Peter. Alabama was worse than he had ever imagined. They were expected to slave in these cotton fields for the rest of their lives. In spite of the harsh life, Peter was determined to make a better life for himself. He practiced self-discipline by abstaining from liquor, tobacco, and bad language.

Then one tragic day in December 1821, Levin, not yet twenty-five years old, was slashed 317 times with a rawhide lash. He had been whipped by his wife's master for visiting her too often at the neighboring plantation. Levin was finally released from slavery. A tearful Peter buried the older brother with whom he had shared so much tragedy.

"Oh, Levin," he cried aloud. "Now you gon' see our mama. Now you be free."

Rather than destroy him, Levin's death strengthened Peter. He renewed his vow not to die a slave. And like Levin, Peter met a woman from another plantation. They fell in love, married, and had a family. Like his parents before him, Peter was determined they would all be free. Like his father, he worked whenever he had free time from his plantation duties. Sometimes during the winter months he earned additional money by freeing flatboats loaded with cotton that had gotten caught on the rocks in the Muscle Shoals. Slowly, as the years went by, he accumulated the money to purchase his freedom. He had saved over $300. Peter's wife Vina feared for the sum of money that Peter was hiding. She knew if anyone found out a slave was in possession of such a substantial amount, he would be whipped or worse, and the money taken away.

Unlike his father, Peter was far from the boundaries of the free state of New Jersey. The state of Alabama would not recognize the freedom of a slave even if it were given by the slave owner.

Then one day a new shop opened up in town. Peter stopped by to see if the new owner needed help. He did, and Peter was hired. The following Saturday when the work was completed, Peter realized that he had been paid more than twice the amount anyone else had ever paid him.

As the weeks went by, Peter came to know and respect Joseph Friedman. One Saturday when Peter's chores were finished earlier than usual, he asked why Friedman and his brother Isaac behaved so different from the other white people in the community. He wanted to know why they treated him like a "real human person" instead of a piece of human chattel.

Joseph Friedman explained to Peter that he was a Jew. He said he understood persecution. He told him that many centuries ago God had delivered his people from slavery under a pharaoh in a place called Egypt. Peter wanted to know if that was the reason some of the townspeople were so often rude to them.

Friedman reflected. "It's ironic. Even when the slavery has ended, the persecution seems to continue."

In spite of Vina's fears, Peter confided in Joseph Friedman. He believed that he had finally found the white man he could trust. Peter would finally acquire his freedom.

The Friedmans decided to purchase Peter's freedom for him even though they were aware they could not set him free in Alabama. For more than a year Peter had been careful to cough, complain, and walk with a stoop around the plantation. Before the offer was made by Friedman for Peter, the new owner, John Hogan, had commented, "You gittin' ole an' broke down, Peter. What use is you 'round here anyway?"

Between January 26, 1849, and April 16, 1850, in five installments, Peter gave Friedman a total of $500 for the purchase of his freedom. "The Man Who Bought Himself" prepared to leave for his long-sought Promised Land,

Philadelphia. He assured his family that once he had gotten to Philadelphia and found his mother, he would raise enough money to buy their freedom and bring them to be with him.

Meanwhile, they all understood they were to go along with the ruse devised by the Friedmans. Joseph would take over the shop, while his brother Isaac made a trip home to Cincinnati, Ohio. Of course he would take their newly acquired slave with him to wait on him during his travels.

Peter would always remember the kindness he received from the Friedman family in Ohio. He spent the night in their home and ate at their table with them. He met their brother Levi who had helped plan the best way for Joseph to "buy" and free Peter.

Peter left Cincinnati and struck out on his life's quest. With $80 in his pocket and a worn carpetbag in his hand, a now white-haired Peter continued his odyssey. He traveled by steamer up the Ohio River to Pittsburgh and then by stagecoach to Philadelphia.

After Peter arrived in Philadelphia, he hoped that by having notices read in the colored churches to the effect that forty-one or forty-two years or so before, two little boys were kidnapped and carried south, one of the older members would recall the circumstance and help him find his family.

Quite by chance Peter was directed to the Byas boardinghouse. There he met the Reverend and Mrs. Byas. It was the Reverend who took him to the Anti-Slavery Society, explaining that it was a place where records of old churches were held. Peter was introduced to the young man working there as a man from the South who was born in Philadelphia.

The young man nodded and asked Peter to have a seat. "Now, sir," he said, "what were your parents' names?"

Peter started slowly, "I—I was stole away from the Delaware River when I was six years old." Then a torrent of information seemed to flow from him: The disappointment of the past days. Not finding the place where he thought the old shanty would be. Not finding anyone who remembered the story of two lost boys. Not finding anyone who knew his mama, whose name was Sidney, or his daddy, Levin. Not finding even a trace of Keturah or Halah. Peter stopped talking. He realized the young man was looking at him in a most curious way. He had been warned that there were white men and colored alike who trapped unsuspecting runaways. They took freed men and women and sold them back down south. Peter bolted toward the door. "Wait!" the young man shouted. Peter froze.

"Listen, Peter, I know you think that I am behaving strangely. I have no intention of harming you in any way. It's just that my own mother's name is Sidney. My father's is Levin. All my life I heard my mother mourn for her two lost boys. Peter, I believe you are my own brother."

Yes, Peter thought, I am your brother, all right—your brother until you can find out if I have any money you can flimflam me outta, 'fore you try to git rid a me.

"Peter, I have an idea. I have an older sister. Come with me to see her. She can tell you more about the family."

Peter nodded. All he wanted was to get out the door. "Her name is Mary. She is a schoolteacher. She keeps a few boarders. Maybe you can stay with her for the night."

"Maybe," Peter said. "Of course, tell me the name of some woman wid a sainted name like Mary. Lure me 'way to some ole bordenhouse and den, bam! Gotcha!"

"I know you don't believe me, Peter. But will you come with me to see Mary?"

Peter relaxed visibly as they stepped into the street. "Do you have a last name?" the young man asked.

"My last name was Friedman," he said. "Before that it was Hogan, before that it was Gist, before that it was Fisher. I had enough of last names. Now I'm free."

"You have a last name," the young man said, "a name of your own. It is the same as mine. My name is William Still. Your name is Peter Still."

The family was fearful of how their mother would react to seeing her lost boy. After all, she was almost eighty years old now. Mahalah, Mary, William, and several other of his family approached the stately house. It was painted white and had many windows framed with long green shutters. Peter learned his mother had had an additional fourteen children.

"Our brother James lives here in Medford, too," William explained. "He is going to Mother's house with us. James is a doctor. The countryside is filled with people he has cured. People come from all over New York, Massachusetts, even Europe for his treatment. Some people call him the cancer doctor."

The siblings drove up to the small farm their father had left to their mother and brother Samuel when he died. In spite of their plan to move slowly, Peter wanted to throw his arms around her and say, "Mama, it's me, Peter. I'm home."

The old woman wondered why her children were not at work on a weekday.

"We've brought someone to meet you," Mary said.

"Always glad to meet friends of my children," the old woman said to Peter. "Come on inside."

Soon the conversation turned to her children. She spoke then of her two lost boys. "Mama," Mary said softly, "he has come back. This is Peter, your son."

The old woman looked at Peter as if she had not heard a word. Then she rose from her chair and walked into the next room. There she knelt to pray. She returned to the room trembling but calm.

"Who are you?" she asked Peter in a quiet voice.

Through his tears Peter answered, "My name is Peter. I had a brother named Levin, but God res' his soul, now he be free. My father's name was Levin, and my mother's name was Sidney."

The mother placed her arms around her child as she wept aloud. "Oh, Father, now let thy servant depart in peace, for mine eyes have seen thy salvation and in these latter days beheld the first fruits of my womb."

Peter returned to Philadelphia a hero. The Reverend Byas had spread the word through the colored section that the six-year-old boy, who had been stolen from his home and had no facts about the state from which he was stolen, had come to the Anti-Slavery office on North Fifth Street and found his brother sitting there behind a desk.

It was during Peter's next visit to the Anti-Slavery office that he met another remarkable man. William introduced Peter to a young Quaker, Seth Concklin, who was an abolitionist. He had read the story of "The Man Who Bought Himself."

Concklin had come forward to volunteer to travel alone to Alabama, to the McKiernan plantation where Peter's wife and children were now staying. He would meet Vina in a secret place and then guide her and the children, Peter, Levin, and Catherine back some six hundred miles through Alabama, Tennessee, and Kentucky to Cincinnati, where the family would be reunited.

But Peter shook his head. "How can I ask this man to risk his own life for me and mine?" William and Concklin presented convincing arguments as to why, and how their plan would work. Finally, after much argument, Peter relented, "If you are willing to risk your life, sir, then I must be willing to risk the lives of Vina and the children."

As soon as sufficient money was raised, Concklin would leave for the South. Meanwhile, Peter would return to Cincinnati where Isaac Friedman had promised him his free papers and a job. On August 23, 1850, Peter Still and Isaac Friedman left the Cincinnati office of Mayor H. E. Spencer. In Peter's hand was a document. He gave it to Isaac to read the words that guaranteed Peter Still was henceforth and forever a free man.

After celebrating Christmas and the New Year with his two sisters, his closest living relatives, Seth Concklin set out on his mission. Peter had given him $80 and an apron of Vina's that she would recognize (Peter had brought the apron north with him) to know that Concklin had been sent by him.

A few weeks later Peter received a letter from a Mr. Miller, the alias that Concklin had chosen to travel under. Isaac had left town, so Peter took the letter to Levi. It had been mailed February 3. Concklin had arrived at the shoe shop on the plantation at one o'clock on Tuesday, January 28. It was rainy and muddy, he said in his letter.

"My pants were rolled up to the knees," he wrote, "in the character of a man looking for employment." The boys were inside the shop making shoes. Concklin made contact with them. Through them he later made contact with Vina. He went on to write: "Our friends in Cincinnati have failed finding anybody to assist me on my return. I find the whole country fifty miles around is inhabited by Christian wolves." He was "trusting nevertheless to a good Providence" that all would go well.

A month passed before Peter received the next letter from Mr. Miller. Friedman scanned the letter and let out a shout. "Listen, Peter. They got a skiff. With Concklin at the helm most of the time and the boys rowing, they have made it to Harmony, Indiana."

"Indiana!" Peter was excited. "Indiana is a free state."

Concklin's letter told how the boys had spotted their slave master on the shore before leaving, "but he didn't see them." Concklin continued to tell how once when he was too exhausted to stand at the helm any longer, two white men "in a skiff near the shore" started calling to the boys and coming near them. "The two men came alongside, demanding where we were going and where from. Are you all black men aboard?" The boys replied, "White massa lyin' thar, sir." At that point, Concklin said, "I arose on my knees, partly throwing off my blankets and staring my assailants in the face. They bowed, with 'How de do, sir,' gave my boat a scrutinizing look, and retired."

Peter sighed with relief. The plan they had devised to keep Vina and Catherine under a stack of old blankets at all times had paid off. "Peter," Friedman reminded him, "the letter is dated March 23. Your family may very soon be arriving in Cincinnati."

On the last day of May, Peter received a message from his sister Mary: Come to Philadelphia!

Was his family there? Would they be waiting there at Mary's house to surprise him? Why hadn't they come to Cincinnati? Why had the telegram not been sent by Mr. Miller himself? Peter left at once.

"Mary."

Mary went to the desk, took out a newspaper, and handed it to him. Peter looked down on it. He could read only the date: Thursday, May 29, 1851. "Mary, you know I can't read this."

"They were . . . taken, Peter. He's dead." She laid her hand on Peter's arm. "Concklin's dead."

"And my family?" the stricken man asked. "What of my family?"

"There is only one line about your family. It says, 'The slaves went back to bondage.'"

Mary also read to Peter that Miller, the white man arrested in connection with the capture of the family, was drowned, with his hands and feet in chains and his skull fractured. "Someone sent these accounts to William. It was he who asked me to tell you what happened. He did not know how to tell you himself."

Peter could not get over his feelings of guilt for agreeing to Seth Concklin's plan. He shared his guilt and grief with the Friedmans upon his return to Cincinnati.

A telegram was sent at once to Joseph. It was a coded message: ANY NEWS OF THE STILLMAN FAMILY? The telegraph operator in Tuscumbia would not know Peter's last name, and using the name Stillman would cause it to sound as if one Jew were inquiring about another.

The telegram was to no avail. They were to discover later that McKiernan and the townspeople assumed a tie-in between the Friedmans and the attempted escape of Peter's family. It was only Joseph Friedman's timely departure that saved his life.

Shortly thereafter Levi Friedman wrote a letter to one of McKiernan's relatives concerning the plight of Peter's family. Peter learned that although they had been whipped, they had all survived.

Later, Levi corresponded directly with McKiernan, making him an offer to purchase Peter's family. A letter finally arrived on August 6, 1851. The most important line was: "You can say to Peter & his new discovered Relations in Philadelphia I will take 5000 for the 4 culerd people & if this will suite him & he can raise the money I will deliver to him or his agent at Paduca at mouth of Tennessee river said negros."

Peter left at once for Philadelphia. William helped him find a job with a wealthy family that paid far more wages than he was earning in Cincinnati. William's observation was that in spite of the increased wages, "it would take three lifetimes for you to save five thousand dollars." Peter had no guarantee that McKiernan would keep his word. Nevertheless, Peter asked William to write a letter to him stating the money was forthcoming. William agreed to write the letter, but he said, "You cannot expect people to give you five thousand dollars to buy your family when so many others equally deserving are just as badly off."

"Look here," said Peter. "I know a heap of men as good and as smart as I am that are slaves now; but I bought my liberty, and my family shall be free."

In November 1851, Peter Still once again resolved to follow a dream and set out to raise enough money to buy the freedom of his family.

He had acquired three letters of introduction. He took them to a Reverend Milliard in Auburn, New York. Peter explained to him how he wanted to raise money for his family. He told him how his family had given him help —the suit on his back and about $150—"but I . . . thought if I could speak to a group of people, not abolitionists, jus' good people, if I could tell them about my Vina, my daughter, my sons—" He stopped.

Milliard frowned. "There are, I have read, over two million slaves in the South. What makes your family special?"

"They're special to me," Peter said softly.

"Look," Milliard said, "this once I'll let you make an appeal from my pulpit, after service tonight. But don't be disappointed to be met by silence —and no contributions at all."

That night as Peter tried to stand in front of the congregation, "his legs turned to water." He was barely able to tell his story. When the collection plate was passed, he had raised $3.05.

But a few churchgoers did come up and talk to him. He was invited to speak at a school, a factory, and a home. Peter seemed to be able to find words in these less formal settings. When he left Auburn a week later, he had added $450 to his fund.

Peter carried letters of introduction across the North and Canada. All through the summer months of 1854 he never slowed his pace: "Hartford, $300; Wethersfield, $21; Middletown, $126; New London, $115; Meridan, $80; Bridgeport, $126; Norwich, $100; Northampton, $45; Buffalo, $80; Toronto, Canada, $15." To anyone, anywhere, the seemingly tireless, aging man would go to tell his story.

After a harrowing two-and-a-half-year journey, Peter returned to Philadelphia. He was weak, ill, and near collapse from exhaustion. His old suit hung like a gunny sack around his thin bones. But Peter Still had raised $5,000.

On December 31, 1854, Peter Still and Levi Friedman stood on a wharf in Cincinnati, and waited for the steamboat *Northerner* to arrive. Suddenly the boat was docked, and there were three decks of passengers yelling and waving greetings to their loved ones.

"I can't see them," Peter cried out in dismay, "I can't see them." Peter was racing around the quay like a madman. This could not happen again. They had had their feet on free soil before, only to— Then he saw Vina. She was waving to him.

Vina! She was here! The children! They were here!

Now they were all seated around the dinner table in Levi Friedman's dining room. There were so many questions. So many answers. Finally Peter asked his son, young Peter, about his wife Susanna.

"She got sick one Sunday mornin', said to me, 'Now you take care our baby.' Den she died."

"There's a baby? I have a grandson!"

The family explained how at the last minute McKiernan had refused to let the baby go. "You'll git this one when I get two hundred dollars."

"Listen, son, I raised five thousand dollars. I'm sure I can raise two hundred dollars more."

"No doubt we can do that tomorrow night, Peter," said Levi Friedman. "The members of our temple are planning a sort of celebration. We want to be sure your family has a proper send-off for the new year."

Everyone at the table joined hands. Peter looked lovingly at his wife and family. "Can't wait for you to meet Mama." He said a silent prayer for his family and for his long-ago Granny Mose.

Spirit of the Dead

Haile Gerima

"Spirit of the Dead" is the powerful poem that sets the tone and introduces the movie *Sankofa,* produced, written, and directed by Haile Gerima. Nine years in the making and truly in the tradition of Black storytelling, this movie's success was accomplished by "word of mouth." Throughout major cities in the United States, audiences after seeing *Sankofa* were literally shouting in the streets: "You must see this movie!"

Sankofa is an Akan word meaning to return to the past in order to go forward. Mona, a contemporary model, is possessed by spirits lingering in the Cape Coast Castle in Ghana and travels to the past, where as a house servant called Shola on a sugar plantation she is constantly abused by the slave master. Nunu, an African-born field hand, and Shango, Shola's West Indian lover, continuously rebel against the slave system. For Nunu this means direct conflict with her son, a mulatto benefiting from the system as a head slave. Inspired by Nunu's and Shango's determination to defy the system, Shola finally takes her fate into her own hands.

Spirit of the dead, rise up.
Lingering spirit of the dead, rise up
and possess your bird of passage.

Those stolen Africans, step out of the ocean
from the wounds of the ships and claim your story.

Spirit of the dead, rise up.
Lingering spirit of the dead, rise up
and possess your vessel.

Those Africans shackled in leg-irons
and enslaved,
step out of the acres of cane fields
and cotton fields and tell your story!

Spirit of the dead, rise up.
Lingering spirit of the dead, rise up
and possess your bird of passage.

Those lynched in the magnolias,
swinging on the limbs of the weeping willows,
rotting food for the vultures,
step down and claim your story.

Spirit of the dead, rise up!
Lingering spirit of the dead, rise up
and possess your vessel.

Those tied, bound, and whipped
from Brazil to Mississippi,
step out and tell your story.

Those in Jamaica, in the fields of Cuba,
in the swamps of Florida,
the rice fields of South Carolina,
you Waiting Africans,
Step out and tell your story!

Spirit of the dead, rise up!
Lingering spirit of the dead, rise up
and possess your bird of passage!

From Alabama to Surinam,
up to the caves of Louisiana,
Come out, you African spirits!
Step out and claim your stories!

You raped, slave-bred, castrated, burned,
tarred and feathered, roasted, chopped,
lobotomized, bound and gagged,
You African spirits!

Spirit of the dead, rise up.
Lingering spirit of the dead, rise up
and possess your bird of passage!

Feet in Water, Song in the Heart

David A. Anderson/Sankofa

This story will be familiar to many. The details and the format are mine, but
Reuben preparing to take his freedom from slavery is a story shared by every
African-American family seeking to preserve its folklore. By contrast, the opening scene represents a recent manifestation of a pernicious tradition, that of
the unconscious adoption of labels that mask identity.

Wade in the water
Wade in the water, children
Wade in the water
God's a-gonna trouble the water

"Mr. Chairman. I move that from now on we start each meeting with the singing of a spiritual."

I figured it was a good motion, in tune with why we had formed the organization in the first place. But right off a couple of big brothers snickered, and some little bitty sister over in the corner cracked, "Is he serious?"

Somebody else asked for clarification, and I could deal with that. I repeated the motion, this time relying on the best buppie English I could conjure up. Then that same little sister said, "You mean like them old-timey songs they used to sing back before affirmative action?" I started to run some corrective history on the sister, but the chairman said that I was out of order. If I'da talked about his next of kin, he woulda knowed what was out of order, but I just held my peace. Figured to get the brother one-on-one over lunch (you know how that game goes).

Well, we had lunch. Do you know, that brother went off on me. Told me it was no wonder I had been *downsized* out of my job. Told me I was out of touch. Told me I don't even dress right. "Next, you'll want us to sport Afros," he said. Now that really hurt.

I went to the next meeting, late, so I wouldn't have to chitchat with nobody. I sat off to one side so I could see everybody's face. Every face in that room had Africa in it—and I don't mean Pretoria. The meeting rolled: committee reports; discussion of résumés, job fairs, mobility, mentors. They definitely had the career thing down. But everything discussed, debated, motioned came off as "minorities could" or "minorities like" or "as minorities we should ask . . ." I jumped in with points of order and all the other little mess I could think of. But the only thing those minorities went for was the suggestion that "the brother's (meaning me) concern be referred to the Subcommittee on the Retention of Archival Messages and Cryptographic Data."

While they discussed that, I scoped the faces again. The African *look* was there, but as I eased on out of the room, it came to me that the look was painted on; painted masks. Could have been water-based paint. But then, minorities don't go near wading water.

Long time back, when I was a little fella, a man told me about people that could deal with water. He said that even though they were in captivity, they was down with the spirituals, too.

"How do water and captive, spiritual-singing people go together?" I asked. The man smiled. Then he told me about this one brother named Reuben. Said that . . .

One night, late, Reuben slipped into the cabin where his mother and three sisters were sleeping. He took hold of the oldest girl's hand. She was but fourteen, but she was the one he was closest to. He could count on her to look after his mother. As she came up out of sleep, he whispered, "I'm goin.' I goin' tonight." Goin'? Goin' where? Why? How? were the questions that raced through her head. But he squeezed her hand so hard, all the questions were choked off. After a minute or two he eased up on her hand and said, "I hear ole Master Hutton tell that there Tollie West fella, he think he got a slave what can read . . . and write. Hutton say he got a good idea who 'tis, and when he ready, he gon sell him to the 'meanest man and the highest bidder in Luzanna.' I 'specs ole Hutton just about got it figured that I'm the one. He gon sell me just like he did Papa." Jane—that was his sister's name—knew he was right. He had to go before Hutton got to him. But she was worried, scared. "But Reuben, where you goin'? *How* you goin'?"

"Jane, I'm gon cross the river and then cut through the swamp that run back o' Hattiesville. Here tell there's some folks there they calls 'abolition-ers'; they works with the underground railroaders. All them is what helps a body what wants to take his freedom git to the North."

She could see that he had studied on it, but she was still scared for him. He knew she was scared from the way she kept stroking his arm and the way she didn't hardly breathe. So he tried to ease her mind: "Jane, maybe they help me find the Yankee army. I join the Yankee army, show them how to whip the Rebs. Then I come back and free you and Mama and all our peoples."

He stood up. This time she couldn't tell whether he was talking to her or to himself: "There's a big river way up north they calls the O-hi-o. If I can get 'cross that river, won't nobody stop me from readin' . . . and writin'!" The cabin seemed to light up as if a million, million fireflies turned on at the same time. And she could see the river and see the freedom on the other side. She followed him out into the moonlit night, and they walked through the woods until they came to the waters of the Tennessee River. He took off his clothes, rolled them into a tight bundle, and bound that to a branch jutting up from a small log. He set the log in the water and stepped in behind it. Holding to the log, he waded forward; he waded in the water. She saw that with each step the water rose higher on his body, and she began to pray: *Please, Lord, guide my brother man (God's a gonna trouble the water). Jus' lead him up to the freedom lan' (God's a gonna trouble the water). Why don' you wade in the water? Wade in the water, chil'ren. Wade in the water, God's a gonna trouble the water.* When she opened her eyes, she couldn't see him anymore.

Did Reuben get to the freedom land? The man who told me the story said, "Maybe. Maybe he got drownded in the swamp. Maybe he got killed whilst he's fightin' 'longside the Yankees. Mama never heard from Reuben. Just don't know what happened to him. We do know that a heap of our people crossed that river, and some other rivers, too. Every one of them that put their feet in the water wanted to know something about this readin' and writin' business. They had a freedom song in their hearts."

Daddy, my storyteller, made his passage some time back, and he is with uncle Reuben and the many thousands that waded in the water. Jane, my grandmother, is with them, too. Water-wading, spiritual-singing people . . . in the majority.

Sojourner Truth Speaks

Alice McGill

I have been performing in a one-woman show called *Sojourner Truth Speaks* for the last ten years. During that time I have portrayed Sojourner Truth over two thousand times. She was a very simple woman and yet a very complicated woman at the same time. While researching her life I found that her strengths could not be numbered, there were so many. Her power to influence cannot be measured. She influenced and is still influencing so many. If I could choose one phrase to describe Sojourner Truth, that phrase would be "love of self." Through self-love she was able to demonstrate, through her work, great love and compassion to others of all colors and creeds.

Sojourner Truth once remarked, in reply to an allusion to the late Horace Greeley, "You call him a self-made man; well, I'm a self-made woman." And she lived the life of a self-made woman.

Sojourner Truth was born to James and Betsey, slaves of one Colonel Ardinburgh in Hurley, Ulster County, New York. Her original name was Isabella. Some encyclopedias list her name as Isabella Van Wagener. Van Wagener, the last name of a couple who paid for her freedom, she used until she renamed herself Sojourner Truth, June 15, 1843. From that date on, Sojourner Truth became a self-made woman.

Sojourner Truth became one of the most prolific and sought-after speakers of the nineteenth century. Being true to her name, she sojourned for over four decades, all the while speaking about the evils of slavery, women's rights, religious experiences, and other issues involving the rights of humankind.

Not knowing how to read or write had no bearing on her ability to stir an audience, large or small. She often said, "I can read de pepul." Wherever was posted *Sojourner Truth Speaks,* the people flocked to hear her speeches, some of which were so impromptu that she jokingly prefaced them with "I'm heah for the same pu'pose ye is heah; I want to heah what I gots to say." And she spoke thus after having been introduced as the eighty-three-year-old Sojourner Truth.

"Well, chilern, I'm glad to see so many together. Ef I am eighty-three years old, I only count my age from de time when I was 'mancipated. Den, I 'gun ter live. God is a-fulfillin', an' my time dat I lost bein' a slave was made up. My mother said to me when I was bein' sole from her, 'I want to tell ye dese tings dat you will allers know dat I have tole you, for dar will be a great many tings tole you after I start out of this life inter the world to come.' An' I say dis to you all, for heah is a great many pepul dat when I step out ob dis existence, dat you will know what you heered ole Sojourn' Truth tell you. I was born a slave in the State of Noo Yo'k, Ulster County, 'mong de low Dutch. W'en I was ten year old, I couldn't speak a word of Inglish, an' I hab no eddicati'n at all. My old marster died, and we was goin' to hab a auction. We was all brought up to be sole. My mother tell me to look up to the stars and moon. She say the same moon and stars shine on me when I am sole from her. Now, I hears all ye say 'bout de home an' de fam'ly. Where's my fam'ly? Where's my home?"

Some of the tender-skinned women were at the point of losing dignity at the women's rights convention in Akron, Ohio. The year was 1851. There had been a storm of protest brewing in the corners of the hecklers and sneerers who attended for the purpose of teaching the women a lesson. There were few women in those days who dared to "speak in meeting."

At her first word there was a profound hush. She spoke in deep tones, which, though not loud, reached every ear in the house. Sojourner Truth spoke for women's rights.

"Well, chilern, whar dar is so much racket, dar must be something out o' kilter. I tink dat 'twixt de niggers of de Souf and de women of de Norf, all a-talkin' 'bout rights, de white men will be a-fix pretty soon. But what's all dis here talkin' 'bout? Dat man ober dar say dat women needs to be helped into carriages and lifted ober ditches, and to have de best place everywhar. Nobody eber help me into carriages or ober mud pubbles, or gives me any best place. And ain't I a woman? Look at me! Look at my arm! I have plowed and planted and gathered into barns, and no man could head me—and ain't I a woman? I could work as much as a man and eat as much as a man when I could get it and bear the lash as well, as well—and ain't I a woman? I have borne thirteen chilern and seen 'em mos' all sold off into slavery, and when I crid out with a mother's grief, none but Jesus heard—and ain't I a woman? Den dey talks 'bout dis ting in de head—what's dis dey call it?"

"Intellect," whispered someone near.

"Dat's it, honey. What's dat got to do with women's rights or niggers' rights? If my cup won't hold but a pint and yurn holds a quart, wouldn't ye be mean not to let me have my little half measure full? Den dat little man in black dar, he say women can't have as much rights as man 'cause Christ wasn't a woman. Whar did your Christ come from? From God and a woman. Man had nothin' to do with him. If the first woman God ever made was strong enough to turn the world upside down all 'lone, den togedder dey ought to be able to turn it back and get it right side up again, and now dey is asking to do it, de men better let 'em."

Amid roars of applause Sojourner took her seat among her friends.

Get on Board and Tell Your Story

Gloria Davis Goode

Spirituals are songs that were created by African Americans who lived in the southern states during the period of captivity called slavery. In the mid-nineteenth century, reports of these unusual poetic melodies reached the North in travelers' journals, novels, and narratives told by fugitive slaves. Charlotte Forten was probably one of the first African-American women to document in her journal writings a few songs that she heard freedmen sing on Saint Helena Island. Forten's writings no doubt captured the attention of William F. Allen, Charles P. Ware, and Lucy McKim Garrison, three northern writers who compiled the first notable collection of spirituals in 1867, *Slave Songs of the United States.*

Even though spirituals appeared in several collections printed after the Civil War, it was not until 1871 that they caught the attention of the American public. A group of eleven singers, an accompanist, and a chaperone from Fisk University, under the direction of Charles White, traveled throughout the northern states on a concert tour, including in their repertoire some folk songs in four-part harmony that had been handed down to them from their parents. Although they encountered difficulties with discrimination and ridicule on some parts of their tour, they made their mark on America at the World Peace Jubilee in Boston when they performed a stirring refrain of Julia Ward Howe's "Battle Hymn of the Republic." Winning the praise of critics, they carried their audiences by storm as they sang before royalty and common people in Europe. When they returned, they had enough money to construct a new building on the Fisk University campus, Jubilee Hall. The tradition of choral concert tours was preserved and carried on by generations of African-American music instructors and students at Black colleges throughout the South.

Jubilee Songs as Sung by the Jubilee Singers, a book-length collection, was published in 1872. The Fisk University singers called their songs "jubilees" after the "year of jubilee," or the year when slavery ended, while the late-nineteenth-century African-American scholar William Edward Burghardt Du Bois, referring to the quiet and plaintive melodies, called the spirituals "sorrow songs." James Weldon Johnson, in his major collection of spirituals in 1926, dubbed the creators of the songs "black and unknown bards of long ago," even though he acknowledged that they were the work of many highly gifted individual musicians. These individuals improvised lines and tunes while their listeners added verses and choruses, all from a common storehouse of knowledge and experiences that African Americans possessed. Therefore, we can say that spirituals were the work of many composers operating within a folk tradition. When we think of the term "folk" in reference to these melodies with texts, we mean that they were disseminated through oral transmission, were composed with individual and group effort, were handed down from generation to generation, were in existence in different variants, and were collected while being performed by singers in a traditional setting.

Spirituals convey a broad range of topics. There are those that were primarily used in Baptist and Methodist churches. "Wade in the Water" is an inspirational melody used during the rite of baptism, and "Let Us Break Bread Together on Our Knees" is sung as a communion hymn. "Get You Ready, There's a Meeting Here Tonight" grew out of the nineteenth-century religious camp meetings where great singers served as the leaders while the camp meeting congregations responded as choruses.

Secret meetings on southern plantations and in wooded areas were convened by the singing of spiritual songs. Spirituals were used as signals for African Americans to steal away to praise meetings where they held religious services and secretly planned slave revolts. Nat Turner's insurrection followed his conversion and a vision in which the Spirit appeared to him as "the thunder rolled in the heavens." His call to become a prophet and deliver his people from bondage is communicated to him through divine inspiration echoing the sound of the trumpet through his soul.

> Steal away, steal away,
> Steal away to Jesus,
> Steal away, steal away home,
> I ain't got long to stay here.
>
> My Lord, he calls me, he calls me by the thunder,
> The trumpet sounds within-a-my soul,
> I ain't got long to stay here.
>
> Green trees a-bending, poor sinner stands a-trembling,
> The trumpet sounds within-a-my soul,
> I ain't got long to stay here.

The great orator Frederick Douglass was one of the first African-American writers to discuss code words in spiritual texts that could be used as secret messages. Some spirituals narrated Bible stories in which the ancient heroes were analogous to the people who played roles in the Underground Railroad. "Moses" may have referred to the renowned conductor Harriet Tubman, who led her people "out of Egypt" into "the Promised Land." These songs told stories of freedom, using words or phrases like the ones listed below with their double entendre.

Code Word	Religious Meaning	Secret Meaning
get on board	become saved	prepare to leave
glory	heaven	freedom
home	heaven	the North, freedom
I ain't got long	I'm ready to die	I'm ready to leave
Jesus	Jesus	freedom
midnight special		escapees leaving at midnight
no extras	unsaved sinners	no extra escapees
steal away	death will come quietly	run away
train	group of saved souls	group of escapees

The spiritual below could announce an escape plan, give the time and circumstances of the trip, and inspire slaves to join the freedom train.

> This train is bound for glory, this train,
> This train is bound for glory, this train,
> This train is bound for glory,
> Get on board and tell your story
> This train is bound for glory, this train.
>
> This train don't pull no extras, this train,
> This train don't pull no extras, this train,
> This train don't pull no extras,
> Don't pull nothing but the midnight special,
> This train don't pull no extras, this train.

As the conductor led his or her passengers on the Underground Railroad, it was important for anyone who was "on board" to "tell your story." In the context of the praise meeting, "telling your story" meant testifying about the trials and tribulations in your life and thanking the Almighty for giving you the guidance to overcome your obstacles and unload your burdens. "Telling your story" inspired others to follow in your footsteps, for most storytellers or testifiers were revered as orators and leaders by members of their spiritual communities. The secret meaning of "tell your story" meant that once you reached freedom, you were obligated to tell the story of your life in slavery, your escape, and your ultimate freedom so that these events could be documented for use as propaganda to further the antislavery cause. During the antebellum period, "telling stories" became a necessary activity of the abolitionists as freedmen orally recounted their life stories in retrospect and scores of fugitive slave narratives were collected, written down, published, and circulated in the North.

Some spirituals were adapted; that is, words were changed to fit different situations that could arise. A collector remembers hearing the spiritual "Follow the Risen Lord," a song that was sung by itinerant evangelists at revivals and camp meetings.

> Follow the risen Lord, follow the risen Lord,
> The best thing the wise men say
> Follow the risen Lord.

The freedom version of the song is known to us today as a spiritual with a coded message, "Follow the Drinking Gourd," which refers to the path that one can take to the North by following the Big Dipper. The text mirrors the West African tradition of fashioning eating and drinking utensils out of gourds. Each African-American family on a southern plantation or farm had a well from which they drew water. Once the water had been collected in a bucket, it was left on a table where family members and even visiting friends could take a drink using a dipper that was carved out of a gourd. The gourd or dipper was also used as a symbol of freedom; it was hung over the doorways of stations along the Underground Railroad.

According to the collector of this spiritual, H. B. Parks, in *Texas Folk and Folklore* edited by Mody C. Boatright, the conductor is an old man, a peg-legged sailor whose trip with runaway fugitives began near Mobile, Alabama. Before dawn he would lead his freedom train along the bend of the Tombigbee River and follow his peg-legged print on the dead trees along the trail pointing north. When the river ended at the divide, he and his freedom train picked up the Tennessee River on the other side and followed it into the Ohio.

> When the sun comes back and the first quail calls,
> Follow the drinking gourd,
> For the old man is a-waiting for to carry you to freedom,
> Follow the drinking gourd.
>
> Now the river bend will make a mighty good road,
> The dead trees will show you the way,
> And there's another river on the other side,
> Just you follow the drinking gourd.
>
> Now the river ends between two hills,
> Follow the drinking gourd,
> And there's another river on the other side,
> Follow the drinking gourd.

Unlike their secular counterparts, the blues, which have remained essentially in oral tradition, spirituals, originally folk songs, are now considered part of the "fine arts" tradition. They have been arranged by noted African-American musicians such as N. Ballanta-Taylor, Hall Johnson, John Work, Jester Hairston, and Margaret Bonds. Composer Harry T. Burleigh acquainted the Czechoslovakian composer Antonín Dvořák with the spiritual genre, which Dvořák used as thematic motives in the second movement of his "New World Symphony." The African-American composer Nathaniel Dett incorporated spiritual melodic materials in his choral compositions. Following the precedent set by contralto Marian Anderson, who sang spirituals on Easter Sunday in 1939 to an estimated seventy-five thousand people at the Lincoln Memorial, divas such as Leontyne Price and Jessye Norman continue to mesmerize audiences with renditions of well-known spirituals. No choral program can be said to be "musically correct" without a spiritual, whether sung by a soloist, an ensemble, a chorus, in a cappella fashion, or with orchestral accompaniment.

The civil rights era revitalized spirituals as folk songs because they were used spontaneously with calls and responses suitable for group participation. The functional context of the songs was recreated as the demonstrators sang for the purposes of inspiring, telling stories, and providing outlets for emotional expression during times of protest. Because of their special qualities, spirituals have been included in many Protestant denominational hymnals and have been performed as part of the standard liturgical repertoire in synagogues and churches.

Today, spirituals have been altered by young composers and incorporated with new texts and musical motifs into African-American expressions such as religious rap and gospel. While some African Americans prefer to forget the spirituals in favor of evangelical songs that speak to contemporary issues, others look to Africa for the authentic music of Black Americans. But forgetting the spirituals is akin to negating one's heritage and unlearning the lessons of the past. When I was a child living on a tobacco farm in rural North Carolina in the 1940s, my grandmother sang spirituals all day while she prepared delicious meals on a gigantic wood stove. Whenever I think of those precious times that I shared with several generations of my people inside the farmhouse on a winding dirt road, singing and telling stories, while the world outside the farmhouse was engulfed in prejudice and intolerance, I am reminded of an old spiritual that reaffirms the need to remember not only our suffering but our joy.

> I've been buked and I've been scorned,
> I've been buked and I've been scorned, children,
> I've been buked and I've been scorned,
> I've been talked about sure's you born.

> There'll be trouble all over this world,
> There'll be trouble all over this world, children,
> There'll be trouble all over this world,
> There'll be trouble all over this world.
>
> Ain't gonna lay my religion down,
> Ain't gonna lay my religion down, children,
> Ain't gonna lay my religion down,
> Ain't gonna lay my religion down.

The spirituals, born in slavery, reared in freedom, and aged in ancestral memories, have reached maturity as American art songs with universal implications; they speak to humankind about the divine and worldly experiences of human life. These musical treasures have been collected, preserved, and catalogued in libraries all over the world as the unique historical and cultural experiences of African Americans in the United States. Today, choirs from African-American colleges continue their concert tours throughout the United States. For the African-American listener, the sound of their spirituals can serve as an awakening, for in the traditional re-creation of these songs, we celebrate the voices of our ancestors in captivity and in freedom. It is through their music that we are renewed.

> Remember me, remember me,
> Oh, Lord, remember me.

The Ballad of the Underground Railroad

Charles L. Blockson

Tonight we ride the underground train.
It runs on tracks that are covered with pain.
The whole of Humanity makes up the crew
And Liberty's the engineer to carry us through.
The North Star will lead us,
And Freedom will greet us
When we reach the end of the line.

The Underground Train,
Strange as it seems,
Carried many passengers
And never was seen.

It wasn't made of wood,
It wasn't made of steel;
A man-made train that
Ran without wheels.

The train was known
By many a name.
But the greatest of all
Was "The Freedom Train."

The Quakers, the Indians,
Gentiles and Jews,
Were some of the people
Who made up the crews.

Free Blacks and Christians
And Atheists, too,
Were the rest of the people
Who made up the crews.

Conductors and agents
Led the way at night,
Guiding the train
By the North Star Light.

The passengers were
The fugitive slaves
Running from slavery
And its evil ways.

Running from the whip
And the overseer,
From the slave block
And the Auctioneer.

They didn't want their masters
To catch them again,
So the men dressed as women
And the women as men.

They hid in churches,
Cellars and barns,
Waiting to hear the
Train's alarm.

Sleeping by day,
And traveling by night,
Was the best way they knew
To keep out of sight.

They waded in the waters
To hide their scent,
And fool those bloodhounds
The slave masters sent.

They spoke in riddles
And sang in codes,
To understand the message,
You had to be told.

Those who knew the secret
Never did tell
The sacred message
Of the "Freedom Train's" bell.

Riding this train
Broke the laws of the land,
But the laws of God
Are higher than man's.

PART III

—◦◦◦—

When the Heart Overflows, It Comes Out Through the Mouth

Memories and Stories About Family and Friends

Sometimes I feel like a motherless chile
Sometimes I feel like a motherless chile
Sometimes I feel like a motherless chile
   A long ways from home
   A long ways from home

(Spiritual)

For us the question should be, What are the specific *forms* of that humanity and what in our background is worth preserving or abandoning. The clue to this can be found in folklore, which offers the first drawings of any group's character. It preserves mainly those situations which have repeated themselves again and again in the history of any given group. It describes those rites, manners, customs, and so forth, which insure the good life, or destroy it; and it describes those boundaries of feeling, thought and action which that particular group has found to be the limitation of the human condition. It projects this wisdom in symbols which express the group's will to survive; it embodies those values by which the group lives and dies. These drawings may be crude but they are nonetheless profound in that they represent the group's attempt to humanize the world. It's no accident that great literature, the products of individual artists, is erected upon this humble base.

—RALPH ELLISON, Shadow and Act

Mother/word, Father/tongue, lovepoem, wordsong, talking drum.
When one is in trouble, one remembers God and Family. (West Africa.)

Even the tongue and the teeth quarrel now and then. (West Africa).

Even a little story brings friendship remembrance. (West Africa)

A father's love and a mother's strength is a multitude of words. (Traditional)

In These Dissenting Times

Alice Walker

I shall write of the old men I knew
And the young men
I loved
And of the gold toothed women
Mighty of arm
Who dragged us all
To Church.

The Tree of Love

Linda Goss

This story is a homage to my family: my mother's voice, my father's singing, my brother's laughter, my granddaddy's stories, and the great tree that once stood in the backyard of my Tennessee family home.

Momma used to say, "Listen, Baby Dear, I can't be around with you always, but I want you to remember that no matter where you go or what you do, I want you to always be able to look out and see the trees."

At first I didn't know what she was talking about—some of her home-spun folklore, I supposed. But I listened because, after all, this was Momma talking.

"Baby Dear, I want you to go out and walk among the trees. Go to the park, the woods where they are, and I want you to find one that appeals to you and then I want you to give it a big hug. Now, I know what you're thinking, even though you ain't saying nothing. I raised you so you wouldn't talk back to me or sass me."

"But Momma—" I interrupted.

"Listen, Baby Dear, I know you are going to worry about folks seeing you hugging trees and thinking you're crazy or something. If they look at you strangely, don't pay them no mind. You go right ahead and hug that tree anyway."

I was beginning to worry about Momma. She had been looking tired lately.

"I'm telling you that no matter how far you climb to the top of the tallest building, you got to be able to come back down and plant your feet on the ground, on the grass, on the dirt. We are a part of nature. Trees are God's gift to us human beings. Sometimes we act foolish and forget how precious life is. A tree is a living thing."

"Momma, I love you," I said, and I kissed her gently on her cheek. Momma was preaching now, so I listened all the more.

"Behold the beauty of a tree. Feel how firm and tough it is. Shake hands with the branches. Kiss the leaves. Don't be embarrassed. Trees have seen it all. They were here before we were. And if they ever disappear from the face of this earth, what hope or beliefs will humankind have then? The tree won't reject your love. Now my mamma, your grandmother, used to say, 'The tree of love gives shade to all.' "

Momma had a sadness in her eyes. She leaned her head back and paused for a moment as if looking at someone, and then she spoke:

Baby Dear, when I was a young child around nine or so, living down in Alabama, there was a great big old weeping willow tree in our backyard. The branches were so long and flowing that the children called them "arms." My oldest brother, Matthew, called the tree "Old Willa."

Now that weeping willow had been standing in back of our farm before my great-great uncle was born, which would have been your great-great-great uncle. My mamma and pappa were married under Old Willa. We would have family gatherings, picnics, and good-time parties under Old Willa. I was named under that tree. I remember [chuckling] one time when Pappa blew his lid. Late one night he caught Baby Sis and one of her sweethearts kissing under Old Willa. Pappa picked up a big stick and chase him away screaming, "Boy, I better not catcha 'round here no mo' 'cause I'm gonna git ya if I do!"

Well, Pappa never caught Mac Ray, but Baby Sis sure did. They were married a year after that. Pappa welcomed him into the family. Good thing, too. Poor old Mac Ray died in the war.

Some folks thought Old Willa had mysterical powers. Miss Sally Mae, a root doctor, thought so. She would stop by every now and then and rubbed Old Willa's trunk. It was a thing to see. Miss Sally Mae would talk to Old Willa and rub right in the middle of her trunk as if she was rubbing her stomach.

Sometimes Pappa would gather all of us 'round Old Willa. Pappa loved to tell stories, you know. He would tell us about Uncle LoveJoy, your great-great-great uncle. He called the story, "The Great Escape." Uncle LoveJoy was a slave, and one night he escaped from the plantation, which was a few miles from the farm. He could hear the dogs and the slave catchers gaining up on him. He ran like the devil. He didn't know which direction to run, but he could hear something or someone whispering to him, "Come, come." So he ran in the path of the whispering. He ran and bumped his head right into that weeping willow tree and hid behind it. Those dogs took another trail. Uncle LoveJoy thanked that tree.

Twenty years later he came back with his wife and children and some of her brothers and sisters, and they bought the land with the tree on it and built the farm. The family took good care of that farm and passed it on down to other family members, and that's how your grandpa and grandma got it.

We'd have some fun times beneath Old Willa—but one day it all came to an end. The city developers came through and said that Old Willa had to be cut down because the tree was standing in the way of progress. Our farm and property was condemned by the city. The highways were coming through. The workers cut Old Willa down. They poured heaps of salt on her trunk so she wouldn't grow back. My mamma was sad after that. You might say she never got over it. Pappa gathered the family around what was left of Old Willa.

"We are going to give this here tree a proper burial," Pappa said.

We held hands around the tree, and Pappa said a prayer. We sang softly, "Like a tree standing by the water, I shall not be moved. I shall not be, I shall not be moved. I shall not be, I shall not be moved. Just like a tree standing by the water, I shall not be moved."

Mamma began weeping, and she cried out, "Old Willa was a love tree, and the tree of love gives shade to all. No matter where you go, children, or what you do, you find a tree and you give it a big hug. It doesn't matter what kind of tree it is. It can be a sycamore, maple, elm, oak, birch—" Mamma kept naming different kinds of trees. We were amazed. We didn't know that she knew the names of so many trees—"magnolia, spruce, fir, holly, banyan, cedar, dogwood, pine, hickory, pecan, chestnut, palm, black walnut—[She named fruit trees:] peach, pear, apple, coconut, cherry, pineapple."

And then she said, "But my favorite is weeping willow."

Mamma clutched her heart as if she had a pain. She walked over to Pappa and collapsed in his arms.

After Mamma's funeral, Pappa was too sad to stay around the area, so he took me and my seven brothers and six sisters up north to Tennessee. We didn't forget Mamma, but we eventually forgot about Old Willa. At least we never talked about the tree.

"Baby Dear, I told you this story now because when I saw you marching down the aisle getting your diploma, you stood tall and proud as a tree. Then I saw an image of Old Willa running through my mind."

I grabbed Momma and hugged her tightly. I felt as though I was hugging Old Willa. "Oh, Momma," I cried, "I thank you dearly for telling me this story. I promise you, Momma, that I will hug and kiss as many trees as I can."

The phone rings, interrupting my daydream. My administrative assistant informs me the board meeting begins in ten minutes. I thank her and go back to my dream. Every time I see Momma, she tells me about Old Willa. For ten years now, since my college graduation, she always has something new to say about the family and the weeping willow.

I sit in a swivel highbacked chair working in a gray-colored office suite on the twenty-second floor in one of the busiest cities in the world, the Big Apple. I haven't seen any apple trees. I do, however, go over to Central Park every now and then. I take my family with me, and sometimes I go alone. I have found an "Old Willa" in the park. It's not a weeping willow tree. I don't even call her Old Willa. I call her "Nuba," a name of African ancestors long forgotten. I talk to her and she listens; she understands. Momma was right. The tree of love gives shade to all.

Dear Sis

Arthenia J. Bates

A letter from home departing from the routine of cataloging the new babies, the new funerals or the new weddings was a relic. It did not matter if Mama, Daddy or one of the other children above the fifth grade answered my letter, it almost always said the same thing:

> Just a few lines to let you hear from me. How are you at this time? Fine I hope. Received your kind and loving letter. Hope when these few lines reach your loving hands will find you enjoying the best of life and health.
>
> We know that you need more but things are tight here in Wedgefield. I couldn't send as much money as you needed but I want you to try and make out. We can't complain because many more are in a worse shape than us.
>
> Take care of yourself and don't worry so your grades can be good.
>
> I'll close this letter but not my love.

But the letter which I received from home on Monday, October 13, 1941, was different. My little brother, Bay Boy, had run away to join the Navy.

This letter deserved a special explanation, but unfortunately, no details were given. I wrote several letters, using the precious few pennies that I could ill afford, to find out how and why Bay Boy became interested in Uncle Sam's Navy.

No answer came.

By now I began to wonder how he had fared on leaving. I only wished that I had been at home when he left. I would have fixed a shoe-box lunch of fried chicken, light bread, oranges, apples, bananas, parched peanuts, and squares of light-colored fudge—Bay Boy didn't particularly like cake or pie. I knew that nothing gave a traveler from Wedgefield more joy than the shoe-box lunch. Some people wrapped the box as if it were a gift, fancied up with ribbons, but everyone knew the secret.

I studied my books as well as I could under the circumstances, but I could not forget Bay Boy, a tender-skinned boy of sixteen, who had known only the meanest corner of Wedgefield (a town not even on the map) before making this venture. He had been considered as the funny one at home because he talked little, asked for nothing, protested nothing. When he became ill—no matter how ill—he wanted to be left alone.

But Bay Boy was now in the Navy, and they said it was a man's Navy and he was only a boy. How could he have made up his mind to join that man's Navy? He was the only one in our family of eleven, ranging in age from seven to twenty-nine, who had never spent a night away from home. But even so, no one cared enough to tell me about Bay Boy's venture.

Time moved on. The war in Europe raged. I found relief in the communal *sanctum sanctorum:* The prayers for peace, the rightful greatness of "God Bless America," the final promise of the parting G.I. voiced even by a three-year-old singing prodigy of the local network: "I'll be back in a year, little darling. Uncle Sam has called and I must go."

At King's College, war was something for me to read about in the newspapers. I had to read the news because ten of the questions out of twenty-five on the semester examination in my Modern European History course were based on current events. I was always prepared to tell Mr. Levant what happened here or there on this date or the other. Sunday afternoon was the only time for actually listening to the news.

On December 7, in the afternoon—I never kept up with the hours on a Sunday afternoon at King's College, for all of the afternoons were one long, solitary hour, with boredom pressing the tips of your elbows as you pored over noble subjects that would make you the world of tomorrow—someone yelled: "The President! the President! The President!"

I could hear feet everywhere.

"Who? President Stone?" someone asked to no one in particular.

"No, fool," someone answered no one in particular. "What's Prexy doing in a girls' dorm on Sunday afternoon?"

"Who?"

Someone snatched my arm as I moved on with the others to Susy Beth's room. And the voice of FDR: "Friends, and you are my friends." The words were spoken with quiet detachment. "I now declare the United States of America in a state of war with Japan."

The war cloud settled over the group of girls huddled in Susy Beth's room. Surely, then, I knew that God must bless America. Bay Boy was somewhere—a part of the Navy. He never even read the news. He was just a boy of sixteen who could get into all kinds of devilment after dark. But now he would have to fight for his country.

The holiday season began on the twentieth of December. I would celebrate Christmas with the family. I would also find out more about Bay Boy's venture.

My hopes rose skyward as the train neared Wedgefield. The wee station, scarcely more than a covered shed to shield the baggage and the few passengers from the elements, was seldom a cheerful place at train time. Knowing that Daddy or Buddy would meet the train relieved me of the fear of carrying my suitcase the whole country mile to the house.

No one met me.

Day had almost come, but enough of the grayness from dawn tarried to make things some distance away indistinguishable. I could not leave my bag under the shed, so I began walking the mile, changing the suitcase from one hand to the other.

The house was dead.

On being admitted, I found the air rife with those before-arising fumes which, along with the cold pot-bellied heater, said everything but "Welcome home." When I kissed Mama, she gave her typical greeting: "Your nose sure is cold. I thought that the college didn't close until day after tomorrow." And Daddy said, "Why didn't you tell us to meet you?"

I moved on toward the mantel, where my letter lay half-opened—the one which I had written telling them when to meet me.

"Where's Bay Boy?"

"A dirty rascal. He sent a dry letter here, his civilian clothes and six pictures. I bet those pictures cost ten dollars. That money could've bought enough groceries for a week."

"Where's Bay Boy, Daddy? I want to see the pictures."

"No need to bother, they're not so good. Looks to me he's scared to death—trying to back away from something."

"Where are they?"

"Muttah, where's Bay Boy?"

"They're on the mantelpiece, behind the clock, I think."

I found the packet.

Here was my brother, standing tall, but without strength. They were signed, every single picture: "All my love, Henry Lee Mingo."

You could not say that he was handsome. He was just a tall, good-looking ginger-colored boy with the typical Booker T. Washington look. He stood between two tall white columns, with his arms dangling to his sides. The sailor suit became him very well, only he stood with his legs far apart, with one foot before the other, as if he were going to walk away as the photographer snapped the pictures. I looked so long at the pictures, until Daddy called.

"Sugar pie."

"Yes, sir."

"Did I tell you that he sent a dry letter. I know that he must have gotten one paycheck by now."

"Yes, sir."

"When I was his age, I was supporting myself, Grandma and Grandpa."

"Yes, sir."

"You making fire."

"Yes, sir."

"Time for the house to stir."

I looked at the return address on Bay Boy's letter: c/o A.P.O., San Francisco, California.

I would write him on returning to King's College, hoping that he might account for his sudden interest in joining the Navy.

February brought a letter from Bay Boy. I received it in the morning mail, but I would not open the letter until after supper, after I had studied all of my assignments for the next day. It was one of several letters which answered my question: Why?

February 5, 1942

Dear Sis,

I received your kind and loving letter and was very glad to hear from you. I am glad that you wrote first because I thought that you would be mad at me also for leaving school. I guess I let everybody down because they wanted me to finish school and be a great man. Right now I don't know about anything.

I'm just glad you wrote. Now I want to tell you that I cry every night because I wish I had stayed in school. I am only sixteen, as you know, so Daddy didn't have to sign the papers.

One day me and Knocker and Buster got in a little trouble at school. Mr. Hasty sent us to the Home Ec room to hang up some drapes. We pulled up one of those long shiny tables to reach high enough. Well a girl started calling Miss Jenkins from the kitchen side to show her how we scratched up the serving table with our shoes. Knocker hauled off and slapped the girl so we left before that lady got out of the kitchen.

Mr. Hasty said he was going to turn us over to the principal. I knew that it was going to be rough because my homeroom teacher knows Miss Janie. You remember I was in her class when Mama turned me over to the truant officer for playing hooky when I was in the seventh grade.

(I'm writing the other part a little later.)

But Sis, I didn't even want to play hooky. I had to slip around the schoolhouse and hide in the toilet. I was glad when they made me go to class because I didn't know what to do. But old Beebee used to pick at me every time I put on those blue pants Mama bought me for Field Day. He started calling me Boy Blue and the children used to point at me and laugh.

One day I went to the board to work my example and he pointed at me and said "Boy Blue" and all of the children laughed. Miss Janie was checking papers and didn't know why they were laughing.

Oh, what I was saying now about us was that we slipped on off the school ground when the children were marching to chapel because we knew the principal was going to call us to the office. You know how mean Prof. Graham can act. He'd have sent us home for good. We just went on to the highway and thumbed on over to Lynchburg to be examined.

(Here we go again.)

I was scared to death but all three of us went on the West End and bummed around Buster's house until the man from Lynchburg wrote to say whether or not we passed for the Navy.

I was the only one who passed.

When Daddy got the papers in the mail, he called me a dirty scoundrel and said if I was man enough to walk off and sign up without asking him he was man enough to sign up for me to go.

So I hope this is enough to tell you how I got in the navy. But I wish I was in school now. 10 B wasn't so bad after all.

Write soon to let me hear from you.

Your brother as ever,

Henry Lee

March 10, 1942

Dear Sis,

Just a few lines to let you hear from me. I am well and hope you are the same. I didn't know that you get lonesome in college too. Daddy used to say that college was a great place to be.

I started to say you ought not to cry when you don't get a letter from home, but I guess you said that to let me know that I wasn't the only cry baby in the family. Anyway, Sis, don't let nobody see you crying.

That's right, you asked me if I miss Knocker and Buster. You know I do. It's so funny. No it's not so funny. We used to swear that we would always stay together until we married.

You know what we used to do with the money we got selling junk to Dirty Red? We used to see the same movie three times so that we could learn some of the parts. Mama used to fuss anyway so I just went right on asking to study with Knocker. She thought I wanted to talk to

Knocker's sister but I wasn't thinking about that girl. She was a blabber mouth.

If we had hung around Knocker's house like we did at Buster's, she would've told everybody.

Look I'm going to send you some money to get yourself an Easter dress. I guess those girls at King's College have some fine clothes.

Tell me some more about the teacher who jumps up on the desk when he starts teaching his class. I sure would like to see that.

That's right, send me a picture of yourself in the next letter. Some of the fellows don't get any mail so they like to hear the rest of us talk about our letters and look at the pictures that we get.

I will close my letter but not my love.

Your brother as ever,

Henry Lee

April 20, 1942

Dear Sis,

That picture is tops. These fellows sure went on when I showed it to them. They say you look like you're going to be a teacher. (Smile)

I like the dress you bought with the money I sent you. They told me that you looked more like sweet sixteen than I do. Did I do wrong by telling them you were twenty?

What I was trying to prove is that you look swell and that you are smart because you're second year in college. I told them that you could even stop and teach after two years and that would make you a school teacher at twenty. A white fellow from Alabama said that he didn't know that colored girls went to college. He was really surprised to see that campus you sent me with all of those girls doing so many wonderful things.

(Stops for the present time.)

Sis, it's sort of hard for me to tell you a tale. Buddy is between us, but we seem to be a little closer though he's next to me. Anyway here's the real dope. I didn't enjoy my trip from Wedgefield to Norfolk. (I'm too old to tell a tale anyway.)

You write back and tell me if you think it's wrong for me to talk about Mama and Daddy. You know Reverend Short used to say you're supposed to honor your mother and father. You know I don't want a curse to fall on me.

Remember when Sonny and Little Pop got drowned down at the pond? Knocker said they had sassed their grandmother. She shook her dog finger after them and said they would have bad luck.

Well, write back soon and tell me what I asked you.

Say hello to all of your friends and send some pictures of the school or any of your friends when you can.

Your brother as ever,

P.S. I have not had a letter from Mama yet written in her own hand writing.

May 19, 1942

Dear Sis,

Thanks for the pictures of the school. It's funny, I didn't know that there was a college that looked that good in South Carolina either. When I get back, I want to go to Charlestown, Fort Jackson, and all those interesting places that the fellows ask me about.

Now about the trip from Wedgefield to Norfolk. Well, I left home almost seven o'clock, the ninth of October. It was sort of cool so I wore my navy blue Sunday suit and put a sweater underneath it. I had heard that there was a lot of water about Norfolk so I wanted to be warm.

Mama got up to cook some breakfast but it wasn't done by the time I got dressed, so I walked on so the bus wouldn't leave me.

I never did spend a night away from home so I felt funny. When I left I told Mama good-bye, but she was busy. I wanted to look back to see if she was in the door, but I wouldn't. I thought I was going to be glad so I wouldn't hear her fuss no more, but I just felt funny.

I went on by the store to see Daddy. He told me how he had done for all of us from the time Granny came on. He told me to never forget that whenever I wanted to throw my money away. He told me to keep myself clean and then he looked at me a long time.

I wanted to touch Daddy. I got the strangest idea that he wanted to touch me too. But we never did. You know I hadn't touched him excepting when he whipped me since I stopped riding Pete and Tom (Daddy's knees—remember?). (You're used to this now.)

I got on the bus about five minutes after seven on a Thursday morning and it was way up in the morning on Friday when I got to Norfolk. I ate the peanuts I got from the store at the bus station and bought a cold drink. When I got to Charlotte, North Carolina, I had spent my quarter. Right then I wished I was back in South Carolina. I could see something in Wedgefield every time I shut my eyes. And I shut them a lot whether I was asleep or not to forget about being hungry. One lady wanted to give me some of her food but I was not used to eating other people's cooking. I was sort of shame too.

Sis, getting in, you know what I mean, is another story.

All I wish is that Mama and Daddy had asked me "why." If they had, I'd have told them. But they never did ask me why I played hooky or why I came home so late or why me and Knocker and Buster ran away from school to try to get in the navy.

I wonder why they never asked me "why," Sis?

I hope that you will pass your examinations and have a safe trip back to Wedgefield.

Your brother as ever,

[signature: Henry Lee]

Dad and Luch

Lucy Hurston

My father, Everette Hurston, was the youngest brother of Zora Neale Hurston. I was a very young child when she died, but I remember the amazing stories Dad told me about her. Aunt Zora spoke to me through her books, such as *Their Eyes were Watching God* and *Dust Tracks on a Road*. Aunt Zora was a strong and determined Black woman. Her courage and persistence inspired me to go back to school, to lecture, to write, and to "jump at de sun."

Her name was Lucy. She was a petite, pretty, brown-skinned girl with two thick braids that hung down and touched each shoulder. The third braid started at her right temple and barely touched her chin. Each part was perfectly straight, and each braid was pulled tight by elastic bands, top and bottom.

As she studied the image in the mirror, she found it necessary to wet the first finger of her right hand and force her eyebrows into position. The traditional Saint Benedict uniform fit her small frame quite well, except perhaps for the way her blouse was tucked tightly, stiffly into her skirt, the collar to hem pulled taut. Maybe next year, eighth grade, she'd bloom. Regardless, the balance of the person in the mirror passed inspection: no ashy knees, socks pulled up and held firmly in place by rubber bands that were hidden by the one-inch folds just below each knee, black-and-white saddle shoes polished with no white on the black and no black on the white. She designated herself "presentable" with a nod.

As she went downstairs, she could hear and smell the morning starting. The gas stove was on, the oven door was open for warmth by the breakfast table. Cream of Wheat was bubbling on the stovetop. Her bowl had been placed on the table with a slice of American cheese in the bottom. She sat at the table, smiling, feeling warm in the nippy kitchen. The plastic on the chair was cold against the back of her thighs, and she let her feet swing without touching the flour. She hummed an old tune they had listened to together.

As her bowl was filled with Cream of Wheat, she closed her eyes and inhaled the steam. By the time she exhaled and opened her eyes, a tall glass of Ovaltine was being placed beside her dish.

With her belly full and mouth wiped clean, she peeled her thighs from the plastic of the chair to gather her book bag and coat for school. Her lunch had been made and brown-bagged for her as she ate breakfast. She scooped it up and headed for the front door.

There sat Pepe, her dog, fifteen years old and lovable. Probably not the best protector but her champion and favorite. She petted and cuddled the old animal as she prepared to leave. The other dog, Fritz, was a much better guard dog, but he was possessed, she was sure! That explained why he had to be kept locked up tight in the cellar.

Lucy waited by the front door, red beret, coat, and scarf on, book bag and lunch positioned comfortably for the three-block walk to school. If it was too cold, they would walk to the corner and descend the steps to the subway and walk underground for the next two blocks while they hummed songs together.

This flood of twenty-one-year-old memories, of simpler and happier times, came every now and then. I was still petite and pretty after two marriages and two sons.

Fragments of the past thirty years fluttered in and out of my consciousness, and I sat in Mount Sinai Hospital. The oncology ward was quiet. Room 726 overlooked Blue Hills Avenue, a main street in Hartford, Connecticut. Although it was 5:30 P.M. and the traffic was at its height, I didn't notice any movement when my eyes wandered to the window. Nor did I notice the rain slamming against the windowpanes or the brief moments when it stopped.

It hurt to look at my watch, to see time leaving, dissipating. It hurt worse to look at the hospital bed. There lay my strength, my world of memories: no more bowls of Cream of Wheat and cheese prepared for me or seven-times-table drills or checkers on the front porch.

Who would call me "Luch"? And say *naught* instead of *zero*? And tell me stories of some ninety years of history lived—laughing widely so the light caught the gold tooth in the front of his smile? I hadn't heard all of the fishing stories or Babe Ruth tales yet, or about being a bounty hunter in Mississippi and riding a motorcycle with a pair of bull horns mounted in the front. These stories that had intrigued me or made me laugh were now vital specimens to be savored, for they would be told to me no more.

Sure, other people died, but I never knew anyone personally who died. This was to be my first encounter with death, and no others would ever matter. In my mind I could list dozens of people who really needed to die, ones who served no purpose on the face of the earth. But not Daddy! It wasn't fair, and I would never be the same.

I drew each breath with Daddy, held it and swore I'd not exhale if he didn't. The simple task kept me on the edge of life with Dad. By 8 P.M. I was light-headed. I was losing control. I knew it and did not care. My blouse was saturated in front but not from crying, not sobbing, just letting my heart drain out through my eyes. You didn't heave to do that. There was no noise associated with this process.

How does life just leave a body? The night before we had talked together. Dad was in a lot of pain—out-of-his-mind pain—but had conversed in brief, sane intervals, calmly. "Take the boxes, Luch. Keep them. The boxes. They're for you. You hold onto them." His eyes were touching mine. The words were pushed from his lips. He would move his lips for the next few minutes with no sounds erupting as his focus on my eyes clouded, faded, and disappeared. I still stood in his line of vision but he could not see me as that alternate personality took over. That other personality, pain, would invade Dad's body until the following evening. They would take turns being dominant. When it was Dad's turn, he would talk to me, touch my hand, and comfort the freckle-faced girl with three braids, emotionally bouncing me on his knee again. But then it was the other one's turn. It would prohibit Dad from focusing or talking except to thrash around without dignity and cry out in pain with yelps and moans. By 1:30 A.M. even the doctors were tired of the other one taking his turn on this fragile ninety-year-old body. With a morphine injection, the doctors decided to silence the other one and allow Dad to rest. I held Dad's wrist and elbow carefully. Several other aides and nurses held all the other moving limbs.

I comforted Dad as the needle's tip pierced his forearm, inches above my hand. Dad's distorted face indicated the heightened state of his nerve endings. He snorted and cried out as this pain-rescuing serum raced through his body. Then he closed his eyes. We would never talk together again.

Once the doctors finished congregating and discussing the situation, they decided that Dad's comfort was all they could control. This could be maintained by continually feeding him morphine through an intravenous drip. Now that he was calmed with the initial dose, they proceeded to maintain his composure by placing an IV in his frail left hand.

As the weather continued to forecast the mood in room 726, I held Dad's right hand. It was cold and clammy to the touch. I cupped it in both of my hands for warmth. Dad's left hand was completely encased in gauze, hiding the IV needle that fed the morphine to the other personality. His eyes were closed, and he looked comfortable, serene.

Dad was sixty when I was born. I grew up in hospital waiting rooms. Having five pacemakers during a thirty-year time frame had to have been a record somewhere. How many times had doctors said he wasn't going to make it? How many times did he have last rites? He said he wasn't ready to go, so he hung in there. I waited for him to say that again, to prove the doctors wrong. But I knew this time Dad wasn't fighting. After all, he had handed over "the boxes." He had never done that before. The contents were a lifetime of family memories, generations of culture, research, and love. Treasures of his sister Zora were in those boxes, books, pictures, birthday cards, old Ella Fitzgerald records, and my third-grade report card. The accumulations of a ninety-year-old Black man known and loved as Daddy.

Many times, after school, homework, and dinner, I would sneak to the attic and go through those boxes. I would look at the collection of old books and try to read the "funny words that had lots of commas in them." I stared at the brown cardboard pictures and old faded newspaper clippings. I would always get caught and punished for going through "Dad's old things." Now I was being given "the boxes" some twenty-one years later. I didn't want them; I wanted Dad instead. But he entrusted them to me—only me—and said, "Keep the boxes, Luch," and of course I would.

His hand had almost returned to normal temperature at 8:15 P.M. His breathing was so sporadic there seemed to be several minutes between the inhales and the exhales now. His slim fingers lay under my hand. He wasn't holding my hand, I was holding his. Then his first two fingers and thumb curved upward, encasing my wrist. There was a slight squeeze, an acknowledgment, a physical motion of thanks and farewell, of appreciation, of understanding. This was accompanied by a smoother, longer intake of air that was not to be released. It was the final polished performance of a gentle man that occurred at 8:25 P.M. that rainy Friday night in Hartford.

By 11 P.M. on Friday, June 26, I was home, totally confused, exhausted, enraged, and drained. Yet I knew there was a task I had to do. In the cool quietness of my living room, I stretched out on the floor with pen, paper, and Kleenex, and began recording the events of the evening. I was documenting history. I had found an outlet for the pain and a purpose for my future.

Grandma

Charlotte Blake Alston

"Grandma" is more a story herself than a storyteller. Based on a character from *One Acre at a Time,* a 1976 production of Philadelphia's New Freedom Theater, she has become a composite of my maternal grandmother, great aunts, and the multitude of older African-American women who were part of my childhood. I offer her in performance as a tribute to all those women whose value was never recognized outside their communities but who were highly regarded and respected within their communities. To those women who were part of *all* our childhoods; those grandmothers, aunts, neighbors, Sunday School teachers, members of the Ladies' Auxiliary who raised us, nurtured us, encouraged us, got after us, prayed for us, held-us-rocked-us-comforted-us in their bosoms, and told us time and time again that they just knew we were going to be something special. It is hard to capture her essence on a printed page. She must be experienced. As she speaks and engages the audience and slowly, gently, and lovingly reveals glimpses of her life to us, she is at once a bridge and a window. She reminds us of what we forget from time to time—that in Black families there has never been a generation gap. For our grandmothers, age and generation have never been barriers to their love for us. "Grandma's" effect on an audience is more powerful and meaningful than any lecture I could give on intergenerational love in African-American families and culture.

Well, Lawd have mercy, Jesus! I'm gon come on in here and seddown. I been workin' in that church kitchen all day, and my feet sure is killin' me! I'm gon seddown right here where ain't nobody can bother me. The first thing I'm gon do is take off these shoes. Well, Lawd, I know ain't nobody gon come in here and bother me now!

But you know, these is some good shoes. They is. They don't make shoes like this no more. When the salesman brought the shoes out to me, he said, "Lady, these heah shoes is gon comfort your corns!" And then he laughed, "Heh, heh, heh." Well, I thought it was the joke time, so I thought I better be friendly and tell him a joke, too. So this is what I say. I say, "Knock, knock!" The salesman, he look up from the floor and say, "Knock, knock?" I say, *"Knock, knock!"* He say, "Well, who's there?" This is what I say. I say, "Mayonnaise." He say, "Mayonnaise who?" I say, (singing) "Mayonnaise have seen the glory of the coming of the Lord!" I love to tell jokes.

But that ain't what I come in heah for. I ain't come in heah for all this foolishness. I was writing me a letter to my Robert. He got a great big house out in California. Let me see what I got heah.

"Dear Son . . . " That's a good start, ain't it? "I know you will be surprised when you receive this letter from me since I just called you last week. But it don't seem like we got enough time to talk with the rates bein' so high and all. How's Janis and Robert, Junior doin'?

"Now I hope Robert ain't wearin' some of them haircuts like them young boys is doin' around heah. I'm glad to heah that Janis has gone on off to college. But she told me she is stayin' in one of those dorms that got the boys and the girls all in the same building. I don't like that. But I told Janis like my mama told me and I told your sisters, I don't care what none of these boys say to you, keep your dress down and your drawers up!

"Your sister Sarah and her husband, Lawd she is pregnant again. What does this make? Four? Five? I think it's five. I can't keep up—the girl is so fast. But, you know, she gets that from her mama. Don't look at me like that. I used to be fast. Listen, just 'cause a grape done turned into a raisin don't mean it still ain't sweet now!

"I hope she don't name him no more of them African names no more! What was the last one—oh, Kuumba. That ain't all—Kuumba Ochiame Oyewolf! Or was it Wolf-ya-owe? I don't know, I just call 'em all Junior. The child be done run out in the street and got hit by a car by the time I get all that name out. I ain't got time to say all that!

"But, you know, they are some beautiful kids! They come over here and turn on the radio and listen to that—whatchacall—rap music! Lawd, that's 'bout to run me out of house and home. But you know, I'm gon get 'em good, 'cause I wrote me a rap, too. I got it right heah. Y'all want to hear it?

> "When the grandkids come to stay with me,
> Jonathan and Beverly and little J.C.,
> They run to the radio and turn it on
> And all the peace I had is gone!
>
> "They say 'Grandmommy, do you like this song?'
> And then they all start to sing along.
> Why they call it singing is beyond me
> 'Cause I can't hear no melody!
>
> "Once I tried to listen to the words they say,
> But I can't understand them to this day.
> And to me it don't make no sense at all
> So I'll leave the understanding to y'all.
>
> "And then they all sound the same to me,
> But the kids say, 'No, that's Heavy D!
> And don't look at us like you're lost
> When we start dancin' to Kriss Kross!'
>
> "So I go on in the kitchen and I let 'em have fun
> They're really good kids so there's no harm done.
> Their parents teach them to understand
> The right way to treat their fellow man
>
> "So you listen to your rappin' and enjoy yourself
> 'Cause your old grandmommy just loves ya to death
> And maybe you'll remember when I'm dead and gone
> That you had a grandmother that wrote a rap song!"

I'm gon mail that as soon as I get a stamp. Well, let me get on back. 'Scuse me, sir, could you help me with my chair? (She singles out a man in the audience.) Now, because you're so nice, I'm gon tell you a joke. Knock, Knock! (The man responds: Who's there?) Canteloupe. (Canteloupe who?) I can't elope with you tonight, my daddy's got the car!

Nightmare

Malcolm X

There's a saying in my neighborhood, "Let the man speak for himself." Much has been said about El-Hajj Malik El-Shabazz, better known as Malcolm X. Malcolm X was a compassionate and dedicated leader. In his own words we bear witness to his childhood pain and realize why he became the man he did.

One afternoon in 1931 when Wilfred, Hilda, Philbert, and I came home, my mother and father were having one of their arguments. There had lately been a lot of tension around the house because of Black Legion threats. Anyway, my father had taken one of the rabbits which we were raising, and ordered my mother to cook it. We raised rabbits, but sold them to whites. My father had taken a rabbit from the rabbit pen. He had pulled off the rabbit's head. He was so strong, he needed no knife to behead chickens or rabbits. With one twist of his big black hands he simply twisted off the head and threw the bleeding-necked thing back at my mother's feet.

My mother was crying. She started to skin the rabbit, preparatory to cooking it. But my father was so angry he slammed on out of the front door and started walking up the road toward town.

It was then that my mother had this vision. She had always been a strange woman in this sense, and had always had a strong intuition of things about to happen. And most of her children are the same way, I think. When something is about to happen, I can feel something, sense something. I never have known something to happen that has caught me completely off guard—except once. And that was when, years later, I discovered facts I couldn't believe about a man who, up until that discovery, I would gladly have given my life for.

My father was well up the road men my mother ran screaming out onto the porch. *"Early! Early!"* She screamed his name. She clutched up her apron in one hand, and ran down across the yard and into the road. My father turned around. He saw her. For some reason, considering how angry he had been when he left, he waved at her. But he kept on going.

She told me later, my mother did, that she had a vision of my father's end. All the rest of the afternoon, she was not herself, crying and nervous and upset. She finished cooking the rabbit and put the whole thing in the warmer part of the black stove. When my father was not back home by our bedtime, my mother hugged and clutched us, and we felt strange, not knowing what to do, because she had never acted like that.

I remember waking up to the sound of my mother's screaming again. When I scrambled out, I saw the police in the living room; they were trying to calm her down. She had snatched on her clothes to go with them. And all of us children who were staring knew without anyone having to say it that something terrible had happened to our father.

My mother was taken by the police to the hospital and to a room where a sheet was over my father in a bed, and she wouldn't look, she was afraid to look. Probably it was wise that she didn't. My father's skull, on one side, was crushed in, I was told later. Negroes in Lansing have always whispered that he was attacked, and then laid across some tracks for a streetcar to run over him. His body was cut almost in half.

He lived two and a half hours in that condition. Negroes then were stronger than they are now, especially Georgia Negroes. Negroes born in Georgia had to be strong simply to survive.

It was morning when we children at home got the word that he was dead. I was six. I can remember a vague commotion, the house filled up with people crying, saying bitterly that the white Black Legion had finally gotten him. My mother was hysterical. In the bedroom, women were holding smelling salts under her nose. She was still hysterical at the funeral.

I don't have a very clear memory of the funeral, either. Oddly, the main thing I remember is that it wasn't in a church, and that surprised me, since my father was a preacher, and I had been where he preached people's funerals in churches. But his was in a funeral home.

And I remember that during the service a big black fly came down and landed on my father's face, and Wilfred sprang up from his chair and he shooed the fly away, and he came groping back to his chair—there were folding chairs for us to sit on—and the tears were streaming down his face. When we went by the casket, I remember that I thought that it looked as if my father's strong black face had been dusted with flour, and I wished they hadn't put on such a lot of it.

Back in the big four-room house, there were many visitors for another week or so. They were good friends of the family, such as the Lyons from Mason, twelve miles away, and the Walkers, McGuires, Liscoes, and Greens, Randolphs, and the Turners, and others from Lansing, and a lot of people from other towns, whom I had seen at the Garvey meetings.

We children adjusted more easily than our mother did. We couldn't see, as clearly as she did, the trials that lay ahead. As the visitors tapered off, she became very concerned about collecting the two insurance policies that my father had always been proud he carried. He had always said that families should be protected in case of death. One policy apparently paid off without any problem—the smaller one. I don't know the amount of it. I would imagine it was not more than a thousand dollars, and maybe half of that.

But after that money came, and my mother had paid out a lot of it for the funeral and expenses, she began going into town and returning very upset. The company that had issued the bigger policy was balking at paying off. They were claiming that my father had committed suicide. Visitors came again, and there was bitter talk about white people: how could my father bash himself in the head, then get down across the streetcar tracks to be run over?

So there we were. My mother was thirty-four years old now, with no husband, no provider or protector to take care of her eight children. But some kind of family routine got going again. And for as long as the first insurance money lasted, we did all right.

Wilfred, who was a pretty stable fellow, began to act older than his age. I think he had the sense to see, when the rest of us didn't, what was in the wind for us. He quietly quit school and went to town in search of work. He took any kind of job he could find, and he would come home, dog-tired, in the evenings, and give whatever he had made to my mother.

Hilda, who always had been quiet, too, attended to the babies. Philbert and I didn't contribute anything. We just fought all the time—each other at home, and then at school we would team up and fight white kids. Sometimes the fights would be racial in nature, but they might be about anything.

Reginald came under my wing. Since he had grown out of the toddling stage, he and I had become very close. I suppose I enjoyed the fact that he was the little one, under me, who looked up to me.

My mother began to buy on credit. My father had always been very strongly against credit. "Credit is the first step into debt and back into slavery," he had always said. And then she went to work herself. She would go into Lansing and find different jobs—in housework, or sewing—for white people They didn't realize, usually, that she was a Negro. A lot of white people around there didn't want Negroes in their houses.

She would do fine until in some way or other it got to people who she was, whose widow she was. And then she would be let go. I remember how she used to come home crying, but trying to hide it, because she had lost a job that she needed so much.

Once when one of us—I cannot remember which—had to go for something to where she was working, and the people saw us, and realized she was actually a Negro, she was fired on the spot, and she came home crying, this time not hiding it.

When the state Welfare people began coming to our house, we would come from school sometimes and find them talking with our mother, asking a thousand questions. They acted and looked at her, and at us, and around in our house, in a way that had about it the feeling—at least for me—that we were not people. In their eyesight we were just *things,* that was all.

My mother began to receive two checks—a Welfare check and, I believe, a widow's pension. The checks helped. But they weren't enough, as many of us as there were. When they came, about the first of the month, one always was already owed in full, if not more, to the man at the grocery store. And, after that, the other one didn't last long.

We began to go swiftly downhill. The physical downhill wasn't as quick as the psychological. My mother was, above everything else, a proud woman, and it took its toll on her that she was accepting charity. And her feelings were communicated to us.

She would speak sharply to the man at the grocery store for padding the bill, telling him that she wasn't ignorant, and he didn't like that. She would talk back sharply to the state Welfare people, telling them that she was a grown woman, able to raise her children, that it wasn't necessary for them to keep coming around so much, meddling in our lives. And they didn't like that.

But the monthly Welfare check was their pass. They acted as if they owned us, as if we were their private property. As much as my mother would have liked to, she couldn't keep them out. She would get particularly incensed when they began insisting upon drawing us older children aside, one at a time, out on the porch or somewhere, and asking us questions, or telling us things—against our mother and against each other.

We couldn't understand why, if the state was willing to give us packages of meat, sacks of potatoes and fruit, and cans of all kinds of things, our mother obviously hated to accept. We really couldn't understand. What I later understood was that my mother was making a desperate effort to preserve her pride—and ours.

Pride was just about all we had to preserve, for by 1934, we really began to suffer. This was about the worst depression year, and no one we knew had enough to eat or live on. Some old family friends visited us now and then. At first they brought food. Though it was charity, my mother took it.

Wilfred was working to help. My mother was working, when she could find any kind of job. In Lansing, there was a bakery, where, for a nickel, a couple of us children would buy a tall flour sack of day-old bread and cookies, and then walk the two miles back out into the country to our house. Our mother knew, I guess, dozens of ways to cook things with bread and out of bread. Stewed tomatoes with bread, maybe that would be a meal. Something like French toast, if we had any eggs. Bread pudding, sometimes with raisins in it. If we got hold of some hamburger, it came to the table more bread than meat. The cookies that were always in the sack with the bread, we just gobbled down straight.

But there were times when there wasn't even a nickel and we would be so hungry we were dizzy. My mother would boil a big pot of dandelion greens, and we would eat that. I remember that some small-minded neighbor put it out, and children would tease us, that we ate "fried grass." Sometimes, if we were lucky, we would have oatmeal or cornmeal mush three times a day. Or mush in the morning and cornbread at night.

Philbert and I were grown up enough to quit fighting long enough to take the .22-caliber rifle that had been our father's and shoot rabbits that some white neighbors up or down the road would buy. I know now that they just did it to help us, because they, like everyone, shot their own rabbits. Sometimes, I remember, Philbert and I would take little Reginald along with us. He wasn't very strong, but he was always so proud to be along. We would trap muskrats out in the little creek in back of our house. And we would lie quiet until unsuspecting bullfrogs appeared, and we would spear them, cut off their legs, and sell them for a nickel a pair to people who lived down the road. The whites seemed less restricted in their dietary tastes.

Then, about in late 1934, I would guess, something began to happen. Some kind of psychological deterioration hit our family circle and began to eat away our pride. Perhaps it was the constant tangible evidence that we were destitute. We had known other families who had gone on relief. We had known without anyone in our home ever expressing it that we had felt prouder not to be at the depot where the free food was passed out. And, now, we were among them. At school, the "on relief" finger suddenly was pointed at us, too, and sometimes it was said aloud.

It seemed that everything to eat in our house was stamped Not to Be Sold. All Welfare food bore this stamp to keep the recipients from selling it. It's a wonder we didn't come to think of Not To Be Sold as a brand name.

Sometimes, instead of going home from school, I walked the two miles up the road into Lansing. I began drifting from store to store, hanging around outside where things like apples were displayed in boxes and barrels and baskets, and I would watch my chance and steal me a treat. You know what a treat was to me? Anything!

Or I began to drop in about dinnertime at the home of some family that we knew. I knew that they knew exactly why I was there, but they never embarrassed me by letting on. They would invite me to stay for supper, and I would stuff myself.

Especially, I liked to drop in and visit at the Gohannas' home. They were nice, older people, and great churchgoers. I had watched them lead the jumping and shouting when my father preached. They had, living with them—they were raising him—a nephew whom everyone called "Big Boy," and he and I got along fine. Also living with the Gohannas was old Mrs. Adcock, who went with them to church. She was a woman who was always trying to help anybody she could, visiting anyone she heard was sick, carrying them something. She was the one who, years later, would tell me something that I remembered a long time: "Malcolm, there's one thing I like about you. You're no good, but you don't try to hide it. You are not a hypocrite."

The more I began to stay away from home and visit people and steal from the stores, the more aggressive I became in my inclinations. I never wanted to wait for anything.

I was growing up fast, physically more so than mentally. As I began to be recognized more around town, I started to become aware of the peculiar attitude of white people toward me. I sensed that it had to do with my father. It was an adult version of what several white children had said at school, in hints, or sometimes in the open, which really expressed what their parents had said—that the Black Legion or the Klan had killed my father, and the insurance company had pulled a fast one in refusing to pay my mother the policy money.

When I began to get caught stealing now and then, the state Welfare people began to focus on me when they came to our house. I can't remember how I first became aware that they were talking of taking me away. What I first remember along that line was my mother raising a storm about being able to bring up her own children. She would whip me for stealing, and I would try to alarm the neighborhood with my yelling. One thing I have always been proud of is that I never raised my hand against my mother.

The Crumb Snatchers

Janice "Jawara" Bishop

An encounter with Ms. Mattie, a neighborhood gossip, prompted the writing and telling of this story. The incident happened the morning after I had received my teaching degree. I was feeling great, and I wanted to go back and visit the old neighborhood. As I stood there on the corner looking around, I noticed a very old woman. She was watching me so intently, I felt compelled to say something to her. As I spoke she approached. A smile of recognition came across her face. Puzzled, I stood there as she circled me, staring me up and down. Finally she shouted, "I know you. I'll be doggone, you're one of Berniece's crumb snatchers, ain't ya? The oldest one, ain't ya gal? Ha! Ha!" As I looked at this elder, I couldn't imagine why she would say such a thing. A crumb snatcher? Was she talking to me, a college graduate? Surely she must be mistaken. She circled me again. "Well, I never," she continued. "It sure is good to know that somebody's child got out of this hellhole." Panic stuck me as I recognized her voice. It was Ms. Mattie, my girlfriend's grandmother.

Throughout my teenage years I had vowed to pay her back for her enduring meanness to the children in our family. She couldn't understand why we were so pleasant and caring toward one another or what we had to laugh about. Now here she stood! As she rattled on and on about the past, I realized the strength I'd gained from her antagonizing ways. Those hard times made us the loving family we are today.

What to do? Cuss her out? Pray for her? Laugh? I simply said, "It was nice seeing you again, Ms. Mattie," and walked away.

Essie waited impatiently for me to finish my chores. We wanted to go to the movies. "Hurry up, Jan! I gotta ask Grandmom if I can go."

My stomach churned. "She may not want you to go with me."

"Girl, don't mind Grandmom. She's like that with everybody." No, she's not, I thought as I slowly followed her.

"Grandmom, can I go to the movies?" Essie shouted. I stood nervously in the vestibule, pulling up my socks, patting my hair.

I could hear Miss Mattie's footsteps. "Sure, Baby, who you goin—?" The footsteps halted, and Miss Mattie stared at me with distaste. "Oh! One of Berniece's crumb snatchers. Sit on that piano stool and don't move; don't want you droppin' no roaches in my furniture," she mumbled. Essie looked at me in distress as tears welled in my eyes. Humiliated, I avoided her comforting hands and bolted from the house.

Later I heard Mom calling, "Circle time!" so the family would form a circle on the floor where she would tell stories diverting attention from our growling stomachs. If the electricity was shut off, we heard stories; if the ice cream truck was nearby, Cousin Betty would start a noisy game like tug-of-war, drowning out the tantalizing music of the truck as we pulled and screamed until we fell exhausted.

"Circle time!" Mom called again and opened the door, expecting to find us all waiting. Instead she found me huddled in a corner. Her eyes widened in sudden fear.

"It's nothing, Ma. Miss Mattie was just talking about us." She gathered me in her arms. Oh, it felt so good!

"Baby, we're poor, and we're a big family. Some folks think that makes us less than them. You just have to learn not to hear them. We are fine people."

Cousin Betty and the younger children came in. She shot Mom a questioning look. Mom yelled, "Circle time!"

As the candles flickered, Mom told stories of great African kings, and stories of proud people, passed down to her by her father. She ended with a song. And quietly the older children carried the younger ones up to bed. In the distance I heard the ice cream truck. Mom and I smiled. Crumb snatchers? Maybe. But crumb snatchers growing up with love.

Zora

Terry McMillan

You know her. You've seen her. She's the woman down the street. She's "real
people." Zora Banks has her own voice and her own story to tell. She's in love
with Franklin Swift. He has plenty to say, too. The talk is frank. The story is
bittersweet, but the emotions underneath the tale hit home.

My Daddy always said, "Work with what you've got."

What I've got is a good set of lungs and vocal cords.

Mount Olive Baptist used to be standing room only when word got out
that I was doing a solo. I used to make people cry and speak in tongues,
and those fans would be swaying so fast you couldn't even see the name
of the funeral parlor on 'em. There is no greater feeling than singing a song
that makes people feel glad to be alive.

Marguerite—that's my stepmother—has always accused me of being too
idealistic. "You always reaching for what you can't see, chile." My real
Mama died in a car accident when I was three years old, which is how I got
stuck with Marguerite as a replacement. Not that she hasn't been a nice
stepmother, but I've never had anyone to compare her to. She did teach
me how to cook, how to shave my armpits and legs, and told me when to
douche. Daddy married her when I was thirteen. She's taller than him,
flat-chested, with an ever-growing behind and hazel eyes. Every six weeks
she dyes her gray hair black, because she says, "I ain't got no time to be
looking old."

My Daddy looks old, but I guess if you'd worked for the railroad for
thirty-six years and married someone who insisted you take all the overtime
you could get, then snatched your paycheck every Friday and lived at Sears,
gave you an allowance, and only closed the bedroom door on Saturday
nights, you'd look old too.

When I told my Daddy I was moving to New York City to sing, he just
blew a cloud of smoke out of his cigar, tapped off an inch of ashes, grinned
—that gold tooth sparkling—and said, "You go 'head, baby. Life ain't
nothin' to be scared of. 'Sides, the Lord'll follow you wherever you go."

I've had my doubts.

The problem is I've been influenced by so many folks that I sound like a
whole lot of singers all rolled up. This has bothered me for too long,
because I don't know what my real voice is. Sure, every now and then I
hear myself with such clarity, with such precision, that I get surprised—
even a bit scared—because what I hear sounds like someone I could envy.
But it's not consistent. I can imitate just about anybody I admire. Joan

Armatrading, Chaka Khan, Joni Mitchell, Laura Nyro, Aretha and Gladys too.

Sometimes I stay after school—since my piano's in layaway and I still owe three hundred dollars on it—and compose. I sit there with my eyes closed, and when my fingers press against the keys and I start to sing, the room often moves. My heart opens up and lets in light. Writing songs allows me to fix what's wrong. And when I'm singing, I'm not lonely, just overwhelmed by desire. I'm not looking for a man; I've found one. Folks aren't starving; I'm giving 'em food from my plate. I invent jobs. Get rid of torment and racism and hatred, and spin a world so rich with righteousness that usually, by the time I finish, I'm perspiring something awful, and I don't even realize how much time has passed until I walk outside and see that it's dark.

As it stands now, I do most of my singing in the shower. I get clean and let out pain at the same time—watch it go down the drain. And not just my pain but everybody else's that I've known who's ever felt or known hurt. And there are millions of us. To tell the truth, sometimes I get scared when I think of myself being in a world where I don't make a bit of difference. Where I could die and the only people who would ever know I was here would be friends, lovers, and relatives. I want to affect people in a positive way, which is one reason why I teach music. But it's not enough. I want to sing songs that'll make people float.

That's why I'm looking for a coach. I need to learn how to control my voice. Find my center. Learn to pay attention to what I feel in my heart so that it comes out of my pen, then my mouth, instead of screaming inside my head. I don't care if I'm never as famous as Diana or Aretha or Liza or Barbra. I don't have to make *Billboard*'s Top 40 either. I'd be just as content squeezing a microphone in my hands in some smoky club, with an audience who came to hear me sing. The only way I'll ever be able to afford a voice coach is by moving out of this expensive-ass apartment, which is precisely why you can have Manhattan and its Upper West Side. I'm going to Brooklyn, where they say you can at least get your money's worth. My Daddy always said, "You gotta give up somethin' to get somethin'." I'm giving up roaches, water bugs, mice, $622 a month, and a view of a brick wall.

Right now I'm staring at the ceiling and can hear birds chirping. This is a good sign. But I can't lie: I am lonely, and it has been almost six months since I've been touched by a man. I'll live, though. Instead of wasting my time wishing and hoping, sleeping with self-pity and falling in love over and over again with ghosts, I'm going to stop concentrating so hard on what's missing in my life and be grateful for what I've got. For instance, this organ inside my chest. God gave me a gift, and I'd be a fool not to use it. And if there's a man out there who's willing to ride or walk or run or even fly with me, he'll show up. Probably out of nowhere. I'm just not going to hold my breath.

March

Clay Goss

This story, originally a letter written to a friend, was developed into a monologue about father-son relationships.

Every year for as long as I can remember, in the month of March I lose my memory. Maybe it's just the way my body responds to the abrupt change of seasons. The days are longer and the sun is out more. There's an expectancy in the air, a whisper slowly growing into a warm mellow roar.

I lose my keys. I lose my money. I misplace papers. I can't remember obvious things like my telephone number. Just the other day I had to dial information to find out what my number was, this after dialing my old number (twenty-five cents), what I thought was my current number, (twenty-five cents), and having to ask someone what the information number was (I thought it was still 411).

Then there's the wind. Me and the wind. Or the wind and me. I'll step outside and the wind will be up, and I'll get this feeling that the wind is going through me or inside me, straight up to my brain where it just blows whatever perception I have of myself away. My head gets to spinning, floating. It's as if I'm a leaf left over from the fall finally getting its chance to fly.

I want to fly a kite. A boyhood dream, I know. I want to fly a kite in a big open space, stand there anchored to the ground with the pull of the string as a tether to the cosmos. And so I get a kite and go up to Belmont Plateau where Ben Franklin flew his legendary kite with the key dangling from its string. I do this every year.

I buy the kite, and it never flies right. The last few years I have taken my son along, and he just looks at me as I try to fly my kite. It goes up and it comes down. It never goes up very far or stays up very long. We always end up looking at all the other kites swaying in the plateau breeze. That's a lot of fun, too. The next best thing to being there.

This year I bought my kite and headed out with Jamaal for our yearly attempt at flying. We went out in the late afternoon. Monsoon winds accompanied us, but still the kite wouldn't fly. We watched the others, some in the oddest shapes one can create, swoop the wind into its wings.

The next afternoon we went out again, because I had no classes to teach. It was a warm day with very little wind. I got the kite off the ground and decided to hand the controls over to Jamaal. I don't know why I did that since he was content to see me fail—by now it had become a joke between us, a fish tale, the one that always got away.

Jamaal began to run with the kite. I told him to slow down, but he kept on running. Soon he was fifty yards away and, *boom,* it was a miracle. The darn thing took flight. It looked like a bird. Then a sea gull. A hawk. An eagle. A Phantom jet fighter. A messenger from God.

Jamaal stood there. It got to him. He was really moved. He told me he could feel the pull of the string from the tug. He screamed out some babble about my mother's dog—the one that was run over by a school bus last September, the dog he had named Amigo, the one we all loved. He screamed out, "Amigo, Amigo," over and over again. And then hollered, "I love you, Amigo," a couple of hundred times. By the time I got over to him, he was deconstructing this incantation back to the kite. He loved the kite now. But I know what I heard.

He handed me the controls, and I let myself be attached to the spirit of the string. It was a wonderful spirit, a pulling upward and outward at the same time. All you had to do was hold your ground and let the kite lead you around. Either way was cool. It was all about the connection.

After about five minutes I gave him back the reins. Man, the kite stayed up there for another thirty-five minutes, extended out as far as the length of the string. Jamaal said something like "This kite goes into my kite Hall of Fame."

Every year for as long as I can remember, in the month of March I lose my memory. I lose car keys. I lose my wallet. I lose my socks and my underwear. I lose my eyeglasses. I lose my way. I lose my bearings. I lose my composure. I lose my head, and I often lose my mind. And then the March winds come along, and I want to fly a kite. I want my son to tag along and watch me connect to the vastness of the universe; let him see me ride the breeze of the great googamooga, drop eighteen thousand splits to the floor right dead in the lap of the alpha and the omega. Recycle a boyhood dream.

This March the kite went up.

Bubba

Sonia Sanchez

Bubba was a real person who lived on my block. He was the leader of a gang on our block in Harlem. He ran everybody's life and told us what to do, what to think, and probably what to be. And he let me, my sister, and some other young sisters pass through the gateway of life without getting raped or attacked.

I wrote this piece because I wanted to show how this country let this boy, this man slip through our fingers merely because he was Black.

I wrote this piece to remember him and keep him in my skin.

How shall I tell you of him, of Bubba, young man of Harlem? Bubba. Of filling stations and handball games; of summer bongo playing; of gang bangs; of strict laughter piercing the dark, long summers that kept us peeled across stoops looking for air. Bubba. Of gangs who pimped a long walk across Harlem and decided who would pass and who would be stopped at the gateway of life.

Bubba. Black as a panther. Bubba. Whose teeth shone like diamonds while he smiled at us from across his dominion. Who stretched his legs until they snapped in two when his days became shorter and schools sent him out among the world of pushcarts and do rags of Seventh Avenue. Bubba. Who gave his genius up to the temper of the times.

While I marched off to Hunter College and the aroma of Park Avenue; while I marched off to Proust and things unremembered; while I read sociology texts that reminded us few Blacks that we were the aberrations of the world, Bubba and others marched off to days of living in a country that said, "I'm the greatest hustler in the world so don't come downtown trying to hustle me. Hustle your own."

And he did. And they did.

"Hey there, pretty lady. Yeah. You strutting yo' young black ass 'cross 125th Street. I be digging on you. See that corner over there baby? Stretch on out on that corner so we can live in the style that we ain't never been accustomed to. Want to be accustomed to."

And she did. And they did. Young girls throwing their souls on Harlem corners. Standing dead on dead avenues. Caged black birds in a country without age or memory.

One summer day, I remember Bubba and I banging the ball against the filling station. Handball champs we were. The king and queen of handball we were. And we talked as we played. He asked me if I ever talked to trees or rivers or things like that. And I who walked with voices for years denied the different tongues populating my mouth. I stood still denying the commonplace things of my private childhood. And his eyes pinned me against the filling station wall and my eyes became small and lost their color.

"I hear voices all the time," he said. "I talk to the few trees we have here in Harlem." And then he smiled a smile that kept moving back to some distant time that I stopped looking at him and turned away. I thought that I would get lost inside his sorcery.

"When I was real small," he continued, "I used to think that the moon belonged to me, that it came out only for me, that it followed me everywhere I went. And I used to, when it got dark there in North Carolina, I used to run around to the backyard and wait for the moon to appear. And when she came out I would dance a wild dance that woke up my father. My father used to scream outside at me and say, 'Stop that foolishness, boy. You ain't got the sense you wuz born with.' " Bubba laughed a laugh that came from a million cells.

"I ain't never told nobody that before. But you so dreamylike girl, always reading, that I thought you would know what it is to walk with drums beating inside you. But you just a brain with no imagination at all. Catch ya later baby. I'm gon go on downtown to a flick."

I nodded my head as he left. I nodded my head as I hit the ball against the wall. I nodded my head as the voices peeped in and out of my ears and nostrils leaving a trail around my waist. I picked myself up from the fear of anyone knowing who I was and went home; never to talk to Bubba again about seeing behind trees and walking over seas with flowers growing out of my head.

Words. Books. Waltzed me to the tune of Hunter College days. I severed all relationships on my block. Each night I drenched myself with words so I could burst through the curtain of Harlem days and nights. My banner was my tongue as I climbed toward the gourds of knowledge and recited a poem of life.

"Hey. There. Girl. How you be? Hear you goin' to Hunter now. How is it?" It was Bubba. Bubba. Of greasy overalls. Of two children screaming for food. Of a wife pregnant with another. Of the same old neighborhood.

"Oh. Hunter's all right Bubba. If you like that sort of thing."

"But what you studying girl? What you studying to be? A teacher? A lawyer? What?"

"Well, I'm studying a little sociology. Psychology. History. Chemistry. I'm not quite sure just what it is I intend to be. Do you understand?"

"Yeah. I understand. Catch you later girl." And he walked his tired footsteps to the corner bar and went inside.

And I stood outside. Afraid to cross the street, abandoned to the rhythms of America's tomtoms.

One day, after graduation, I returned to the old neighborhood. I recognized a few faces and sat and talked. I was glad to sit down, I had taught all day long. I answered the questions of my former neighbors. And the tension of the years dissolved in our laughter. Just people. Remembering together. Laughing.

"Does Bubba still live 'round here?" I finally asked. The women pointed to the minipark. And I called out good-bye and walked past the filling station to the park. There he sat. Nodding out the day. The years.

As long as I have hands that write; as long as I have eyes that see; as long as I can bear your name against silence, I shall never forget our last talk Bubba. That September day when I sat next to you and told you my dreams and my prayers.

The air froze as you raised your head and spoke, "Hey there girl.

How . . . " And I continued to talk. Holding your hand, your silence, re-membering for you the laughter you gave us so freely, thanking you for the conversations and protection you gave me.

"Hey there girl," he sniffled, "Wanna play some handball and . . . "

And I waited with him on that bench. Watched the sun go down. Saw the moon come out.

"Bubba," I said. "There she is, your old friend the moon. Coming out just for you."

He finally pulled himself up off the bench. He stood up with the last breath of a dying man.

"How 'bout a few bucks girl? Gotta see a man 'bout something."

I handed him $20. He put it in his pocket, scratched his legs and nodded good-bye.

Bubba. If you hadn't fallen off that roof in '57, you would have loved the '60s. Bubba you would have loved Malcolm. You would have plucked the light from his eyes and finally seen the world in focus.

Bubba. Your footsteps sing around my waist each day. I will not let the country settle into the sleep of the innocent.

Thank You, M'am

Langston Hughes

When Langston Hughes was fourteen years old, his classmates elected him class poet. That same day he went home and wondered what he should write about. "That was the way I began to write poetry." Luckily for the world Langston Hughes never stopped writing. He loved Black people, and he made us feel proud to be Black and Beautiful. He also showed us our good side and our bad side. He was a romantic and a realist. Ted Joans, another great African-American poet, has said that one has "nothing to fear from the poet except the truth." Langston Hughes will forever be loved because he showed us that truth.

Published in 1958 in *The Langston Huges Reader,* "Thank you, M'am" (al-most half a century later) tells us as we approach the next century that under-standing and communication between the old and the young is crucial in our crime-infested society.

She was a large woman with a large purse that had everything in it but a hammer and nails. It had a long strap, and she carried it slung across her shoulder. It was about eleven o'clock at night, dark, and she was walking alone, when a boy ran up behind her and tried to snatch her purse. The strap broke with the sudden single tug the boy gave it from behind. But the boy's weight and the weight of the purse combined caused him to lose his balance. Instead of taking off full blast as he had hoped, the boy fell on his back on the sidewalk and his legs flew up. The large woman simply turned around and kicked him right square in his blue-jeaned sitter. Then she reached down, picked the boy up by his shirt front, and shook him until his teeth rattled.

After that the woman said, "Pick up my pocketbook, boy, and give it here."

She still held him tightly. But she bent down enough to permit him to stoop and pick up her purse. Then she said, "Now ain't you ashamed of yourself?"

Firmly gripped by his shirt front, the boy said, "Yes'm."

The woman said, "What did you want to do it for?"

The boy said, "I didn't aim to."

She said, "You a lie!"

By that time two or three people passed, stopped, turned to look, and some stood watching.

"If I turn you loose, will you run?" asked the woman.

"Yes'm," said the boy.

"Then I won't turn you loose," said the woman. She did not release him.

"Lady, I'm sorry," whispered the boy.

"Um-hum! Your face is dirty. I got a great mind to wash your face for you. Ain't you got nobody home to tell you to wash your face?"

"No'm," said the boy.

"Then it will get washed this evening," said the large woman, starting up the street, dragging the frightened boy behind her.

He looked as if he were fourteen or fifteen, frail and willow-wild, in tennis shoes and blue jeans.

The woman said, "You ought to be my son. I would teach you right from wrong. Least I can do right now is to wash your face. Are you hungry?"

"No'm," said the being-dragged boy. "I just want you to turn me loose."

"Was I bothering *you* when I turned that corner?" asked the woman.

"No'm."

"But you put yourself in contact with *me,*" said the woman. "If you think that that contact is not going to last awhile, you got another thought coming. When I get through with you, sir, you are going to remember Mrs. Luella Bates Washington Jones."

Sweat popped out on the boy's face and he began to struggle. Mrs. Jones stopped, jerked him around in front of her, put a half nelson about his neck, and continued to drag him up the street. When she got to her door, she dragged the boy inside, down a hall, and into a large kitchenette-furnished room at the rear of the house. She switched on the light and left the door open. The boy could hear other roomers laughing and talking in the large house. Some of their doors were open, too, so he knew he and the woman were not alone. The woman still had him by the neck in the middle of her room.

She said, "What is your name?"

"Roger," answered the boy.

"Then, Roger, you go to that sink and wash your face," said the woman, whereupon she turned him loose—at last. Roger looked at the door— looked at the woman—looked at the door—*and went to the sink.*

"Let the water run until it gets warm," she said. "Here's a clean towel."

"You gonna take me to jail?" asked the boy, bending over the sink.

"Not with that face, I would not take you nowhere," said the woman. "Here I am trying to get home to cook me a bite to eat, and you snatch my pocketbook! Maybe you ain't been to your supper either, late as it be. Have you?"

"There's nobody home at my house," said the boy.

"Then we'll eat," said the woman. "I believe you're hungry—or been hungry—to try to snatch my pocketbook!"

"I want a pair of blue suede shoes," said the boy.

"Well, you didn't have to snatch *my* pocketbook to get some suede shoes," said Mrs. Luella Bates Washington Jones. "You could of asked me."

"M'am?"

The water dripping from his face, the boy looked at her. There was a long pause. A very long pause. After he had dried his face and not knowing what else to do, dried it again, the boy turned around, wondering what next. The door was open. He could make a dash for it down the hall. He could run, run, run, *run!*

The woman was sitting on the day bed. After a while she said, "I were young once and I wanted things I could not get."

There was another long pause. The boy's mouth opened. Then he frowned, not knowing he frowned.

The woman said, "Um-hum! You thought I was going to say *but,* didn't you? You thought I was going to say, *but I didn't snatch people's pocket- books.* Well, I wasn't going to say that." Pause. Silence. "I have done things, too, which I would not tell you, son—neither tell God, if He didn't already know. Everybody's got something in common. So you set down while I fix us something to eat. You might run that comb through your hair so you will look presentable."

In another corner of the room behind a screen was a gas plate and an icebox. Mrs. Jones got up and went behind the screen. The woman did not watch the boy to see if he was going to run now, nor did she watch her purse, which she left behind her on the day bed. But the boy took care to sit on the far side of the room, away from the purse, where he thought she could easily see him out of the corner of her eye if she wanted to. He did not trust the woman *not* to trust him. And he did not want to be mistrusted now.

"Do you need somebody to go to the store," asked the boy, "maybe to get some milk or something?"

"Don't believe I do," said the woman, "unless you just want sweet milk yourself. I was going to make cocoa out of this canned milk I got here."

"That will be fine," said the boy.

She heated some lima beans and ham she had in the icebox, made the cocoa, and set the table. The woman did not ask the boy anything about where he lived, or his folks, or anything else that would embarrass him. Instead, as they ate, she told him about her job in a hotel beauty shop that stayed open late, what the work was like, and how all kinds of women came in and out, blondes, redheads, and Spanish. Then she cut him a half of her ten-cent cake.

"Eat some more, son," she said.

When they were finished eating, she got up and said, "Now here, take this ten dollars and buy yourself some blue suede shoes. And next time, do not make the mistake of latching onto *my* pocketbook *nor nobody else's*— because shoes got by devilish ways will burn your feet. I got to get my rest now. But from here on in, son, I hope you will behave yourself."

She led him down the hall to the front door and opened it. "Good night! Behave yourself, boy!" she said, looking out into the street as he went down the steps.

The boy wanted to say something other than, "Thank you, m'am," to Mrs. Luella Bates Washington Jones, but although his lips moved, he couldn't even say that as he turned at the foot of the barren stoop and looked up at the large woman in the door. Then she shut the door.

Miss Wunderlich

Hugh Morgan Hill (Brother Blue)

I've given my life to storytelling; it's sacred to me. We can touch human hearts forever. It's my life, being I want to change the world—to ease the burden of those who suffer, to feed the hungry, to lighten the struggle.

My kind of theater can be presented anywhere, in any setting, with nothin' but a place to stand—an imagination. I can take it to the poorest people. I can take it to one person or many. I can take it anyplace. It's in my body, in my soul. I've told my stories by candlelight, at high noon beside the sea, in convents, in hospitals, in college classrooms and graduate seminars, in Sunday schools, in public schools, in nursery schools, in theaters, in halls, in prisons—I like to work in prisons.

I tell stories wherever people are—even in the streets. And when you're there in the streets, you meet the street people. The people who are suffering, dying, lost, some going mad, some drunk. "Tell the drunk a story, Blue." You know, you can sober up a man with a story. Stories are healing. But people are in a hurry in the streets. You've got to make things concise. Boom! You can talk all you want, but how does the recipe taste in your mouth and your belly? Did you give them something they can use?

You want to know why *I* tell stories? If I never get another response from anyone—no one ever again tells me that they like my stories—I've got that memory. And whenever I see someone tryin' to get out of the cocoon of loneliness, sadness, trouble, I always think of my brother. There is always a beautiful soul, a butterfly, within.

For, you see, storytellin' has become a sacred mission. Ever' time I tell a story, I risk all on that deep feelin'—tryin' to do somethin' real, from the middle of me, movin' in the spirit, trustin' completely with my life. For my work is like that of an old jazz musician: blowin' an old song but blowin' it ever new.

Did you ever fall in love with your teacher? It happened to Blue. It was like this, you see. I was eight years old and I hated school. The kids were cruel to me. I was one black button in a field of snow. They called me everything but Blue. And I cried. I wanted somebody to look past my eyes and see somethin' beautiful in me.

Hey, people. You wanna hear a secret? In the middle of you and in the middle of me there's some kind of magic. It's there for love. If someone don't love you, you can cry. You could even die. I almost did, but she come along. Like a rainbow song. Her skin was like snow. Inside was her bright soul. She had magic eyes. She could look through the muddy water when children cry and see the beautiful soul, the butterfly. Well, in school I was cryin' all the time.

At home I say, "Mama, kiss me once, kiss me twice. It be nice." You know how mamas do when they kiss you. They mostly miss ya. Talkin' 'bout "blow you nose" and "don't tear your clothes."

Daddy seemed so tall. Like a brick wall. He was a bricklayer when he could get work. Didn't wear no gloves on his hands, you understand. I asked him for a kiss, but instead he had a trick, squarin' off my face. Gonna turn it into a brick and put it in a wall someplace. And I cried. That's when she come along—when I was dyin'.

Miss Wunderlich. Like an angel. On my first test in arithmetic I almost failed. I almost died. She said, "Come on, Blue, give me that paper. Let's play peek-a-boo." She's lookin' inside me. She's sayin', "Blue, I love you. In you I see something beautiful, a butterfly. Don't cry, don't die." She took my paper, and she put somethin' on there like a kiss.

I heard music. I fell in love with the woman. I did numbers in my sleep. One plus one is two. I love you. Two times two is four. I won't be late no more.

Next test, guess what I got? A-plus. That's what happened to Blue. If they only knew what love can do. I fell in love with school—with the ceiling, the floor, the window, and the door—'cause she was in there. I fell in love with the sky 'cause it was blue like her eyes. It can happen to you. All you have to do is fall in love with someone who can look through your eye and see the butterfly in you, in your soul, and you become what that person sees in you. And that saved my life.

"Miss Wunderlich, I'm Brother Blue. I love you. I'm playin' peek-a-boo in the streets, in the jailhouses, in the hospitals, in the subways. I'm lookin' past the colors, past the eyes, past the skin. I'm lookin' past the eyes of the people I meet for the wonderful within. I pray someday before I die, before I blow away, that I'll save one life, maybe two, like you saved Blue.

"Good night, Miss Wunderlich. Good mornin', too. I'm Brother Blue. I love you my whole life through, the next one, too. I'm a storyteller travelin' around the world. All I do when I tell stories is play peek-a-boo, like you did with Blue. I'm lookin' for the beautiful within, the butterfly in all people. Every night I think of you. Every morning, too. I'll love you forever, Miss Wunderlich. You taught me what to do. I believe in *love*. And that's *you*."

Cheese

E. J. Stewart

Katie Missouri is a fictitious character in "Cheese," created for an advanced fiction-writing class in the spring of 1991. However, Katie Missouri resembles several of my aunts and family friends. As a matter of fact, the name Katie Missouri is a combination of two very real people (but that is another story).

Later the same year, while visiting my parents in Kinston, North Carolina, after talking with my parents and while listening to them laughing, singing hymns, and recounting some family history, I sat in the back bedroom of their trailer home and wrote this delightful monologue swiftly and without hesitation.

Hello! Who there? *Who!* Sister Leona, that you? What you sayin' out there? Woman, get your old bones in here. I can't hear what you sayin' out there on the porch.

Why ain't I called you? Don't you even come in here talkin' no mess. You ain't even in the house good 'fore you start in on me. Shucks, woman, I been busy—had company about all week. Watch out there. Don't be stompin' on my peas. But you knowed it although I ain't called. Hum huh! I knowed you knowed. That nosy Ella Mae knowed. The entire countryside should know by now. Hum huh. I know they know. Mouth almighty quick as lightnin' and twice as deadly. So don't come in here talkin' no stuff to me about not callin'.

That why you here, anyhow, with your in-qui-si-tive self? Well, sit down. You ain't goin' get no taller, thought you seem to be wider than the last time I seen you. Oh, don't take it so personal. I jest making a joke. You church folks so touchy! Make yourself useful and shell some of these dry field peas. Your rheumatiz botherin' you again? Hummm. Never mind then. That's okay. No need to 'pologize. I'm 'bout finished anyhow. You shoulda come sooner so you could be some help. Looks like you always a day late and a dollar short.

Hold on a minute! I'm goin' get to my company! Don't rush me. What your hurry? You ain't got nowhere to go or nothin' to do, do you? That's what I thought. Well then. Ella Mae told the truth for once. I had company all right. My granddaughter from New York came to visit. She jest left this morning. I was hopin' you could get to see her, but she was in such a hurry. She never stays too long. Which one? You deaf or somethin'! The one livin' in New York. I ain't got but one grandgal livin' in New York. I thought you knowed that. The rest of them scattered all over. Let's see: Baltimore, Texas, Georgia, Chicago, and Cal-i-for-ni-a—oh, yeah, Denver. That should be about it. *Wait!* No, there's one more. I even got me a boy livin' in my name state. Almost forgot about him. My baby boy is still out there in Missouri.

What that? Wait a minute! Who tellin' this story? Yeah, I thought I was. Then you need to shut up and let me tell it. So I gets off the path once in a while. Now where was I? See what you did. You made me forget. What that? Oh, yeah, my grandgal. She my boy Rufus knee baby gal. The one talk real fast. Yeah, that's the one. I thought you shoulda remembered her. She what? Didn't she always think she was too pretty? Wont she homely, *mercy!* Looked like more than a few hanks chased after her. Hum, hum, hum. But you betta not have said so. Ha, ha, ha! She did turn out to be right nice-lookin' now. With all that makeup and store-bought hair. She come in here with hair down to her whatyoumacallit, and the fanciest-lookin' rags you ever seen.

Sure, it was some kind of good seein' her again. She come in here with what she called "goodies." She brought in all kinds of things that don't mean much to me, but it made her happy.

Un huh, girl! You know how they do. They go up the road someplace, start makin' a little bit of money, then they start thinkin' about all the things they didn't have when they was comin' up and all. You got it. Then we have to suffer through all their fooliness. They think of all kinds of stuff they think we want or need. This one, she come in here yesterday with all this *cheese*. That's right, *cheese*. The kind in the round wooden box. She told me how much I use to love this old-fashion cheese in the wooden box. Said how I used to love cheese toast, 'nilla wafers with cheese, macaronies with cheese, cheese in coffee. To hear her tell it, I was a cheese-lovin' fool.

What that, sister? You knows it! I ain't never loved no cheese. Cheese always did keep me clogged up. I don't know why she come in here with all that stuff! She musta been the one who loved cheese so. Now let's see, it was her or one of her sisters who use to say that when she went up north and made her own money how she was goin' to eat all the cheese she wanted. Said how she was gonna have a special room jest for all the foods she loved so.

That musta been her. Hum! Sounds like her. Now she tryin' to impose her will on me. But you know how they do. I couldn't tell that crazy gal I ain't never loved no cheese. I had to be the one 'cause she remembered. So I finally had to jest eat a hunk of that there cheese with some of them awful 'nilla wafers. You know, so her feelings won't be hurt. She thought she done something special for me, you know. Yeah. Then I went and took me a physics. Otherwise I'd be stopped up for a week. That was yesterday, and that physics ain't worked me yet. May take some of this herb tea my great grandboy brought on his last visit.

I ain't complainin'! I was plum tickle to see her drivin' up in the yard with one of them fancy big cars. Bright pretty red one. What, drive from New York? Nay, she don't drive from no New York City! This one got to fly. That car come from the jetport, over yonder. Rented, I reckon. She says that road trip takes too long. Her time too val-u-ble to waste that many hours on the road, you know. She much too important for that!

They tells me she got some bigtime job up there, though, ordering folks around. She got that from her daddy and grandpappy. She must make good money, too, 'cause she always sendin' me somethin'. One thang or the other. No-o-o! Nothin' I much wants and for sure nothin' I needs. But she thinks she doin' somethin' so I jest lets her.

I ain't being no ingrate. But you tell me what in the world I needs with gold watches, all kinds of whatnots to collect dust. Look at this place. Then there's sets of glasses, sets of dishes, all kinds of electrical stuff, TVs, and even a CRV?

What that? What you saying? A VCR? Oh, so it's called a VCR. Well, whatever it is, what she 'pose I'm goin' to do with it? More movies come on this cable TV thing here than I'm goin' to watch. The time before last she come in here with thin, low-cut nightgowns with no sleeves. No sleeves as big as my arms is and as cold as I stays. Girl, I know I got central heat, but I still stays cold! Old women like us need some warm, long-sleeve flannel gowns if anything. That thin frilly stuff is for them young gals. I ain't courtin' nobody right now. 'Sides, my courtin' days is about over.

Yeh, you heard me right: My courtin' days about over! What you say? You ain't got to tell me. I know I'm old and don't move too swift no more, but I still abreathing, ain't I? That's what I thought! Well then, I will court again if I takes the notion. Even when I do take the notion, I don't need no low-cut, thin sleeveless nothing to do it in. I never did need that frilly fooliness. Shucks, girl. Ha, ha, ha! I got my other husbands without all that womanly wiles frilly fooliness. And when I decides to get me another one, I can do it jest as good in a warm flannel as I can in nothin' at all. Hell, the fellows I knows don't care nothin' about no frilly gown nohow.

Nasty! I ain't talkin' nasty. I'm statin' the facts as I sees them. Now you gettin' ready to go! Well now, if you don't like this kind of talk, then you need to go on home with your holy and righteous self. You church folks can be downright aggravating.

I ain't crit-i-ciz-ing nobody. The gift's all right. I knows my grandgal means well. They all means well, bless their little hearts. Don't I always take all the things they brings me and say thanks? You know, so they feelings don't get hurt. 'Sides, this my family, and I can say whatever I please about them. So don't you come tryin' to make me feel bad about what I says. I'm way past grown. You the one don't want to hear my kind of talk. You don't like it. Home is where you needs to be, woman!

Well, go on if you was goin' anyhow. Make sure you ain't got no at-ti-tude. Um huh! Jest so we don't have no misunderstanding about what I says about my folks or anythin' else.

Wait a minute! Don't be too quick to leave. I thought you 'spose to be my friend. Yeah, I know that what you claim. Well then, you need to act like it. Go down the hallway into the first bedroom. Look under the bed in there and get a box of that there cheese. Don't get that piece of box neither. Get a full box. Watch out there. Don't step on my peas on that newspaper. Watch where you going. Damn if half of you is deaf and that other half is blind.

You got it? Can you carry it? Hold on. Let me get the door for you. Uh humm. I knowed you always loved cheese, girl. That why I wanted you to take a full box. Be careful on those old porch steps. Don't you fall and hurt yourself 'cause I ain't got no money. But then you know that. Oh, well, you welcome, honey. I sure hope you enjoys it. Anythin' for my friends.

Beside, I jest as soon you be clogged up as me. Ha, ha! Jest jokin'. Damn, you sure is touchy. You get home safe. But remember, I still got a mess of that herb stuff my great grandboy bought from overseas there. You know, jest in case!

Christmas

Anonymous

Overheard at a shopping mall:
Will you be home for Christmas, Daddy?
Or will the AIDS monster take you away?

PART IV

What's the 411? You Got It Goin' On

Rhythm Talk

When you go into any culture, I don't care what the culture is, you have to go with some humility. You have to understand the language, and by that I do not mean what we speak, you've got to understand the *language*, the interior language of the people. You've got to be able to enter their philosophy, their world view. You've got to speak both the spoken language and the metalanguage of the people.

—WOLE SOYINKA,
Myth, Literature, and the African World

   I came to play
I twirl and pearl/dribble the ball
behind my back/between my legs.
   Why, I jump so high
sometimes I need a parachute to land safely.
They used to call me U.F.O.
because the Air Force radar
thought I was from outer space.
   I can run so fast that one time,
during a game, I ran to the store,
bought a juice/drank it
and got back before anyone knew I was gone
. . . And I had the ball.
   I helicoptered around
and dunked so hard, I tore the basket down.
   My name is Lonnie Boo
and I CAN DO THE DO.

—ISAAC L. MAEFIELD,
"Lonnie Boo," a basketball rap

We Real Cool

Gwendolyn Brooks

THE POOL PLAYERS.
SEVEN AT THE GOLDEN SHOVEL.

We real cool. We
Left school. We

Lurk late. We
Strike straight. We

Sing sin. We
Thin gin. We

Jazz June. We
Die soon.

Jazz Scene

Miles Davis with Quincy Troupe

"Listen. The greatest feeling I ever had in my life . . . was when I first heard Diz [Dizzy Gillespie] and Bird [Charlie Parker] together in St. Louis, Missouri, back in 1944. I was eighteen years old."

Miles made up his mind to be a musician. He came to New York to study at Juilliard but really wanted to study with jazz great Charlie Parker. He soon had his chance and began playing with Bird at nineteen, getting a musical education no school could teach.

Back in New York, The Street was open again. To have experienced 52nd Street between 1945 and 1949 was like reading a textbook to the future of music. You had Coleman Hawkins and Hank Jones at one club. You had Art Tatum, Tiny Grimes, Red Allen, Dizzy, Bird, Bud Powell, Monk, all down there on that one street sometimes on the same night. You could go where you wanted and hear all this great music. It was unbelievable. I was doing some writing for Sarah Vaughan and Budd Johnson. I mean everybody was there. Nowadays you can't hear people like that all at once. You don't have the opportunity.

But 52nd Street was something else when it was happening. It would be crowded with people, and the clubs were no bigger than apartment living rooms. They were so small and jam-packed. The clubs were right next to each other and across the street from one another. The Three Deuces was across from the Onyx and then across from there was a Dixieland club. Man, going in there was like going to Tupelo, Mississippi. It was full of white racists. The Onyx, Jimmy Ryan's club, could be real racist, too. But on the other side of the street, next to the Three Deuces, was the Downbeat Club and next to that was Clark Monroe's Uptown House. So you had all these clubs right next to each other featuring people like Erroll Garner, Sidney Bechet, Oran "Hot Lips" Page, Earl Bostic every night. Then there would be other jazz going on at other clubs. That scene was powerful. I'm telling you, I don't think we will ever see anything like that ever again.

Lester Young used to be there, too. I had met Prez when he came through St. Louis and played the Riviera before I moved to New York. He called me Midget. Lester had a sound and an approach like Louis Armstrong, only he had it on tenor sax. Billie Holiday had that same sound and style; so did Budd Johnson and that white dude, Bud Freeman. They all had that running style of playing and singing. That's the style I like, when it's running. It floods the tone. It has a softness in the approach and concept, and places emphasis on one note. I learned to play like that from Clark Terry. I used to play like he plays before I was influenced by Dizzy and Freddie, before I got my own style. But I learned about that running style from Lester Young.

Anyway, after laying around for a while, I did a record with Illinois Jacquet in March 1947. We had a hell of a trumpet section, with me, Joe Newman, Fats Navarro, and two others—I think Illinois's brother Russell Jacquet and Marion Hazel. Dickie Wells and Bill Doggett played trombone, and Leonard Feather, the critic, played piano. I liked playing with Fats again.

Dizzy was packing them in with his big band, playing bebop. He had Walter Gil Fuler, who used to write for B's band, as his musical director. . . . There was a lot of excitement with what Dizzy's band was doing. Then, in April, Dizzy's manager, Billy Shaw, booked his big band into the McKinley Theatre up in the Bronx. What made this gig so special in my memory is that Gil Fuller hired the best trumpet section that I think has ever been in any one band. He had me, Freddie Webster, Kenny Dorham, Fats Navarro, and Dizzy himself. Max Roach was on drums. Just as we were about to do the gig, Bird came back to New York and joined the band. He had got out of Camarillo in February and hung around Los Angeles long enough to record two albums for Dial and pick up his drug habit again. But those were terrible records that Ross Russell made Bird record. Now, why did Ross do Bird like that? Man, that's the reason I didn't like Ross Russell. Anyway, when Bird came back to New York he wasn't as bad off as he had been in Los Angeles, because he wasn't doing too much drinking and he wasn't shooting up as much then as he would later.

But, man, the trumpet section. . . . That music was all over the place, up in everyone's body, all up in the air. And it was so good to play with everybody like that. I loved it and was so excited about playing with everybody I didn't know what to do. It was one of the most exciting, spiritual times I have ever had, next to that first time I played with B's band in St. Louis. I remember the crowd on the first night listening and dancing their asses off. There was an excitement in the air, a kind of expectation of the music that was going to be played. It's hard to describe. It was electric, magical. I felt so good being in that band. I felt that I had arrived, that I was in a band of musical gods, and that I was one of them. I felt honored and humble. We were all there to do it for the music. And that's a beautiful feeling.

Dizzy wanted to keep the band clean and felt that Bird would be a negative influence. On the night we opened at the McKinley, Bird was up on stage nodding out and playing nothing but his own solos. He wouldn't play behind nobody else. Even the people in the audience were making fun of Bird while he was nodding up there on stage. So Dizzy, who was fed up with Bird anyway, fired him after that first gig. Then Bird talked to Gil Fuller and promised him he would stay clean, and he wanted Gil to tell this to Diz. Gil went to Dizzy to try to talk him into letting Bird stay. And I went to Diz and told him that it would be good to keep Bird around to write some tunes for a little money; I think it was a hundred dollars a week. But Dizzy refused, saying he didn't have no money to pay him and that we would just have to get along without him.

I think we played the McKinley Theatre for a couple of weeks. Meanwhile, Bird was forming a new band and asked me to come with him, and I did. The two records Bird had recorded for Dial out in Los Angeles had been released. I was on one and Howard McGhee was on the other, I think. They had been released in late 1946 and were now big jazz hits. So, with 52nd Street open again and Bird back in town, the club owners wanted Bird. Everybody was after him. They wanted small bands again and they felt that Bird would pack them in. They offered him $800 a week for four weeks at the Three Deuces. He hired me, Max Roach, Tommy Potter, and Duke Jordan on piano. He paid me and Max $135 a week and Tommy and Duke $125. Bird made the most he had ever made in his life, $280 a week. It didn't matter to me that I was making $65 a week less than what I had made in B's band; all I wanted to do was play with Bird and Max and make some good music.

I felt good about it, and Bird was clear-eyed, not like the crazed look he had in California. He was slimmer and seemed happy with Doris. She had gone out to California to get him when he got out of Camarillo, and accompanied him east on the train. Man, Doris loved her Charlie Parker. She would do anything for him. Bird seemed happy and ready to go. We opened in April 1947, opposite Lennie Tristano's trio.

I was really happy to be playing with Bird again, because playing with him brought out the best in me at the time. He could play so many different styles and never repeat the same musical idea. His creativity and musical ideas were endless. He used to turn the rhythm section around every night. Say we would be playing a blues. Bird would start on the eleventh bar. As the rhythm section stayed where they were, then Bird would play in such a way that it made the rhythm section sound like it was on 1 and 3 instead of 2 and 4. Nobody could keep up with Bird back in those days except maybe Dizzy. Every time he would do this, Max would scream at Duke not to try to follow Bird. He wanted Duke to stay where he was, because he wouldn't have been able to keep up with Bird and he would have messed up the rhythm. Duke did this a lot when he didn't listen. See, when Bird went off like that on one of his incredible solos all the rhythm section had to do was to stay where they were and play some straight stuff. Eventually Bird would come back to where the rhythm was, right on time. It was like he had planned it in his mind. The only thing about this is that he couldn't explain it to nobody. You just had to ride the music out. Because anything might happen musically when you were playing with Bird. So I learned to play what I knew and extend it upwards—a little *above* what I knew. You had to be ready for anything.

A week or so before opening night, Bird called for rehearsals at a studio called Nola. A lot of musicians rehearsed there during those days. When he called the rehearsals, nobody believed him. He never had done this in the past. On the first day of rehearsal, everybody showed up but Bird. We waited around for a couple of hours and I ended up rehearsing the band.

Now, opening night, the Three Dueces is packed. We ain't seen Bird in a week, but we'd been rehearsing our asses off. So here this nigger comes in smiling and asking is everybody ready to play, in that fake British accent of his. When it's time for the band to hit, he asks, "What are we playing?" I tell him. He nods, counts off the beat and plays every tune in the exact key we had rehearsed it in. . . . Didn't miss one beat, one note, didn't play out of key all night. It was something. We were amazed. And every time he'd look at us looking at him all shocked, he'd just smile that "Did you ever doubt this?" kind of smile.

After we got through with that first set, Bird came up and said—again in that fake British accent—"You boys played pretty good tonight, except in a couple of places where you fell off the rhythm and missed a couple of notes." We just laughed. That's the kind of amazing thing that Bird did on the bandstand. You came to expect it. And if he didn't do something incredible, *that's* when you were surprised.

Bird often used to play in short, hard bursts of breath. Hard as a mad man. Later on Coltrane would play like that. Anyway, so then, sometimes Max Roach would find himself in between the beat. And I wouldn't know what Bird was doing because I would never have heard it before. Poor Duke Jordan and Tommy Potter, they'd just be there lost . . . like everybody else, only more lost. When Bird played like that, it was like hearing music for the first time. I'd never heard anybody play like that. Later, Sonny Rollins and I would try to do things like that, and me and Trane, playing those short, hard bursts of musical phrases. But when Bird played like that, he was outrageous. I hate to use a word like "outrageous," but that's what he was. He was notorious in the way he played combinations of notes and musical phrases. The average musician would try to develop something more logically, but not Bird. Everything he played—when he was on and *really* playing—was terrifying, and I was there every night! And so we couldn't just keep saying, "What? Did you hear *that!*" all night long. Because then *we* couldn't play nothing. So we got to the point where, when he played something that was just so outrageous, we blinked our eyes. They would just get wider than they were, and they already were *real* wide. But after a while it was just another day at the office. . . . It was unreal.

I was the one who rehearsed the band and kept it tight. Running that band made me understand what you had to do to have a great band. People said it was the best bebop band around. So I was proud of being the band's musical director. I wasn't twenty-one years old yet in 1947, and I was learning real quick about what music was all about.

My Friend Bennie

Rex Ellis

Like many people, I have friends who grew up with me who abused drugs. While none of them, thank God, have died from that abuse, many lives have been ruined, and permanent damage has been done to those who have used them. "My Friend Bennie" was my attempt to create something that was not "preachy," that could reach young people and hopefully motivate them to listen. My decision to use verse was inspired by Horace "Spoon" Williams, a man I wish I'd had the pleasure of meeting.

I just got back from the hospital
and I saw a terrible sight.
My friend Bennie was there and
I stayed with him most of the night.
I had to leave a few minutes ago
'cause he'd taken a turn for the worse,
and I got this weird feeling, that the next time I see him,
he'd be riding in the back of a hearse.

Bennie and me have been best friends
since before I was five.
We lived on the same street corner,
'cept we lived on opposite sides.

Bennie and me shared everything
when we were growing up.
He watched my back . . . I watched his,
we brought each other luck.

Like that time when Russell Jimmerson said,
"I'm gon beat your tail!"
Bennie said, "don't worry, I got a plan
and I know that it won't fail."

When Russell came at me that day after school,
the boys thought that I would run.
They didn't know that Bennie and me
was gon have ourselves some fun.

Russell made his move (guess he thought he was cool),
by talkin' about my mama.
I told him that at least the ma I had
didn't wear big ragged pajamas.
This got him mad and he took a swing
that almost reached my head.
But I ducked just in time and pushed him back,
and he landed in a flower bed.

Old Bennie saw him fall from the third-floor window
where he promised me he'd be.
He dropped a bag of manure on Russell's big head,
and boy was he a sight to see!

That bag dropped down on him
and that manure came out,
and crowned ol' Russell king.
He jumped all around trying to shake it all down,
and he looked like a puppet on a string.

The boys laughed so hard they fell on the ground,
and tears came from their eyes.
Ol' Russell would stand, and then fall again,
'cause that manure made him slip and slide.

Well he ran to the bathroom as fast as he could
and ran water in the sink,

But that didn't help 'cause the smell was spreading,
and Russell was starting to stink.

So he ran on home and stayed there alone
until his daddy arrived;
And they tell me when his father asked him what had happened,
Russell looked down and he lied.

After that day everyone knew
if you messed with either of us,
one would find a way to help the other
and we'd get you back or bust.

Bennie and me was like red beans and rice,
we naturally went together,
and I guess I was foolish but I chose
to believe we'd stay that way forever.

So you can imagine my surprise when they called me last month
and told me my buddy was sick;
And when they told me it was drugs that he had been takin',
I thought someone was playin' a trick.

See, Bennie and me shared everything,
the good news and the bad,
but he never told me about those drugs,
and that's what made me so sad.

Maybe if I'd known it, I could have helped him out.
At least I could have talked to him,
together we could have figured what it was all about.
But Bennie never let me in.

I've been thinking about this thing for days and days,
it's been so hard for me to take,
why didn't he tell me, why didn't he try?
Didn't he know that his life was at stake?

It's hard to watch someone you love
tremblin' and moanin in pain,
but it's worse if you think that you could've stopped
that life from going down the drain.

I don't know if Bennie will ever be well,
they say drugs will make you a slave,
but if it happens to you, think it through and through,
don't neglect a life *you* might save.

Nut-Brown: A Soul Psalm

Clay Goss

I was a student at Howard University in the late sixties, during the Vietnam War. My friends and I would sit around after classes listening to R&B tunes on the radio and jazz albums on the record player at the same time. Sometimes the TV (with the sound off) was on also.

John Coltrane, the late great jazz saxophonist, was the center of our musical universe. He was an icon, our idol. We chanted his masterpiece, "A Love Supreme," daily. Most of us were seemingly headed for success, yet we worried about the future. This story is a reflection of those times, a lament of the sixties. The rapist in the story is a symbol of the evil that is always lurking around all of us.

Technicolored bluebrown statue coming up ahead on the road. Sand is sandy windy. Nut-brown Mud Woman lion's body showing. And stars are very far away, digging on their faraway distance from me. From us. From everything else.

It was one of those short but sweet things, you know, she said. Seems so ridiculous now. You know. You know what. That's what it is. Delfonics sing "The Shadow of Your Smile." Just remembering, you see, I should have been married two years ago, you see, she said to me.

Yet all I saw was bluebrown statue closer ahead on the road. Do lions bite? She had stayed alone with me just two hours, rapping and digging on the TV. Look at this picture of him, she said to me. And this cat in the picture in her hand was a boss cat who could really do her boss. And you knew he could have been married just two months beforehand.

Still, all I saw was bluebrown Sphinx statue of Bunny. Of Life. Of Beginning. She had blown my mind just before I got into the conversation with who I was looking at now. She who now talks of what could have been. Delfonics sang "Alfie" on the record player. Are we meant to be kind, Alfie? Are only fools kind, Alfie? God? Allah? Om? Life? Huh! Huh!

But Bunny's face was a Nubian queen interested in outer space. So far away from me. Can nonbelievers believe in love, Alfie? Huh? Bluebrown statue is a woman. She stares at stars, at animals, at parks with rapists in it. And her man is known but not found. She will not be deterred in finding her star, her man, her life, herself. We look each other in the eye without ever glancing. We just rapped on about ourselves becoming one within the without of ourselves. Love is the blue of night in which the stars reside. Love is the black backdrop of space. Without ourselves. Within ourselves. Each knowing and proud of ourselves. Becoming one in ourselves. Ourselves. Speeding with blue. Dionne Warwick sings "It's the End of the World." "Valley of the Dolls" comes on next. Dionne cries, "When will I, where will I, who will I, how will I know. . . . Why?"

So this girl Bunny she told me good night and opened the door to her room. The Sphinx had been passed again. Ourselves. Within and without ourselves. Our. Selves. Ourselves. And I dug me. And I dug her. And I dug we within and without. Rapist breathing easy in the park.

But back to now while JoAnn tells me that she really wanted to marry that cat in the picture. She said his letters were so very, very beautiful. That she had burned every one of them. They didn't seem like they were addressed to her. He sent ten letters to her even when he was in Vietnam. He always signed his letters "A Love Supreme, A Love Supreme." And JoAnn started crying. She started crying, forgetting that I was in the room. Looking off into the ceiling, seeing clouds, so it seemed. Seeing the Sun. The Sun over California where she said this cat lived. And JoAnn got up and grabbed the phone. Dialing long distance to the Source. To the Mediator. To the lost and yet always found. To the always Cat who two years ago in the face of death still remembered her and wrote ten letters saying, "A Love Supreme, A Love Supreme."

Yet all I saw was Bunny back on the road, still as the statue of the Sphinx. So beautiful. So beautiful. So beautiful when you got in front of her and looked at her. Without and within. Looked and listened as she said she dug outer space. Dug on what she was. And you knew you had dug on yourself. And you were you. Right here. She was there. Right there. Within and without by yourself yet with her. Ourselves. Yet. . . . Our. Selves. Each digging outer and inner space. Out there Us. Yet her there, me here. Blue background love with us residing thereof. In thereof. Out there of. We. Us. Alone. Together. Yet so very far apart. She back down the road, lion's body showing. Who was her Sun? Me. Yeah, me. Yet I was any girl's Sun. She any man's Sphinx. She anyone's Queen. Me anyone's Sun. Love Supreme. Stars millions of miles away from each other. Out and without and further without. Blue is where we resided. Sending parallel beams of light. Vibrations. She black and absorbing yet radiating parallel beams. Blue was love backdrop where we resided. I had returned to my apartment and was now talking to another Mary. She, Bunny, was reacting to life outside. Being her own thing. Her own reflection of the Sun. Her own self, light place in Blues Land. Blue People Yeah! Blues People. Yeah! We! A Love Supreme. A Love Supreme. A Love Supreme. And I wondered who would be her man? Who would be my woman. Knowing already that she was my woman. I her man. Yet still millions of miles apart. Doing Our Thing. Residing and sharing the backdrop of Blue. Of park. Of night. So if life belongs to the strong, Alfie, I guess I just be weak. 'Cause what are words? Nonbelievers can believe. I believe in love. 'Cause I know people just exist being strong. Just exist being weak. Just exist being something except stars shining their own, own way. Their own beautiful way. Shining as a man. Not being a man. Not being strong, not being weak. Shining and posing like a woman. Not being a woman. Not being strong like a lion. Not being the Sphinx. Just shining and attracting like the Sphinx. Shining and attracting like a woman. And I am black, black and absorbing. Black and original. Black and original riding on a sightseeing bus through the cosmic universe. And I see the stars. And I feel the stars. And I know the Sphinx digs on me. And sees through me. And knows who I am. I know that she can. A Love Supreme. A Love Supreme. Temptations sing, "With Their Hands." Next they sing, "There's a place for us. . . . I'll take you there. Somehow. Somewhere. Someplace. Some way. Hold my hand, universe, and we're halfway there. I'll take you there. Somehow. Someplace. Somehow." I will, she will. Bunny will. I will. Temptations sing "Try to Remember." Yeah! It's nice to remember dreams. Experience. You. Who and how. Without and within. Love and ember about to be alone. She. Me. Together. Apart. Together. Apart. Blue background town of love where we live. Who will be her man? Who will be my woman? Uniques of the only unique. Apart and without, within and without, within and without yet within. Within-apart. She digging on outer space. Me being me past the jungle beyond myself to then. Try to remember. Temptations sang "Who Can I turn To?" Well, Bunny, you can turn to me. Damn the rapist hiding in the park. 'Cause I'm your Sun yet not your man yet maybe your man. I am 'cause I'm not. You are 'cause you're not. And in being not both of us are so very are. 'Cause we reside in Blue. Blues People living the Blues. Black people living in Blues. Blues shining Blues on black people trying to love and do their thing. Their particular respective common yet uncommon, group, communal, universal thing. Their thing. Together Together-apart. Touching without and within without touching at all. A guitar strums electric Blues from Watts's 103rd Street Band. The Mediator speaks next, saying, "Remember. Remember the Drums." The you's of yesterday relative to today. And somedays I knew I loved Bunny. And somedays she probably loved me. And today we love. Without touching. Both going our separate yet common ways to ourselves. Together-apart. Knowing it. Knowing it. Dig it. Knowing it. Out in outer-inner space. Lost but already found. Found but digging on being lost. Knowing it. Without touching. Without knowing. Without feeling while holding hands and running away from the rapist in the park. Today. What about tomorrow? Caught up in outer space, innerly and outerly. Why did we run, girl? Why? Where? Why did we run, girl? Artistics sing "I'm Gonna Miss You." Jay Wiggins sings, "Sad Girl. You look so sad. Did he break your heart? That's too bad. I guess you see how love can be. Come on, girl. Forget that guy. Forget that guy." Love is apart-together brown dirt statue up and down the road of stars in the blue love sky where you and I reside. Within yet without.

Without touching. Everybody's somebody's fool. You're no exception to the rule. A Love Supreme. A love Supreme.

JoAnn goes off to sleep dreaming of what could have been two years ago. Bunny closes the door to the dormitory in my face. She says good night with a smile on her face. Her paws show out between her smile. While I dig on myself alone yet together with her. Not her man. Yet her man. A Love Supreme. A Love Supreme. Sleep comes into my mind. Everyone waits together for the future. Sleep is a mere trivia, soothing times against tides. Within and without. The Sun rises in the West. Sets in the East which in some places West. West. West. And the North Star shines bright, digging on itself in vain. Bunny doesn't. I don't. We do dig the North Star and the West. The Sun. North Pole. South Pole. Two opposite directions, yet each is cold. So alike and cold. So common to each other, yet apart. Apart and without from each with the equator as their source. Their origin. Sun rises every morning in our hearts, girl. Sun sets every night in our minds, girl. Within and without. Without touching. Yet touching. Without knowing. Within knowing. What is us? What is nothing? What is real? What is us? What is really nothing yet everything something nothing? We. Us. Apart so together, nothing everything. JoAnn dreams. We you I dream. Without touching. Within touching. Together apart knowing and being ultra cool. All digging outer space and steadfast in who will be our man. Who will be our woman. Who will be our woman? Who will be our our? Ourselves. Ourselves. Blues people inhabitants of a background-colored love. So within yet so without that we're both together while neither apart Bunny and I. She together-apart. . . . Blues peoples. . . . Apart. . . . Rapist in the park. . . . In the jungle. . . . Outer space. . . . Without touching. . . . Ten letters signed:

A Love Supreme   A Love Supreme
A Love Supreme   A Love Supreme
A Love Supreme   A Love Supreme
A Love Supreme   A Love Supreme
A Love Supreme   A Love Supreme
A Love Supreme
A Love Supreme

Without touching. Without. Touching. JoAnn dreams. Bunny lives. I live. We all love. A Love Supreme. . . .

Why are we so close without touching? Without touching. Why do we walk down the street holding hands? Without touching. Why do we look at each other's soul and spirit? Without touching. Why do we love and get married and have kids? Without touching. Why do we touch and feel our bodies and souls? Without touching. Without touching without knowing ourselves. Without knowing within within and without without touching. Without knowing why we do everything without knowing who and why we love. And why we are. And why we laugh. And why we cry. And why we look at each other with dreams in our eyes, and stars in our dreams and happiness in our hearts without knowing without touching without and within so close 'cause we're so apart without thinking. Without digging on we within and we without shining and living and crying and trying to be free and really we touching within and touching without loving everything like ourselves. Understanding understanding why we we apart and together touching without touching together in love. A Love Supreme. A Love Supreme and touching. And loving. And crying. And trying to be free and trying to be we touching touching if not really together together starting starting all over all over again one time like the first that is the last time love time touching within and without touching. . . . Tomorrow A Love Supreme. A Love Supreme.

Hello, girl, will you be my woman right now without touching? Without touching without touching a thing supreme, so fine. So clean. Like rust clouds speeding on ahead of the group. Cars chasing up the highway heading for a lost honeymoon. Rice stains on some bride's teeth. Two vacant seats at a never-happened reception. Ice cream for the kids. Live music for phantom dancers tired of working all week. In at eight, out at five. In. Out. Within. Without. Live music. FM radio. Coltrane chanting revelation in the background on thirty-three and a third. Wife over at the piano keeping up him. With even him. Now he's dead. Dead and said. Said and apart. Apart and within. Within and without yet within from her, too, like us in the past. Me in the past. JoAnn in the past. Bunny in the past. Me in the past in the jungle beyond myself to then. Rapist still hiding in the park ignored. Blues still where we lived.

Yet all I saw was technicolored bluebrown statue coming up ahead on the road. Sandy was sandy windy. Nut-brown Mud Woman lion's paw showing. While Dyke and the Blazers sang "We Got More Soul."

Lady in Brown

Ntozake Shange

"Lady in Brown" was first presented at the Bacchanal, a woman's bar just outside Berkeley, California. . . . We just did it. Working in bars waz a circumstantial aesthetic of poetry in San Francisco from Spec's, an old beat hangout, to "new" Malvin's, Minnie's Can-Do Club, the Coffee Gallery, & the Rippletad. With as much space as a small studio on the Lower East Side, the five of us, five women, proceeded to dance, make poems, make music, make a woman's theater for about twenty patrons. This was December 1974. We were a little raw, self-conscious, & eager. Whatever we were discovering in ourselves that nite had been in process among us for almost two years.

> *lady in brown*
> de library waz right down from de trolly tracks
> cross from de laundry-mat
> thru de big shinin floors & granite pillars
> ol st. louis is famous for
> i found toussaint
> but not til after months uv
> cajun katie/pippi longstockin
> christopher robin/eddie heyward & a pooh bear
> in the children's room
> only pioneer girls & magic rabbits
> & big city white boys
> i knew i waznt sposedta
> but i ran inta the ADULT READING ROOM
>   & came across
>   TOUSSAINT
>   my first blk man
> (i never counted george washington carver
> cuz i didn't like peanuts)
>   still
> TOUSSAINT waz a blk man a negro like my mama say
> who refused to be a slave
> & he spoke french
> & didn't low no white man to tell him nothin
>   not napolean
>   not maximillien
>   not robespierre
> TOUSSAINT L'OUVERTURE
> waz the beginnin uv reality for me
> in the summer contest for
> who colored child can read
> 15 books in three weeks
> i won & raved abt TOUSSAINT L'OUVERTURE
> at the afternoon ceremony
> waz disqualified
>   cuz Toussaint
>   belonged in the ADULT READING ROOM
>   & i cried
> & carried dead Toussaint home in the book

he waz dead & livin to me
cuz TOUSSAINT & them
they held the citadel gainst the french
wid the spirits of ol dead africans from outta the ground
TOUSSAINT led they army of zombies
walkin cannon ball shootin spirits to free Haiti
& they waznt slaves no more
                    TOUSSAINT L'OUVERTURE
became my secret lover at the age of 8
i entertained him in my bedroom
widda flashlight under my covers
way inta the night/we discussed strategies
how to remove white girls from my hopscotch games
& etc.
TOUSSAINT
waz layin in bed wit me next to raggedy ann
the night i decided to run away from my
              integrated home
                   integrated street
                        integrated school
1955 waz not a good year for lil blk girls

Toussaint said 'lets go to haiti'
i said 'awright'
& packed some very important things in a brown paper
     bag
so i wdnt haveta come back
then Toussaint & i took the hodiamont steetcar
to the river
last stop
only 15¢
cuz there waznt nobody cd see Toussaint cept me
& we walked all down thru north st. louis
where the french settlers usedta live
in tiny brick houses all huddled together
wit barely missin windows & shingles uneven
wit colored kids playin & women on low porches
     sippin beer

i cd talk to Toussaint down by the river
like this waz where we waz gonna stow away
on a boat for new orleans
& catch a creole fishin-rig for port-au-prince

then we waz just gonna read & talk all the time
& eat fried bananas
> we waz just walkin & skippin past ol
>> drunk men

when dis ol young boy jumped out at me sayin
"HEY GIRL YA BETTAH COME OVAH HEAH N
> TALK TO ME"
well
i turned to TOUSSAINT (who waz furious)
& i shouted
"ya silly ol boy
ya bettah leave me alone
or TOUSSAINT'S gonna get yr ass"
de silly ol boy came round de corner laughin all in my
> face
"yellah gal
ya sure must be somebody to know my name so quick"
i waz disgusted
& wanted to get on to haiti
widout some tacky ol boy botherin me
still he kept standin there
kickin milk cartons & bits of brick
tryin to get all in my business
> i mumbled to L'OUVERTURE "what shd I do"
finally
i asked this silly ol boy
"WELL WHO ARE YOU?"
he say
"MY NAME IS TOUSSAINT JONES"
well
i looked right at him
those skidded out cordoroy pants
a striped teashirt wid holes in both elbows
a new scab over his left eye
& i said
> "what's yr name again"
he say
"i'm toussaint jones"
"wow
i am on my way to see
TOUSSAINT L'OUVERTURE in HAITI
are ya any kin to him
he dont take no stuff from no white folks

& they gotta country all they own
& there aint no slaves"
that silly ol boy squinted his face all up
"looka heah girl
i am TOUSSAINT JONES
& i'm right heah lookin at ya
& i don't take no stuff from no white folks
ya dont see none round heah do ya?"
& he sorta pushed out his chest
then he say
"come on   lets go on down to the docks
& look at the boats"
i waz real puzzled goin down to the docks
wit my paper bag & my books
i felt TOUSSAINT L'OUVERTURE sorta leave me
& i waz sad
til i realized
TOUSSAINT JONES waznt too different
from TOUSSAINT L'OUVERTURE
cept the ol one waz in haiti
& this one wid me speakin english & eatin apples
yeah.
toussaint jones waz awright wit me
no tellin what all spirits we cd move
down by the river
st. louis 1955   hey wait.

Courtin' Tales: The Wolf, the Gator, and the Sweet Potato Vision Pie

Debbie Wood Holton

Courtin' Tales, a series of short love fables, continues the genre of African-American storytelling popularized by William J. Faulkner, Langston Hughes, Zora Neale Hurston, and Harold Courlander. In *Courtin' Tales* the authors juxtapose agrarian and tropical characters (wolf, alligator, fox, barracuda, and so forth) living within the contemporary urban experience, thus sharing and extending a special legacy of creative writing, moral living, social commentary, and entertainment by Black people throughout the diaspora.

Christmas time in Chicago was always special. The window decorations in Marshall Field's on State Street and along Michigan Avenue's Magnificent Mile always delighted the Wolf. The lights were dazzling, sparkling and

winking reds, greens, golds, and blues, as she trotted the downtown territory. The Wolf was on the hunt for something special for Gator, that
smooth-scaled, sweet-talking Philly lizard she had grown to love. She had
a Gator-jones, no doubt about it. "Gator likes to cook," she remembered,
"so I'll get him a cookbook." Stopping in Kroch & Brentano's bookstore,
she spotted *Spoonbread and Strawberry Wine* and noted the wonderful
recipes he could try out on her and stories they could read together. The
Wolf loved to eat Black folk food and had gained a little weight when she
was in grad school in Atlanta because of her voracious soul-food appetite.
Now that she was back in the North, having reclaimed her carnivorous
ways while working on her doctorate, she hungered for those choice sweet
potato croquettes and pan-fried white cornbread she used to "sample" so
often. She bought the cookbook and got on the number 3 King Drive bus,
making her way back to the Chicago Southside, to her den in that elegant
high-rise overlooking the lake.

Gator lived on the Westside (pronounced Wess-side). It was a wilderness
by Southsiders' standards, a bleak environment, they thought, peopled by
creatures who had no dreams, education, or business acumen. So what a
forward-thinking, sophisticated lizard, A.B.D. like herself was doing with
those legendary Hyenas baffled her Southside sensibilities sometimes.
"Must be the community-building he's doing; trying to uplift the masses
and all that." Yet she also knew from the stories he told her that dreams
come true on the Westside, too. "What do you get when you cross a
Southside Chicago Wolf educated at a historically black institution of higher
learning with a Westside Philly Gator educated at a historically black institution of higher learning?" she joked to herself. "An expanded vision of
apartheid," she answered herself, laughing. "Ah, the joys of double consciousness." Her quick mind moved from under the sobering weight of
these truths to another image altogether—Gator and his girlfriends.

Now, she knew he had Kittens, Chicks, and a Fox or two eating from the
palm of his hand. He didn't mention them, but she knew. One even lived
in her neighborhood. So although they had been seeing each other occa-
sionally since Wynton Marsalis, the Wolf knew that she may not see him on
Christmas day. He may have other plans, she reasoned. Besides, a blizzard
was brewing; the Hawk had brought his extended family to stir the snow.
Who wanted to be out in all that?

The Gator had been promising his vintage BMW a new battery for some
time. The tiny web of rust on the passenger-side floor made the wind sing
through the car when he traveled. Gator had made serious plans for himself
for Christmas. First he would call his Philly family, then he would go see
the Fox, his main squeeze, for she had invited him to dinner. But the battery
never came, so the car disappointedly said, "No more, not another mile will
me and my rust travel with you." Dashed were Gator's eating and socializ-

ing plans, for the blizzard was supposed to be bigger than the biggest snowstorm in Chicago history—one for the books—and public transportation was out of the question. Gator waxed philosophical, however, and recognizing fate put on his favorite sweatshirt and slippers, turned on the television, and ate peanuts. It would be a meager Christmas after all.

At that moment the phone rang. It was the Wolf. She enjoyed talking on the phone with Gator. In fact, that was one of the few ways they were sure to communicate, for their schedules were always in conflict and they both were afflicted with workaholic type A syndrome, an unfortunate but necessary disease they had both acquired to complete their Ph.Ds.

"What are you doing?" she asked.

"Well," he hedged, "I had made some plans, but my car got mad at me and died."

"Did your plans include that Fox whose name you called me by the other day, or was it that cute Chick at your office?" she pried. "If it's the Bird, I think she's cute."

He hated it when she acted like she knew his business, especially with that liberated feminist tone. I have to watch this Wolf, he vowed to himself.

"Well, actually, yes, it was the Fox." He figured playing it straight up would be the best defense.

"I was hoping you could stop by for cocktails before you went to dinner," she whispered seductively.

"Sounds like an intriguing idea, cocktails with a Wolf before dinner with a Fox, but I don't think so. My car died, remember?"

The chitchat continued a few more minutes.

"Merry Christmas," she said; "Merry Christmas," he replied. And then they hung up.

The Wolf, who had been wrapping presents most of the day, turned her attention to the promise she had made to herself if she ever felt she had found the righteous beast of her dreams—the pie other prey had prayed for, the ultimate snare in her lair. She would make him the quintessential Sweet Potato Vision Pie. Ranking second only to her secret spaghetti, the making of the Wolf's Sweet Potato Vision Pie was a rare and solemn act, requiring deep concentration, incantation, and emotional control. She decided to make three: one for the family, one for him, and one for herself. After all, her food was power, and she could use some to win Gator from the Fox; and she knew she could cook like a baaaad somebody when she wanted to, and nobody enjoyed it more than she did.

Sweet smells from neighborhood kitchens poured forth. The family feast was going to be so big several kitchens were required. Pies almost complete, the feast was ready to begin. On the outside the blizzard was moving in fast. Great snow clouds, rushed by the breath of the Eagles, Crows, Buzzards, and other members of the Hawk's clan moved to their destination quickly: the Greater Chicago area. The Wolf, emerging from deep sweet potato meditation, knew at that moment what had to be done. She had heard a voice, a soft yet strong voice that was her intuition and guide. The voice said, "Go to the Westside. Go to the Gator." But being rational and trained in empirically verifiable reasoning, the Wolf shook off the feeling and ignored the voice. The voice spoke again, stronger and firmer than before, "Go to the Gator." The Wolf ignored it again. This time the message was loud and clear: "Get your big, black fuzzy wuzzy in a cab and take that Gator some dinner! He needs his presents! No one should be alone for Christmas. Not even a Philly Gator can withstand that kind of loneliness."

Finally acknowledging this as a sign from above and beyond, the Wolf made her apologies to her family—a courageous act in itself—and fixed the biggest plate she could carry. She already had a shopping bag full of niceties for Gator. Since he was into bachelor living, she thought practical gifts would be appreciated. Bundling up in her goose down coat (she was sensitive about wearing fur), she got in one of the few cabs running, and together she and the cabdriver plowed through the billowing swirls of snow and wind into the Westside Wilderness.

"That food sure does smell good," said the cabdriver, a type-A Bear who seemed nice enough. She was glad he wasn't in hibernation tonight.

"I know what you mean," said the Wolf, making sure a sinister ring laced her sonorous voice. She didn't want any trouble on the way.

"Must be something mighty powerful taking you this far on tonight of all nights," he offered.

"I got the Call, and the Lord is with me," she replied simply and left it at that. In case he considered her an easy mark, he might reconsider if she began articulating to him her understanding of the Black Cosmos. She also though about naming some orishas in case the Bear had any doubts. She prepared lectures in her mind.

Once off the highway, they passed dilapidated houses, abandoned buildings, rib joints, Missionary Baptist churches, and a mansion or two, all quiet and blanketed with still-falling snow. She saw blinking Christmas lights, some slow, some frenetic, and creative window and yard decorations that rivaled the Black folk art she had seen at museums. Reminds me of the Southside in its way, she reflected, filing the knowledge away for future reference. The ride didn't take as long as she expected. Soon they were in front of the Gator's house, and the Bear was counting his tip. Seventeen miles she had traveled into the wilderness on Christmas in the middle of a shivering cold blizzard for the one she knew she loved.

She rang the doorbell. He let her in. When she had called to say she was coming over, he was excited but not surprised. She was different, unpredictable. This behavior was yet another thing to ponder, although the theories of behavior that he had studied were not enough to explain this phenomenon, this Wolf. The smells from the bag and the glitter of the paper caught his attention.

Welcome to my humble home, he growled softly. Still dressed in slippers and sweatshirt, but looking absolutely gorgeous to her, he took her coat and led her through the kitchen. There she emptied the bag of food. The plate she had prepared was humongous. Turkey was creeping off the sides; mustard and turnip greens with chunks of turnips sat next to the turkey, between the dressing and cranberry sauce. Corn pudding, made with the original Petersburg, Virginia, recipe, was spooned out on a second plate along with the green beans and Virginia ham. Big pieces of cornbread and homemade yeast rolls were wrapped in aluminum foil, still warm. All this and much more she spread out on the table, and then she reached into a plastic bag she had held carefully while he admired the board.

"I want you to know," she said as she pulled out the warm pan, "that this, what you are about to receive, is from the very essence of my being."

"It's a sweet potato pie," he said matter-of-factly, wondering why all the theatrics. She was weird.

"This, my dear Gator-sweetie, is not just any old sweet potato pie. The crust I made from scratch with sweet butter and pastry flour. The filling has been soaking up spices since yesterday. This is a two-day process. Before you eat anything, taste this."

Remembering her spaghetti, he consented. He didn't know what she had put in that concoction, but it was unlike any spaghetti he had eaten before or since. If this pie was as good as that spaghetti, he reasoned, he would have to reconsider his courting criteria. He took a bite.

Wow! he shouted in his head. Baby, baby, baby, I got the feeling, baby! He saw himself doing a James Brown move. Damn, this is good! Taking a moment to regain his composure, he said aloud to her, "This is exceptional." Feeling a little awkward, off balance and blissful, he could not help keeping his singular attention turned to the pie. He was hooked.

"Take another bite," she purred. Wolves can purr when they want to. She started humming the refrain from a blues tune she knew he recognized, something about hoodoo or somesuch.

After savoring every chew and contemplating each swallow, an energy soon rose up within him that must have been what he imagined was the spirit of Christmas itself. For although not an avid Jimi Hendrix fan, the Gator called up out of nowhere a variation on the lyrics she was waiting for, surprising himself with the correct cadence and guitar effects. He got down on his alligator knees and cried, " 'Wild Thing, I think I love you.' Da-da da-da. 'But I want to know for sure.' Da-da da-da. 'Give me another bite, one more time, yeah.' " He took another bite. " 'Oh yes, I love you.' " Moving through the kitchen as if on wings, he knew this was it. He had the *vision* now; they were in it for the long haul. Slowly the glaze in his eyes disappeared, and he returned to normal. It seemed as if time had stood still.

"Can we eat now?" She was smiling, having already fixed her plate. "And can you turn up that heat?"

"Sure, Wolfie," he said affectionately, for now he had a better appreciation for her appetite, warm blood requirements, and culinary Zen. "Let's watch some channel 9 Christmas movies. *It's a Wonderful Life* is on again."

Outside the blizzard raged on, piling high drifts against the doors and windows. Maybe the Westside's not so bad, she thought. After all, I'm here now. She helped herself to another piece of cornbread and visualized the sweet little negligee she had hidden in her purse. Later, later, later, she reassured herself. There's a blizzard outside. Little did they know that at that very moment the predaceous Barracuda was planning her attack.

Frog Went A-Cruzin'

Morton Brooks

What I love about Black storytelling is that you can always update an old tale. In my travels I have heard many versions of "A Frog Went A-Courtin' " performed in different regions throughout the U.S.A. What strikes me is the various rhythms. I decided to "take a poke at it" so I could put on my own brand of blend of hip-hop rap flavor that is part of the contemporary music scene.

Frog went a-cruzin' and he did ride,
An '89 Escort he did drive.
Parked in the lot, walked through the front door.
Picked up the phone and dialed 714.
He said, "Yo! Miss Mouse, do you be in?"
She said, "yes, I'll buzz the door to let you in."
Frog took the elevator to the seventh floor.
Got off, knocked—she opened the door.
He kissed her very gently, then dropped to his knees.
Said, "Yo! Miss Mouse, please marry me."
She said, "Yes, my man, but 'fo' we do that,
We gotta tell my father, Rat."
Well Father Rat soon came home.
Said, "Who's been here since I've been gone?"
She said, "My baby came to see me
And he asked to marry me."
Father Rat laughed and split his side.
And said, "Oh, my baby is gonna be a bride."
A cry went out across the land.
Hey, Miss Mouse is gonna marry her man.

Where, where, where will the wedding be?
At the church and lodge near 20th and T.
The Preacher said, "Do you take?" Both said, "I do!"
"Now you're married, may God bless you."
After the wedding, the fun began.
Who came to the 'ception? Why, all their friends.
The first to arrive was D. J. Bee
With the biggest sound system you ever did see.
He set up the equipment, put on the disc,
Flicked the switch, and he was in the mix.
Oh the sound pumped all over the town
As friends of the couple came to get down.
While the music was pumpin' the best man Wren
Was dancing it up with the bridesmaid Hen.
Now we see Cool Daddy Flea
Hoppin' to the tunes played by D. J. Bee.
Then we see Slim Slam Snake
Shaking to the rhythm with his slammin' date.
Don't forget Brother Louse
Break dancin' and shoutin', "I'm in the house!"
Now in the corner was Homeboy Tick
Who ate, jammed, and drank till he got sick.
They called Doctor Sistah Cleo Fly.
She said, "Too much funnin', but ya ain't gonna die.
Dance with me, Tick, around and around,
Around and around, shake it on down."
A cat came to where the action was at.
When they saw him, someone hollered, "Scat!"
Frog grabbed mouse and ran away
To another town, where now they stay.

Strawberry, Strawberry

Harriette Bias Insignares

"Strawberry, strawberry" is a jump-rope game for three or more persons. As a child growing up in Savannah, Georgia, during the early 1950s, I would play this type of game with my friends or relatives. We especially enjoyed playing under the streetlights at night after we had had our baths and eaten dinner. It was a treat from our parents to play outside for a little while before bed. I included it in my collection, *Juba's Folk Games,* for the National Storytelling Festival held in Jonesborough, Tennessee, in 1976.

> Strawberry, strawberry, sweet and tart,
> Tell me the name of your sweetheart.

Say the letters of the alphabet until the person misses a step and stops the rope. That letter represents the initial letter of the name of the sweetheart. This can be followed through a series of names beginning with that letter or may move to the following lines.

> Strawberry, strawberry, red and sweet,
> Tell us the month of the wedding feast.

Say the months of the year over and over in the same manner as described above.

> Strawberry, strawberry, wild and sweet,
> How many children will there be?

Count from one to one hundred or until the person misses a step.

> Strawberry, strawberry, ripe and sweet,
> Tell us the name of their street.
> Strawberry, strawberry, ripe and sweet,
> Tell us the name of their street.

Children use familiar street names or make them up.

> Strawberry, strawberry, red and pretty,
> Tell us the name of their city.

Children name different cities from the States or from around the world.

> Strawberry, strawberry, cream and cake,
> How much money will they make?

Children count by hundreds, thousands, and so forth. The game ends with the "red hot" round, which speeds up the rope to make the jumper go so fast that he or she tires and quits or trips on the rope. Then the next jumper begins the game again.

PART V

—◦◦◦—

If I'm Lying, I'm Flying

Humorous Tales

Dream singers,
Story tellers,
Dancers,
Loud laughers in the hands of Fate—
   My people.
Dish-washers,
Elevator-boys,
Ladies' maids,
Crap-shooters,
Cooks,
Waiters,
Jazzers,
Nurses of babies,
Loaders of ships,
Rounders,
Number writers,
Comedians in Vaudeville
And band-men in circuses—
Dream-singers all,—
   My people.
Story-tellers all,—
   My people.
   Dancers—
God! What dancers!
   Singers—
God! What singers!
Singers and dancers.

Dancers and laughers.
   Laughers?
Yes, laughers . . . laughers . . . laughers—
Loud-mouthed laughers in the hands
   Of Fate.

—LANGSTON HUGHES, "Laughers"

Humor is laughing at what you haven't got when you ought to have it. Of course, you laugh by proxy. You're really laughing at the other guy's lacks, not your own. That's what makes it funny—the fact that you don't know you are laughing at yourself. Humor is when the joke is on you but hits the other fellow first—because it boomerangs. Humor is what you wish in your secret heart were not funny, but it is, and you must laugh. Humor is your own unconscious therapy.

LANGSTON HUGHES,
The Book of Negro Humor

Some folk de gift fe lie. (Gullah)

Is Anancy Meck it! (Anansi the spider started it all.) (Jamaica)

De Day Anancy Beat Pan

Paul Keens-Douglas

Since returning to Trinidad, his native home, in 1974, Paul (Tim-Tim) Keens-Douglas has focused on highlighting the Trinidad and Tobago and eastern Caribbean vernacular in poetry, storytelling, and dramatic presentations, both as a writer and a performer. *Tim-Tim* means "I'm going tell a story." This phrase comes from the French West Indies of the Caribbean which includes countries such as St. Lucia, Haiti, Martinique, Guadaloupe, and Grenada (where he was raised).

Pan is the steel pan, a musical instrument that is made by engraving notes on a steel drum (traditionally a pan or large oil can) cut to varying lengths. The steel pan was invented in Trinidad. The pans all together are known as the steel band. A panorama is a steel band competition. These occur during the carnival celebrations in Trinidad and Tobago. There is nothing more hypnotic than Trinidad carnival. As the folks say, "Make noise easy," "lift yuh leg up and jump," "We like it so," and "Let the mas start." In 1993 the steel pan was declared the National Instrument of Trinidad and Tobago.

> We gonna tell a story,
> A story 'bout Anancy
> Anancy the Spiderman.
> That little tricky spider
> Who cross the sea from Africa
> And will always try to trick you if he can.
>
> *Chorus*
> Anancy, Anancy,
> Anancy, Anancy,
> Anancy the Spiderman.
> Anancy, Anancy,
> Anancy, Anancy,
> That tricky little Spiderman.
>
> Anancy likes to make you do
> The things you really shouldn't do
> And he knows just how to
> Make you do them too.
> He's got himself a trickster's bag
> With quite a trick or two,
> Anancy's always trying something new.

Chorus

So when you see Anancy
Be sure you listen carefully
To all the things he's going to say to you.
And if you know it's wrong to do
Then do what's right and do what's true,
Just look him in the eye and tell him . . . shoooo!

Chorus

Once upon a time, before my time, before your time, before anybody time, all de panmen in Trinidad and Tobago decided to have a contest to see who could beat de bes' pan in de whole worl'. An' as allyu know, Trinidad and Tobago is de home ah de steelband. Yes, man, dat's de place where de steelband was born. But dat's another story.

Anyway, everybody was excited, because de first prize was ten thousan' dollars an' ah free trip to Egypt to see de Pyramids. Why Egypt? Ah don't know an' don't bother to ask me, ah only tellin' yu de story as ah know it.

So Pan Trinbago, de big steelband organization in Trinidad and Tobago, make ah grand announcement on de TV. If yu hear dem, "Be it known to all the people of Trinidad and Tobago, that a big steelband competition will be held on the first of October, to see who could beat the best tenor pan in the whole wide world. The first prize will be ten thousand dollars and a free trip to Egypt to see the Pyramids." Now ah tenor pan is one ah de lead instruments in ah steelband. Is ah small pan wit' plenty notes, an' does usually carry de melody, an' yu have to be real good to play it.

Now Anancy, de Spiderman, who come from Africa to de Caribbean wit' de slaves, an' who could do all kind ah tings like change he shape, an' talk in different voices, an' who does always be tryin' to trick people, was sittin' on he roof watchin' de neighbor TV through ah open window. Now remember ah tell allyu dat Anancy was ah trickster. Well, he was also very cheap. Anancy didn't want to spend too much money on electricity, so he used to put off his TV, an' climb up on his roof, an' watch de neighbor TV through de window.

As a matter ah fact, Anancy even used to invite he friends over to watch TV through de neighbor window. He used to tell dem how he have a drive-in TV, fully airconditioned, an' when dey arrive he used to charge dem five dollars, an' was roof time. Anyway, from de time Anancy hear dat de first prize was ten thousan' dollars, he say to heself, "I in dat!," an' is enter he want to enter de people competition.

De only trouble was dat Anancy didn't own ah tenor pan. So he decide dat de best ting to do was to buy one. But remember, Anancy don't like to spen' money, he cheap. So he decide to ring up all de big bands an' ask how much for ah tenor pan. He ring up Despers, he ring up All Stars, he ring up Invaders, he ring up Phase Two Pan Groove. He even get in touch wit' ah band call' Guava Stick Satans who have dey panyard way up on top El Tucuche, the highest mountain in Trinidad. As a matter of fact, is only Anancy who know how to get in touch with de Guava Stick Satans, because dem fellas don't come down town at all, at all. Dem is de last of de "Bad-john" steelbandmen, an' de say dey eh have no time wit' no "sponsor Band," dey playin' for deyself.

Dem Guava Stick boys real harden yu know, dey does tune pan wit' dey bare hand, ah mean dey hand real hard. Dey does cuff pan into shape. Dey don't use fire, an' hammer, an' tuner, an' dem kind ah ting. Is one set ah cuff in dem pan tail, an' is to hear dem pan soun' sweet. Well, boy, when all dem people tell Anancy how much ah tenor pan costin', Anancy say, "Nah, I not spendin' my good money on no pan. I go' get one for free."

Well it so happen dat ah lady name' Miss Cartar had jus' get ah new dustbin from de Solid Waste people, dem people who does collect de garbage an' keep de place sanitary. De dustbin mark "Litter Me." Well Miss Cartar decide that she go' do she bit to keep de city clean, an' she start puttin' all kind ah garbage in she new dustbin.

From quite where he was sittin' on top ah coconut tree teatin' coconut, Anancy spot Miss Cartar puttin' out she garbage. Anancy take one look at de new dustbin, an' he say to heself an' de coconuts on de tree, "Dere is my tenor pan!" An' as soon as Miss Cartar turn she back an' gone inside, is because Anancy run down de tree, throw all Miss Cartar garbage on de groun', an' take off wit' de lady brand-new dustbin.

Miss Cartar in de meantime comin' back wit' ah nex' set ah garbage, throw it where she thought de dustbin was; an yu know is because she throw de garbage on de groun'. Ah "police" happen to be passin', see dat, charge Miss Cartar wit' litterin'. Well is now confusion start, because Miss Cartar now want to know wha' happen to she dustbin, an' was endless bacchanal.

In de meantime Anancy runnin' down de road wit' Miss Cartar dustbin on he head, an' laughin' like he jus' win de National Lottery. He jump two fence an' ah culvert, an' cut across ah pasture. Den he stop to rest under ah mango tree. An' who yu tink spot him? Brer Monkey. Brer Monkey was on top de mango tree bitin' mango to see if dey ripe, when he see Anancy wit' de dustbin on he head. Well you know how Brer Monkey farse, an' like to mind people business. He forget de mango for ah minute an' shout out, "But ae, ae Anancy, is what you have dey? Dat's not Miss Cartar dustbin?"

Anancy almost drop de dustbin when he hear Brer Monkey voice, but he recover quick, an' he answer back as bright as ever, "Miss Cartar dustbin? Yu mad or wha'? Dis is ah brand-new steel drum I jus' buy from de oil company. Is ah barbecue pit I goin' to make. Is ah surprise for me wife birthday, so don't tell anybody. You is one monkey mus' get invite to de surprise barbecue party. Soon as tings fix up, ah go' send an' tell yu."

Well is nothin' Brer Monkey like more dan to hear dat he gettin' invite to party. So he promise Anancy not to say nothin', an' he gone back to bitin' de people mango on de tree. In de meantime Anancy pick up de dustbin, put it on he head, an' head for a quiet place in de forest where he figure nobody could see him, or nobody could recongize Miss Cartar dustbin.

At last Anancy came to ah big banyan tree, an' he put down de dustbin, an' sit down to tink about how he go make he tenor pan. He had de steel drum which was only recently Miss Cartar dustbin, but he didn't have no tools to cut it to make de tenor pan. Because to make de tenor pan, he had to cut away de bottom of de drum about six inches from de top, an' tune up de top. But to do dat he needed certain tools. So he sit down dey rackin' he brains to figure out how to get de pan cut.

Suddenly Anancy hear somebody whistling comin' through de forest. Who yu tink it was? Brer Mongoose! An' what yu tink Brer Mongoose had in he hand? A brand-new hammer an' chisel. Well, from de time Anancy spot de hammer an' chisel, he get a bright idea. So he shout out, "But ae, ae Brer Mongoose, is where yu goin' wit' dat rusty ole chisel?"

Well yu know Brer Mongoose have ah bad temper. He get vex immediately an' tell Anancy, "Brer Anancy, yu better ketch yu fallin' self. Dis is ah brand new chisel, made in de greatest part of Great Britain. So hush yu mout', an' mind yu business!" Anancy hit back wit', "Greatest part of Great Britain? Boy yu don't know Britain on de decline? Ah bet yu chisel can't even make ah dent in dis ole, rotten, dustbin!"

Well is now self Brer Mongoose get vex, he shout out, "Oh yeah? Bring yu dustbin here, let me mash it up for you." An' Brer Mongoose take up he hammer an' chisel, an' wit' all de strength of he vexation, start to rain blows on Anancy drum. Bam! Bam! Bam! An' every time he hit it he bawlin', "Take dat! An' dat! An' dat!"

An' dat is exactly what Anancy wanted him to do. Because every time Brer Mongoose hit de drum Anancy turn it. Mongoose hit it, he turn it. Mongoose hit it, he turn it, Mongoose hit it, he turn it, an' before you could say "Tim Tim," Brer Mongoose cut off de whole top of de steel drum. An' dat is exactly what Anancy wanted.

When Brer Mongoose see de top of de drum fly off, he hold he belly an' he start to laugh. If yu hear him, "Anancy, boy, is like yu go need ah new dust bin. Ha, ha. It serve yu right. You should ah never laughed at me new chisel. Ah tell yu dis chisel make in de greatest part of Great Britain. Ha, ha. But don't take it too hard. De best ting to do is to throw yu dustbin in ah dustbin," an' is down de road he gone, laughing at Anancy.

All dis time Anancy fakin' an' playin' how he vex, but from de time Brer Mongoose get out ah sight, he pick up de top of de drum, an' start to dance an' sing at de top of he voice, "Mongoose tink he hold me, but he don't know is I hold he!" Yu have to get up early to put one on Anancy." After a while he quiet down an' begin to tink of what he goin' to do nex'. He suddenly realize dat although de pan cut, it still have to tune. An' it not easy to tune ah tenor pan. Yu have to get ah expert, an' expert does charge money. An', of course, Anancy don't want to spend no money.

Now de only place he know where he could get ah pan tune in ah hurry, is way up on El Tucuche by de Guava Stick Satans. Dem is de fellas who does tune pan wit' dey bare hand. But yu have to be real brave to go up by dem witout ah invitation. Anancy decide to take ah chance because he had to get de pan tune right away.

So he take de pan top, throw way de bottom part, an' head up El Tu- cuche. When he reach up dey he enter de Guava Stick Satans Panyard. He was frighten, but he only studyin' 'bout gettin' de pan tune. When he see de set ah tough Bad-johns in de yard, he feel like turnin' back. But it was too late. Dey spot him. An' everybody surround him. De leader of de Guava Stick Satans was ah fella about eight foot tall, an' weighin' 'bout three hundred pounds. An' he was de smallest.

He pick up Anancy by he collar, an' he growl, "Wha' yu want up here!?" Anancy brains start to work overtime, if yu hear him. "Ah come up here for allyu to tune ah pan for me. Ah hear allyu is de best pan tuners in de whole of Trinidad & Tobago an' de worl'." De leader say, "Yu have money?" Hear Anancy, "Money is no problem, ah have plenty, 'bout ten thousan' dollars!" De leader smile like ah alligator, an' he say, "Gimme de pan, ah go' give yu ah special!"

Anancy hand over de pan like was ah egg an' he 'fraid it break. De Leader take it from Anancy, an' start to tune it wit' some serious big cuff. If yu see him. Do . . . cuff, re . . . cuff, me . . . cuff, cuff . . . cuff, fa . . . cuff, so . . . cuff, cuff, cuff, cuff, la . . . cuff, te . . . cuff, cuff, doh . . . cuff, cuff, cuff, cuff . . . cuff. In no time at all de pan tune sweet like syrup. Anancy eye get bright when he hear de sweet notes. Den de Guava Stick Satans leader give back Anancy de pan, an' he say, "Yu pan well tune. Where de money?"

Now Anancy was so involved in gettin' de pan tune, dat he had forget all about payment. Anancy brains start to tick over like ah ole Mercedes-Benz. He decide to try an' confuffle the Leader brains wit' ole talk an' logic. If yu hear him, "Well, yu see, when ah say ah had de money, wha' ah really mean was dat ah judge in de Savannah holdin' it for me, because ah bound to win. So, yu see, in actuality, de money really mine, ah jus' eh collect it yet. But soon as ah get it, which is right after de competition, your money sure!"

Anancy should ah known better. Tryin' to reason with a Guava Stick Satan is like tryin' to reason wit' ah big stone. De Guava Stick Satans' leader start to change color one time, fus he vex. He start to swell up like ah

Craupaud, an' he shout out for de rest ah de band, "Allyu come quick, ah smartman tryin' to teaf we!" Nex' ting 'bout two hundred Guava Stick Satans come out of de bush, with one set ah big stick, an' iron bold, an' chain link, an' young boulder. One shout out, "Is dat smartman, Anancy, get him!"

When Anancy hear dat, he grab de pan, an' run for he life, if you see speed, Ben Johnson couldn't catch him. De Guava Stick Steelbandmen pick up one set ah stone, an' start to pelt dem behind Anancy. If you see stone goin' down dat hill was like "stone rain." Poor Anancy. All he could ah do was put de pan on top he head, to shelter from dem stone. Stone start to hit de pan ping! pang! pong! pow! podow! So much stone hit de pan, dat by de time Anancy reach de bottom of de hill de whole pan untune.

Anancy get vex, vex, vex. De pan untune an' he don't have time to get it tune again, because de competition was only ah few days off. So Anancy sit down outside Lal shop to tink. He tink, an' he tink, an' he tink. Den he say, "Ah ha, ah have dem!" Anancy get ah bright idea. So he go down de road an' he climb through ah lady name Miss Lezama window, to use she telephone when she wasn't lookin'. Because Anancy don't like to pay for telephone calls, he always usin' people telephone when dey not lookin'. Nex' ting de people get some big, big bill from all kind ah places like Africa, New Zealand, an' Acapulco, an' dey don't know how dat happen.

Anyway, Anancy pick up Miss Lezama good, good phone, an' he call up Brer Dog, Brer Cat, Brer Corbeau, Brer Fowl-Cock, Brer Goat, an' Brer Donkey. He tell dem meet him by de Savannah, he have ah big surprise for dem. In no time at all, all man-jack reach down by de Savannah to see wha' Anancy have to offer. Because yu know how some people like freeness an' complimentary. Some ah dem so cheap, dey wouldn't even "spend ah holiday."

When dey reach, Anancy greet everybody in fine style, an' put everybody to sit down like de Savannah belong to him, an' start strut 'bout de place like he in deep thought, an' have so much important tings to say, dat he don't quite know how to start. Is Brer Donkey who start him up, because Brer Donkey leggo one long, steups an' say, "Hear, nah, Brer Anancy. But is wha' really goin' on? Yu bring we down here to tell we someting, but up to now yu eh tell we nutten. Yu turn politician or what? Say wha' yu have to say now, or all ah we gone, yu hear?"

Anancy pause in midstep, den he spin round like a ballet dancer for dramatic effect, an' he say, "How would allyu like to make plenty, plenty easy money?" All ah dem shout out, "Yes, man, we in dat!" So Anancy continue, he say, "Well it simple. I go' pay allyu two hundred dollars each, if allyu help me win de pan competition nex' week. You see my pan out ah tune, an' ah can't get it tune-up in time, but ah have ah idea. I go' play ah tune call' "Big Stone Falling on a Pan." All allyu have to do, is hide underneath the stage, an' make allyu mout' sounds like ah pan, an' I go pretend dat I beatin' de pan. Nobody go notice de difference, an' ah bound to win. Because allyu go soun' like big stone fallin' on ah pan in trut!"

Brer Donkey say, "Two hundred dollars?" Anancy say, "Yes, man, two hundred dollars, plus ten percent if rain fall an' allyu get wet." When de res' ah dem hear dat, all man get excited, an dey start to hold big discussion among demselves like is summit conference dey havin'. Den dey tell Anancy, "All right, we go' do it, but we want we money immediately after we done play!" Anancy say, "No problem, dat money in allyu pocket already!"

Well boy, dem animals practice for about ah week, till dey had de whole ting organize properly. Of course Anancy was head an' foot wit' dem, gettin' on as if he study music at de Royal Academy. At last de night of de show reach. Show supposed to start at eight o'clock, 'bout six o'clock Anancy partners neak under de grandstand, an' go an' hide under de stage.

In no time at all de stands start to full up wit' people. About thirty thousand people come to see de show. Ten thousand pay, ten thousand get complimentary, an' ten thousand climb over de fence. Later on de promoters say how dey eh make no money, because de ten thousand who pay ask back for dey money. About forty panmen turn up to take part in de competition. Dey was some ah de best panmen in de world, an' dey had some ah de fanciest tenor pans yu ever hope to see in yu life, all chrome-up an' shinin', an' tune so fine, dat if yu put yu ears near de pan, yu could hear some notes playin' by deyself.

Well, boy, show start, an' man start to beat pan. Crowd gone wild. About twenty fellas play before Anancy. If you hear sweet pan. Men only beatin' classics; Tocata an' Fugue, Moonlight Sonata, Waltz of de Flowers. One fella even beat Beethoven Fiftieth Movement. Nobody in de world ever knew dat Beethoven had ah Fiftieth Movement, but dat fella beat it. De crowd give him ah standin' ovation.

Well, boy, time reach for Anancy to play. Anancy walk on stage wit' he out-ah-tune pan. If yu see him. He dress up in scissors-tail coat, ruffle shirt, stripe pants, patent leather shoe, top hat, black bow tie, an' white gloves. He put in five extra false teet to give him a broad smile, so dat de whole grandstand could see it, an' he even pay a fella two dollars to blow ah trumpet as he make he entrance. An' don't talk 'bout de "out-ah-tune pan." Anancy put so much decorations on it, dat people thought he had invented a new kind a pan. Most people say it looked like ah cross between ah frying pan an' ah satellite. De girls start to whistle, de men get jealous.

Anancy set up he pan right over de spot where he partners hidin' under de stage. He whisper to dem, "Allyu ready?" De partners whisper back, "Yeaaaaaaah!" Den Anancy put on he best broadcaster voice, like how he does hear dem readin' de news on TTT, de TV station, an' he say, "Ladies and gentlemen, fellow artiste, distinguished guests, it gives me great pleasure to be here tonight participating in this historic pan competition. For my contribution I have chosen an original piece called 'Big Stone Fallin' on a Pan' in G Minor!" De crowd gone wild, dey stamp, dey clap, den dey quiet down.

Anancy pick up de panstick, an' he stamp he foot three times for he partners under de stage to know dat he ready. Den he bow to de audience, lift up de sticks high like he is ah conductor, den he bend down over de pan an' start to pretend he playin'. As soon as he do dat, he partners under de stage start up wit' dey mout'. Bang, bang, plinket plink, ping, ponky-pong, pam, pam!" If you hear noise. People never hear nothin' bad so in all dey life.

Dis time if you see Anancy play imaginary pan. He bendin' an' weavin', duckin' he head lef' an' right, stampin' he foot like he keepin' time, an' he two hand flyin' over de pan like he killin' ants. Meantime under de stage Fowl-Cock crowin', Donkey brayin', Cat meowin', Dog barkin', Goat baain', an' Corbeau flappin' he wing, keepin' time an' conductin'. All ah dem tryin' to soun' like ah tenor pan playin' "Big Stone Fallin' on a Pan."

After ah time de crowd can't take it no more. Dey start to boo. Nex' ting yu know dey start to pelt all kind ah ting at Anancy—orange, paper cup, mango skin, programs, bite-up hops-bread, an' de people from de South pelt some expensive rolls of toilet paper, dey had flowers on dem. Even de judges throw tings at Anancy, first dem partners sound bad.

Anancy get so vex, he forget all about he partners under de stage. He jus' put de pan over he head, an' he take off like ah jet. All dis time de partners under de stage don't know dat Anancy gone, so dey still playin' pan wit' dey mout', "pang, plilkety, pimm, ding ding, buup." De crowd amaze. Dey hearin' pan, but dey eh have no pan on de stage. Den somebody peep under de stage an' spot de partners.

Well, if you tink dey stone Anancy, yu should see wha' dey do to de partners. Dey pelt everyting dey could find. Ah man even pelt ah bicycle dat ah nuts vendor was usin' to sell nuts. Dem partners run for dey life. Brer Goat get he head bust. Brer Dog twist he ankle. Brer Fowl-Cock lose half he feathers goin' through de fence. Brer Cat fall in ah pool ah water, an' yu know how cat hate water. Brer Donkey get he ears bend, it take him six weeks to get dem straighten out. Brer Corbeau fly straight into ah Jep nest, an' he get sting all over he bare neck. Someting happen to every one ah dem partners. Dey eh stop runnin' till dey reach ah little way outside Toco, which as yu know, is one ah de furthest parts of Trinidad.

An' who yu tink dey see cock up on ah big stone, drinkin' ah "ice-coconut?" Anancy, of course. Hear Anancy, "But is where you fellas been? Yu know how long I waitin' on allyu? Ah even buy some coconut water for allyu." Anancy lie, Anancy jus' finish teafin' de coconuts off Mr. Latchman-Singh tree. Brer Donkey say, "Anancy, you an' yu stupidness nearly get us kill. Dis is de last time I goin in any plan wit' you. Ah don't want no coconut water, jus' give us de two hundred dollars yu promise us, an' we go let bygones be bygones!"

Anancy drop de coconut he was drinkin', he open he eye big, big, like he in shock, an' he bawl out. "Two hundred dollars? Yu mad or wha'? Is allyu make me lose de competition wit' allyu bad singin'. If ah had win de ten thousand dollars ah would ah pay allyu five hundred each, because I is ah generous soul, but ah eh win. So no win, no pay!"

When Brer Donkey hear dat, he get so vex, he spin 'roun' an' he fire ah back-kick at Anancy. He send Anancy flyin' through de air like ah football, an' when yu see Anancy hit de groun', he take off like ah jet, if you see speed. Anancy run so fast he foot eh touch de groun' yet. Den all de other animals get vex wit' Brer Donkey. Dey tell him, "If you didn't kick Anancy so far, we could ah catch him an' get we money. Now he gone, an' money gone!" An' big argument break out among dem.

Anancy in de meantime eh stop runnin' till he reach safe an' soun' where he livin'. An' from dat day to dis, he never try to enter no steelband competition again.

De moral of de story is, "If you can't do it right, don't do it at all!" Crick . . . Crack . . . monkey break it back for ah penny Pommerack!

Riley's Riddle

Margaret Taylor Burroughs

What Anansi the spider is to African folklore, the cunning rabbit is to African-American folklore. During the period of slavery, the rabbit in outwitting and tricking the other animals was often identified as the slave outwitting his master.

These animal stories are the heritage of all American children. Many of them I heard as a child. Some I have collected from adults who recalled them from their childhood lore. Others I have sought out from the folklore journals. Purposely, I have retold these stories without the dialect so that they might be intelligible to children and an aid to them in reading. I have made a conscious effort to retain the humor and folk idioms which, I believe, is an invaluable contribution of the African American to American life and culture.

One day Riley decided to earn his own living, so he laid off a piece of ground and planted himself a potato patch. Fred Fox saw all of this going on, and he figured that Riley had suddenly calmed down because he was afraid. Fred decided that this would be a good time to pay Riley back for all the tricks that had been played on him. He decided to harass Riley about the potato patch.

One time he left the draw bars down. Another night Fred flung off the top bars. The next night he tore down a panel of the fence. Fred kept on this way until Riley didn't know what to do. When Fred saw that Riley did nothing, he was convinced that Riley was afraid. He decided that it was just about time to gobble Riley up, so one day he called on Riley and invited him to go for a walk.

"Where to?" asked Riley.

"Oh, right out yonder," said Fred.

"Where is right out yonder?" asked Riley.

"Out yonder in the orchard," said Fred, "where there are some mighty fine peaches. I want you to climb the tree and fling them down."

"Oh well, said Riley, "I don't care if I do." So the two of them set out. After a while they came to the peach orchard. Riley picked out a good tree and climbed it while Fred sat at the foot. He figured that since Riley would have to come down the tree backwards, this would be a good time to nab him. But Riley saw what Fred was up to before he went up the tree. Riley began pulling the peaches.

"Fling them down here, Riley," said Fred, "Fling them where I can catch them."

"If I fling them down where you are, Fred," hollered Riley, "and you should chance to miss them, they will be squashed, so I'll just pitch them out yonder in the grass where they won't get busted." So Riley flung the peaches out in the grass, and when Fred Fox went after them, Riley shinnied down and out of the tree. When he was a little way off, Riley called to Fred that he had a riddle for him to read.

"What is it, Riley?" asked Fred.

"This," said Riley. "Big bird rob and little bird sing. The big bee zoom and the little bee sting. The little man leads and the big horse follows. Can you tell what's good for a head in the hollow?"

Fred Fox thought and thought. He scratched his head and thought some more. The more he studied, the more he got mixed up with the riddle, and after a while he said, "Riley, I give up. Tell me the answer to the riddle."

"So you can't read a simple riddle like that," said Riley. "Come along with me and I'll show you how to read that riddle. Before you read it, you'll have to eat some honey, and I know just the place where we can find some fine honey."

"Where is that?" asked Fred.

"Up at Bobby Bear's beehive."

"I don't have much of a sweet tooth, Riley," said Fred, "but I would like to get to the bottom of this riddle, so I guess I'll go along." They started out, and it wasn't long before they came to Bobby Bear's beehives. Riley rapped one of them with his cane. He tapped one after the other until he came to one that sounded as if it was full of honey.

"This one is full, Fred," said Riley. He went behind the hive. "I'll tip it up, and you put your head inside and get the drippings."

Riley tilted the hive up, and Fred jammed his head underneath it. Then Riley turned it loose, and the hive came right down on Fred's neck and there he was! Fred kicked and squealed, danced and pranced, buzzed and prayed but all to no avail for there he was! Riley got off some distance and then he called back, "Don't you get the riddle yet, Fred? Honey is good for a head in the hollow!" Riley then went off and told Bobby Bear that Fred Fox was trying to rob his beehives. When Bobby heard that, he got a handful of hickory switches and let Fred have it, and then he turned him loose. Fred never forgot Riley's riddle after that.

Br'er Rabbit and the Peanut Shells

Maxine A. LeGall

When I was about eight or nine (1949 to 1950), I visited my grandmother's friend in Lafourche Parish, Louisiana. For many people in that area, the building of a room, as some would say, "to put the outhouse in" was an important event that attracted many onlookers. This story, through the character and voice of Br'er Rabbit, tells what happened to me that day.

In those days all the animals had gotten it into their heads that they needed toilets inside their houses. They were copying off Miz Meadows and the girls who had had Br'er Bear put an inside toilet just behind the front room of their house. Good for business, they said. But that was back in October, and now it was the middle of the hottest summer on record and Sis Turtle was having Br'er Bear put one in her house.

Of course, to put in a toilet, you first have to dig a deep hole in the ground. And that's just what Br'er Bear was doin'. He was standing up on his hind legs down in the hole. He throwed shovelful after shovelful of dirt into the air until he had dug himself a hole about four feet deep.

Just about this time Br'er Rabbit appeared. He just stood there with all the other animals watching the goings-on. Pretty soon he took a handful of peanuts out of his pocket. Lookin' at Br'er Bear do all that work made him hungry, and he began to shell the peanuts, one at a time. He threw the peanut shells on the ground in that hole. He was so content watching Br'er Bear doing all that work and shelling and eating those peanuts that he didn't notice Br'er Fox pacing around that hole.

Br'er Fox had his mouth open a little bit. He was looking at those peanuts Br'er Rabbit was poppin' into his mouth, but most specially he was looking at those shells Br'er Rabbit was tossing into the hole and onto the ground.

"Stop throwing those shells on the ground, Br'er Rabbit," he said. "Don't you know that throwing peanut shells on the ground will start an argument?" Br'er Fox was gettin' real hot under his heavy red coat, and walking around wasn't helping him any.

Before Br'er Rabbit could answer, Br'er Bear put his shovel down and wiped his forehead. "Now Br'er Fox," he hollered out from down in the hole, "don't you start no lies. Br'er Rabbit, you can throw as many shells as you want down in this here hole and onto this here ground. I don't mind one bit!" And he grinned at Br'er Rabbit while at the same time he snapped his eyes at Br'er Fox.

Br'er Rabbit pulled another peanut out of his pocket and proceeded to snap the shell in two.

Br'er Fox was really sweating now. He moved his hot body closer to Br'er Rabbit and, with his mouth open wider still, shouted, "Don't throw those shells on the ground. It causes folks to argue, I said!" He was looking mighty agitated, and his tongue was hanging out.

Br'er Bear pushed his hat back on his head. "It does not cause folks to argue. Br'er Rabbit, throw those shells on the ground if you want to!" He made a motion as if to step out of that hole.

Br'er Rabbit rolled his eyes over to Br'er Fox, who looked like he was ready to chew Rabbit's hand off if he threw another shell on the ground. He rolled his eyes over to Br'er Bear, who looked like he would tear Br'er Rabbit limb from limb if he didn't throw the peanut shells on the ground.

By now Br'er Bear was out of the hole and gesturing with both his hands and the shovel.

Br'er Fox rushed past Br'er Rabbit and shouted at Br'er Bear, "I say it does cause an argument!"

"I say," said Br'er Bear, "it doesn't cause an argument!"

"It does!" Br'er Fox had his mouth wide open now. Br'er Rabbit could see all his sharp teeth.

"It does not!" In one quick movement Br'er Bear had fallen onto all four legs and was pushing his face up close to Br'er Fox's. "It does not! It does not! *It does not!*"

Br'er Rabbit's nose began to twitch. He could smell a good fight coming on, and he didn't want to be anywhere near Br'er Bear or Br'er Fox when this one started. Before anyone could even see what he was doing, Br'er Rabbit was gone—boogedy, boogedy, down the road away from there.

You probably want to know what happened to the peanut shells Br'er Rabbit had in his hand. Why, Br'er Rabbit put those things back in his pants pocket, and he never ate peanuts outside again, leastways not around Br'er Bear and Br'er Fox.

> Br'er Rabbit ran in his hole.
> This story has been told.

Br'er Rabbit Builds a Home

Jackie Torrence

My Grandpa and I were walkers. We walked to his garden every day. We walked up the hill to see his brother, Uncle Fred. We walked to his sister Aunt Sally's house and down the road to see Aunt Mag, his sister in-law.

Pa would sometimes wait until Grandma had me busy somewhere else or I was down for a nap before he would leave. I never understood that maybe he didn't want my company all the time. But when I discovered he had left without me, there was just no living with me until he returned.

Early morning walks were the best. The road was shaded by the trees. The sun was not yet beaming down on us, and the day was quiet and still. The birds and other animals in the woods were still running about—deer, chipmunks, foxes, raccoons, possums, rats, squirrels, rabbits—especially rabbits. They were always with us on the road. When we'd spot one running ahead of us or behind us or right beside us, Pa would say Br'er Rabbit was going about his daily business.

I remember asking Pa if Br'er Rabbit had a house to live in like me and him. In reply, he related the story of how Br'er Rabbit built a home.

All the creatures in the Big Wood—Br'er Possum, Br'er Bear, Br'er Coon, Br'er Wolf, and Br'er Rabbit—decided they should go in together and build themselves a house.

They each took different jobs. Br'er Rabbit insisted that he'd have to do something on the ground because he couldn't climb ladders, which made him dizzy in the head. And he couldn't work outside because the sun made him shiver. So he got himself a ruler and stuck a pencil behind his ear and started measuring and marking, marking and measuring. He was in and out, all around, so busy that the other creatures really thought he was putting down a whole passel of work. Yet all the while, he was just marking time, doing absolutely nothing.

The critters that was workin', was workin'. They built a fine house, the likes of which nobody in those parts had ever seen. Why, if the truth be known, it was a splendid house: plenty of upstairs rooms, plenty of down-stairs rooms, a whole heap of chimneys, fireplaces, and all sorts of other wonderful things.

After the house was finished, each critter picked a room. Old Br'er Rabbit picked one of the upstairs rooms and proceeded to furnish it. While all the other critters were busy finishing their rooms, Br'er Rabbit was slipping three things into his room: a shotgun, a big black cannon, and a big tin tub of water.

When everything was all finished in the house, they cooked a big supper to celebrate. Then everyone took a seat in the parlor.

Br'er Rabbit sat for awhile, and then he yawned and stretched and excused himself for bed. The other creatures stayed on and laughed and talked and had a good time in their new parlor.

While they were talking and laughing, Br'er Rabbit yelled from his room, "When a big feller like me wants to sit down, whereabouts do you think he ought to sit?"

All the other critters just laughed and said, "When a big feller like you can't sit in a chair, he better sit on the floor."

"Watch out down there, 'cause I'm fixing to sit right now," yelled Br'er Rabbit. He pulled the trigger of the shotgun. *Ka-boom!*

Well, all the critters looked at one another and wondered, what in the world was that? But everything was quiet then, and nobody said anything for a long time.

After a while, the critters forgot the noise and started talking and laughing again.

Then Br'er Rabbit stuck his head out the door again and said, "When a big feller like me wants to sneeze, whereabouts can he sneeze?"

The other creatures turned and hollered up the stairs, "When a big feller like you can't hold a sneeze, he can sneeze where he pleases."

"Watch out down there cause I'm gonna sneeze right here," said Br'er Rabbit. And he lit the fuse on the cannon. *Ka-boom!*

Well, the sound of the cannon knocked the critters out of their chairs. The glass shook in the windows, the dishes rattled in the cupboard, and Br'er Bear hit the floor, right on his bottom.

"Lordsey be," said Br'er Bear, "I think Br'er Rabbit has a powerful bad cold. I think I'm gonna step outside for a breath of fresh air."

All the critters settled down again and were talking among themselves when Br'er Rabbit yelled out another time, "When a big feller like me wants to take a chew of tobacco, whereabouts is he supposed to spit?"

The other critters hollered back to Br'er Rabbit, mad as they could be, "If you be a big man or a little man, spit where you please."

"Look out down there!" yelled Br'er Rabbit, "I'm gonna spit!" About that time he turned over the tub of water and it came rolling down the steps. *Ker-splash!*

Well, every one of the critters heard it coming at the same time. They all took off in different directions. Some jumped out of the windows, some bolted through the doors, everyone went in a different direction, but they all cleared out of the house.

Old Br'er Rabbit locked the doors, closed the windows, went to bed, and slept like he owned the world.

Why Women Always Take Advantage of Men

Zora Neale Hurston

Mules and Men, published in 1935, was the first book of African-American folklore written by an African American. The book is both entertaining and anthropological. It is a collection of folktales within folk life based on her field research in Florida. The narrator is a storyteller and the townspeople are storytellers, and the dialect and rhythmic language patterns create a down-home, sit-back, living-room atmosphere.

In her essay, "Characteristics of Negro Expression," published in Nancy Cunard's anthology *Negro,* Zora Neale Hurston states that black people's "greatest contribution to the English language is (1) the use of metaphor and simile; (2) the use of the double descriptive such as 'hot-boiling'; and (3) the use of verbal nouns such as 'she won't take a listen' or 'uglying away.' " She felt that our "very words are action words." Our "interpretation of the English language is in terms of pictures. One act described in terms of another. Hence the rich metaphor and simile. . . . Negro folklore is not a thing of the past. It is still in the making."

In "Why Women Always Take Advantage of Men" the listener or reader is eavesdropping in the middle of a conversation.

Gene rolled his eyeballs into one corner of his head.

"Now Gold call herself gettin' even wid me—tellin' dat lie. 'Tain't no such a story nowhere. She jus' made dat one up herself."

"Naw, she didn't," Armetta defended. "Ah *been* knowin' dat ole tale."

"Me too," said Shoo-pie.

"Don't you know you can't git de best of no woman in de talkin' game? Her tongue is all de weapon a woman got," George Thomas chided Gene. "She could have had mo' sense, but she told God no, she'd ruther take it out in hips. So god give her her ruthers. She got plenty hips, plenty mouf and no brains."

"Oh, yes, womens is got sense too," Mathilda Moseley jumped in. "But they got too much sense to go 'round braggin' about it like y'all do. De lady people always got de advantage of mens because God fixed it dat way."

"Whut ole black advantage is y'all got?" B. Moseley asked indignantly. "We got all de strength and all de law and all de money and you can't git a thing but whut we jes' take pity on you and give you."

"And dat's jus' de point," said Mathilda triumphantly. "You *do* give it to us, but how come you do it?" And without waiting for an answer Mathilda began to tell why women always take advantage of men.

You see in de very first days, God made a man and a woman and put 'em in a house together to live. 'Way back in them days de woman was just as strong as de man and both of 'em did de same things. They useter get to fussin' 'bout who gointer do this and that and sometime they'd fight, but they was even balanced and neither one could whip de other one.

One day de man said to hisself, "B'lieve Ah'm gointer go see God and ast Him for a li'l mo' strength so Ah kin whip dis 'oman and make her mind. Ah'm tired of de way things is." So he went up to God.

"Good mawnin', Ole Father."

"Howdy man. Whut you doin' 'round my throne so soon dis mawnin'?"

"Ah'm troubled in mind, and nobody can't ease mah spirit 'ceptin' you."

God said: "Put yo' plea in de right form and Ah'll hear and answer."

"Ole Maker, wid de mawnin' stars glitterin' in yo' shinin' crown, wid de dust from yo' footsteps makin' worlds upon worlds, wid de blazin' bird we call de sun flyin' out of yo' right hand in de mawnin' and consumin' all day de flesh and blood of stump-black darkness, and comes flyin' home every evenin' to rest on yo' left hand, and never once in all yo' eternal years, mistood de left hand for de right, Ah ast you *please* to give me mo' strength than dat woman you give me, so Ah kin make her mind. Ah know you don't want to be always comin' down way past de moon and stars to be straightenin' her out and it's got to be done. So give me a li'l mo' strength, Ole Maker and Ah'll do it."

"All right, man, you got mo' strength than woman."

So de man run all de way down de stairs from Heben till he got home. He was so anxious to try his strength on de woman dat he couldn't take his time. Soon's he got in de house he hollered "Woman! Here's yo' boss. God done tole me to handle you in whichever way Ah please. Ah'm yo' boss."

De woman flew to fightin' 'im right off. She fought 'im frightenin' but he beat her. She got her wind and tried 'im agin but he whipped her agin. She got herself together and made de third try on him vigorous but he beat her every time. He was so proud he could whip 'er at last, dat he just crowed over her and made her do a lot of things she didn't like. He told her, "Long as you obey me, Ah'll be good to yuh, but every time yuh rear up Ah'm gointer put plenty wood on yo' back and plenty water in yo' eyes."

De woman was so mad she went straight up to Heben and stood befo' de Lawd. She didn't waste no words. She said, "Lawd, Ah come befo' you mighty mad t'day. Ah want back my strength and power Ah useter have."

"Woman, you got de same power you had since de beginnin'."

"Why is it then, dat de man kin beat me now and he useter couldn't do it?"

"He got mo' strength than he useter have. He come and ast me for it and Ah give it to 'im. Ah gives to them that ast, and you ain't never ast me for no mo' power."

"Please suh, God, Ah'm astin' you for it now. Jus' gimme de same as you give him."

God shook his head. "It's too late now, woman. Whut Ah give, Ah never take back. Ah give him mo' strength than you and no matter how much Ah give you, he'll have mo'."

De woman was so mad she wheeled around and went on off. She went straight to de devil and told him what had happened.

He said, "Don't be dis-incouraged, woman. You listen to me and you'll come out mo' than conqueror. Take dem frowns out yo' face and turn round and go right on back to Heben and ast God to give you dat bunch of keys hangin' by de mantelpiece. Then you bring 'em to me and Ah'll show you what to do wid 'em."

So de woman climbed back up to Heben agin. She was mighty tired but she was more outdone that she was tired so she climbed all night long and got back up to Heben agin. When she got befo' de throne, butter wouldn't melt in her mouf.

"O Lawd and Master of de rainbow, Ah know yo' power. You never make two mountains without you put a valley in between. Ah know you kin hit a straight lick wid a crooked stick."

"Ast for whut you want, woman."

"God, gimme dat bunch of keys hangin' by yo' mantelpiece."

"Take 'em."

So de woman took de keys and hurried on back to de devil wid 'em. There was three keys on de bunch. Devil say, "See dese three keys? They got mo' power in 'em than all de strength de man kin ever git if you handle 'em right. Now dis first big key is to de do' of de kitchen, and you know a man always favors his stomach. Dis second one is de key to de bedroom and he don't like to be shut out from dat neither and dis last key is de key to de cradle and he don't want to be cut off from his generations at all. So now you take dese keys and go lock up everything and wait till he come to you. Then don't you unlock nothin' until he use his strength for yo' benefit and yo' desires."

De woman thanked 'im and tole 'im, "If it wasn't for you, Lawd knows whut us po' women folks would do."

She started off but de devil halted her. "Jus' one mo' thing: don't go home braggin' 'bout yo' keys. Jus' lock up everything and say nothin' until you git asked. And then don't talk too much."

De woman went on home and did like de devil tole her. When de man come home from work she was settin' on de porch singin' some song 'bout "Peck on de wood make de bed go good."

When de man found de three doors fastened what useter stand wide open he swelled up like pine lumber after a rain. First thing he tried to break in cause he figgered his strength would overcome all obstacles. When he saw he couldn't do it, he ast de woman, "Who locked dis do'?"

She tole 'im, "Me."

"Where did you git de key from?"

"God give it to me."

He run up to God and said, "God, woman got me locked 'way from my vittles, my bed and my generations, and she say you give her the keys."

God said, "I did, man, Ah give her de keys, but de devil showed her how to use 'em!"

"Well, Ole Maker, please gimme some keys jus' lak 'em so she can't git de full control."

"No, man, what Ah give Ah give. Woman got de key."

"How kin Ah know 'bout my generations?"

"Ast de woman."

So de man come on back and submitted hisself to de woman and she opened de doors.

He wasn't satisfied but he had to give in. 'Way after while he said to de woman, "Le's us divide up. Ah'll give you half of my strength if you lemme hold de keys in my hands."

De woman thought dat over so de devil popped and tol' her, "Tell 'im, naw. Let 'im keep his strength and you keep yo' keys."

So de woman wouldn't trade wid 'im and de man had to mortgage his strength to her to live. And dat's why de man makes and de woman takes. You men is still braggin' 'bout yo' strength and de women is sittin' on de keys and lettin' you blow off till she git ready to put de bridle on you.

B. Moseley looked over at Mathilda and said, "You just like a hen in de barnyard. You cackle so much you give de rooster de blues."

Mathilda looked over at him archly and quoted:

> Stepped on a pin, de pin bent
> And dat's de way de story went.

Funeral

Mary Carter Smith

Over the years I have attended many wakes and funerals. Sometimes I was on that first row, reserved for the closest members of the family. This is a very important part of the African-American experience. My feelings about funerals have been inside me for years. I have shared these with many groups and have found that other people have their memories of funerals. Many emotions are evident; grief, humor, and curiosity are only a few. There are often many comments made behind hands or fans at funerals. I am not being irreverent, just truthful. One of the most sincere compliments heard at the end of the traditional funeral is; "They put him/her away real nice."

Don't walk so fast, Lillie Mae. My legs ain't what they used to be. Lord, here we are going to another "wake." Lillie Mae, why in the world do they call it a "wake"? Seems to me a "sit and watch" would be more fitting. Whole lot of cars around the church. I see Mr. Williams has a brand-new family car. That's it right behind the hearse. Um-m! One of them stretched-out Cadillacs. That's a l-o-n-g car. But he may as well get rid of them smoky windows. When folks pay as much as he charges to ride in those cars, they want some clear, clean windows, so folks can look in and see 'em as they ride past. Lord, these funeral directors can charge you some fancy prices. Not funeral directors? I know you don't call them undertakers anymore. Oh, so they're morticians. Well, just so they do a decent job and charge you a decent price, I don't care what they're called. One thing for sure. They will never run out of customers.

There's a big crowd here. Inez has been a member here for over forty years. And she's an Eastern Star, too. I see some of the Elks here, too. Years ago she was a member.

I'm thankful they have handrails 'cause these steps and my knees don't get along so well.

The usher right there is giving out programs. Good evening, sister. I'd like a program. Am I staying for the service or just coming to the wake? That's none of your business. I'm here because the dear deceased was a friend of mine, and I'll just *take* one of these programs. Thank you. I'll never understand why they don't have enough programs made so everybody can have one without having to go through the third degree. Let's squeeze into this line and go around and view the remains and greet the family. Lord, there's a heap of folks here tonight. (Walking and waving, kissing, and so forth.) Oh, she looks so natural. That's a lovely pink dress she has on. I've already told my family to put me away in my blue dress I wore to my daughter's wedding, and don't let that "mortician" talk them into buying a new one. Inez looks so calm and peaceful. She was a good woman. I'm gon miss her. (A quiet tear.)

Look at all these flowers! There's an empty chair. A clock, stopped at the exact time she passed, and a bleeding heart and baskets and baskets and baskets. Poor Inez can't enjoy them now. I wonder if anybody gave her even a handful of dandelions and daisies when she was alive. (Greets the family.) Lillie Mae, I'm glad we got here early so we can get a seat. (Going into pew.) Excuse me, I didn't mean to step on your feet. But that's what you expect when you take the seat on the end and everybody has to climb over you to get in. (Sits.) We've got a good view from here. Just look at how that huzzy Jeweletta is switching down the aisle in that tight dress, showing off her big hips. Look at her, holding on to his hand and drooling over Brother Johnson. And poor Inez ain't hardly cold.

Now we can read the obituary. Let's see what this one says. Lillie Mae if you want to *see* some lies, you just read some of these obituaries. Lies of omission especially. Some second wives won't even put in the name of the first wife. Yet you see the oldest of the man's children marching in with the family. And you *know* the children had a mother. There's no date of birth on this one. Now let me see. Inez came out of high school three years before I did. And she was a *big* girl when she came up here from South Carolina. And you see all these grown children. Honey, she had to be way up in her sixties! (Reading.) "Only daughter of the late James and Mary Jones." The way I heard it, there was something else "late." They were late getting married. Had lived together for years. But they couldn't get their social security without a marriage certificate. So they slipped across the state line and had a very quiet ceremony. Like I say, "Better late than never." (Reading.) "Inez Johnson was the mother of four children." True. But only three of those belong to Brother Johnson. She "broke her leg" and had one before she married. But Brother Johnson understood and gave the child his name, and they are one loving family.

Who's that up there whooping and hollering and falling out? Humph! Her sister Annie. No wonder she's carrying on so. Guilty conscience. Poor Inez sent and sent for her. But Annie was too "busy" with her big beauty salon in New York. Now here she comes in her big fox fur with her big guilt complex. She ought to sit down and shut up.

Here comes Sister Smith with her third husband limping behind her. She's buried two already, and this one looks mighty weak. You think what they say about her is true? I don't know. Could be. Well! And here's that rascal Charles Williams in *church!* He always jokes and says he won't come to church because they throw things. "When I was a baby, they threw water on me. When I got married, they threw rice on me." I told him if they could find a church to take him, the next time they'd be ready to throw dirt on him. Well, they're closing the casket.

"Life is like a mountain railway." (Sings.) That choir can *sing!* No sense in that man reading all of John 14 . . . and reading it *slow!* When some folks get in front of a microphone, they just hate to give it up! All these resolutions! There are *ten* preachers on the platform. Just supposed to take three minutes each. It'll never happen! They finally got to the eulogy. (Amen, and so forth, comments.) Lillie Mae, that was an uplifting sermon! They're really putting her away nice. You going to the cemetery? Me, too. Then we'll come back to the church and eat. I can smell that chicken frying downstairs. I hope that they have some ham and candied sweets. And I saw folks bringing in lots of cakes and pies. Inez's Missionary Circle is serving. That's the way I want it when I go. Nobody better not serve no punch and sandwiches. You only die once, and I want to be put away in *style!* This has been one beautiful funeral. I really enjoyed it. (Leave singing "Soon and Very Soon.")

Uglyrella

Jose Pena

I live with my mother and stepfather and sister and brother. My mother was born in the United States. My father's parents were born in Puerto Rico. I plan to go to Puerto Rico one day. I also want to learn to speak Spanish when I get older. I like to write because it makes me feel good. After I write my stories I read them to my family. One of my favorite stories that I have written is "Uglyrella" because it's funny. I was in the sixth grade when I entered this story in the Zora Neale Hurston storytelling competition and won second place.

Once upon a time there lived a girl named Uglyrella. She was one ugly girl. She had a beautiful stepmom and two beautiful stepsisters, and they hated her. One day a letter came to the door. It was an invitation to a ball from the prince. The prince was one ugly dude, and he wanted to find a wife. The stepsisters and stepmother said, "Good. We can get ugly and he will take one of us, then we can have his money."

Uglyrella had to do a lot of work. She had to make everybody ugly. When she was done, she asked if she could go, too. The stepmother said, "No! You're too beautiful to go, and you have a lot of work to do."

The stepmom and stepsisters left, and Uglyrella began to cry. Suddenly an old ugly witch was standing there! And Uglyrella said, "Man, are you ugly!" The witch said, "Thank you. Do you want to go to the ball?" Uglyrella said, "Yes! Can you get me the stuff?" The witch said, "Yes. Get me a very rotten tomato." And she turned it into an ugly red carriage. Then she said, "Get me two big roaches." She made them large enough to pull the carriage. Then the witch said, "Get me a rat." She made that into an ugly man to drive the carriage. "Now," said the witch, "get me a beautiful dress." She turned it into an ugly dress. Now Uglyrella was ready. "Leave the ball by one o'clock or everything will turn back the way it was," said the witch. "Okay," said Uglyrella, and she went to the ball.

Everybody was looking at her. They said, "Man, she is ugly!" Then her eyes met the prince's, and they fell in love. They danced. The prince did not dance with anyone else. Suddenly, while they were dancing, they bumped into the punch, and it splashed on the stepsisters' faces. Their ugly makeup came off, and everybody said, "Eeeeew! Look how beautiful they are." They were embarrassed the rest of the night. Suddenly the clock struck one, and Uglyrella ran. The prince was running after her, crying out, "Is it my cologne? Does it smell too good?" "No," she said, "it smells rotten." The prince called out, "Thank you." Uglyrella disappeared from sight. She was a good runner. She left behind a huge smelly shoe. It was green and red with frogs painted on it. The prince said, "I will find her and then marry her."

He went out the next day and traveled to every house. The shoe did not fit anyone. The stepsisters' and stepmother's feet kept slipping out of it because it was so big. Then Uglyrella tried it on. It fit her just right. The prince said, "Wow, you have big feet!" Uglyrella said, "Thank you." The prince took Uglyrella to the castle to marry her. Her stepsisters and stepmother had to be servants in the castle.

Uglyrella and the prince lived ugily ever after.

Nho Lobo

As told by Len Cabral

I am the great grandson of a Cape Verdean Whaler whose family immigrated to America in 1910. Many Cape Verdeans came to America and settled in New England because of the Portuguese whaling industry. Cape Verde, located off the west coast of Africa, was a Portuguese colony up until 1975. Cape Verdeans built and worked the cranberry bogs of southern New England, many coming here first as seasonal workers and then returning to Cape Verde, only to come back for another season of strawberry, blueberry, and cranberry picking.

Nho Lobo (pronounced Lobe) is the ever-popular character in many Cape Verdean folktales. He is the trickster who lacks common sense. He is silly, greedy, and lazy all at the same time. I first heard this story from my godmother and later from my mother.

Before I tell you the story, I have to introduce some characters to you.

The main character of the story is Nho Lobo. Nho Lobo is lazy. Nho Lobo is tricky. Nho Lobo is cunning. Nho Lobo wants something for nothing . . . all the time. Now Nho Lobo has a nephew, and his nephew's name is Tubino. Tubino is different. He is always working in the garden, repairing the windows, fixing the fence, helping his neighbors. He is busy, busy. That's Tubino.

There is another character in the story, a monkey named Shabene. In the Cape Verdean Islands there is a vegetable called a manioc plant, which grows under the ground and which the people love to eat.

One day Tubino went into his garden. Tubino always had a song in his heart. Whenever he worked, he always sang, and he sang his favorite Cape Verdean folk song: "I'm so glad, I'm so glad, I'm so glad that you are here. I'm so glad. What a wonderful day it is." Then he said, "Today I am going to plant some manioc, and I hope my lazy uncle, Nho Lobo, does not come by because, you see, he likes to eat manioc but he does not like to work. I am going to start working."

Tubino went into the garden, and he started to plant manioc. He planted row upon row upon row of manioc. All of a sudden, as he was planting, he heard the voice of his uncle coming down the mountain trail. "Ah yeh, it's Nho Lobo." He could hear Nho Lobo singing his favorite song: "I tunga, I tunga, I tunga, tunga, tunga, tunga, I tunga, I tunga, tunga, tunga." "Ah yeh, it's Nho Lobo. Nho Lobo, don't want you here. Ba casa, Nho Lobo. Go, Nho Lobo."

Nho Lobo came down and said, "Ah, Tubino, my nephew, you are planting manioc."

"Yes, but they are not for you, Uncle. Ba casa. I know you don't like to work. You just like to eat."

"No, no, I know how to plant manioc. You know how to work. I know how to work. Let me help you."

"Okay, but don't you eat any."

"Don't worry I won't eat any."

"Go on, get busy now so we can finish this job."

Tubino went across the field. He started to plant row upon row of manioc across the field. As soon as he turned around, Nho Lobo started to eat the manioc plants. Then he went back to work as if he were planting.

Tubino turned around and said, "Ah yeh, Nho Lobo, you have eaten my plants here."

Nho Lobo said, "No, Tubino, I have been busy working over here. Look at all the rows I planted here. You know something, Tubino? You are out here working in this hot sun. You don't have a hat on your head. You are forgetting what you have done. You ought to go home and rest, and I will finish work for you."

"You will plant for me?"

"Yes, I will plant for you. Ba casa, ba casa."

Tubino went ba casa. Well, as soon as Tubino was gone, Nho Lobo ate all the manioc plants, every one of them. All of them. And then he started walking home, rubbing his belly, singing, "Ah tunga, ah tunga, ah tunga, tunga, tunga, ah tunga, ah tunga, tunga."

Well, Tubino came back. He looked. "Ah yeh yeh. That lazy uncle of mine ate all my manioc. Ah, I have to get even with him. Let me think." Tubino got an idea.

Tubino walked down to the docks where the boats were tied and he got some rope. He placed the rope over his shoulders and then walked up that dusty mountain trail by Nho Lobo's house. Nho Lobo was sleeping on the porch as Tubino rushed by and made noise. Nho Lobo woke up and said, "Ah, Tubino, ah boy, eh boy, speta, speta . . . Wait, where are you going in such a hurry. Speta. Where are you going?"

Tubino said, "Uncle, you haven't heard?"

"Heard what? I have been sleeping."

"Well, Uncle, while you have been sleeping a big storm has been gathering, and the storm is going to be so ferocious, the wind is going to be so powerful, it is going to blow everything away, everything that is not tied down. So, Uncle, I am going to tie myself to this banana tree so that I will not get blown away."

"Nephew, tie me to this tree."

"Oh, no, Uncle, this is the only rope I have."

"Oh, Tubino, come on. . . . Tie me to this tree. I am a poor thing. Come, come."

I told you that Nho Lobo is convincing. He convinced Tubino to tie him to this banana tree. Tubino said, "Okay, Uncle, I will." As soon as he agreed to tie his uncle up, his uncle started giving orders.

"Tie me tight now, come on, tie me good and tight now. Ah yeh, ah yeh, that's good, that's good enough. Okay."

"Okay, Uncle, now listen. I have to get some more rope for myself." And Tubino went ba casa.

Well, Nho Lobo is tied to that tree. He said, "Good thing I woke up when I did. Yeh, yeh. I don't want to get blown away. Yeh, yeh." He looked up in the tree and up in the tree he saw Shabene the monkey eating bananas. Nho Lobo said, "Ah, boy, Shabene. Shabene. Ah, boy, Shabene." Now Shabene knew all about Nho Lobo, and he was ignoring Nho Lobo, but Nho Lobo was very cunning. "Shabene. Shabene. Can I have a banana?" I told you he was convincing. Well, he convinced Shabene to give him one banana. "Hummm, thank you, obrigad, Shabene. Obrigad. Hummm. Shabene, another banana. Obrigad, Shabene. Hummm. Obrigad. Shabene, do you see any clouds in the sky? No. You feel any wind or rain? No. Hummm. Shabene, my nephew Tubino, I think he fooled me. He told me a storm is coming, and anything that is not tied is going to get blown away. So I allowed him to tie me to this banana tree, and now I can't get— It's not funny, Shabene. Shabene, don't you laugh at me. Oh, no, Shabene, I am not yelling at you. You are my friend. Oh, yes, I love you, Shabene. Shabene, will you untie me? Please, Shabene, please."

I told you Nho Lobo was convincing. Well he convinced Shabene to come down from that tree and untie him. Shabene untied Nho Lobo's arms and then he untied Nho Lobo's hands and then he untied Nho Lobo's feet, and as soon as Nho Lobo's feet were untied, he reached down and grabbed hold of Shabene. "Ah, Shabene, I am going to eat you up now. Ah yeh, gotcha. Going to eat you up."

Well, just then Tubino came back. Nho Lobo said, "Yeh, Tubino, you tried to fool me. Tried to tell me a storm was coming. Yeh, yeh, sure. Look here. I have this monkey, Shabene. I am going to eat Shabene, and I am not going to share it with you."

"That's okay, Uncle. But do you know the best way to eat monkey?"

"The best way to eat monkey? How?"

"Well, take the rope and tie the monkey up, and then throw the monkey in the air as high as you can—the higher the better. When that monkey comes down, open your mouth nice and wide, as wide as you can, and swallow that monkey in one gulp. It tastes good."

"Yeh?"

"Yeh, yeh." And Tubino went ba casa.

Well, Nho Lobo tied up Shabene. He went one, two, three, and he threw Shabene way up in the air, way up in the air. At least he thought he threw Shabene way up in the air. Shabene landed in the tree. But Nho Lobo did not see him land in the tree, so Nho Lobo was waiting like this. "Ahhh, ahhh" . . . five minutes. "Ahhh, ahhh" . . . ten minutes. "Ahhh, ahhh" . . . fifteen minutes. "Ahhh, ahhh" . . . twenty minutes.

Finally, Tubino came back and said. "Nho Lobo, are you still waiting?"

"Yes, I am still waiting."

"Ahh. You know, Uncle, you are so strong. You threw Shabene up so high that the wind is going to blow it across the ocean to America, and if I were you, Uncle, I would rush over to America and get your food before someone else gets it."

"Ah, okay."

Nho Lobo ran down to the docks where all the boats were tied. But all the boats were gone . . . even the *Ernestina*. But that did not stop Nho Lobo. Nho Lobo dove into the water, and he started to swim. He swam and he swam and he swam and he swam, clear out of sight. That is the last time anyone on the Cape Verdean Islands ever saw Nho Lobo. But rumor has it that if you should go to New England and all the states along the eastern seaboard, and if you go to places like New Bedford in Massachusetts or down the Cape by the cranberry bogs or into Rhode Island, all the way up to Nova Scotia, through Maine, way up to all those old whaling seaports, you might see someone walking along with his hands over his head, his mouth wide open, looking up at the sky . . . going "Ahhhhhhhh." That's Nho Lobo.

Willi and Joe Joe and the Pamper Diaper

Temujin the Storyteller

The characters Willi and Joe Joe were born around 1977. They are very loosely based on characters from the movie *Cotton Comes to Harlem* and the West Indian people I came to know, love, and respect when I lived in New York in late 1969 and early 1970. Willi and Joe Joe became part of a game I used to play with my young cousin Danielle. She loved to hear me speak in a West Indian accent. Because I'm blessed with a good ear for languages and accents, I have found it easy to pick up a smattering of many tongues and accents from all over the world in my twenty-six-year career. Willi and Joe Joe are my "everymen" and are done out of love and respect, as are all the accents I do in homage to my extended global family.

This a West Indian story because me like West Indian stories.

Now me got two friends, Willi and Joe Joe, and them love to go fish. One day Willi him go to Joe Joe's house and him say, "Joe Joe, you go fish?"

Joe Joe say, "Man, me can't go."

"Why you can't go?"

"Me got to watch the baby."

"Bring the baby!"

"Man, me can't bring the baby."

"Why you can't bring the baby?"

"The baby only do a few things: him eat, him sleep, him cry, him mess up diaper. Man, me wash dirty diaper all day long."

"You ain't never hear of them Pamper diaper?"

"Pamper diaper? Pamper diaper? What kind of diaper is that?"

"Oh, man, it a wonderful thing. You put it on the baby, the baby mess it up, and you throw it away."

"Throw it away? Throw it away? Where me get something like that?"

"You got to go down to Kingston—any grocery store, them got Pamper diapers."

Three days later, Willi go back and knock on Joe Joe's door.

"Joe Joe, you go fish?"

"Man, me been waiting for you three days. Me got them Pamper diaper, and them a fine, fine thing."

"You got one on the baby now?"

"Yah, boy, go show Uncle Willi them Pamper diaper."

The baby walk out. Pamper diaper dragging along the floor. Willi look and shake he head and say, "Man, you go to change that thing."

Joe Joe say, "No, me read the box. It say good for twenty-five pounds. Ain't but ten pounds in there now."

Willi and Joe Joe Them a Go to Mardi Gras

Temujin the Storyteller

Do ya remember me two friends, Willi and Joe Joe? Well, them a love to party, them a love to have a good time. Them especially love to go to carnival—you know, the one before Lent.

Well, them a been to carnival in Jamaica. Them a been to carnival in Trinidad. Them even been to carnival in Brazil.

One day Willi and Joe Joe them hear about the Carnival in the United States, me think it call Mardi Gras.

Well, Willi and Joe Joe, them poor boys, and them don't have a lot of money so them a get a job working on a ship going to the States.

Them a work hard night and day, day and night.

Until them a get to the United States and the ship docks at New Orleans.

Them a take their pay and them a go party.

Them a have too much fun.

Them a eat up everything.

Them a drink up everything.

Them a chase every girl in sight.

Then them a get tired, and they a want to go to sleep.

So, them a walk into a big, pretty Hilton Hotel, and them a ring the bell.

The man him a come to the counter an' him say, "May I help you?"

And Willi him say, "Yes I—we want a room."

The man him say, "Do you have reservations?"

And Willi him say, "We don't got no reservations. We got money and we want a room."

The man say, "Obviously, sir, you do not understand. In order to have a room at this or any hotel during Mardi Gras, you have to contact us in advance, let us know when you plan to arrive, and we would reserve— that is, hold—a room for you. Since neither you nor your friend did that, there is no room available for you."

And Willi him say, "Wait, wait, wait. Let me ask you a question. What called the man that run the country here?"

The man say, "We call him the president."

And Willi him say, "And what's the man's name?"

The man say, "Bill Clinton."

And Willi him say, "Well, if Bill Clinton, president of the United States, were to walk in here right now an' say, 'Me want a room,' what would ya do?"

The man say, "Well, now, if that were to happen, we would of course find him a room."

And Willi him say, "Well, me know for a fact that the man ain't comin', so we want the man's room!"

PART VI

As Restless as the Tempestuous Billow on the Boundless Sea

Stories, Songs, and Poems of Protest and Change

For, while the tale of how we suffer, and how we are delighted, and how we may triumph is never new, it always must be heard. There isn't any other tale to tell it's the only light we've got in all this darkness. . . . And this tale, according to that face, that body, those strong hands on those strings, has another aspect in every country, and a new depth in every generation.

—JAMES BALDWIN, "Sonny's Blues"

There is no greater agony like bearing an untold story inside you.

—ZORA NEALE HURSTON

A storyteller's resources are the world and the word.

The profoundest commitment possible to a Black creator in this country today—beyond all creeds, crafts, classes, and ideologies whatsoever—is to bring before his people the scent of freedom. He may rest assured his people will do the rest.

—OSSIE DAVIS

We Shall Overcome

Guy and Candie Carawan

The story behind a song that people struggling for their freedom sing every-where.

This modern adaptation of the old Negro church song *I'll Overcome Someday* has become the unofficial theme song for the freedom struggle in the South. The old words were: I'll be all right . . . I'll be like Him . . . I'll wear the crown . . . I will overcome.

Negro Food and Tobacco Union workers in Charleston, South Carolina, adapted the song for picket line use during their strike in 1945 and later brought it to Highlander Folk School. It soon became the school's theme song and associated with Zilphia Horton's singing of it. She introduced it to union gatherings all across the South. On one of her trips to New York, Pete Seeger learned it from her and in the next few years he spread it across the North. Pete, Zilphia, and others added verses appropriate to labor, peace, and integration sentiments: We will end Jim Crow . . . We shall live in peace . . . We shall organize . . . The whole wide world around . . . and so forth.

In 1959, a few years after Zilphia died, I went to live and work at Highlander, hoping to learn something about folk music and life in the South and to help carry on some of Highlander's musical work in Zilphia's spirit. I had no idea at that time that the historic student demonstrations would be starting in the next few years and that I would be in a position to pass on this song and many others to students and adults involved in this new upsurge for freedom. As Wyatt Tee Walker said,

One cannot describe the vitality and emotion this one song evokes across the Southland. I have heard it sung in great mass meetings with a thousand voices singing as one; I've heard a half-dozen sing it softly behind the bars of the Hinds County prison in Mississippi; I've heard old women singing

it on the way to work in Albany, Georgia; I've heard the students singing
it as they were being dragged away to jail. It generates power that is
indescribable.

Royalties derived from this composition are being contributed to the We Shall Overcome
Fund.

We are not afraid, we are not afraid,

We are not afraid today.

Oh, deep in my heart, I do believe,

We shall overcome someday.

We are not alone . . . (today)

The truth will make us free . . .

We'll walk hand in hand . . .

The Lord will see us through . . .

Black and white together (now)

We shall all be free.

Martin Luther King: A Story Poem

Charlotte Blake Alston

Several years ago I was invited to tell stories on Martin Luther King Day at a Jewish day care center. The audience consisted of two-and-a-half- to five-year-olds and their families. I wondered what I might say to two-and-a-half-year-olds that would give them any meaningful, in-depth understanding of who Martin Luther King was beyond the image they probably held: a person with a crown on his head. My own experience with children taught me that even two-and-a-half-year-olds with day care experience have probably heard and felt the pain of such comments as "You're not my friend!" or "You can't come to my birthday!" They surely had experienced and could identify with that *emotion.* Given that, the logical place to begin the story of King was in his childhood, with an experience that would resonate with both the oldest and the youngest audience member. The language is simple but not condescending. The audience chants with me: Mm-mm-mm! Martin Luther King!, using claps and arm waves. This allows children to participate actively in the telling from beginning to end.

Chorus

Mm—mm—mm!
Martin Luther King!
He knew that with the love of God
He could do 'most anything!

Mm—mm—mm!
Martin Luther King!
He said, "We must be fair to all—
We must let freedom ring!"

Martin had a little friend
With whom he loved to play.
They'd played together all their lives
Each and every day.

Baseball, football,
Tag, hide 'n' seek,
They wrestled and they rolled around
And laughed till they were weak.

Well, Martin went to see his friend
One bright and sunny day.
The mother said, "He's busy now—
You'll have to go away."

The next day he went back again,
His friend did not come out.
Martin did not understand
What this was all about.

Martin went home feeling sad
"Just what is going on?
My best friend will not play with me
And I feel so alone.

"Maybe Mom will understand.
Can you explain to me?"
When Martin heard his mother's words
They stung worse than a bee.

"His mother does not want you there
Because your skin is brown.
And white and black boys cannot
Play together in this town."

She gave Martin a great big hug
And sat him on her knee.
Martin said, "That isn't right.
It isn't fair to me!

I'm a good and honest friend
I do not cheat or lie.
When I grow up, I'm gonna
Change these things—at least I'll try!"

Chorus

Well Martin studied hard in school,
He did his very best,
And he was just a little more
Determined than the rest.

He went to college at fifteen,
He gave it all he had.
Then he went to learn to be
A preacher like his dad.

When Martin spoke to people,
He gave them such a lift
That people used to think that
God gave him that special gift.

Some people came and said,
"We need a preacher for our church.
If you would be our minister,
Then we could end our search."

Martin felt so good inside
He thought that he would burst.
Now he was a minister
Who also had a church!

Martin loved the people and
They loved to hear him speak.
And hundreds came to listen to him
Every single week.

"The laws down here are just not fair,
They're meant to keep us down.
They're based on hatred, not on love,
We must turn them around."

Chorus

Well, one day Mrs. Rosa Parks
Had worked a long hard day.
Her feet were really hurting,
How much, I couldn't say.

A bus pulled up, Mrs. Parks got on
And sat down on a seat.
All she wanted was to sit
And soothe her tired feet.

The bus got crowded and the driver
Came to where she sat
And said, "This white man wants to sit—
Get up, move to the back."

"I'm tired and I won't get up.
You can't treat folks this way."
The driver said, "I'll call the law,
You'd best do what I say."

The people all looked at Mrs. Parks
To see what she would say:
"Call the law," Miss Rosa said,
" 'Cause I won't stand up this day."

Well, you know, they called the law,
They put Mrs. Parks in jail.
Friends from her community
Went down and paid her bail.

But they were really angry.
Mrs. Parks was not a crook.
"We've got to put a stop to this!"
And that was all it took.

Dr. King said, "I agree
We can't let this go on.
So we won't ride the buses
Because the law is wrong."

The people walked, they shared their cars,
They did this for a year,
Till finally the law was changed
Never to reappear!

Chorus

Now other laws were not so fair,
And people fought each day,
Not with guns or fists
But by refusing to obey.

People from all over
Began to lend a hand.
They couldn't believe these kinds of things
Were happening in this land.

Some were beaten, some were killed,
Some were thrown in jail.
They sang to keep their courage up.
They knew they would not fail.

Then one day in Washington
Thousands gathered 'round
To hear King tell about his dream.
He said, "We won't bow down.

I have a dream," Dr. King said,
"That one day in this land
Black and white will all be free
And will walk hand in hand."

Chorus

He went to Memphis, Tennessee,
To help the people there.
Martin and his helpers went
Because they really cared.

They went out on a balcony—
Thought of the day ahead.
They heard a shot, and when they looked,
Martin—was—dead.

Oh, what a sad time.
People everywhere
Could not believe what happened there.
Our hearts just felt so bare.

"We are each a child of God,"
Martin used to say,
"And if we work together,
We can make a better day."

Now it's up to us to carry on
What he began.
We must work hard to live in peace,
But Martin knows we can.

Chorus

"Over My Head I See Freedom in the Air": The Albany Movement

Bernice Johnson Reagon

I found my voice and my stance as a fighter, and earned the right to change traditional songs to new freedom songs in the Movement, as a member of the first Youth Chapter of the NAACP in Albany, Georgia. I was the secretary. This was spring 1959, and I was a senior in high school.

My consciousness about Black people struggling for freedom went back further. I had felt the change in the air in my home when in 1954 Emmet Till and Charles Mack Parker were lynched in Mississippi; the Supreme Court had handed down the *Brown* v. *Topeka Board of Education* decision, and our teachers were telling us we had better get ready because integration was coming.

As a junior high school student in 1954–55 I had lived daily with Autherine Lucy, who through a suit launched by the NAACP integrated the University of Alabama. I fantasized going to school with her every day.

In December 1955, the Montgomery Bus Boycott was born when Rosa Parks refused to get out of her seat on a Montgomery, Alabama, bus and was arrested. She, with E. D. Nixon, Ralph David Abernathy, Martin Luther King, Jr., Mary Ethel Jones, and all the Black people of Montgomery made us believe that we could stand because they walked for a year to draw a new line in the dirt in their hometown of Montgomery.

The Little Rock, Arkansas, school desegregation case, in which nine Black students attended the formerly White Central High School, took place in 1957, and I learned my first military division unit. President Dwight David Eisenhower sent in the 101st Airborne Division to ensure the admission and protection of the Little Rock nine attending Central High School. It was forced integration.

An initial action of the first NAACP Youth Chapter in Albany in 1959 was to send a delegation to the White owner of the Harlem Drugstore (located in the Black community with Black clientele) to request that a Black clerk be hired—he refused. Early in 1960, during my second quarter as a college student at Albany State College, the Sit-In Movement erupted. All over the South, beginning with the February 1 Greensboro, North Carolina, sit-ins, Black students (sometimes joined by White students) sat in lunch counters, movies, restaurants, churches, and racially segregated establishments that served the public. There were supportive demonstrations all over the nation; there was even a bus boycott in Johannesburg, South Africa. The country was in an uproar, and Black students were moving out of the classrooms into the streets in growing numbers.

Julian Bond, then a student at Morehouse College and a member of the Atlanta Student Movement, called the student government office at Albany State and asked for sympathy demonstrations on Black campuses across the South. I was in the small group of students who got together to demand that our president, William H. Dennis, take a stand. He did take a stand; he suspended student government for the rest of the year and forced the dean of students to resign for supporting us. Understanding a little more about taking stands, we went into the summer waiting for the next opportunity.

In the fall of 1961, I met the Reverend Charles Sherrod from Virginia and Cordell Hull Reagon from Nashville, field secretaries for the Student Nonviolent Coordinating Committee. SNCC had come to town, and it would change my life. This was an organization formed by students who had been involved in their local sit-ins; many of them had been sent to jail during the Freedom Rides. The organization was led by Charles McDew, Diane Nash, and James Bevel out of Nashville and Marion Barry, James Farmer, Charles Sherrod, and Bob Moses. Ella Baker and Howard Zinn served as advisors.

The group decided to move out using two strategies: direct action, in which local people would be mobilized to move in demonstrations against local segregated institutions, and voter registration drives, which would be launched in key Black-Belt areas of the South where Blacks outnumbered Whites.

Sherrod and Cordell had been sent into southwest Georgia to start a voter registration drive because in most of the counties, although Blacks outnumbered Whites, they were not registered voters because of terrorism and fear for their lives and the lives of their families. The threat was there every day. It was the local police, it was the employee who refused to serve you, it was every White person a Black person had to face in trying to survive. Voting was not one of the things you did in Terrell, Mitchell, Baker, and Sumter counties if you were a Black American citizen. A voter registration drive in the late forties and early fifties, however, put a large number of Blacks on the rolls in Dougherty County, where I lived. SNCC decided that they would set up an office in Albany and work from there into the surrounding target counties.

Sherrod was accompanied by Cordell Hull Reagon, a veteran at seventeen of the Nashville sit-ins, the Freedom Rides, six weeks in Parchman State Penitentiary, the McComb, Mississippi, voter registration drive, and the Cairo, Illinois, campaign. He had a singular energy about him when he was trying to get people involved in Movement activity, whether for joining a demonstration, registering to vote, or attending a workshop on nonviolence. He was a beautiful singer with a warm high tenor voice and was passionate about the struggle for freedom. We fell in love, working and singing together in the Albany Movement. We were married two years later and have two children, Toshi and Kwan Tauna.

SNCC set up its office in the beginning of the fall quarter of 1961. In my first discussions with Cordell and Sherrod, I often asked about the name of the organization, the Student Nonviolent Coordinating Committee. I had no cultural reference for the term "nonviolent." It did not compute for me as a word or as a concept. I could not figure out why anyone would name their organization that. "Coordinating" wasn't much better. The only part of the name that made sense to me as part of an organization's name was "student." These men who were my age were already moving in the world in new ways that I knew nothing about. The thing I understood was that I wanted to be a part of the Movement developing throughout the South. I wanted to participate in changing Albany, Georgia. I wanted to find a way to stand with my life.

By Christmas 1961, I had participated in nonviolent workshops (I had settled for a functional definition: if someone hit me, I was not to hit him or her back), argued with the NAACP about whether SNCC was a responsible group and whether NAACP members should work with SNCC, gone to jail, been suspended from school, sung freedom songs, and found a new voice.

Sherrod and Cordell organized workshops in nonviolence. They talked about nonviolence as love, turning the other cheek. They made it clear that if I wanted to participate in the Movement, I could not fight. It wasn't a major problem for me since I did not have a history of getting into physical fights.

One evening in the fall of 1961, state representatives from the NAACP came to town to tell us of the Youth Chapter in Albany that we could not be in SNCC and in the NAACP simultaneously. They said that following SNCC would land us in jail and that the NAACP, which was testing court cases and had the financial resources, would have to get us out. They told us to choose between the two organizations. Mr. Thomas Chatmon, our advisor, spoke to us quietly, saying that he would be with us no matter what, so we took a vote. Blanton Hall and Bertha Gober voted to go with SNCC, and I think I voted to stay with the NAACP or did not vote at all. The process was so painful, I only remember sitting there feeling that someone was telling me there was a choice for me to make that I could not see or feel. Why couldn't we work together? We were all working for freedom, weren't we? I didn't have the courage to vote with SNCC and against the NAACP, because they were one in my soul; their existence as two groups meant nothing to me. I was so angry with Rubye Hurley for putting the question to us and asking me to choose that I stopped attending NAACP meetings altogether. It would be another twenty-five years before I would become a life member of the NAACP.

In November 1961, I learned the name of my first agency of the federal government. The Interstate Commerce Commission (ICC) ruled that any commerce that involved transportation across state lines was in its bailiwick and could not operate or use segregated facilities. It was during Thanksgiving break when student members of the NAACP Youth Chapter went to the Trailways bus station to test the ruling. They were arrested when they tried to buy tickets from the White waiting room window and were bailed out by the NAACP as planned.

However, it was different with Bertha Gober and Blanton Hall, who went as SNCC representatives to buy tickets. They were arrested, refused to pay bail, and stayed in jail. I think I was still mad at being split between the NAACP and SNCC, but the arrest of Bertha and Blanton settled it for me. Clearly, the action in Albany was going to be led by SNCC and I was going to be involved. I learned an important lesson. Groups who should be partners will often jeopardize the overall struggle over issues of control and power. The divisiveness between these two organizations with the same goal of increased freedom for our people was painful, and their blunt way of demanding that we choose between them was a scarring process.

That winter in 1961 I decided to work where the key battle was going to take place, the one I wanted to be in, the one that was attacking racism in my community. When Sherrod and Cordell, who had been joined by a third SNCC field worker, Charlie Jones, called for a support demonstration on Albany State's campus for Blanton and Bertha, I joined in. We were marching to protest their arrest and to give them support while they were in jail.

There was no singing as we walked through the halls of the campus buildings trying to get students to join us in support of Bertha and Blanton. We were quiet as we walked the blocks up the hill to the Flint River bridge. I walked with my best friend, Annette Jones. I felt as if we had failed because there were so few, so I just kept my head in front and kept walking. When we got almost to the bridge, Annette said, "Bernice, look back!" But I wouldn't and I kept walking. Then she said, "Bernice, just look back!" I turned around and almost shouted out loud, because from the bridge to the campus there was nothing but students. It was the same feeling I had when I watched TV reports during the Montgomery Bus Boycott, when every day the buses would still be empty as my people held it together and kept walking—only this time it was me, it was Annette Jones, Janie Culbreth, Bobby Burch, Cordell Reagon, Charlie Jones. It was Albany's time now.

We walked silently, two by two, twice around the courthouse and then headed back to the campus. When we got to the corner, Charlie Jones asked the Reverend William Boyd if we could meet at Union Baptist because it was obvious we could not go to the campus. The administration had shown its hostility to all efforts related to the growing activism of Black students the year before when it suspended the student government. Inside the church, Charlie Jones said, "Bernice, sing a song," and I began to sing "Over my head I see . . ." Usually in the opening line I always sang "trouble in the air"; however, since Albany had just had its first march that wasn't a homecoming or thanksgiving parade, I did not see any "trouble." I saw "freedom," so I switched the words as I sang, and everyone followed, raising up the song.

> *Over my head I see Freedom in the air*
> *Over my head I see Freedom in the air*
> *Over my head I see Freedom in the air*
> *There must be a God somewhere.*
>
> *Over my head I see glory in the air . . .*
>
> *Over my head I see music in the air . . .*

It was the first time my living had changed a song even as it came out of my body. Freedom!

OVER MY HEAD

Over my head I see trouble in the air
Over my head I see trouble in the air
Over my head I see trouble in the air
There must be a God somewhere.

Sung very slowly & freely, (without accompaniment)

Elizabeth Eckford

Martin B. Duberman

One evening in the late summer of 1957 I sat with my family transfixed as images of angry white mobs screaming at a lone black girl flashed across the TV screen. I remember feeling knots in my stomach and praying that she would not be harmed. We live in a time when young people take for granted many of the rights and privileges they enjoy but feel no connection to the civil rights struggle of the 1950s and 1960s or to the people who blazed the trail *for them.* While most students are familiar with such names as Jesse Jackson, Andrew

Young, and Martin Luther King, they don't seem to realize—and we fail to teach them—that the vast majority of people who exhibited enormous courage and put their lives on the line and sometimes lost their lives were everyday folks like you and me. Many of them were children. We cannot neglect to tell the stories of and for countless unnamed and unsung heroes of so significant a struggle. I believe one of the most powerful ways to tell those stories is by sharing the personal testimony of a participant or eye witness. I speak this piece without what I refer to as "dramatics." It needs nothing else. The words and images are powerful enough. I use this in my programs for high school and adult audiences.

This monologue recounts the ordeal experienced by Elizabeth Eckford who set out to enter Central High School in Little Rock, Arkansas, in the fall of 1957. Elizabeth was one of nine African-American students who were to be the first to attend the all-white school. There had been so many threats, so much talk of mobs forming and potential violence that a decision was made by Daisy Bates, then president of the local chapter of the NAACP, not to send the students on the first day. The students were called. By the time Elizabeth Eckford left for school, she had not received a call. I share this piece often with high school students to underscore the fact that most of the people who were involved in marches, demonstrations, sit-ins, who exhibited enormous courage and put their lives on the line for things we now take for granted, were everyday people such as themselves. Many were young people their age.

—Charlotte Blake Alston

The night before, I was so excited, I couldn't sleep. The next morning I was about the first one up. While I was pressing my black-and-white dress—I had made it to wear on the first day of school—my little brother turned on the TV set. They started telling about a large crowd gathering at the school. The man on TV said he wondered if we were going to show up that morning. Mother called in from the kitchen where she was fixing breakfast: "Turn that TV off!" She was so upset and worried. I wanted to comfort her, so I said, "Mother, don't worry!"

Dad was walking back and forth, from room to room, with a sad expression. He was chewing on his pipe and he had a cigar in his hand, but he didn't light either one. It would have been funny, only he was so nervous.

Before I left home, Mother called us into the living room. She said we should have a word of prayer. Then I caught the bus and got off about a block from the school. I saw a large crowd of people standing across the street from the soldiers guarding Central. As I walked on, the crowd suddenly got very quiet. For a moment all I could hear was the shuffling of their feet. Then someone shouted, "Here she comes. Get ready!" The crowd moved in closer and then began to follow me, calling me names. I still wasn't afraid, just a little bit nervous. Then my knees started to shake all of a sudden, and I wondered if I could make it to the center entrance a block away. It was the longest block I have ever walked in my life.

Even so, I still wasn't too scared because all the time I kept thinking that the guards would protect me.

When I got right in front of the school, I went up to a guard. He just looked straight ahead and didn't move to let me pass him. I stood looking at the school—it looked so big! Just then the guards let some white students go through.

The crowd was quiet. I guess they were waiting to see what was going to happen. When I was able to steady my knees, I walked up to the guard who had let the white students in. He, too, didn't move. When I tried to squeeze past him, he raised his bayonet, and then the other guards closed in and raised their bayonets.

They glared at me with a mean look, and I was very frightened and didn't know what to do. I turned around, and the crowd came toward me. They moved closer and closer. Somebody started yelling, "Lynch her! Lynch her!"

I tried to see a friendly face somewhere in the mob. I looked into the face of an old woman, and it seemed like a kind face, but when I looked at her again, she spat on me.

They came closer and closer, shouting, "No nigger bitch is going to get in our school. Get out of here!" Then I looked down the block and saw a bench at the bus stop. I thought, "If I can only get there, I will be safe." I don't know why the bench seemed a safe place to me, but I started walking toward it. I tried to close my mind to what they were shouting and kept saying to myself, "If I can only make it to the bench, I will be safe."

When I finally got there, I don't think I could have gone another step. I sat down and the mob crowded up and began shouting all over again. Someone hollered, "Drag her over to this tree! Let's take care of the nigger!" A white man was sitting on the bench. I don't know what made him do it, but he leaned over, patted me on the shoulder, and whispered in my ear, "Don't let them see you cry." Then the bus came and I got on.

I can't remember much about the bus ride, but the next thing I remember I was standing in front of the School for the Blind, where Mother works. I ran upstairs, and I kept running until I reached Mother's classroom.

Mother was standing at the window with her head bowed, but she must have sensed I was there because she turned around. She looked as if she had been crying, and I wanted to tell her I was all right. But I couldn't speak. She put her arm around me and I cried.

The Golden Bandit

Toni Cade Bambara

If I'm asked to give a lecture on hunger, I prefer to provoke discussion on the politics of food by presenting a refashioned version of that great tale of famine "Hansel and Gretel" rather than by quoting data. In the 1980s, while working on the *Atlanta Missing and Murdered Children's Case* (a novel) and the *Philadelphia Police Bombing of MOVE* (a documentary), I fashioned "The Golden Bandit" to remind people to question the official version of things, to put the authorized tale, a con text, into a critical context. I often use it as an intro to public readings from my novel about Atlanta.

So there's this little yellow-haired gal, whom I think you all know, and she's walking through the woods. What's her name?

> Goldilocks.

The very one. She comes upon a lovely house and knocks on the door, but no one is at home. Does she go away?

> No.

What does she do?

> She went on in.

She broke in.

> Yeah.

What do you call people who break in other people's houses?

> Burglars. Felons. Uninvited.

This yellow-haired burglar chile then went into the folks' living room, where her attention was arrested by some fine-crafted furniture. Three chairs in particular caught her eye. Did she behave herself?

> Nawww.

What did she do?

> Laid up all over the people's furniture.

And?

> Broke it up.

What do you call people who come in uninvited and then commence to wreck the joint?

Vandals. Bush-whackers. Cops.

Ahunh. So this burglar-chile vandal then went into the folks' kitchen where a Panama fruit salad was in the fridge and rice-and-peas à la Grenada was cooking in the crock pot.

I heard that!

And she turned up the burner under the greens till the lid started rattling with steam, and she turned up the heat on the skillet till the chicken was popping in the polyunsaturated-low-cholesterol fat.

Like at my house.

And turned up the oven till the baked macaroni and cheese started puffing up and oozing down the sides of the earthenware all crusty and brown.

Have mercy!

Well, did she act like she had some good home training?

Noooooo.

What'd she do?

Ate like a natural fool.

So whattya call a person who ain't even invited in the first or second place who proceeds to apply a scorch-and-destroy policy on other people's food crops?

Colonialists! Imperialist invaders! Fascist dogs! Thiefing thieves! Unnatural disasters!

Ahunh. So then this burglar-chile-vandal-thief went upstairs to the folks' bedroom. Did you hear what I said, Good People? Can you say "shameless hussy"?

Ohhhh, the shameless hussy.

And got in the folks' bed.

Hmph, hmph, hmph.

With her shoes on.

The nasty heifer.

Rock-a-long, rock-a-long, and the folks come home. Does she beg their pardon for all these antisocial goings-on?

No, she does not, the unrepentant little criminal.

Does she offer to call her daddy to run on by with his carpentry box and fix that door?

Naww, she don't.

Does she call her mama to replace those chairs on her charge-a-card?

You know she didn't.

Having messed with the folks' groceries, does she consult the Yellow Pages under *R* to have some supper brought round?

Nooo.

Does she rip off those nasty sheets and hurry 'em down to the speed-wash?

Noooooo.

Does she even say, "Good evening"?

Not a mumbling word, the heathen.

So what'd she do?

She jumped out the window and ran away like the little sneak-thief she is.

Now. When she came bounding into her own home, out of breath, hair kind of mashed on one side, chicken bones clinging to her clothes, did she 'fess up by way of explaining her greasy appearance?

No.

Did she elicit the help of her parents, presumably grown-ups, presumably grown and capable of analyzing the normative values of their tribe/community/household that have given rise to the sociopathic behavior of their warped little offspring—in short, Good People, did this retrograde little heifer seize the time and engage in principled self-criticism?

None of that, naww.

She said some bears were chasing her.

A liar on top of everything else.

Wellll, errr, rahhh, I heard tell that this little yellow-haired gal was a child-hood hero of yours.

> No way. Puhleeze. I'll admit it, but I was young and foolish at the time.

Well, then, do you think it is hip, healthy, or wise to inflict little children with the *official* version of the golden bandit before we have assumed the necessary task of encouraging and equipping the young in a critical habit?

> No, no, no.

A critical habit is crucial, wouldn't you say, afflicted as we are every day with, err, rahh . . .

> Authorized versions. Lies. Cover-ups. Disinformation.

Are you saying, Good People, that an official text is often a con text?

> Got that right.

That's exactly what three convicted bears and their lawyer claimed on appeal. The end.

On the Horizon

Serious Bizness

Serious Bizness is Jaribu and Ngoma Hill, a husband and wife composing, singing, and performing team. They are committed to justice and leave no sociopolitical stones unturned.

Many times they write a song on the way to an event, sing it there, and hope they don't forget it by the time they return home. Their songs tell stories about current events, Black history, and even about areas as yet untouched. They are not afraid to speak their minds or tackle the world: "This song was not intended to merely entertain you. Hard facts are often omitted from the menu."

"On the Horizon" was written following the tragic drowning of thirty-three Haitians whose bodies washed up on the shore in Miami, Florida, when Reagan turned their boats back as they tried to seek refuge from repression. These men, women, and children were forced to return to certain death. Their rickety boats could not withstand the trip back, and so the vessels gave out and the Haitians died.

On the horizon, crystal and blue,
I see a horrible view.
Thirty-three lives lost oh so brutally.
Thirty-three lives lost oh so callously.

Turn 'em back, oh, you betta turn 'em back.
We're overcrowded, so the government said,
So the government said.

Miami, land of sunshine,
There's another side to this nursery rhyme.
DisneyWorld, fun in the sun,
There's another story for people on the run.

Turn 'em back, oh, you betta turn 'em back.
We're overcrowded, so the government said,
So the government said, so the government said.

It makes you wonder, how it makes you speculate
Was it just another case where they discriminate.
They turned back all that was black
We're overcrowded, so the government said,
So the government said.

Oh, oh, turn 'em back, oh, oh, you betta turn 'em back.
We're overcrowded, so the government said, so the government
    saidddddd . . . so the government said.

High-Rise Tenements

Serious Bizness

The reason we raise the issues is our love of the people, our love of freedom. We never leave on a down note. We always talk about struggle. Struggle will ease your pain. In the words of Marcus Garvey, we love to sing, "Up you mighty people."

High-Rise Tenements
No sentiments for the residents

Rats and roaches running wild
Out the window falls a child
Just because there was no rail
And the window sill was frail

High-Rise Tenements
No sentiments for the residents

Brother Johnson froze in bed
Boiler broke, paint filled with lead

Asbestos hanging above his head
At 39 shy is he dead

High-Rise Tenements
No sentiments for the residents

Landlord wants to raise the rent
Inflation up eighteen percent
Con Ed sucks your pocket dry
Oil bills rising to the sky

High-Rise Tenements
No sentiments for the residents

We can stop and start anew
Something good for me and you
Organize it's time to fight
For decent housing is our right

High-Rise Tenements
No sentiments for the residents

Old Glory's Story

Serious Bizness

"Old Glory's Story" was written after the Atlanta child murders began to hit
the news wires. We have since revised it to include other victims of the racism
and brutality constantly visited upon our people from the cradle to the grave.
The song was written almost ten years ago, and yet the issues remain current
and the list of victims continues to grow.

Sit down and let me tell my story
Sit down and listen to my song
Sit down and let me tell my story
about repression under old glory

Don't tell me about the red, white, and blue
What's it ever done for me and you
Don't tell me about the Bill of Rights
What about the crosses burnin' in the night

This is a story 'bout a sister
Eleanor Bumpurs was her name
This is a story 'bout her murder
and a people filled with rage

This is a story 'bout Miami
Young black men who lost their lives
This is a story for their families
their children and their wives

This is a story for every promise,
broken promise, that's been made
This is a story for every life
Every life that's been taken away

This is a story 'bout a people
fighting against the Klan
This is a story 'bout a people
united to take a stand

This is a story servin' notice
that these murderers cannot hide
This is a story given warnin'
that they'll pay for their crimes

When you think about the children
whose lives have been taken away
When you think about the martyrs
the martyrs who have been slain

Dry your eyes, take a stand
struggle will ease your pain
Dry your eyes, take a stand
struggle will ease your pain

Roslyn Malamud: The Coup

Anna Deavere Smith

Roslyn Malamud is a Lubavitcher resident of Crown Heights, Brooklyn, New York. The Lubavitchers are members of an Orthodox Jewish sect that fled the Nazi genocide of Jews in Europe during World War II.

At 11:30 P.M., three hours later and five blocks away from where Gavin Cato was killed, Yankel Rosenbaum, a visiting twenty-nine-year-old Hasidic history professor from Melbourne, Australia, is stabbed. He dies at Kings County Hospital. Lemrick Nelson, Jr., a sixteen-year-old Trinidadian American, is arrested and charged with the second-degree murder of Yankel Rosenbaum. On October 29, 1992, Lemrick Nelson, Jr., is acquitted of all counts against him in the killing of Yankel Rosenbaum.

(Spring, Midafternoon. The sunny kitchen of a huge, beautiful house on Eastern Parkway in Crown Heights. It's a large, very well equipped kitchen. We are sitting at a table in a breakfast nook area, which is separated by shelves from the cooking area. There is a window to the side. There are newspapers on the chair at the far side of the table. Mrs. Malamud offers me food at the beginning of the interview. We are drinking coffee. She is wearing a sweatshirt with a large sequined cat. Her tennis shoes have matching sequined cats. She has on a black skirt and is wearing a wig. Her nails are manicured. She has beautiful eyes that sparkle and are very warm, and a very resonant voice. There is a lot of humor in her face.)

Do you know what happened in August here?
You see when you read the newspapers.
I mean my son filmed what was going on,
but when you read the newspapers . . .
Of course I was here
I couldn't leave my house.
I only would go out early during the day.
The police were barricading here.
You see,
I wish
I could just like
go on television.
I wanna scream to the whole world.
They said
that the Blacks were rioting against the Jews in Crown Heights
and that the Jews were fighting back.
Do you know that the Blacks who came here to riot were not my
neighbors?
I don't love my neighbors.
I don't know my Black neighbors.
There's one lady on President Street—
Claire—
I adore her.
Salazarhe's my girl friend's next-door neighbor.
I've had a manicure
done in her house and we sit and kibbitz
and stuff
but I don't know them.
I told you we don't mingle socially
because of the difference
of food
and religion

and what have you here.
But
the people in this community
want exactly
what I want out of life.
They want to live
in nice homes.
They all go to work.
They couldn't possibly
have houses here
if they didn't
generally— They have
two,
um,
incomes
that come in.
They want to send their kids to college.
They wanna live a nice quiet life.
They wanna shop for their groceries and cook their meals and go to
their Sunday picnics!
They just want to have decent homes and decent lives!
The people who came to riot here
were brought here
by this famous
Reverend Al Sharpton,
which I'd like to know who ordained him?
He brought in a bunch of kids
who didn't have jobs in
the summertime.
I wish you could see *The New York Times,*
unfortunately it was on page twenty,
I mean, they interviewed
one of the Black girls on Utica Avenue.
She said,
"The guys will make you pregnant
at night
and in the morning not know who you are."
(Almost whispering)
And if you're sitting on a front stoop and it's very, very hot
and you have no money
and you have nothing to do with your time
and someone says, "Come on, you wanna riot?"
You know how kids are.

The fault lies with the police department.
The police department did nothing to stop them.
I was sitting here in the front of the house
when bottles were being thrown
and the sergeant tells five hundred policemen
with clubs and helmets and guns
to duck.
And I said to him,
"You're telling them to duck?
What should I do?
I don't have a club and a gun."
Had they put it—
stopped it on the first night
this kid who came from Australia . . .
(She sucks her teeth)
You know,
his parents were Holocaust survivors, he didn't have to die.
He worked,
did a lot of research in Holocaust studies.
He didn't have to die.
What happened on Utica Avenue
was an accident.
JEWISH PEOPLE
DO NOT DRIVE VANS INTO SEVEN-YEAR-OLD BOYS.
YOU WANT TO KNOW SOMETHING? BLACK PEOPLE DO NOT DRIVE
VANS INTO SEVEN-YEAR-OLD BOYS.
HISPANIC PEOPLE DON'T DRIVE VANS INTO SEVEN-YEAR-OLD BOYS.
IT'S JUST NOT DONE.
PEOPLE LIKE JEFFREY DAHMER MAYBE THEY DO IT.
BUT AVERAGE CITIZENS DO NOT GO OUT AND TRY TO KILL
(Sounds like a laugh but it's just a sound)
SEVEN-YEAR-OLD BOYS.
It was an accident!
But it was allowed to fester and to steam and all that.
When you come here do you see anything that's going on, riots?
No.
But Al Sharpton and the likes of him like *Dowerty,*
who by the way has been in prison
and all of a sudden he became Reverend *Dowerty*—
they once did an exposé on him—
but
these guys live off of this,
you understand?

People are not gonna give them money,
contribute to their causes
unless they're out there rabble-rousing.
My Black neighbors?
I mean I spoke to them.
They were hiding in their houses just like I was.
We were scared.
I was scared!
I was really frightened.
I had five hundred policemen standing in front of my house
every day
I had mounted police,
but I couldn't leave my block,
because when it got dark I couldn't come back in.
I couldn't meet anyone for dinner.
Thank God, I told you my children were all out of town.
My son was in Russia.
The coup
was exactly the same day as the riot
and I was very upset about it.
He was in Russia running a summer camp
and I was very concerned when I had heard about that.
I hadn't heard from him
that night the riot started.
When I did hear from him I told him to stay in Russia, he'd be safer
there than here.
And he was.

Carmel Cato: Lingering

Anna Deavere Smith

Carmel Cato lives in Crown Heights, Brooklyn, New York. He is originally from Guyana. He is the father of seven-year-old Gavin Cato who was killed at the intersection of Utica Avenue and President Street in Crown Heights on August 19, 1991, when a station wagon carrying Lubavitcher Grand Rebbe Menachem Schneerson careened into him and his cousin Angela, who suffered a broken leg. This dramatic and moving work is from *Fires in the Mirror,* conceived and performed by Anna Deavere Smith. She creates her characters and their stories by interviewing them and later using their own words in her performances. Her goal has been to find the American character in the ways that people speak.

Cornel West states in the foreword to *Fires in the Mirror* that it is "the most significant artistic exploration of Black-Jewish relations in our time. . . . In the midst of the heated moment of murder, mayhem, and madness of the Crown Heights crisis, [Anna Deavere Smith] gives us poignant portraits of the everyday human faces caught up in the situation."

(7:00 P.M. The corner where the accident occurred in Crown Heights. An altar to Gavin is against the wall where the car crashed. Many pieces of cloth are draped. Some writing in color is on the wall. Candle wax is everywhere. There is a rope around the area. Cato is wearing a trench coat, pulled around him. He stands very close to me. Dark outside. Reggae music is in the background. Lights come from stores on each corner. Busy intersection. Sounds from outside. Traffic. Stores open. People in and out of shops. Sounds from inside apartments, televisions, voices, cooking, etc. He speaks in a pronounced West Indian accent.)

In the meanwhile
it was two.
Angela was on the ground
but she was trying to move. Gavin was still.
They was trying to pound him.
I was the father.
I was 'it, chucked, and pushed,
and a lot of
sarcastic words were passed towards me
from the police
while I was trying to explain: It was my kid!
These are my children.
The child was hit you know.
I saw everything, everything,
the guy radiator burst
all the hoses,
the steam,
all the garbage buckets goin' along the building.
And it was very loud,
everything burst.
It's like an atomic bomb,
That's why all these people
comin' round
wanna know what's happening.
Oh it was very outrageous.
Numerous numbers.
All the time the police sayin'

you can't get in,
you can't pass,
and the children laying on the ground.
He was hit at exactly eight-thirty.
Why?
I was standing over there.
There was a little child—
a friend of mine
came up with a little child—
and I lift the child up
and she look at her watch at the same time
and she say it was eight-thirty.
I gave the child back to her.
And then it happen.
Um, Um . . .
My child, these are the things I never dream about.
I take care of my children.
You know it's a funny thing,
if a child get sick and he dies
it won't hurt me so bad,
or if a child run out into the street and get hit down,
it wouldn't hurt me.
That's what's hurtin' me.
The whole week
before Gavin died
my body was changing,
I was having different feelings.
I stop eating,
I didn't et
nothin',
only drink water,
for two weeks;
and I was very touchy—
any least thing that drop
or any song I hear
it would affect me.
Every time I try to do something
I would have to stop.
I was
lingering, lingering, lingering, lingering,
all the time.
But I can do things,
I can see things,

I know that for a fact.
I was telling myself,
"Something is wrong somewhere,"
but I didn't want to see,
I didn't want to accept,
and it was inside of me,
and even when I go home I tell my friends,
"Something coming I could feel it
but I didn't want to see,"
and all the time I just deny deny deny,
and I never thought it was Gavin,
but I didn't have a clue.
I thought it was one of the other children—
the bigger boys
or the girl,
because she worry me,
she won't et—
but Gavin 'ee was 'ealtee,
and he don't cause no trouble.
That's what's devastating me now.
Sometime it make me feel like it's no justice,
like, uh,
the Jewish people,
they are very high up,
it's a very big thing,
they runnin' the whole show
from the judge right down.
And something I don't understand:
The Jewish people, they told me
there are certain people I cannot be seen with
and certain things I cannot say
and certain people I cannot talk to.
They made that very clear to me—the Jewish people—
they can throw the case out
unless
I go to them with pity.
I don't know what they talkin' about.
So I don't know what kind of crap is that.
And make me say things I don't wanna say
and make me do things I don't wanna do.
I am a special person.
I was born different.
I'm a man born by my foot.

I born by my foot.
Anytime a baby comin' by the foot
they either cut the mother
or the baby dies.
But I was born with my foot.
I'm one of the special.
They're no way they can overpower me.
No there's nothing to hide,
you can repeat every word I say.

Showdown in L.A.

Rex Ellis

When I was making the transition to my new job at the Smithsonian Institution in 1992, I rented a very small efficiency apartment in Rossyln, Virginia, just across the river from Washington, D.C. Each morning I had a routine of listening to the "Today" show as I prepared for my day. One morning Bryant Gumbel came on with a very glum face as he discussed the Rodney King verdict and the furor it had caused. I immediately thought of my eleven-year-old son and wondered how I was going to explain this to him when I didn't fully understand it myself. "Showdown in L.A." was my attempt to communicate the frustration, hurt, anger, and dismay I felt when the news was given that justice had not prevailed.

I woke up one Thursday morning in my itty bitty room
and as usual I turned on the news;
But the newsman's spirit was low, as he showed us a video
of a black who had been violently abused.

Some policemen took turns kicking and beating on him,
as he lay helplessly on the ground;
and here one year later, a jury of his peers
turned his plea for justice down.

Well some young people got mad and set buildings on fire.
From L.A. it spread to other states,
And I sat there surprised, at what I saw with my own eyes;
how one action could cause so much hate.

I'm a black man, you see, and I've tried in my way
to follow the path you have marked;
but my blood runs cold, though I'm 41 years old,
when I think of what can happen in the dark.

I know that could have been me bleeding there on the ground;
with no one to hear my cries;
I could have been maimed by those people who are hired
to protect and defend our lives.

Are we hated that much, are we so despised
that justice has no meaning for us?
Where is the promise that a new day will come;
in what can we put our trust?

Is it fear that we bring; are we doomed to repeat
the horrors of our past history?
Should we apologize for being alive,
are we really truly free?

I know we have our faults but all of us do
whether we are white, brown, or red.
But is this what I will see, whenever we disagree;
can we only hope for justice when we're dead?

What is the answer I give to my son
when he sees this scene of horror?
How do I explain, how do I assure him
that he will have a brighter tomorrow?

How do I continue to see life's benefits,
when all about me falls apart?
How do I keep the love that you teach,
in the uppermost corner of my heart?

What do I say to those who hate,
and those who fear my face?
How do I keep my son from believing
that his humanity is tied to his race?

Help me, dear Father;
I need your guidance to make sense of this travesty.
Show me the way that I must go
so a brighter tomorrow I'll see.

The Chronicle of the Sacrificed Black Children

Derrick Bell

Derrick Bell, a distinguished legal scholar and civil rights activist, employs a
series of dramatic fables and dialogues in his teachings to probe the foundations

of America's racial attitudes and raise disturbing questions about the nature of our society. Vincent Harding, historian, states, "Mr. Bell has chosen to engage the often harsh realities of the Black struggle for justice in America through the use of a storytelling technique filled with imagination, fantasy, and unabashed spirituality."

All the Black school-age children were gone. They had simply disappeared.

No one in authority could tell the frantic parents more than they already knew. It had been one of those early September days that retain the warmth of summer after shedding that season's oppressive humidity. Prodded perhaps by the moderate weather, the pall of hateful racial invective that had enveloped the long desegregation battle lifted on what was to be the first day of a new school year. It was as well implementation day for the new desegregation plan, the result of prolonged, court-supervised negotiations. Plaintiffs' lawyers had insisted on what one called a "full measure" of racial balance, while the school board and the white community resisted, often bitterly, every departure from the previous school structure.

Now it seemed all for nothing. The black students, every one of them, had vanished on the way to school. Children who had left home on foot never appeared. Buses that had pulled away from their last stop loaded with black children had arrived at schools empty, as had the cars driven by parents or car pools. Even parents taking young children by the hand for their first day in kindergarten, or in pre-school, had looked down and found their hands empty, the children suddenly gone.

You can imagine the response. The media barrage, the parents' anger and grief, the suspects arrested and released, politicians' demands for action, analysts' assessments, and then the inevitably receding hullabaloo. Predictable statements were made, predictable actions taken, but there were no answers, no leads, no black children.

Give them credit. At first, the white people, both in town and around the country, were generous in their support and sincere in the sympathy they extended to the black parents. It was some time before there was any public mention of what, early on, many had whispered privately: that while the loss was tragic, perhaps it was all for the best. Except in scruffy white neighborhoods, these "all for the best" rationales were never downgraded to "good riddance."

Eventually they might have been. After all, statistics showed the life chances for most of the poor children were not bright. School dropouts at an early age; no skills; no jobs; too early parenthood; too much exposure to crime, alcohol, drugs. And the city had resisted meaningful school desegregation for so long that it was now possible to learn from the experience of other districts that integrating the schools would not automatically insulate poor black children from the risks of ghetto life.

Even after delaying school desegregation for several years, the decision to proceed this fall with the now-unneeded plan had been bitterly opposed by many white parents who feared that "their schools" would have to have a 50 percent enrollment of black children to enable the school system to achieve an equal racial balance, the primary goal of the desegregation plan and its civil rights sponsors. So high a percentage of black children, these parents claimed, would destroy academic standards, generate discipline problems, and place white children in physical danger. But under all the specifics lay the resentment and sense of lost status. Their schools would no longer be mainly white—a racial status whites equated with school quality, even when the schools were far from academically impressive.

Black parents had differed about the value of sending their children to what had been considered white schools. Few of these parents were happy that their children were scheduled, under the desegregation plan, to do most of the bus riding—often to schools located substantial distances from their homes. Some parents felt that it was the only way to secure a quality education because whites would never give black schools a fair share of school funds, and as some black parents observed: "Green follows white."

Other black parents, particularly those whose children were enrolled in the W. E. B. DuBois School—an all-black, outstanding educational facility with a national reputation—were unhappy. DuBois's parents had intervened in the suit to oppose the desegregation plan as it applied to their school. Their petition read:

> This school is the fruit of our frustration. It is as well a monument of love for our children. Our persistence built the DuBois School over the system's opposition. It is a harbor of learning for our children, and a model of black excellence for the nation. We urge that our school be emulated and not emasculated. The admission of whites will alter and undermine the fragile balance that enables the effective schooling black children need to survive societal hostility.
>
> We want our children to attend the DuBois School. Coercing their attendance at so-called desegregated schools will deny, not ensure, their right to an equal educational opportunity. The board cannot remedy the wrongs done in the past by an assignment policy that is a constitutional evil no less harmful than requiring black children to attend segregated schools. The remedy for inferior black schools sought by others from the courts we have achieved for ourselves. Do not take away our educational victory and leave us "rights" we neither need nor want.

The DuBois School's petition was opposed by the school board and plaintiffs' civil rights lawyers, and denied by the district court. Under the desegregation plan, two-thirds of the DuBois students were to be transferred to white schools located at the end of long bus rides, to be replaced by white children whose parents volunteered to enroll them in an outstanding school.

In fact, DuBois School patrons were more fortunate than many parents whose children were enrolled in black schools that were slowly improving but lacked the DuBois School's showy academic performance. Most of these schools were slated for closure or conversion into warehouses or other administrative use. Under a variety of rationales, the board failed to reassign any of the principals of the closed black schools to similar positions in integrated schools.

Schools in white areas that would have been closed because of declining enrollment gained a reprieve under the school-desegregation plan. The older schools were extensively rehabilitated, and the school board obtained approval for several new schools, all to be built in mainly white areas—the board said—the better to ensure that they would remain academically stable and racially integrated.

Then, in the wake of the black students' disappearance, came a new shock. The public school superintendent called a special press conference to make the announcement. More than 55 percent of the public school population had been black students, and because state funding of the schools was based on average daily attendance figures, the school system faced a serious deficit during the current year.

There were, the superintendent explained, several additional components to the system's financial crisis:

Teacher Salaries. Insisting that desegregation would bring special stresses and strains, the teacher's union had won substantial pay raises, as well as expensive in-service training programs. A whole corps of teacher aides had been hired and trained to assist school faculties with their administrative chores. Many newly hired teachers and all the aides would have to be released.

School Buses. To enable transportation of students required by the desegregation plan, the board had ordered one hundred buses and hired an equal number of new drivers. The buses, the superintendent reported, could be returned. Many had made only one trip; but the new drivers, mechanics, service personnel, and many of the existing drivers would have to be laid off.

School Construction. Contracts for rehabilitation of old schools and for planning and building new schools had placed the board millions of dollars in debt. The superintendent said that hundreds of otherwise idle construction workers were to have been employed, as well as architectural firms and landscape designers. Additional millions had been earmarked for equipment and furniture suppliers, book publishers, and curriculum specialists. Some of these contracts could be canceled but not without substantial damage to the local economy.

Lost Federal Funds. After desegregation had been ordered by the courts, the board applied for and received commitments for several million dollars in federal desegregation funds. These grants were now canceled.

Lost State Funds. Under the court order, the state was obligated to subsidize costs of desegregation; and, the superintendent admitted, these appropriations, as well as the federal grants, had been designated to do "double duty": that is, while furthering school-desegregation efforts, the money would also improve the quality of education throughout the system by hiring both sufficient new teachers to lower the teacher-pupil ratio, and guidance counselors and other advisory personnel.

Tax Rates. Conceding that the board had won several increases in local tax rates during the desegregation process, the superintendent warned that, unless approval was obtained for a doubling of the current rate, the public schools would not survive.

Annexations. Over the last several years, the city had annexed several unincorporated areas in order to bring hundreds of additional white students into the public school system and slow the steady increase in the percentage of black students. Now the costs of serving these students added greatly to the financially strapped system.

Attorney Fees. Civil rights attorneys had come under heavy criticism after it was announced that the court had awarded them $300,000 in attorney fees for their handling of the case, stretching back over the prior five years. Now the superintendent conceded that the board had paid a local law firm over $2,000,000 for defending the board in court for the same period.

Following the school superintendent's sobering statement, the mayor met with city officials and prepared an equally lengthy list of economic gains that would have taken place had the school-desegregation order gone into effect. The president of the local chamber of commerce did the same. The message was clear. While the desegregation debate had focused on whether black children would benefit from busing and attendance at racially balanced schools, the figures put beyond dispute the fact that virtually every white person in the city would benefit directly or indirectly from the desegregation plan that most had opposed.

Armed with this information, a large sum was appropriated to conduct a massive search for the missing black children. For a time, hopes were raised, but eventually the search was abandoned. The children were never found, their abductors never apprehended. Gradually, all in the community came to realize the tragedy's lamentable lesson. In the monumental school desegregation struggle, the intended beneficiaries had been forgotten long before they were lost.

My Dungeon Shook

James Baldwin

"Can I get a witness?" the black preacher shouts from the pulpit in a dramatic delivery. He or she repeats this refrain over and over and over again, causing the congregation to "jump up and say." Traditionally, the Black storyteller's style and delivery is powerful because the storyteller "leaps out" at the audience and forces the listener to "wake up!"

James Baldwin's literary style and delivery is like the traditional Black storyteller. He was a prophet of ancient lore, he was a storefront preacher, and he was a traveling bluesman who wanted America to "testify" and "confess" its sins.

Letter to My Nephew on the one-hundredth anniversary of the Emancipation:

Dear James:

I have begun this letter five times and torn it up five times. I keep seeing your face, which is also the face of your father and my brother. Like him, you are tough, dark, vulnerable, moody—with a very definite tendency to sound truculent because you want no one to think you are soft. You may be like your grandfather in this, I don't know, but certainly both you and your father resemble him very much physically. Well, he is dead, he never saw you, and he had a terrible life; he was defeated long before he died because, at the bottom of his heart, he really believed what white people said about him. This is one of the reasons that he became so holy. I am sure that your father has told you something about all that. Neither you nor your father exhibit any tendency towards holiness: you really *are* of another era, part of what happened when the Negro left the land and came into what the late E. Franklin Frazier called "the cities of destruction." You can only be destroyed by believing that you really are what the white world calls a *nigger*. I tell you this because I love you, and please don't you ever forget it.

I have known both of you all your lives, have carried your Daddy in my arms and on my shoulders, kissed and spanked him and watched him learn to walk. I don't know if you've known anybody from that far back; if you've loved anybody that long, first as an infant, then as a child, then as a man, you gain a strange perspective on time and human pain and effort. Other people cannot see what I see whenever I look into your father's face, for behind your father's face as it is today are all those other faces which were his. Let him laugh and I see a cellar your father does not remember and a house he does not remember and I hear in his present laughter his laughter as a child. Let him curse and I remember him falling down the cellar steps, and howling, and I remember, with pain, his tears, which my hand or your grandmother's so easily wiped away. But no one's hand can wipe away those tears he sheds invisibly today, which one hears in his laughter and in his speech and in his songs. I know what the world has done to my brother and how narrowly he has survived it. And I know, which is much worse, and this is the crime of which I accuse my country and my countrymen, and for which neither I nor time nor history will ever forgive them, that they have destroyed and are destroying hundreds of thousands of lives and do not know it and do not want to know it. One can be, indeed one must strive to become, tough and philosophical concerning destruction and death, for this is what most of mankind has been best at since we have heard of man. (But remember: *most* of mankind is not *all* of mankind.) But it is not permissible that the authors of devastation should also be innocent. It is the innocence which constitutes the crime.

Now, my dear namesake, these innocent and well-meaning people, your countrymen, have caused you to be born under conditions not very far removed from those described for us by Charles Dickens in the London of more than a hundred years ago. (I hear the chorus of the innocents screaming, "No! This is not true! How *bitter* you are!"—but I am writing this letter to *you,* to try to tell you something about how to handle *them,* for most of them do not yet really know that you exist. I *know* the conditions under which you were born, for I was there. Your countrymen were *not* there, and haven't made it yet. Your grandmother was also there, and no one has ever accused her of being bitter. I suggest that the innocents check with her. She isn't hard to find. Your countrymen don't know that *she* exists, either, though she has been working for them all their lives.)

Well, you were born, here you came, something like fourteen years ago; and though your father and mother and grandmother, looking about the streets through which they were carrying you, staring at the walls into which they brought you, had every reason to be heavyhearted, yet they were not. For here you were, Big James, named for me—you were a big baby, I was not—here you were: to be loved. To be loved, baby, hard, at once, and forever, to strengthen you against the loveless world. Remember that: I know how black it looks today, for you. It looked bad that day, too, yes, we were trembling. We have not stopped trembling yet, but if we had not loved each other none of us would have survived. And now you must survive because we love you, and for the sake of your children and your children's children.

PART VII

If You Holler Too Loud, You'll Wake Up the Ghosts

Ghost Tales and Superstitions

My father was good at telling ghost stories.
He told us one about the time when
He was cook for a levee gang and whenever
He went into the cooks' shanty, how the skillets
And pots had been moved from the stove with
Not a soul around. He had seen many spirits
And ghosts, having been born with a veil over his eyes.

—MARGARET TAYLOR BURROUGHS,
"Memorial for My Father," January 1942

If you walk through a graveyard and you see a ghost, offer it a glass of whiskey. If you don't have any whiskey, then you better *run!*

Bury my bones but keep my words.

The old-time talk we still de talkem here! (Gullah)

To cure whooping cough, get a chicken to fly over a person's head.

To cure a fever, wrap a damp cloth with peach leaves inside it around the person's head.

To cure a chest cold, fasten a pad of fried onions to your pajama top and sleep on it. Make sure the onion pad is hot.

Ol' Ben

Rex Ellis

"Ol' Ben" was inspired by my work at Colonial Williamsburg. It was the result of research and my desire to teach history in a way that made meaningful connections with the public. Ben illustrates the ways enslaved Africans and African Americans used stories and their "motherwit" to teach one another how to cope and survive an oppressive institution that never expected them to do either.

Let me see here now. There's the story of Br'er Rabbit, there's the story of Anansi the spider. I think I'm goin' to tell you the story about Titus. You see, during the time of slavery there was a young slave boy named Titus. He worked along with an older slave called Brother Tom. Brother Tom was a coachman who worked for Robert Carter (I'm talking about Robert King Carter, the man with all the land and all the money). Now Robert King Carter had Brother Tom as his coachman, but that was not what Tom did best. He knew more about roots and herbs than anybody else around here. Brother Tom was an herb doctor. Fact is, he knew so much about roots and herbs the governor of the state—his name was Gooch—offered Brother Tom his freedom if he was to give him his cure for any disease known during that time.

Well now, when Brother Tom told this to Titus, Titus got all excited about it. He said, "I know you gonna tell him, right? I know you're gonna tell 'em 'cause you'll get your freedom."

Brother Tom looked at Titus like he was crazy and then decided that he better tell Titus the story of the slave and the skeleton head:

It seems this slave was walking through the woods one night when he came upon a skeleton head. Well, he walked on past it until he thought he heard it speak. So he walked up to it, and sure enough the skeleton head said, "Mouth brought me here, and it's gonna bring you, too." Well, the slave was so excited about hearing a skeleton head speak, he ran home to tell his slavemaster about it. His master was lying up in the bed all nice and ready to go to sleep. The slave runs in and tells him about the skeleton head. Well, the "old massa" gets excited, too. He's superstitious, too. So he puts on his shirt, his shoes, his pants (he decides he'd leave his wig at home, you know, it was nighttime and nobody would see him anyhow). As they are goin' through the woods, the master says to the slave, "Now you listen here, if you aren't telling me the truth, this is the last time you will ever tell a lie."

The slave ain't paid that no mind, he knew he heard the skeleton head speak. Sure enough there was the clearing. Sure enough there was the skeleton head. The slave said, "Hello, Head." The skeleton said nothing. The slave said it again, "I'm talking to you, Head. I said hello." The skeleton head said nothing. "I said—" Now at that very moment as the slave was speaking a big branch came across his head and knocked him down dead. The master threw the branch into the creek and walked back to his house. The skeleton head turned to the dead slave and said, "I told you mouth brought me here, and it was gonna bring you, too."

Brother Tom looked at Titus and said, "So you see, Titus, if you wants to live in this life, you don't say all you see and you don't tell all you know."

The Talking Skull

Traditional from West Africa

Now that you have heard the story about Titus and Brother Tom, let me tell you one of the "original" versions of that tale which comes from Nigeria. The "talking skull" motif appears under different titles such as "Talk" and "Talking Brought Me Here." It is one of hundreds and hundreds of folk stories that Black people brought with them in the slave ships across the waters to the Americas. In African-American folklore the setting and character reflects the experience of slavery. It is also known as one of the "John and Old Massa" tales.

A hunter finds a skull in the bush. He asks, "What brought you here?" The skull replies, "Talking brought me here, and talking will bring you here." The hunter runs off to tell the king about the talking skull.

"I have never heard a dead skull speak," said the king. "Bring me the skull." The hunter gets the skull and brings it to the king. The hunter commands the skull to talk: "Speak, skull, speak!" The skull's jaws do not move. Over and over again the hunter tries to make the skull talk. The skull does not move. Finally the king said, "You have wasted my time with your lies." He tells his guards to take the skull and the hunter back to the bush with orders to kill the hunter.

The guards complete their orders and return to the king. Once they're out of sight, the skull asks the dead man's head, "What brought you here?" The dead hunter's head replies, "Talking brought me here."

The 11:59

Patricia C. McKissack

From 1880 to 1960—a time known as the golden age of train travel—George Pullman's luxury sleeping cars provided passengers with comfortable accommodations during an overnight trip. The men who changed the riding seats into well-made-up beds and attended to the individual needs of each passenger were called Pullman car porters. For decades all the porters were African Americans, so when they organized the Brotherhood of Sleeping Car Porters in 1926, theirs was the first all-black union in the United States. Like most groups, the porters had their own language and a network of stories. The phantom Death Train, known in railroad language as the 11:59, is an example of the kind of story the porters often shared.

Lester Simmons was a thirty-year retired Pullman car porter—had his gold watch to prove it. "Keeps perfect train time," he often bragged. "Good to the second."

Daily he went down to the St. Louis Union Station and shined shoes to help supplement his meager twenty-four-dollar-a-month Pullman retirement check. He ate his evening meal at the porter house on Compton Avenue and hung around until late at night talking union, playing bid whist, and spinning yarns with those who were still "travelin' men." In this way Lester stayed in touch with the only family he'd known since 1920.

There was nothing the young porters liked more than listening to Lester tell true stories about the old days, during the founding of the Brotherhood of Sleeping Car Porters, the first black union in the United States. He knew the president, A. Philip Randolph, personally, and proudly boasted that it was Randolph who'd signed him up as a union man back in 1926. He passed his original card around for inspection. "I knew all the founding brothers. Take Brother E. J. Bradley. We hunted many a day together, not for the sport of it but for something to eat. Those were hard times, starting up the union. But we hung in there so you youngsters might have the benefits you enjoy now."

The rookie porters always liked hearing about the thirteen-year struggle between the Brotherhood and the powerful Pullman Company, and how, against all odds, the fledgling union had won recognition and better working conditions.

Everybody enjoyed it too when Lester told tall tales about Daddy Joe, the porters' larger-than-life hero. "Now y'all know the first thing a good Pullman man is expected to do is make up the top and lower berths for the passengers each night."

"Come on, Lester," one of his listeners chided. "You don't need to describe our jobs for us."

"Some of you, maybe not. But some of you, well—" he said, looking over the top of his glasses and raising an eyebrow at a few of the younger porters. "I was just setting the stage." He smiled good-naturedly and went on with his story. "They tell me Daddy Joe could walk flatfooted down the center of the coach and let down berths on both sides of the aisle."

Hearty laughter filled the room, because everyone knew that to accomplish such a feat, Daddy Joe would have to have been superhuman. But that was it: To the men who worked the sleeping cars, Daddy Joe was no less a hero than Paul Bunyan was to the lumberjacks of the Northwestern forests.

"And when the 11:59 pulled up to his door, as big and strong as Daddy Joe was. . . ." Lester continued solemnly. "Well, in the end even he couldn't escape the 11:59." The old storyteller eyed one of the rookie porters he knew had never heard the frightening tale about the porters' Death Train. Lester took joy in mesmerizing his young listeners with all the details.

"Any porter who hears the whistle of the 11:59 has got exactly twenty-four hours to clear up earthly matters. He better be ready when the train comes the next night . . ." In his creakiest voice, Lester drove home the point. "All us porters got to board that train one day. Ain't no way to escape the final ride on the 11:59."

Silence.

"Lester," a young porter asked, "you know anybody who ever heard the whistle of the 11:59 and lived to tell—"

"Not a living soul!"

Laughter.

"Well," began one of the men, "wonder will we have to make up berths on *that* train?"

"If it's an overnight trip to heaven, you can best be believing there's bound to be a few of us making up the berths," another answered.

"Shucks," a card player stopped to put in. "They say even up in heaven *we* the ones gon' be keeping all that gold and silver polished."

"Speaking of gold and silver," Lester said, remembering. "That reminds me of how I gave Tip Sampson his nickname. Y'all know Tip?"

There were plenty of nods and smiles.

The memory made Lester chuckle. He shifted in his seat to find a more comfortable spot. Then he began. "A woman got on board the *Silver Arrow* in Chicago going to Los Angeles. She was dripping in finery—had on all kinds of gold and diamond jewelry, carried twelve bags. Sampson knocked me down getting to wait on her, figuring she was sure for a big tip. That lady was worrisome! Ooo-wee! 'Come do this. Go do that. Bring me this.' Sampson was running over himself trying to keep that lady happy. When we reached L.A., my passengers all tipped me two or three dollars, as was customary back then.

"When Sampson's Big Money lady got off, she reached into her purse and placed a dime in his outstretched hand. A *dime!* Can you imagine? *Ow!* You should have seen his face. And I didn't make it no better. Never did let him forget it. I teased him so—went to calling him Tip, and the nickname stuck."

Laughter.

"I haven't heard from ol' Tip in a while. Anybody know anything?"

"You haven't got word, Lester? Tip boarded the 11:59 over in Kansas City about a month ago."

"Sorry to hear that. That just leaves me and Willie Beavers, the last of the old, old-timers here in St. Louis."

Lester looked at his watch—it was a little before midnight. The talkfest had lasted later than usual. He said his good-byes and left, taking his usual route across the Eighteenth Street bridge behind the station.

In the darkness, Lester looked over the yard, picking out familiar shapes —the *Hummingbird,* the *Zephyr.* He'd worked on them both. Train travel wasn't anything like it used to be in the old days—not since people had begun to ride airplanes. "Progress," he scoffed. "Those contraptions will never take the place of a train. No sir!"

Suddenly he felt a sharp pain in his chest. At exactly the same moment he heard the mournful sound of a train whistle, which the wind seemed to carry from some faraway place. Ignoring his pain, Lester looked at the old station. He knew nothing was scheduled to come in or out till early morning. Nervously he lit a match to check the time. 11:59!

"No," he said into the darkness. "I'm not ready. I've got plenty of living yet."

Fear quickened his step. Reaching his small apartment, he hurried up the steps. His heart pounded in his ear, and his left arm tingled. He had an idea, and there wasn't a moment to waste. But his own words haunted him. *Ain't no way to escape the final ride on the 11:59.*

"But I'm gon' try!" Lester spent the rest of the night plotting his escape from fate.

"I won't eat or drink anything all day," he talked himself through his plan. "That way I can't choke, die of food poisoning, or cause a cooking fire."

Lester shut off the space heater to avoid an explosion, nailed shut all doors and windows to keep out intruders, and unplugged every electrical appliance. Good weather was predicted, but just in case a freak storm came and blew out a window, shooting deadly glass shards in his direction, he moved a straight-backed chair into a far corner, making sure nothing was overhead to fall on him.

"I'll survive," he said, smiling at the prospect of beating Death. "Won't that be a wonderful story to tell at the porter house?" He rubbed his left arm. It felt numb again.

Lester sat silently in his chair all day, too afraid to move. At noon someone knocked on his door. He couldn't answer it. Footsteps . . . another knock. He didn't answer.

A parade of minutes passed by, equally measured, one behind the other, ticking . . . ticking . . . away . . . The dull pain in his chest returned. He nervously checked his watch every few minutes.

Ticktock, ticktock.

Time had always been on his side. Now it was his enemy. Where had the years gone? Lester reviewed the thirty years he'd spent riding the rails. How different would his life have been if he'd married Louise Henderson and had a gallon of children? What if he'd taken that job at the mill down in Opelika? What if he'd followed his brother to Philly? How different?

Ticktock, ticktock.

So much living had passed so quickly. Lester decided if he had to do it all over again, he'd stand by his choices. His had been a good life. No regrets. No major changes for him.

Ticktock, ticktock.

The times he'd had—both good and bad—what memories. His first and only love had been traveling, and she was a jealous companion. Wonder whatever happened to that girl up in Minneapolis? Thinking about her made him smile. Then he laughed. That *girl* must be close to seventy years old by now.

Ticktock, ticktock.

Daylight was fading quickly. Lester drifted off to sleep, then woke from a nightmare in which, like Jonah, he'd been swallowed by an enormous beast. Even awake he could still hear its heart beating . . . *ticktock, ticktock* . . . But then he realized he was hearing his own heartbeat.

Lester couldn't see his watch, but he guessed no more than half an hour had passed. Sleep had overtaken him with such little resistance. Would Death, that shapeless shadow, slip in that easily? Where was he lurking? *Yea, though I walk through the valley of the shadow of death, I will fear no evil* . . . The Twenty-third Psalm was the only prayer Lester knew, and he repeated it over and over, hoping it would comfort him.

Lester rubbed his tingling arm. He could hear the blood rushing past his ear and up the side of his head. He longed to know what time it was, but that meant he had to light a match—too risky. What if there was a gas leak? The match would set off an explosion. "I'm too smart for that, Death," he said.

Ticktock, ticktock.

It was late. He could feel it. Stiffness seized his legs and made them tremble. How much longer? he wondered. Was he close to winning?

Then in the fearful silence he heard a train whistle. His ears strained to identify the sound, making sure it *was* a whistle. No mistake. It came again, the same as the night before. Lester answered it with a groan.

Ticktock, ticktock.

He could hear Time ticking away in his head. Gas leak or not, he had to see his watch. Striking a match, Lester quickly checked the time. 11:57.

Although there was no gas explosion, a tiny explosion erupted in his heart.

Ticktock, ticktock.

Just a little more time. The whistle sounded again. Closer than before. Lester struggled to move, but he felt fastened to the chair. Now he could hear the engine puffing, pulling a heavy load. It was hard for him to breathe, too, and the pain in his chest weighed heavier and heavier.

Ticktock, ticktock.

Time had run out! Lester's mind reached for an explanation that made sense. But reason failed when a glowing phantom dressed in the porters' blue uniform stepped out of the grayness of Lester's confusion.

"It's *your* time, good brother." The specter spoke in a thousand familiar voices.

Freed of any restraint now, Lester stood, bathed in a peaceful calm that had its own glow. "Is that you, Tip?" he asked, squinting to focus on his old friend standing in the strange light.

"It's me, ol' partner. Come to remind you that none of us can escape the last ride on the 11:59."

"I know. I know," Lester said, chuckling. "But man, I had to try."

Tip smiled. "I can dig it. So did I."

"That'll just leave Willie, won't it?"

"Not for long."

"I'm ready."

Lester saw the great beam of the single headlight and heard the deafening whistle blast one last time before the engine tore through the front of the apartment, shattering glass and splintering wood, collapsing everything in its path, including Lester's heart.

When Lester didn't show up at the shoeshine stand two days running, friends went over to his place and found him on the floor. His eyes were fixed on something quite amazing—his gold watch, stopped at exactly 11:59.

Ligahoo

Lynn Joseph

The Ligahoo has great supernatural powers. The spelling and pronunciation of this creature's name are derived from the French words *loup garou,* meaning werewolf, and in Trinidad the name is pronounced *"Lag*-a-hoo.'' Ligahoo is the name given to the old medicine man of a village. Like medicine men in many other cultures, Ligahoo is well respected and feared. He can proclaim curses as well as offer protection. Ligahoo's greatest power is his ability to change his shape. This shape-changing power is believed to be hereditary in some old Creole families. To see a ligahoo without his seeing you, you must take some *yampee* (sleep) from the corner of a dog's eye and put it in your own eye. Then at midnight, peep out of a keyhole.

Every year starting in May, the rainy season comes and sits like a heavy bushel basket on my head. With the rain comes Auntie Hazel to keep Mama company. Auntie Hazel is Cedric's and Susan's mother. The best part about her coming over is that Cedric and Susan come too. Then Avril, who lives right down the street from me, joins us. We could have plenty of fun then, except that now we have two grown-ups telling us no instead of only one.

No, we can't go to Maracas Bay where the waves are big. No, we can't play cricket in the Savannah. And no, we can't go down to Four Roads River and watch the tadpoles turn into baby frogs.

"With all this rain, that river could overflow anytime," says Auntie Hazel, with her hands on her big hips.

"No playing by de river," says Mama, shaking a long finger at us.

But like cousin Avril used to say, "What else is there to do during de rainy season 'cept watch de river water rise high high and see if de place flood?"

So that's just what we'd do. After the long morning rain, we'd wait until Mama and Auntie Hazel fell asleep on the back porch. Then we'd tiptoe out the front door and run down to the river.

The riverbanks are yellow and wide and slant down to the riverbed. In the dry season, snails and frogs crawl and hop about. And the river is small enough for us to jump across. But in the rainy season, the river grows fat and full. Sometimes the water climbs all the way up the slanted yellow bank and out into the streets.

Most times during the rainy season we'd just stand on the riverbank and watch the thick, red-brown water swoosh on by, carrying tree branches and old tires.

One day though, Tantie changed all that. She was visiting, and we thought she was asleep like Mama and Auntie Hazel on the back porch.

The afternoon was smelling clean and fresh from the rain and the sun was shining strong strong on our backs. Avril, Cedric, Susan, and I stood on the riverbank squishing the muddy grass into little points with our toes. Two big rainbows filled up the sky with Carnival colors. Everything was quiet except for the river, which was groaning like an old cow horn.

Then all of a sudden we heard a voice behind us. "All yuh must be waiting to see Ligahoo?"

We spin around so fast we almost tumbled down into the river.

Avril was the first one to speak. "Tantie," he said, "what you doing here? We thought you sleeping like everyone else."

It was the wrong thing to say. Tantie face set up and she say, "I look like an old fool to you, chile? I know all yuh children were going to come check on de river. But I didn't know you'd be waiting for Ligahoo."

"Tantie, who's Ligahoo?" I asked, feeling a tiny bit scared in case Ligahoo was someone like the soucouyant.

"We not waiting for anybody," said Cedric, who is always truthful.

"Chile, shhh," Tantie said and put a finger to her lips. "Ligahoo not a *anybody*. If he hear you talking so, I don't know what could happen. Last time Ligahoo get vex he cause a flood worse than de madness on de first day of Carnival."

Tantie wrung her hands and then she picked up the hem of her dress and bent down to wipe her face. "I can feel Ligahoo right here," she said.

"Where?" I asked.

"Down there," Tantie said, pointing to the brown rushing water.

"Tantie, ain't nobody down there," said Cedric, peering over the edge.

Tantie closed her eyes and shook her head. "I see all yuh never meet up with Ligahoo before. Or maybe all yuh did and didn't know him."

"What he look like?" I asked.

Tantie smiled a mysterious smile. "Ligahoo," she said, "can look like anything he wants."

Then she began walking away from the riverbank. We followed behind her because Tantie had that look on her face that means a story coming.

"Near here," she started, "there lives a man who knows more than anyone else. He knows how to cure bellyaches. He knows how to put goat mouth on people just by saying their name, so then something bad happens to them. He even know how to tell de river what to do. That man is de one we call Ligahoo."

"How does he tell de river what to do?" whispered Susan.

Tantie laughed. Then her face got serious. "We must be very respectful," she said. "Ligahoo has power over many things. When Ligahoo was a young man just learning about his powers, this island had so much confusion. Nobody knew what Ligahoo would do next. One night all streetlights went out and de whole place in darkness till morning. Another time, de island shook like crazy and trees and lampposts fell down. And another time, Ligahoo get vex 'cause we didn't want to make him King of the Carnival, so he make a storm rage over de place for three days with rain and thunder and lightning. Nobody dare go out in de street to jump up, so Carnival cancel that year. That was when we realize that Ligahoo mean business. After that ain't nobody so much as stick out a big toe against him.

"Ligahoo is de one that set up this six-months rain, six-months dry plan. And is he self say that we cahn come down to de river during rainy season."

Tantie smiled then like the story finish, but I knew my cousins were wondering the same thing I was. So I asked Tantie, "Why Ligahoo don't want nobody to see de river?"

"Because," she answered, "de river is Ligahoo's home in de rainy season. De scary thing about Ligahoo is that he can change his shape to be any animal he wants. His favorite is de fish, so every year he spends six months being a fish in de river. And he don't like people to come down to his home to look for him. When they do, he get so mad he spit and spit till de river flood."

"That's how de floods start, Tantie? From Ligahoo's spitting?" Avril asked.

"That's how," Tantie said, and she sighed real soft.

Avril, Cedric, Susan, and I looked at each other and shook our heads. It didn't seem as if anyone could spit enough to make a whole river flood. Tantie must be read our minds 'cause she say, "When fish spit, is a whole lot of water coming from their mouths. Not like if *you* spit."

We figure Tantie know what she talking about, but I'd seen fish before, and I never saw one spit.

Just then, Tantie turned around to say something else, but she just stared and pointed back toward the river. Before we could turn around she shouted, "Oh no, all yuh close your eyes. Close them quick."

"Why, Tantie?" we asked, getting scared because of the look on her face.

"Is Ligahoo! He changing shape. He coming out de river. Close your eyes, I say!"

Avril, Cedric, and Susan closed their eyes fast. Susan shouted, "Tantie, Ligahoo coming? He coming, Tantie?"

"Hush, chile, let me deal with him," Tantie said. "I know him long time. Just don' look."

The last thing I see before I close my eyes was Tantie put her two hands on her hips and square her feet like she mean business.

Then I heard Tantie talking words I couldn't understand. It sounded like magic to me. I just held Susan's and Avril's hands tight and didn't dare open my eyes.

When Tantie finally say that Ligahoo gone back to the river, Avril, Cedric, Susan, and I opened our eyes and ran home fast like a pack of mongoose was on our heels. That was the last time we went down to the river during the rainy season.

Although sometimes we climb up on the roof and look at the river from up there. Tantie say Ligahoo can't see us there but we should still be careful. And if we see a big fish rising up from the river, we must close our eyes and turn in the other direction. That way Ligahoo won't think we looking at him.

If Your Right Hand Itches

Willie Louise Martin McNear

I pray every night, I work hard, and I help my friends and neighbors. I also don't walk under ladders. I'm not superstitious, just cautious. I have always told my children and grandchildren to believe in God, get a good education, do the best you can do, and knock on wood every now and then. I'm not superstitious, and I don't talk fire or nothing like that; however, some of these folks around here used to say that Sally Mae could "talk fire" because she was still in her mama's womb when her daddy was killed. "Talking fire" meant that if a person was in a fire or burned badly, then Sally Mae could talk the fire or the pain out of the wound. I don't know how true it is. I never saw anybody do it. We used to laugh at that kind of talk when we, my sisters and I, were young. Of course we didn't laugh in front of my mother or grandmother. We didn't dare tell them that we didn't believe in those sayings. If you drop your dish cloth, that meant that somebody was coming. My oldest sister never did drop her dish cloth, 'cause she didn't want anybody coming to the house. If a child's nose bled, a midwife would put a string around a pair of scissors or a set of keys and drop them down the child's back. Now that seemed to work. As I got older I would hear my mother's voice inside my head every time I saw a black cat. If you see a cat, any kind of cat, and if it crosses your path, you are to stop, walk backward ten paces, and make an X with your right foot in front of you and spit on the X. I never did that. My sisters and I would do it as a children's game. I'm not superstitious. I'm well educated and very religious, but I will say this, if you dream about fish, somebody in your family is pregnant. Now that is the truth! I'll tell you something else, too. Don't ever put two spoons in the same cup. That's really bad. My mother used to tell us that all the time, and that is the one thing I won't do even now. It means a death in the family or the death of a friend. Those two are real. All that other stuff is just plain old-timey superstitions. Of course, if your right hand itches, you're going to shake hands with a stranger, and if you left hand itches, you're going to receive some money.

Depending on what neck of the woods you are from, your right hand itching might mean something else. Caroliese I. Fink Reed collected these sayings:

If your right hand itches, you'll get money; but if your left hand itches, you'll get a letter.

Put a box of salt in a new home before you move in, and you'll have good luck.

Clip your hair on the new moon, and it will grow.

If your foot itches under the bottom, you will travel soon.

If the tail of your dress turns up, you will get a new one.

If your nose itches, someone will come to your house.

If your right eye jumps, you will become happy about something; if your left eye jumps, you will become angry about something.

Don't let anyone touch your feet with a broom while sweeping or you will go to jail.

Don't put shoes under the bed; you'll dream all the time.

When you want somebody to leave your house, put a broom behind the door.

Do not wash clothes on the first day of the year.

A leftover cut onion in your house will cause a fuss.

If you stump your foot, turn around three times or you will have bad luck.

If you dream about losing your teeth, there will be a death in the family.

It is bad luck to walk in one shoe.

Hang a horseshoe over your door, and you will have good luck.

Removing the Veil

Caroliese I. Frink Reed

Have you ever heard the expression "born with a veil over the face"? What does it mean to be "born with a veil over the face"?

In the African-American community it has special significance. In the physical world, the "veil" is a caul or membrane that covers the baby's face at birth. This person will be endowed with a special spiritual intuitiveness that allows him or her to "see" what cannot be seen with the naked eye, to "know" what cannot be known through normal observation, and sometimes "hear" what others cannot hear. The person "born with a veil over the face" has been given a special gift of communication with the ancestral spirits.

But what if this person is not sensitive enough or spiritually endowed to manage the gift? In hospital delivery rooms or birthing rooms the physical veil is removed by doctors or nurses. But how is the "spiritual veil" removed? When pregnant women were primarily attended by midwives, the mother was told that her child was "born with a veil over the face." But how does a family know now if the child has been given a special gift?

My brother Cecil was born January 23, 1953, in Brewster Hospital, Jacksonville, Florida. My parents, Neal and Catherine Frink, brought him home to Fernandina Beach shortly after. But in the tradition of the extended African-American family, Cecil spent many days and nights with Mama Nora and PaPa Russel, our great-aunt and uncle and also his godparents.

As Cecil grew into a toddler, Mama Nora began observing that Cecil would become anxious, frightened, and sometimes cry for no apparent reason. These occurrences would happen day or night with alarming frequency. My mother said sometimes he would wake at night crying and say something was in the corner of the room. Mama Nora felt he was "seeing something." She told my mother that he was born with a veil over his face and that she was going to remove it.

Mama Nora had a large kitchen with two stoves—wood and gas. As my mother sat in the kitchen around midday and watched, this is what happened:

As the sun streamed through the large window at the back of the kitchen, Mama Nora took a large cast-iron frying pan and placed about two large tablespoons of Crisco shortening in it. She turned the fire on under the gas burner and watched until the shortening became very, very hot. She picked Cecil up and held him close to her apron-covered bosom. She then turned him in her arms and made him face the frying pan with the hot grease. She held him tightly and passed his face over the pan quickly but determinedly, making sure he saw his reflection in the hot grease and also making sure there was a shadow cast in the grease.

The spiritual veil was removed.

I am told that midwives used to collect the membrane from the newborns and sell them to sea captains. The sea captains valued these birthly treasures. They would put them on the bow of the ship just inside the window. This would enable them to see through the storm, fog, and bad weather.

Were you "born with a veil over the face"?

The Liar's Contest

Ed Shockley

This play was inspired by my belief that the complexity of Afro-American storytelling was not appreciated largely because it was an oral tradition. I was searching for a vehicle to demonstrate the poetic and literary merits of our traditions. I chose the Faustian myth (man against the devil) because of its long history in world literature. The fact that this story has been told repeatedly hopefully focuses attention on the cultural peculiarities of my rendition, that is, the storytelling. Also, by including "Old Bill" with Henry and John I can contrast an educated, linear, logical storytelling style with the metaphor-laden African-influenced contructs that are characteristic of many Black American tales.

I relied heavily on Zora Neale Hurston's *Mules and Men* and various works by Julius Lester. Naturally I also drew heavily on my Yorktown, Virginia, roots, but then they are in every character I pen from south of the Mason-Dixon line. The challenge was to acquaint myself with the variations in storytelling styles. The "dozens," for example, means direct verbal attack in urban African culture but can be a marvelous verbal sparring in its rural manifestation, as in Henry's ill-fated first attempt at bettering Beale. These little lies are significantly different from the myth that Henry spins explaining why the sun rises in the East and sets in the West. This story is wider in scope than most; it utilizes different verbal devices, employs an element of truth at its center, and even allows room for literary references (the most extreme being Velicovski's *World in Collision* which suggests the *imagery of* "oceans washing up over the land and changing places").

Ultimately *The Liar's Contest* attempts to chronicle the meeting of two cultures. Beale is urbane and European. He talks of Don Juan and theology. He deceives with his stories in the tradition of the "forked tongue." Henry, by contrast, is rural and American. His tales are morally coded lessons at best and, equally as often, just innovative verbal scats. His lies are not to be believed but rather to be appreciated. They are therefore laden with metaphor, wit, and horse sense. They are distant cousins of ancient tales told around fires in a long deforested West African bush. And if there's more to say, then I'll save it for tomorrow.

(Beale uncovers the four of diamonds.)

      JOHN
I knew it!
      HENRY
It ain't possible!
      JOHN
I knew it!

HENRY

How could you . . .

JOHN

From the first minute I eyeballed this drifter I knew he was up to something.

HENRY

Shut up, John.

JOHN

The hell you say. Listenin' to you's what got me into this mess.

HENRY

Listenin' to me?

JOHN

Tellin' me they's no way to lose.

HENRY

If you had read the card right . . .

JOHN

I did read the card right.

HENRY

You couldn't have.

BEALE

It is quite possible that he did read it correctly, Henry.

HENRY

You tellin' me you pulled a cheat?

BEALE

You ain't cheatin' till you caught.

JOHN

What have we done?

HENRY

We just won ourselves a wagon full of money.

JOHN

What you fixin' to do?

HENRY

I'm fixin' to cut me a cheat.

JOHN

You don't understand yet, do you?

HENRY

I understand that there's two thousand dollars on the table, a shikker in my hand, no sheriff, and nair a witness.

JOHN

Don't you realize who he is and what we've done?

HENRY

He's some Yankee cardshark, and we done got ourselves softchair tickets outta here.

JOHN

He's the Devil, and we done lost our souls to him.

HENRY

When I'm through cuttin', he won't have a soul his own self.
(Henry starts for Beale. Magical effect.)

HENRY (continued)

I done bit off a hog's portion this time for sure.

BEALE

Indeed you have, Henry.

JOHN

It ain't fair.

BEALE

Fair is a word that you will soon forget. And now I must go.

HENRY

What's your hurry?

BEALE

My job here is complete.

HENRY

Couldn't we work something out?

BEALE

Such as?

HENRY

I heard you was a sportin' man.

BEALE

I have already won your souls; what have you to wager?

HENRY

There must be somethin' else that you want.

BEALE

I can think of nothin' . . .

HENRY

Come on, give a guy a break.

BEALE

. . . except . . .

HENRY

I like the sound of that. Go on.

BEALE

Perhaps your lives.
(John tries to exit)

HENRY

Where you skootin' to, John?

JOHN

Anywhere away from here. You done lost my soul, now you fittin' to git me killed.

HENRY

Sit back down here, loggerhead, and think for a minute.

JOHN

I don't want to think 'cause when I think I remember, and when I remember I feel like a blamed fool for lettin' you gamble away my soul.

HENRY

All right, I pulled a short straw.

JOHN

That's so undersaid it's almost a lie.

HENRY

All right, but what's done is done, and unless we win our souls back, then what good is our life anyway?

JOHN

I must be crazy as a hoot owl at high noon.

HENRY

Why?

JOHN

'Cause you sound like you talkin' sense.

HENRY

Don't worry, John, we gonna get out of this hog trough yet.

JOHN

What's there to worry about? I just lost my soul, and now I'm only tryin' to gamble away my life, too? What's the worry?

HENRY

Okay, Bill, you got a deal. Our lives against our immortal souls.

BEALE

Five-card stud?

HENRY

Naw.

BEALE

Draw?

HENRY

No cards. You worked some magic on 'em last time, and you could do it again.

BEALE

What shall it be then?

HENRY

Hold on to your pitchfork. . . . Lyin'.

JOHN

What?

HENRY

When I was too young to even count fingers, my granmomma used to say that I could lie to beat the Devil. Well, now we gonna find out 'cause we gonna have us a lyin' contest.

JOHN

I know you crazy now.

HENRY

Any other kind of game he could hoodoo, but he can't touch what comes out of my head.

JOHN

Pass me that coondick bottle.

HENRY

What for? You don't drink.

JOHN

Now's as good a time to start as any.

HENRY

What do you say, Bill? I heard tell you was the pappy of a lie, or was that all just beangas?

BEALE

How would we recognize the best lie?

HENRY

You can feel it! I know 'cause I been lyin' all my life. Like the time me and Joe Johnson got into a round of the uglies. He said, "I knew a man once was so ugly he could stop a clock." And I said him right back, "I knew a man once was so ugly the clock would run backwards." Now I had the leg up, but Joe Johnson ain't one quick to call uncle so he tried me again. "I knowed a gal so homely she bring tears to your eyes." But I come right back, "They got a gal over in Tennessee so homely she make you wish for blind." Then Joe tried one he'd been savin' up: "Looky here," says he, "I seen a Buckra boy so 'figured till rainwater wouldn't fall on his face." But see, I had been holdin', too, so I shot back fast as a barnfire: "Hell, that ain't nothin', Joe. Why, we got a geezer right here in black mountain who got to cover his face with a sheet and a pillow just so sleep can sneak up on him." See what I'm sayin'? It's clean as a barber shave.

BEALE

This may well prove worth the bother. We shall have a contest of lies. The winner shall have life, the loser death and damnation. And you, my friend, shall be the judge.

JOHN

Why me?

BEALE

Because you lack the wherewithal to lie.

JOHN

Give me that bottle again.

BEALE

The one who tells the greatest lie claims the prize.

HENRY

'Greed. Now, what we gonna lie on?

BEALE

The choice is yours.

JOHN

I'm gettin' that feelin' again.

HENRY

John, they ain't a man alive can beat me lyin'.

JOHN

But this ain't no man.

HENRY

You ever heard of the dozens, Bill?

BEALE

I believe so.

HENRY

Well, the dozens is like little lyin'. Take hard times, for example. Now, if I was to tell you times is so hard that yesterday I saw a chicken eating scrambled eggs, what would you say?

BEALE

Perhaps that in the same field I observed a late-night worm eating an early bird.

HENRY

And if I was to say that that weren't nothin' 'cause I knew a bobcat once to catch and eat his own shadow, what might you say then?

BEALE

I might say that I knew a hog once who started at his own squiggly tail and ate himself right up to his head, then swallowed his tongue and died.

JOHN

I got that feelin'.

HENRY

Well, you just forget about your feelings 'cause I ain't never lost at lyin', and I ain't about to start now. I was just testin' Bill out. We ain't gonna do the dozens nohow.

JOHN

Whatever you do, it'd better be awful special cause old Bill here been lyin' since before man fell.

HENRY

The story I'm 'bout to tell is awful special. It goes all the way back to the third day of creation. I got to go back that far so I can 'splain why the sun rises in the East of the sky and sets in the West. It weren't always so, mind you. In the beginning de sun rose up at the top of the world and set at the bottom. Dat was the way the good Lord intentioned it to be for always. He wanted everybody to rise up at the same hour everywhere so nobody

would get no dichty ways. And everything was goin' puddin' pie till somebody, I won't say who, put the idea into the slickheads that they could pull
short shift just by movin' the sun from the top on over to the far side of the
world. So the slacks got hatchets and log saws and went to workin' fiercer
than they ever had before nair since. Over in the oakwood they was,
choppin' an' sawin' an' hammerin' nails till by setsun they had made them
a great big old wood bat. And they all gathered together at one end and
grunted that long wood all the way up into the air till it reached right past
the rising moon. Then, just as Mister Sun was about to shut his eyes for a
night's sleep, that bat whopped him upside the head and sent him flyin'
across the sky till he ended up standin' over Africa in de East, too disjointed
to move. So the heat started burnin' down without relief. It dried up all the
trees and water and turned the dirt to sand. Got so hot finally till the people
started to burn. That's when the moon got scared and figured somethin'
had to be done. So she flew way out into space, picked up speed, then
slammed head-on into the earth. The oceans washed up over the lands and
changed places. Mountains fell and valleys rose up into the air high as
eagles headin' home to nest. And that old moon huffed and puffed till the
earth started turnin' real slow so the sun didn't burn quite so long over
China as it had over Africa and the people there ain't get so black nair their
hair so kinky dry. And as the earth picked up speed, dat sun only singed
the Indian and barely warmed the white man. And that's why we all is the
color that we is and why the sun rise East then set West. And if that ain't
the truth, they's a hole in the roof.

BEALE

That is quite a lie, Henry.

HENRY

Thank you.

BEALE

Don't you agree, John?

JOHN

Best I ever heard, and I done had my hair cut every two weeks since Hector
was a pup.

HENRY

I wasn't braggin' on myself when I told you 'bout my lyin', John.

JOHN

Looks not.

HENRY

Well, Bill, what you got to say?

BEALE

There is nothing as colorful as that in my repertorie.

JOHN

Then you give us back our souls?

BEALE

It appears that I must.

JOHN

Great day in the morning! You did it, Henry; you lyin' son of a gun.

BEALE

But for amusement's sake let me tell you a simple story.

JOHN

Say all you want. Hell, I got a lifetime to listen.

HENRY

Don't drop your guard, John.

JOHN

What? What you mumblin', Henry?

HENRY

Nothin'. Pass me the bottle.

JOHN

Go ahead, Bill.

BEALE

There once was a man named Juan, a magnificent sinner who lived a life of excess from beginning to end and died by the gun of a vengeful husband whose wife Juan had driven to madness.

JOHN

Nice guy.

BEALE

As wretched a specimen as any who had ever lived without a day's repentance. Consigned to hell in the minds of men, and indeed he was, in death, made my ward. For three hundred years unmarked by season or sunlight, he suffered the torments until one day he felt that his debt had been paid and asked forgiveness.

JOHN

From who?

BEALE

From the Lord.

JOHN

What Lord?

BEALE

In heaven.

JOHN

But he was in hell.

BEALE

He had no concern for that fact. Though he had long been dead and damned, Juan believed in a forgiving Lord and repented before him from his place beside the fires of hell. How he came to this belief I do not know, else I might have prevented it. Anyway, he did, and his call was answered, his sins forgiven, and now he dwells in the other kingdom.

JOHN

You mean to tell me he got saved after he died?

HENRY

Careful, John.

JOHN

Of course! Why didn't I think of it?

HENRY

Stop talkin', John.

JOHN

You and your liar's contest. You think you're so blamed smart. Risking our lives when all we had to do was beg Jesus to wash us.

HENRY

Close your trap, John.

JOHN

I'm wise to you, Henry. You just don't like me callin' your wood.

HENRY

There wasn't no Juan. No damned soul repentin'.

JOHN

Didn't you hear what he just said?

HENRY

He's lyin', John.

JOHN

What do you mean, lyin'?

HENRY

It was a story.

JOHN

A story?

HENRY

Just like mine, and you fell for it.

JOHN

You mean we ain't won back our souls?

HENRY

No.

JOHN

And we can't be saved like Juan was?

HENRY

All a lie, John, and you bit all the way up to the float. That's why he made you judge.

JOHN

Jesus.

HENRY

It's too late for Jesus.

JOHN
What we gonna do?

HENRY
We gonna burn in hell, looks like.

JOHN
Ain't you got no more lies?

HENRY
I got more lies than a hound got teeth. That ain't the problem.

JOHN
What's the problem then?

HENRY
I ain't sure I got nothin' better than that one he just schooled you wit'.

JOHN
Didn't you tell me that you was the best liar this side of sunrise?

HENRY
I know what I told you, but Bill here lies different than nobody I know.

BEALE
Do you concede?

HENRY
If that means call uncle, I must confess I'm mighty near.

JOHN
Uh uh! You ain't throwin' down my life without a scrap.

HENRY
I do got one more story to tell.

JOHN
Let's hear it then.

Brother Anancy and Brother Tiger

Charlene Welcome Hollis

I was born in Honduras, a country in Central America connected to Guatemala, El Salvador, and Nicaragua. Most Hondurans have Spanish and Indian ancestors, and some also have African ancestors. Most of the Black Hondurans live on the Bay Islands. My great grandfather, John Nelson, sold salt from the ocean so his son John, my grandfather, could go to college in New Orleans. This was in 1890. He majored in agriculture. He returned to Honduras and bought two hundred acres of land. Grandfather Nelson was appointed attorney judge for the Bay Islands. He was a brilliant man. He wrote a will that was so well written it became a popular tourist attraction. People come from all over to Tegucigalpa, the capital of Honduras, to read his will where it is on public display.

Reading, writing, and storytelling were strong traditions in my family. My godsister often told me stories after church on Sundays about Anancy and his friend Tiger.

Once upon a time Brother Anancy and Brother Tiger went out one night for a walk. "The moonlight is *pre pre* [pretty]," said Brother Anancy.

"You can't speak *propere* [proper]," said Brother Tiger.

"You *nara* [neither]," said Brother Anancy.

"Sssh. Did you hear something?" said Brother Tiger.

"It sounds like a baby."

"You're right," said Brother Tiger.

Brother Anancy said, "Should we go and see?"

Brother Tiger said, "It might be a ghost!"

"Ghost! The moonlight is too bright for ghosts to be seen. You look first," said Brother Anancy.

"Why don't you look first!"

They went into the bush. "There he is. It is a baby," shouted Brother Tiger.

"Let's pick him up," said Brother Anancy.

"Okay, you pick him up."

"No, you pick him up."

So Brother Tiger picked up the baby, and they started walking, heading back to town.

"You think baby hungry?" said Brother Anancy.

"Let's get him some johnnycake," said Brother Tiger.

"He might not like it."

"But Baby has to eat!"

They keep walking toward town. Brother Tiger stops and says, "Brother Anancy, this baby's getting heavy."

"Let me help carry him." They continued walking until Brother Anancy said, "This baby is getting heavy."

"Let's put him down," said Brother Tiger. They try to put the baby down, but they can't. Baby's getting heavier. So they pass him from one to the other. Brother Anancy and Brother Tiger both hold Baby, but Baby's getting heavier and heavier. They spend the whole night carrying this heavy child. They can't make it into town. Heavy baby is making them walk slower and slower.

Brother Anancy and Brother Tiger keep trying to put Baby down, but Baby's getting heavier and heavier and the sun will be out soon. Baby starts crying out in a low, deep voice, "Put me back where you take me from. [Louder] Put me back where you take me from! [Louder] PUT ME BACK WHERE YOU TAKE ME FROM!"

Brother Anancy and Brother Tiger turn back and run as fast as they can back to the spot where they found the baby. He disappears into the ground. Brother Anancy said, "That was no baby."

"This is a burial ground, Brother Anancy," said Brother Tiger. "I told you he was a ghost."

"Well," said Brother Anancy, "my mama always told me—don't pick up strangers!"

PART VIII

Now That Takes the Cake

Soul Food and Food Memories

Kosher pickles from a barrel
Pizzas and pig feet
Corn beef on rye
Curly chittlins
Swirly spaghetti
Chicken hot from a deep deep fry
Soul food from behind a counter
Soul food from a corner stall
Soul food from my mama's kitchen
I just love to taste them all

MARY CARTER SMITH, "Soul Food"

Little by little the plantains grow. (Jamaica)

A half loaf is better than no bread. (South Africa)

What's cooking, good looking? (African-American)

A sweet plum might contain a worm. (African-American)

Your eyes are bigger than your stomach. (African-American)

Gravy on my grits. (African-American)

Hard times made even the monkey eat red pepper. (Trinidad)

Sunday Family Dinner

E. J. Stewart

While I was a student in a 101 English class at Queens College in Flushing, New York, twelve years ago, Professor Peter Weiss gave the assignment to write a descriptive paragraph depicting the five senses and reflecting a warm, loving memory. Thus was born Stewart Sunday Family Dinner. The descriptive paragraph of the dinner table and all its fixings has long been lost: the family memory lives on, however, and was resurrected into a full-length short story when I became a professional storyteller.

The scene is a farming community in the eastern part of North Carolina on a hot summer day in the early to middle 1960s. The small wooden three-bedroom house sits nearly a quarter of a mile down a narrow dusty path. Ditch banks overgrowth and tobacco and corn fields obscure much of the view of the main dirt road. The house is perched nearly a foot atop cement blocks. The beautiful brown collie mutt sleeps underneath the left edge of the front porch. Sitting on the porch are two teenage boys. The eighteen-year-old is picking an old guitar. The thirteen-year-old is playing with the tabby cat. The screen door opens, and the short, heavyset woman steps onto the porch, looks down at the boys, and says:

"Boys! Get your dusty rumps up off this porch and go build a hot fire around that old black iron wash pot. Then go and kill me about half a dozen chickens. Don't go killing no roosters or none of my laying hens, neither. We want to have fried chicken and not chicken pastry. You boys plenty old enough to know the difference in chickens. I'm not going to keeping y'all. I want y'all to kill me some young, plump pullets. When that's finished, go out in the cornfield and bring me two, three dozen ears of that tender young corn. Make sure that the silk ain't too dry, neither. Don't bring me no hard corn. Then go see how many okras need cutting, and don't forget to check the tomatoes. Don't forget to gather up some potatoes and onions. All you children know to do is play! Do I have to tell y'all everything?"

The good-looking, slightly gray-headed woman called "Mama" started to reenter the house but stopped abruptly. She turned and looked out past the front yard, down the narrow dirt path heading toward the main dirt road. Squinting her eyes, she yelled, "Vic-tor, Vic-tor! Boy, is that you? Put those marbles down and go next door and tell that Joyce she better bring her narrow behind back here and help Brenda pick those butter beans. I send her someplace, and she go and stays like she grown. She know better. The sweet potatoes still got to be grated for the potato pudding—if you'll want a pudding, that is. All this work! Before y'all come back, go to the back field and bring me two or three full-headed cabbages. Vic-tor, boy, did you hear me? Boy! If you don't put those marbles down right now! Don't let me have to come off this here porch after you," she threatened. "Tell that gal I mean for her to get back here right now. She don't want me to have to walk over there to Ms. Bessie after her." *Slam!* went the screen door. Bodies scattered. The Stewart Sunday Family Dinner was under way. However, it was not Sunday. It was Saturday afternoon.

The three-year-old grandson dropped his marbles in the dust and headed toward the house, running as if a thousand haunts were chasing him. He hopped on the porch, skipped through the house, out the back door, around the two-seated outhouse to the wide ditch banks where his short little legs and tiny feet barely touched the wooden plank board that served as a bridge. This was the shortcut he used in pursuit of his sixteen-year-old aunt who had been sent over to the neighbors' more than three hours earlier to borrow a pot. As usual she had decided to visit for a while.

The thirteen-year-old started gathering twigs to build a hot fire around the old iron wash pot while the eighteen-year-old went into the kitchen to get bread crumbs to lure the ill-witted chickens into slaughter. Oh, he knew they were ill-witted. He always marveled at how stupid chickens were. Nearly every week he would use bread as bait to catch Sunday dinner chickens, and every time the chickens would run up to him and peck at the bread, getting just close enough for him to grab them and wring their little necks. What a sad ritual, he thought. Didn't any of the chickens hear their friends and relatives squackling, and didn't they see them flapping and hopping around headless until they moved no more? Didn't they see them being dipped in boiling water? What did they think plucking feathers out of their skin meant? "Dumb, dumb chickens," he mumbled as he stepped out the back door of the sparsely furnished house heading toward the unsuspecting chickens, clucking all the way.

Victor and his aunts Joyce and Brenda returned to the kitchen with six cabbages and a bushel of butter beans. Victor forgot how many cabbages he was supposed to bring, but being from a large family, he knew more was better. In the kitchen they joined the other children who were eagerly awaiting the licking of the infamous cake batter pans.

Before nightfall the chickens were killed, plucked, gutted, singed, cleaned, seasoned, and readied for frying. Corn was shucked, silked, washed, decobbed, and prepared for the pot. Butter beans would be shelled, washed, and prepared for cooking in fatback meat or leftover grease. Okras, tomatoes, cabbages, sweet potatoes, ice potatoes, onions, and so forth, would be readied for cooking.

In the midst of the preparations the tall, thin, handsome man called Daddy would return home with a string of fish so fresh that when you looked at them they would almost jump off the line. We would have a fish dinner and drink lemonade or soda. Daddy would pass around the penny candies and cookies (sometimes ice cream). Afterwards, we would sing hymns. And if the old secondhand television was willing, we watched "Gunsmoke." If not Daddy would spin tall tales of life when he was a youngster. We would sit and listen as he told of life as the youngest of twenty children. We would be giggling with mischief, thinking, There go Daddy telling those tales again about Aunt Mamie, Aunt Minnie, Uncle Tom, Grandaddy Hillery, and the gangs.

Times were hard for sharecroppers in and around Kinston, North Carolina, in the early sixties. Still, we didn't know we were poor.

Sunday morning the family was busy with breakfast, putting finishing touches on Sunday dinner, and rushing to attend Sunday school and church. After church we would only have to warm up the dinner, maybe make a pan of biscuit or corn bread. Within minutes the house would be pungent with the aroma of golden brown fried chicken, potato salad, small okras floating in the butter beans, fried corn swimming in butter, a slab of fresh-fried pork atop the boiled cabbage, sliced cucumbers, sliced tomatoes, a tomato bread pudding, two platters filled with chocolate and pineapple cake, and a big dish of sweet potato pudding. Ice water, Kool-aid, or ice teas topped off the meal. If Besty said so, there would be a bucket of fresh cool milk.

By the time we were ready to eat, just as Daddy was saying the dinner prayer, a neighbor's child or two or three would come a-calling, maybe some adults. They would sort of linger around the porch until Daddy would hear and say. "What y'all doing out there? You might as well get in the house." They would pile in, and Mama would round up more chairs or the children would fill their plates and sit around on the front-room floor partaking of the goodies. Daddy would say the dinner prayer, and as we raised our forks to eat, Mama would say, *"Wait!"* Then each person would say a Bible verse. We would all begin to eat, and Daddy would partake of his favorite ritual, a spelling bee. You see, my father believed that you shouldn't eat anything you couldn't spell. Me and my brother didn't eat biscuits for a long time, and I was about grown before I tasted spaghetti.

Finally, we could enjoy the Stewart Sunday Family Dinner. Believe me the dinner was worth the wait and anticipation. Although it was summertime, the living wasn't that easy. Tobacco wasn't selling too good. Cotton was no longer "king." The world was discovering mixed blends and polyester.

There were no fancy cars, new furniture, or fine clothes (most times no TV or radio). Still, this sixteen-year-old would sit around trying to boss the little ones while beaming with pride. Oh, yes, pride. For I knew what the neighbor who came a-calling around dinnertime knew. As long as Tyson

Stewart had chickens, vegetable gardens, hogs, meat in the smokehouse, mason jars in the pantry, molasses in the can, dry beans and peas on the shelf—they knew as long as my daddy had anything at all, no child would go hungry.

I was proud indeed that our house was the house people could come to when hard times were hardest, for my father taught his children that in the leanest of times, when the dinner bell rings, there's always room for one more.

Anancy and the Plantains

Pamela Miller Facey

I was born in Manchester, Jamaica. As a child I remember when the whole family would gather at my grandmother's house. When I say the whole family, I'm talking about the extended family: parents, sisters and brothers, aunts, uncles, and my cousins coming together on Saturdays. The women and the older girls would have a fish fry late at night. They would cook snapper. The boys played marbles and made things such as catapults (slingshots) and calbans (bamboo traps). I was one of the young ones, so we played on the barbecue in the moonlight. The barbecue was a large concrete area used for drying pimentoes and coffee seeds. We sang and played games such as:

> There's a brown girl in the ring, tra-la-la-la-la.
> There's a brown girl in the ring, tra-la-la-la-la.
> There's a brown girl in the ring, tra-la-la-la-la.
> For she likes sugar and I like plum.

> Then you skip across the ocean, tra-la-la-la-la.
> Then you skip across the ocean, tra-la-la-la-la.
> Then you skip across the ocean, tra-la-la-la-la.
> For she likes sugar and I like plum.

> Then show me your motion, tra-la-la-la-la.
> Then show me your motion, tra-la-la-la-la.
> Then show me your motion, tra-la-la-la-la.
> For she likes sugar, and I like plum.

Everybody gathered around and listened to my grandmother tell a story, especially if it was about Anancy the spider.

Anancy, his wife, and three children lived in a Jamaican village called Breadnut Hill. Anancy was known far and wide as a "big ginal" or "samfie man" because he conned people to make himself a living and was lazy and shiftless.

Once there was a great famine in Breadnut Hill. During a long drought all the crops had dried up, and most people had little or nothing to eat. Anancy was in the worst position because, having done no work all year, he had nothing saved for hard times.

One morning after he and his family had eaten the last slice of bread in the house, Anancy set out for the village square to see if he could "samfie" someone out of money or food. On the way he met a neighbor taking plantains to the market for sale. Knowing Anancy's career of trickery and ginalship, to avoid much conversation, the neighbor offered Anancy four plantains, one each for his wife and three children, but none for the lazy father, who gladly accepted the gifts.

Anancy ran home with glee to his starving family. He quickly baked the plantains and had his family take their places at the table. As he placed a plantain in each plate, he repeated dolefully, "One for you, none for me. One for you, none for me," until the four plates were served. The crafty Anancy sat with his head bowed before his empty plate.

He protested fiercely (acting like he didn't want any) as his wife offered him half of her plantain, but finally he accepted. Then each child, in turn, gave Anancy half of his plantain.

When they eventually began to eat, the wily Anancy had two plantains, while his family had only one-half each. Once again Anancy had won by his wits.

Fried Green Plantain

One large green plantain
Cooking oil
A pinch of salt, to taste

Cut plantain in half and remove skin. Heat about 2 tablespoons of cooking oil in skillet. Split plantain halves in two. Apply a little salt, place in skillet, and cover. Let plantains brown on both sides. Remove and place on paper towels. Roll plantains flat with a rolling pin. Place in a skillet and fry lightly until browned. Serve with ackee (a fruit that looks like a mango) and codfish or fried fish.

Pulling That Yam

Baba M. Jamal Koram, the Story Man

Martha Ruff, a dear friend and one of my favorite storytellers, gave me the idea to do the story about "picking those yams." I saw her tell a story about pulling a big turnip, based on a Russian folktale. I enjoyed the repetition and pattern in the story. I decided to use yams mixed with African rhythms and drums, and the audience responded "right on cue" when I called out certain parts. The story has become so popular that just about every storyteller has added it to his or her repertoire.

It was one of those days on the farm. The cat wasn't getting along with the dog. The rats weren't getting along with the mice. The cow and the pig were smacking each other in the face with their tails. And the horse and donkey were throwing up their fists at one another. And Ma Jefferson and Pa Jefferson were sitting on the front porch rocking back and forth, back and forth, and Pa said to Ma: "Ma, you mean to tell me that I got to go and pick those yams today?"

And Ma said, "Yeah, Pa, you got to pick those yams today."

And Pa said, "But Ma, I don't feel like getting that basket and picking those yams out there in that hot sun today."

And Ma said, "Now look at me, Pa. You better pick those yams today!"

So Pa Jefferson got up, got the basket, and went out into the field, and he began:

(Drums.)

> Picking those yams and putting them in the basket.
> Picking those yams and putting them in the basket.

(Drums beat faster.)
STORYTELLER: Help me out now!
AUDIENCE: Picking those yams and putting them in the basket.
STORYTELLER AND AUDIENCE: Picking those yams and putting them in the basket. Picking those yams and putting them in the basket. Picking those yams and putting them in the basket.

Now Pa Jefferson came across this great big yam. *Oo—ew! Oo—ew! It was a big yam!* He started pulling that yam and pulling that yam, but he couldn't pull it out, so he hollered, "Hey, Ma, come over here and help me pull this yam out of the ground."

Ma came running over, running over, running over, and Ma grabbed Pa around the waist, and they started *pu——lling that yam!*

(Drums.)

STORYTELLER: And Pa was pulling that yam.
AUDIENCE: Oh yeah!

STORYTELLER: And Ma was pulling that yam.
AUDIENCE: Oh yeah!
STORYTELLER: And Pa was pulling that yam.
AUDIENCE: Oh yeah!
STORYTELLER: And Ma was pulling that yam.
AUDIENCE: Oh yeah!
STORYTELLER: And Ma stopped and said—
(loudly)
STORYTELLER AND AUDIENCE: O—ew! *This is hard work!*

When Ma said that, the cat and the dog heard her, and they came running over, running over, running over. And the cat grabbed Ma around the waist. And the dog grabbed the cat around the waist, and they started *pu——lling that yam!*

(Drums.)
STORYTELLER: And Pa was pulling that yam.
AUDIENCE: Oh yeah!
STORYTELLER: And Ma was pulling that yam.
AUDIENCE: Oh yeah!
STORYTELLER: And the cat was pulling that yam.
AUDIENCE: Oh yeah!
STORYTELLER: And the dog was pulling that yam.
AUDIENCE: Oh yeah!
STORYTELLER: And the dog stopped and said—
STORYTELLER AND AUDIENCE: Ou—ew *Ruff! Ruff! This is hard work!*

The rats and the mice heard him, and they came scurrying over, scurrying over, scurrying over. And the mice grabbed the dog around the waist. And the rats grabbed the mice around the waist, and they started *pu——lling that yam!*

(Drums.)
STORYTELLER: And Pa was pulling that yam.
AUDIENCE: Oh yeah!
STORYTELLER: And Ma was pulling that yam.
AUDIENCE: Oh yeah!
STORYTELLER: And the cat was pulling that yam.
AUDIENCE: Oh yeah!
STORYTELLER: And the dog was pulling that yam.
AUDIENCE: Oh yeah!
STORYTELLER: And the mice were pulling that yam.
AUDIENCE: Oh yeah!

STORYTELLER: And the rats were pulling that yam.

AUDIENCE: Oh yeah!

STORYTELLER: And the rats stopped and said—

STORYTELLER AND AUDIENCE: *Ou—ew! Squeeeeee—ak! Squeeeeeee—ak!*
This is hard work!

The horse and donkey heard them, and they came galloping over, galloping over, galloping over. And the donkey grabbed the rats around the waist. And the horse grabbed the donkey around the waist, and they were *Pu——lling that yam!*

(Drums.)

STORYTELLER: And Pa was pulling that yam.

AUDIENCE: Oh yeah!

STORYTELLER: And Ma was pulling that yam.

AUDIENCE: Oh yeah!

STORYTELLER: And the cat was pulling that yam.

AUDIENCE: Oh yeah!

STORYTELLER: And the dog was pulling that yam.

AUDIENCE: Oh yeah!

STORYTELLER: And the mice were pulling that yam.

AUDIENCE: Oh yeah!

STORYTELLER: And the rats were pulling that yam.

AUDIENCE: Oh yeah!

STORYTELLER: And the donkey was pulling that yam.

AUDIENCE: Oh yeah!

STORYTELLER: And the horse was pulling that yam.

AUDIENCE: Oh yeah!

STORYTELLER: And the horse stopped and said—

STORYTELLER AND AUDIENCE: *Ou——ew! Heeeeeeeeeeeeeeee! This is Hard*
work!

The cow and the pig heard him, and they came scampering over, scampering over, scampering over. And the pig grabbed the horse around the waist. And you know, sometimes pigs have those curly tails. Well, the cow grabbed that pig's tail with his hoof and stre-t-ched it and stre—t—ched it and threw that long tail over his shoulder, and then he grabbed the pig around the waist and they were PU——LLING THAT YAM!

(Drums.)

STORYTELLER: And Pa was pulling that yam.

AUDIENCE: Oh yeah!

STORYTELLER: And Ma was pulling that yam.

AUDIENCE: Oh yeah!
STORYTELLER: And the cat was pulling that yam.
AUDIENCE: Oh yeah!
STORYTELLER: And the dog was pulling that yam.
AUDIENCE: Oh yeah!
STORYTELLER: And the mice were pulling that yam.
AUDIENCE: Oh yeah!
STORYTELLER: And the rats were pulling that yam.
AUDIENCE: Oh yeah!
STORYTELLER: And the donkey was pulling that yam.
AUDIENCE: Oh yeah!
STORYTELLER: And the horse was pulling that yam.
AUDIENCE: Oh yeah!
STORYTELLER: And the pig was pulling that yam.
AUDIENCE: Oh yeah!
STORYTELLER: And the cow was pulling that yam.
AUDIENCE: Oh yeah!

And they pulled, and they pulled, and they pulled, and *bam!* That yam came out of the ground. Ma and Pa rolled it back to the house, and Ma cut it up into little pieces. Ma cooked yam soufflé, yam fries, yam croissants, yam pies, yam cakes, and yam hotdogs.

Let me tell you something. This happened about five years ago. Now last night I went over to Ma and Pa Jefferson's house, and do you know what they gave me? *Yam pizzas!*

Oh yeah!

Brownlocks and the Bears

Vickey Lusk

There were eleven of us in the family. We each had our favorite story. Brownlocks was my favorite. My father told us the story to remind us of the importance of obeying our parents and having pride in who we were. Nowadays I tell the story to my children to remind them of the same values. When I make spoon bread, I use my mother's recipe but I never write it down, and there is one ingredient I always forget. So I call her three thousand miles away (from Pennsylvania to California) and ask her for the recipe.

Many years ago a proud Bear family lived in the middle of a forest near where a stream ran with clear, crisp water. In the Bear family there was a very big Poppa Bear, a middle-sized Momma Bear, and two small Baby Bears.

The Bears all lived in a beautiful cabin with a blue door and blue shutters. Around midday in the early weeks of fall, Momma Bear cooked a large deep dish of delicious spoon bread. She scooped a big dish for Poppa Bear, a small dish each for Baby Bears, and finally a middle-sized dish for herself. Poppa Bear tasted his spoon bread and with a loud voice said, "THIS SPOON BREAD IS TOO HOT!"

Momma Bear put on her loveliest bonnet and said, "Let's go out for a while until the spoon bread cools."

Not long afterward a little girl walking beside the clear, cool stream saw the beautiful cabin with the blue door and blue shutters. She was called "Brownlocks" because of her beautiful brown hair.

Now all the animals loved Brownlocks. The birds in the air sang to please her. The willow trees stretched out their long, thin leaves to capture her attention.

Brownlocks loved animals and flowers and was so excited about a wild flower called "The Pink Ladies Slipper" that she had wandered too far downstream. She had not listened to her Mother when she was told to stay near their home. Brownlocks was tired, hungry, and slightly chilled when she reached the cabin and knocked on the door.

"Is . . . is anyone home?" she asked in a timid voice. But there was no answer. She knocked again. On the third knock, the door opened slowly. Brownlocks walked in, still chilled from the brisk fall air. Once inside the cabin she noticed four rocking chairs sitting by a warm fire. She tried to sit in the big-sized chair, but it was too high. She tried the middle-sized chair, but there were too many pillows in it. "Well," said Brownlocks. "I will sit in the smallest chair." And she did. But the chair began to crack, and then it broke into small pieces because it wasn't strong enough for Brownlocks.

Brownlocks saw four bowls on the table. A big bowl, a middle-sized bowl, and two very small bowls, all of them filled with spoon bread. The big bowl was too spicy, the middle-sized bowl was too sweet, but the small bowls were just perfect. It was so good that she ate it all!

Brownlocks was *so* tired after her bowl of spoon bread. She said, "I will find a nice place to take a short nap." She walked slowly up the lovely staircase. Upstairs she found four "sleigh beds": one very big bed, a middle-sized bed, and two very small beds. Brownlocks wanted to try the very big bed, but it was too high to climb up to. She tried the middle-sized bed, but when she sat on it, the springs squeaked.

"Oh, no!" she cried, "this bed is too noisy! Well, I will try this very small bed. Yes, this bed is perfect! Oh," she said, yawning, "I'm really tired." Before she could stop yawning, Brownlocks fell fast asleep.

Just about that time, the Bear family thought their spoon bread would be ready to eat. At the cabin door, Momma looked up while taking off her bonnet and cried, "The door, it's open!"

Poppa Bear rushed in past Momma and roared. "Arrrrrrgh! Momma! Somebody's been sitting in my chair!"

Momma Bear said, "Mercy me, Poppa! Somebody's been sitting in my chair, too."

The two baby bears cried, "Oh, no, somebody's broken our chairs!"

Poppa Bear said, "I'll make you another chair." Poppa Bear roared, "Arrrrrrrrrgh! Momma! Somebody has tasted my spoon bread."

Mamma Bear looked at her bowl and said, "Someone's been tasting my spoon bread."

The two baby bears looked at their empty bowls and cried, "Momma! Poppa! Someone has eaten *all* our spoon bread!"

"Now, now," Poppa said, "Momma will make us some more. Stand aside." Poppa Bear rushed upstairs, looked at his bed, and roared, "Momma, somebody's been near my bed!"

Then Momma said, "Somebody's been in my bed!"

The two baby bears cried, "Somebody is in our bed sleeping *right now!*"

The loud cries of the baby bears awakened Brownlocks. She looked up and saw the bears standing over her and became very frightened. She sat up and begged, "Oh, please, please, don't eat me! I'm sorry I broke your chair, ate your spoon bread, and slept in your bed! I was just so hungry, and tired, too. Oh, please, please, don't eat me. I'm really very sorry."

Brownlocks slid slowly out of the little bed and ran as fast as she could down the stairs, out the door, and away from the cottage as fast as her legs would carry her.

The Bear family, so struck by her beauty, just stared at Brownlocks because they had never seen such a beautiful little girl!

Brownlocks went back home. Happy to be there she never disobeyed her mom again!

The Bear family looked out over the forest for weeks hoping to see Brownlocks. The baby bears told the story and told the story of that beautiful little girl with lovely brown hair, but they never saw her again.

Spoon Bread

2 cups self-rising cornmeal
1 tablespoon hominy grits
1 tablespoon all-purpose flour
$1/4$ teaspoon ground cinnamon
$1/3$ cup buttermilk

$^1/_3$ cup warm water
3 tablespoons honey or sugar (If sugar is used, blend with dry
    ingredients)
$^1/_2$ stick butter, melted

Preheat oven to 350°F. Mix dry ingredients together. Add remaining
ingredients and blend. Batter will appear slightly lumpy. Allow batter
to sit 2 to 3 minutes. Pour batter into a deep pre-oiled dish (only
half-full). Bake 25 to 30 minutes, or until golden brown. Serve warm.

The Little Cornbread Man

Baba M. Jamal Koram, the Story Man

When I was a little boy, I remember my schoolteacher saying one day, "Today,
class, I am going to tell you a story about the little gingerbread boy." "Gingerbread Boy!" I said. "What's that?" I thought it was when you pour ginger ale
on top of some biscuits or something. My classmates laughed because they
knew who the gingerbread boy was. She told the story, and I liked it. But you
know, I love cornbread better. Ha, ha, ha, hee, hee, hee!

There once was a husband and a wife. It was the husband's birthday, so
the wife said, "I'm gonna make my honey something good for his birthday.
Now what can I make him? He loves that cornbread. I'm going to make him
a little cornbread man."

The wife pulled out her mixing bowls, baking pans, flour, cornmeal, and
whatnot, and she started making that little cornbread man. She made a little
cornbread head, a little cornbread body, two little cornbread arms, and she
put three fingers at the end of each arm. She made two little cornbread
legs, and she put three toes at the end of each leg. Then she took some
California raisins and made two little eyes. She took some chocolate chips
and made three buttons. She took two more of those chocolate chips and
made two ears. She took a carrot stick and made a nose. She took a licorice
stick and made a nice little smiley mouth, and she said, "My, my, my,
that's a handsome little cornbread man." She turned on the oven, put the
cornbread man in it, and that cornbread man started cooking.

Well, in a little while her husband came home. "Baby, what's that I smell
that smells so good in here?"

"You don't smell nothin'. Go on back outside now, Honey."

"Naw, Baby." He sniffs. "I smell something good in here." The husband
went over to the oven and he looked in, and there he saw the little cornbread man lying all stretched out in the pan. The husband said, "Aw shucks,

my wife has made me a little cornbread man. Come on, Baby, let's eat it now! He looks too good lying in that pan like that."

As soon as the husband said that, the little cornbread man sat straight up in the pan and said,

> "Ha, ha, ha! Hee, hee, hee!
> You may be fast, but you can't catch me.
> Run, run as fast as you can
> You can't catch me. I'm the little co——rnbread man."

He slapped his hands together. Phe—ow! Boogie-a-dee-boogie! That little cornbread man was gone out the door. "Come on, Baby," said the husband. "We got to catch him." They ran after him, but they couldn't catch him. He was too fast.

A horse was sitting by the side of the road. He jumped up when he saw the cornbread man. "Heeeeeeeeee, hey, little cornbread man. Slow down! You look too good to be running around like that."

"Oh, no. I outran the husband and his wife, and I can outrun you, too."

Now let me hear you. (The audience joins in.)

> "Ha, ha, ha! Hee, hee, hee!
> You may be fast, but you can't catch me.
> Run, run as fast as you can.
> You can't catch me. I'm the little co——rnbread man."

Pheow! Boogie-a-dee-boogie-a-dee! That little cornbread man was gone. The horse ran gal-lop-a-dee, gal-lop-a-dee. He couldn't catch him because he was too fast.

The cornbread man ran until he came across a great big elephant sitting by the side of the road. "Ruuuuumph! Hey, little cornbread man, slow down. You look too good to be running around like that."

"Oh, no. I outran the husband and his wife, I outran the horse, and I can outrun you, too."

Now what did he say?

> "Ha, ha, ha! Hee, hee, hee!
> You may be fast, but you can't catch me.
> Run, run as fast as you can.
> You can't catch me. I'm the little co——rnbread man.

Phe—ow! Boogie-a-dee-boogie-a-dee! That little cornbread man was gone. The elephant put one foot up, ba-lop, ba-lop. He put one foot down, ba-lop, ba-lop. He couldn't catch him because he was too fast.

This went on and on and on. The little cornbread man outran a little boy. He outran a little girl. He outran the antelope. He outran the leopard. He even gave the lion a run for his money.

Well, later on that day the fox was standing in his kitchen. He had just finished cooking a great big meal. "Humph, I got some black-eyed peas simmering in the pot. I got a crock of collard greens swimming in pot liquor [juice of the greens]. But something is missing." The cornbread man came running around the corner. The fox looked out his window and said, "Heeey! Little cornbread man, come here. Let me talk to ya."

"Oh, no sireee! I outran the husband and his wife. I outran the horse. I outran the elephant. I outran the little boy, little girl, an antelope, a leopard, and a lion. I outran all of them, and I can outrun you, too—"

The fox put his hand behind his ears. "Are you talking to me, boy? Come here. I can't hear a word you're saying. Talk to me." The cornbread man got so mad, he strutted right up to that fox's face and said, "Ha, ha, ha. Hee, hee, hee—"

The fox grabbed those two little cornbread legs. He put one down in them collard greens and one down in them black-eyed peas. He started munching. "Uuuum hummm, this is some good cornbread!"

The cornbread man was still talking: "You may be fast—"

The fox grabbed those two little cornbread arms. He put one down in them collard greens and one down in them black-eyed peas. He started munching. "Scrum-didee-scrum-didee, this sho is delicious."

And that little cornbread man was still running his mouth: "But you can't catch me—"

The fox grabbed that cornbread body, and those chocolate chips melted in his mouth. "Yum, yum, yum. Whoever cook this, can cook!"

And that cornbread man's mouth was still running "Run, run as fast as you can—"

The fox grabbed that cornbread head with those chocolate chip ears, those California raisin eyes, carrot stick nose, and licorice stick mouth, and put it into his mouth.

And do you know that cornbread man was still talking (munching, talking, and chewing with your mouth full of food): "Youcan'tstopmeI'mthelittleco——rnbreadman."

The fox ate all them black-eyed peas and them collard greens, and drank all that pot liquor to wash down that cornbread. Which just goes to show you: No matter how fast you are, there's always someone faster than you!

Cornbread Sticks

1¼ cups yellow cornmeal
¾ cup all-purpose flour

1 tablespoon sugar
2¹/₂ teaspoons baking powder
¹/₂ teaspoon salt
1¹/₄ cups low-fat buttermilk
1 egg, lightly beaten
2 tablespoons Crisco (butter-flavored)

Heat oven to 425°F. Grease two cornstick pans. Place in oven to warm. Combine cornmeal, flour, sugar, baking powder, and salt in a medium bowl. Combine buttermilk, egg, and Crisco. Add to dry ingredients and stir until moistened. Spoon batter into cornstick pans. Bake 15 to 18 minutes. Makes 14 cornsticks.

Sorry, I couldn't find a recipe for a cornbread man. If you know one, pass it on.

Philadelphia, Mrs. Greenstein, and Terrapins

Vertamae Smart-Grosvenor

Our house on Erdman Street in Philadelphia had a coal stove in each room except for the kerosene heater in the living room which we rarely used. Erdman Street was on a dead end. We paid seventeen dollars a month and used to be behind in the rent (most of the time). We had two rooms on each floor, three stories. The third floor was all mine. I used to play school and give plays. I was actor, director and audience all in one. In the winter we all slept in the bedroom on the second floor 'cause we didn't have enough money to make fires in all the stoves. My mother used to get a basket of wood and a bag of coal from Mr. Daniels. They was twenty-five cents apiece and mostly we got credit and would pay him when the eagle flew on Saturday. We had two stoves in our kitchen—one gas, one wood. When they cut off our gas, we could still take care of business on the wood stove. Sometimes Mama would cook on the wood stove anyhow. She said it seem like the food just taste better on it.

During those days, I was one of those "key" children. I wore the house key around my neck. After school I' d let myself in and I wasn't supposed to let nobody in. Nobody. If God came I was supposed to say that "my mother is not home, and I'm not allowed to have any company." God never came by, but some kids would try to get me to come out. Sometimes I'd sneak out and old Mr. Simmons would always tell my mother who would tell my father who would knock the hell out of me. I did not like Mr. Simmons.

Miss Tinnie, Mr. Simmons' daughter, was the only one on the block who had a telephone and she let us get calls there, but we had to pay her ten cents when we received a call. Being an only child and being alone in the house gave me lots of time to experiment with cooking. Since nobody could come in and I couldn't come out, I had lots of time. I used the time to raise hell. I got into a lot of things and lots of trouble. Once I gave a dance concert in the backyard. We had a portable gramophone and a few race records. Most of the records were gospel. I danced to them. Sure enough Mr. Simmons told my mother that I was committing blasphemy dancing to church music.

Another time I set the house on fire. It was my birthday, but it was a Thursday and we didn't have any money. My mother said to wait until Saturday but I just couldn't. I wanted it when it was. I had no faith. Because the same thing had happened at Christmas. They told me that Santa would come on the Saturday after Christmas but the rent was due on that Saturday and he didn't come at all. So I had lost the faith and I wanted my party then.

Mama brought me some pink-coated cupcakes and she went back to work for Mrs. Krader on Ridge Avenue. I was supposed to go back to school at 12:45. Took me five minutes to find some birthday candles for the cupcakes and have a party of one. I put the candles in the window and started singing "Happy Birthday" to me. As I was singing a gentle spring breeze was blowing, and the shade danced over the candles and caught on fire. In a minute the shade was blazing. I started spitting on the fire but nothing happened, so I ran to get a bucket of water. I couldn't find the bucket. Then I remembered that Mama had loaned it to Mrs. Wilson so I ran downstairs to get a big pot but all the pots were soaking in the sink. My mother would be so tired when she came home from cleaning up Mrs. Krader's house all day that she didn't feel like scrubbing pots and she didn't trust me to clean them well enough. If she found a speck of grease on a glass or a dish, she scalded it three more times. We had no hot water and had to heat water for dishes and baths. Yet Mother washed the dishes twice and scalded them three times.

Anyhow I ran back downstairs to get the icebox pan under the icebox— it was always full 'cause I'd forget to empty it—and ran to throw it on the fire, but by this time the whole window frame was on fire and rapidly spreading across the wall. Good old Mr. Simmons had already called the fire department and I heard them coming up the street. I decided that there wasn't nothing I could do for the fire so I dropped the basin, shut the bedroom door and ran up to the third floor and got under the bed. The firemen put out the fire. It was the first time they had been on our street in four years and all the neighbors were there. One of them ran to Ridge Avenue to tell my mother that the house was on fire and her daughter was missing.

Mama almost had a heart attack cause that was always her biggest fear while I was alone. Mama came running. Meantime I'm still under the bed. I heard the firemen ask, "Where is the bad little boy that did it?" The neighbors said, "It weren't no bad boy, it was that child." The firemen said, "Well if we find that child she will go to jail." I was trembling and worried cause I was late getting back to school. My teacher was real mean. Old lady Eaton would make you stay after school for thirty minutes if you were late coming from lunch, and my father would raise hell if I was late coming from school. I was uptight. Just then my mother arrived and came directly to the third floor to look for me. She hugged and kissed me and asked me to explain what happened. I was a real bright reader, and I had read that a doctor said that children had traumas. I thought a trauma was something that could happen to make you speechless and hysterical. So I tried that. I stuttered and stammered and got hysterical and cried and said that I couldn't remember because I had a traumatic experience. My mother gave me two minutes to recover my memory or else receive an emotional experience on my behind. She had never read that book. I recovered in thirty seconds.

After that all the neighbors used to ask me when I was going to have another birthday party, and to be sure to invite them. They said, "This time that child has taken the rag off the bush." Oddly enough that was my only fire. It is odd too, cause I used to cook all the time. Poor Mother never complained about all the food I messed up.

Mrs. Greenstein (of late my mother's former employer) now lives in Miami, and during one of her visits to Philadelphia, she visited my mother. She sent this recipe via my mother to me.

Sponge Cake

1 box Duncan Hines Yellow Cake Mix
1 3-ounce box lemon-flavor Jell-O
²⁄₃ cup milk
²⁄₃ cup Wesson oil
4 eggs

Preheat oven to 325°F. Combine all ingredients except the eggs. Beat the eggs, add to the other ingredients, and mix. Bake 50 minutes.

My best friend on Erdman Street was Shirley Daniels. We had a good time growing up together. We used to get in more trouble than even my daughters Kali and Chandra do now. We were that far out.

Miss Lessie (Shirley's mother) could really make good banana pudding.

Banana Pudding

1 pint milk
3 eggs (separated)
1 cup sugar
1 teaspoon vanilla extract
pinch of salt
5 bananas
2 dozen vanilla wafers

Make a custard with the sweet milk, egg yolks, and sugar. Add the vanilla and salt. Slice the bananas and place alternately in a baking dish with the vanilla wafers and the custard. Beat the whites of the eggs into a meringue, add a bit of sugar, and place on top of the bananas and custard. Bake in a moderate oven 12 minutes.

My daddy belonged to the 20th-Century Motorcycle Club. I remember *Harley-Davidson. Chrome. Shiny Chrome. Real Fox Tails Hanging from Each Handle Bar. Leather Jackets with Shiny Studs.*
One time he had one with a sidecar. That was the one I liked the best. Nobody else on our street had one and no other eight-year-old could go flying through the air like me. I loved to ride fast. I would scream, "Faster! Faster!" and my father would laugh and say we are already doing 250. Are you trying to get to outer space? I guess I was cause now I go there with Sun Ra and his Solar Myth Science Orkestra.
Some Sundays the whole 20th-Century Motorcycle Club would go over to New Jersey to Lawnside to party. Everything was closed on Sundays in Pennsylvania because of the blue laws. They could cook some barbecue in Lawnside. Lord give me strength, it was out of this world. This is the closest I could come to it.

Lawnside Barbecue Sauce

1 bulb garlic, diced
1 cup sugar
3 whole lemons (use juice and rind)
2 cups chopped onions
1 bottle tomato catsup
1 bottle Louisiana Hot Sauce
little bit dry mustard
some vinegar
some water
some butter

Mix all ingredients together well and cook until it looks like it wants to come to a boil, but don't let it. Use on ribs—pork or beef. That's up to you.

Mary McLeod Bethune: Memories

Dorothy L. Height

Mary McLeod Bethune was born in 1875 and died in 1955. She was a great leader, a great educator, and a great cook. She founded Bethune-Cookman College in Florida. Prior to her death, she dictated to an editor of *Ebony* magazine her "Last Will and Testament," known as the Bethune Legacy. The last paragraph of this treasured work will forever be a bell ringing in our ears:

> *I leave you, finally, a responsibility to our young people.* The world around us really belongs to youth, for youth will take over its future management. Our children must never lose their zeal for building a better world. They must not be discouraged from aspiring toward greatness, for they are to be the leaders of tomorrow. Nor must they forget that the masses of our people are still underprivileged, ill-housed, impoverished and victimized by discrimination. We have a powerful potential in our youth, and we must have the courage to change old ideas and practices so that we may direct their power toward good ends.

Mary McLeod Bethune was a great inspiration to Dorothy L. Height, who carries on in her footsteps. Through anecdotes and recipes Dr. Height fondly remembers her.

Once when Mrs. Bethune was traveling on a train during the dark days of segregation, she was seated in what we called "Lower 13" where any Black traveler with a first-class ticket was placed. It was also a time when there were those who would not call a Black woman missus or address her with respect. The conductor came to her and asked, "Auntie, can you make good biscuits?" Mrs. Bethune said that she looked up and replied, "I am an advisor to President Roosevelt. I am the founder of a four-year accredited college. I am an organizer of women. I am the organizer and founder of the National Council of Negro Women. I am considered a leader among women. And, I make good biscuits."

When our founder, Mary McLeod Bethune, needed money in 1904 to keep the school doors open, she baked and sold sweet potato pies. This is her recipe.

MARY MCLEOD BETHUNE'S SWEET POTATO PIE

Filling:

9 medium sweet potatoes or yams (about 4 pounds)
1 cup (2 sticks) butter or margarine, softened
$\frac{1}{2}$ cup granulated sugar
$\frac{1}{2}$ cup firmly packed brown sugar
$\frac{1}{2}$ teaspoon salt
$\frac{1}{4}$ teaspoon nutmeg
3 eggs, well beaten
2 cups milk
1 tablespoon vanilla extract

Crust:

3 unbaked 9-inch single crusts

Heat oven to 350°F.
For filling, boil sweet potatoes until tender. Peel and mash.
Combine butter, granulated sugar, brown sugar, salt, and nutmeg in a large bowl. Beat at medium speed of an electric mixer until creamy. Beat in the sweet potatoes until well mixed. Beat in the eggs. Beat in the milk and vanilla slowly.
Spoon into three unbaked pie shells, using about 4 cups of filling per shell.
Bake 50 to 60 minutes, or until set. Cool to room temperature before serving. Store in refrigerator.

Variation:

Bake filling as a pudding in a greased $12\frac{1}{2}$ x $8\frac{1}{2}$ x $\frac{3}{4}$-inch glass baking dish. Bake for about 1 hour, or until set. Sprinkle with 2 cups miniature marshmallows. Return to oven 5 to 10 minutes, or until marshmallows are lightly browned.

Watching Uncle Shocum Eat

Margaret Ramsey

When I want to see a picture from my childhood, I don't have to turn to old black-and-white photographs in a scrapbook. I just look at my paintings. I tell stories about my Georgia childhood, and I paint those stories. One painting I did, a scene in which children are making ice cream, came about from a favorite memory. I remember my sister's free labor deal. My mother would always make a churn of ice cream on Sundays during the summers, and my sister would invite all the neighbor kids to help with the churning. But the harder it got to turn the crank, the crankier and more difficult my sister got. She would get upset and pick fights with the kids until our momma would make them all go home. I loved it, because it meant there was more ice cream for us to eat.

Another painting I did was "Watching Uncle Shocum Eat."

When I hear the lonesome sound of the freight train as it passes nearby, blowing its whistle and rattling its box cars as if to say, "Hear me out, I'm passing through," I think of my uncle Shocum. Uncle Shocum, whose real name was Emanuel, worked at a railroad shop in South Georgia. He was a hardworking man who worked six days a week as a mechanic's helper. He was tall, dark, and handsome, a very mannerable type of man.

He walked to work early every morning and returned home late in the evening. He lived in the old home place with his sister, who was my mother, her husband, and all of the children. My uncle Bum, whose real name was Willie, and his wife also lived with us in the old house. Sometimes Uncle Jack would live with us when he returned home riding his bicycle from his hobo trips and told us all about his adventures on the fright train.

The old house was tired and weak because it had been standing there weathering the storms and bearing the hot and cold weather since the late 1800s. It would shake, rattle, and roll with the least pressure from Mr. Wind. Now when the icy cold winds of winter came to visit us, the old house would freeze up and bring shivers to all her inhabitants. It would get so cold inside, the dipper would freeze in the water bucket, which sat on a shelf against the wall in the kitchen between the back door and a shuttered window on the back side of the house.

When the rains came, we were entertained by the orchestrated musical sounds of the raindrops falling through the leaking roof and tapping on the bottom of pans and empty syrup cans, in concert. Sometimes it seemed to rain as much inside the old house as it fell outside. We played house inside as it rained by peeling and cutting up some of the sweet figs and serving them in our tin tea sets. We would pick a panful of figs before the rain came.

The old house on the home place was surrounded by an assortment of nut- and fruit-bearing trees. There were six pecan trees of assorted nuts, from the hard shell to the soft paper shell, which were easy to crack. There were plum trees, fig trees, chinaberry trees, where robins built their nests, and a large harbor of sweet scuppernongs, not to mention the sugarcane

patches. There were winter and summer gardens of vegetables and straw-
berries on each side of the house. We shared the playing space in the yard
with the chickens and a well flowing with cool, clear water. The well was
shaded by a large mulberry tree, which was a haven for small insects
and silk worms. Of course there was a cover over the well, and later a
hand-operated pump was added.

My uncle Shocum, being a railroad man, wore blue denim overalls, bro-
gan shoes, and a blue railroad cap to work every day. The railroad shop
provided a commissary for its workers, and my uncle Shocum was one of
its best customers. He allowed us to go shopping at the commissary whenever my mother needed something for the house. On Fridays Uncle Shocum
brought home the groceries to last the family for a week. He would come
home carrying on his back two big croaker sacks full of groceries. He knew
exactly what we needed. It was a joyous time to see him coming down the
sandy path leading to our house. The path was bordered on one side by
rows of palmetto fans and on the other side by crops of huckleberry bushes.
We knew he was bringing plenty of goodies for all as he approached the
house. He would enter the house, set the bags down, and we would unload
each bag, making joyful noises over the contents lining the kitchen table.
There were fish, chicken, and other meats; vegetables, canned fruits, cookies, nuts, candies, bread, potatoes, and other foods.

The kitchen was the highlight of the house because we knew it would
not be too long before we would enjoy a scrumptious meal. The table,
which was covered with a pink-covered oilcloth, sat right in the middle of
the floor near the wall that divided the kitchen from the bedroom. There
was a chair and a bench at the table. My mother was a good cook, and
when Uncle Shocum brought the groceries, she would immediately begin
to prepare the evening meal. She cooked on an old wood-burning stove
that stood on red bricks to make it level on a wooden floor that was not
level. The stove had a compartment on top that was called a warmer. Heat
coming from the top of the stove would keep food placed in that element
warm for serving. Located on the side of the stove was a part called the
reservoir for keeping water hot. We used this hot water mostly for washing
dishes. The stove pipe ran through the shingled roof to the outside, and as
children we loved to stand out and watch the smoke billow upward into
the sky. Hanging against the kitchen walls were pots, pans, skillets made
of cast iron, rolling pins, and bread bowls used by my mother, the cook.
There in the kitchen was a cabinet called the "safe," where dishes, tin pans,
tin cups, and water glasses were kept. The knives, spoons and forks were
kept in the drawer of the safe. To prevent breakage of dishes and glasses,
we were fed in tin pans and used tin cups instead of glassware. The grocery
box was also part of the kitchen furniture. It was built by my mother to act
as a pantry.

Now, as the aroma of the cooking food filled the air, our taste buds shifted to a mode of fine-tuning. We waited with anticipation, but we knew this was the beginning of a long wait before the defining moment presented itself. Like Old Faithful, this was a Friday evening ritual. At this very moment Uncle Shocum was in the back room taking his bath in a tin tub, getting ready to get dressed up to go visiting with his friend. Sometimes he would give up his blue denim overalls for a seersucker outfit and replace his blue railroad cap with a straw brim. Most times he would change into a new set of blue denim overalls.

Mama's frying the fish in the kitchen, and Bessie Smith is belting out a song on a 78 on the old hand-wound gramophone in the living room. The music blasts loud and clear through the Victorian horn of the machine until the gramophone has to be hand-cranked again. We, the children, are sent out of the kitchen and into the yard to play games. We played Little Sally Walker:

Little Sally Walker sitting in a saucer, rise, Sally, rise. Wipe your weeping eyes. Put your hands on your hips and let your back bone slip. Ah, shake it to the East, ah, shake it to the West. Ah, shake it to the very one that you love the best, Sally, you love the best, Sally, you love the best.

After a line or two of this game, some of us stretched our wings and, like a boomerang, we landed right back in the kitchen and waited for supper to finish cooking. Uncle Shocum would take his place in a chair at the table and get ready to eat his supper. Mama would fix his plate, piling it up with food. His appetite was great, and he was a big eater who took his time and chewed his food well. He closed his eyes as he ate slower and slower and slower. Our taste buds raced with desire to sample the food as we watched Uncle Shocum. We kneeled on the bench at the table watching with excitement, hoping he would hurry up and finish. We were always fed after Uncle Shocum because he was the one who bought most of the food for everyone at home. He was the man of the hour.

When he finally finished eating, it was our time to feast. Our tin pans were filled with food. Like Mrs. Sparrow's tree house family, we filed to the table and sat on the doorsteps on a bench outside near the well and enjoyed the catch of the day. The feast was worth the wait, and sometimes we even went back for seconds or refills. As the years went by, my uncle Shocum got married and moved away to another state. The old house remained with us for many years. Though it stood the forces of the elements, it could not, in later years, endure the works of the fire marshal and the power of the bulldozers as it met its fate in the hands of the urban renewal projects that swept it off its feet and into oblivion. It made way for a metal fence surrounding wild growth of Mother Nature's garden of weeds.

Having the Last Say

One Day...

John Edgar Wideman

One day neither in the past nor in the future, and not at this moment, either, all the people gathered on a high ridge that overlooked the rolling plain of earth, its forests, deserts, rivers unscrolling below them like a painting on parchment. Then the people began speaking, one by one, telling the story of a life—everything seen, heard, and felt by each soul. As the voices dreamed, a vast, bluish mist enveloped the land and the seas below. Nothing was visible. It was as if the solid earth had evaporated. Now there was nothing but the voices and the stories and the mist; and the people were afraid to stop the storytelling and afraid not to stop, because no one knew where the earth had gone.

Finally, when only a few storytellers remained to take a turn, someone shouted: Stop! Enough, enough of this talk! Enough of us have spoken! We must find the earth again!

Suddenly, the mist cleared. Below the people, the earth had changed. It had grown into the shape of the stories they'd told—a shape as wondrous and new and real as the words they'd spoken. But it was also a world unfinished, because not all the stories had been told.

Some say that death and evil entered the world because some of the people had no chance to speak. Some say that the world would be worse than it is if all the stories had been told. Some say that there are no more stories to tell. Some believe that untold stories are the only ones of value and we are lost when they are lost. Some are certain that the storytelling never stops; and this is one more story, and the earth always lies under its blanket of mist being born.

Praise Poem

Amiri Baraka/LeRoi Jones

Walk through life
beautiful more than anything
stand in the sunlight
walk through life
love all the things
that make you strong, be lovers, be anything
for all the people of
earth.

You have brothers
you love each other, change up
and look at the world
now, it's
ours, take it slow
we've long time, a long way
to go,

We have
each other, and the
world,
don't be sorry
walk on out through sunlight life, and know
we're on the go
for love
to open
our lives
to walk
tasting the sunshine
of life.

Praise Poem

Maya Angelou

Here on the pulse of this new day
You may have the grace to look up and out
And into your sister's eyes,
And into your brother's face,
Your country,
And say simply
Very simply
With hope—
Good morning.

Biographical Notes

CHINUA ACHEBE is from eastern Nigeria, where he is president of the town council. His first novel, *Things Fall Apart,* a modern classic, sold over three million copies. His other works include *No Longer at Ease, A Man of the People, Arrow of God, Anthills of the Savannah,* and *Hopes and Impediments: Selected Essays.*

CHARLOTTE BLAKE ALSTON is a storyteller born and currently living in Philadelphia, Pennsylvania. She is president of Keepers of the Culture and festival director for the 1996 National Festival of Black Storytelling. She was awarded a Pew Fellowship in 1994.

DAVID A. ANDERSON/SANKOFA is the author of the award-winning book *The Origin of Life on Earth.* His other works include *The Rebellion of Humans* and *Kwanzaa: An Everyday Resource and Instructional Guide.* His oral and written stories punctuate themes across the span of human history.

MAYA ANGELOU, beloved poet, read her historic poem "On the Pulse of Morning" at the inauguration of President Clinton. Her works include her best-selling autobiography *I Know Why the Caged Bird Sings, And Still I Rise, I Shall Not Be Moved,* and *Wouldn't Take Nothing for My Journey Now,* a collection of essays.

JAMES BALDWIN, international literary figure, wrote over twenty books, including *Go Tell It on the Mountain, Notes of a Native Son, Giovanni's Room, Nobody Knows My Name, Another Country, The Fire Next Time, Blues For Mister Charlie* (a play), *Tell Me How Long the Train's Been Gone, The Amen Corner* (a play), *If Beale Street Could Talk, Little Man* (a children's book), and *Just Above My Head.* He was awarded the Legion of Honor of France in 1986.

TONI CADE BAMBARA is the author of *Gorilla, My Love; The Salt Eaters; The Black Woman; Tales and Short Stories for Black Folk;* and *The Sea Birds Are Still Alive.* She is based in Philadelphia, Pennsylvania, where she conducts scriptwriting workshops and assists community organizations in using video as an instrument for social change at the Scribe Video Center. She is currently scripting a biography on W. E. B. Dubois.

AMIRI BARAKA (LeRoi Jones), at the forefront of the Black Arts Movement during the sixties and seventies, is the author of over twenty plays, two jazz operas, seven nonfiction books, and thirteen volumes of poetry. He and his wife Amina coauthored *Confirmation.* His other works include *Blues People, Black Music, Home, Tales, The System of Dante's Hell, The Dead Lecturer, Preface to a Twenty-Volume Suicide Note,* and plays "Dutchman," "Slave Ship," "The Baptism," and "The Toilet."

ARTHENIA J. BATES (Millican), the author of *Seeds Beneath the Snow,* was born in Sumter, South Carolina, where she currently lives. Her other works include "The Deity Nodded" (part of the Literature of the World anthology) and *Hand on the Throttle: In the Light of*

Lionel Lee, Sr., volume I, "Holding On," and vol II, "Holding Out." She taught for a number of years at Southern State in Baton Rouge, Louisiana.

DERRICK BELL is a visiting professor at New York University Law School. He was dismissed by Harvard from his position as Weld Professor of Law for refusing to end his two-year leave protesting the absence of minority women on the law faculty. He is the author of *And We Are Not Saved, Faces at the Bottom of the Well,* and *Confronting Authority.*

MARY MCLEOD BETHUNE, born to former slave parents, was the fifteenth of seventeen children. She became one of the most important forces of her time in the emerging struggle for civil rights. She founded Bethune-Cookman College and The National Council of Negro Women. She was the first woman to be honored with a monument in a public park in the nation's capital. Her famous "Last Will and Testament" is known as *The Bethune Legacy.*

JANICE BISHOP "JAWARA" is a Philadelphia public school teacher. She is cofounder of Keepers of the Culture. She has received several grants and fellowships for her work in Gullah and Geechee history, and she is listed in *Who's Who in American Education.*

CHARLES L. BLOCKSON is the curator of the Charles L. Blockson Afro-American Collection, which contains more than 80,000 artifacts at Temple University in Philadelphia, Pennsylvania. He is the author of *The Underground Railroad in Pennsylvania, The Underground Railroad: First Person Narratives, The Hippocrene Guide To The Underground Railroad,* and a cover story on the Underground Railroad for *National Geographic.*

GWENDOLYN BROOKS is the first Black American to have received the Pulitzer Prize, for her book of poetry *Annie Allen* in 1949. She is the author of *Selected Poems, The Bean Eaters, A Street in Bronzeville, Bronzeville Boys and Girls, Maud Martha,* and *Blacks.* She currently lives in Chicago.

MORTON BROOKS, JR., was born and raised in Richmond, Virginia. He is currently based in Washington, D.C., where he has performed with Back Alley Theater, the Paul Robeson Theater, Spoken Word Poetry Ensemble, Encore Theater, Voices from the Street, and The Nubian League. He has been featured at the National Festival of Black Storytelling.

BROTHER BLUE: See **HUGH MORGAN HILL.**

MARGARET TAYLOR BURROUGHS is a commissioner for the Chicago Park Service. Completely dedicated to cultural and historical organizations, she was a founder of the Museum of Negro History and Art, which became the DuSable Museum of African-American History in Chicago. She was the museum's executive director for a number of years. She is the author of *Jasper the Drummin' Boy, Did You Feed My Cow, What Shall I Tell My Children Who Are Black, Whip Me Whop Me Pudding,* and *Africa, My Africa.*

LEN CABRAL lives in Cranston, Rhode Island, where he is the cofounder of Sidewalk Storytellers. He has been featured at the Smithsonian Institution's Discovery Theater, the National Storytelling Festival, and the National Festival of Black Storytelling.

GUY CARAWAN is a multi-instrumentalist, folk singer, and collector. He, along with his wife Candie, has been based at the Highlander Research and Education Center in Tennessee for more than twenty-five years. They are authors of *Sing for Freedom: The Story of the Civil Rights Movement Through Its Songs* and *Ain't You Got a Right to the Tree of Life?*

WALTER DALLAS, Emmy-nominated director, is the artistic director of Philadelphia's Freedom Theatre. He has directed works on Off-Broadway and regional theaters throughout the U.S.A. He worked with James Baldwin on his last play, *The Welcome Table*.

JULIE DASH wrote and directed the film *Daughters of the Dust,* the first nationally distributed feature by an African-American woman released in the U.S.A. She is the author of the book *Daughters of the Dust; The Making of an African-American Woman's Film*. Other works she has directed include *Lost in the Night* and *Praise House*.

MILES DAVIS, jazz trumpeter and jazz legend, formed one of the greatest musical groups featuring John Coltrane and Cannonball Adderley in the mid-1950s. Known for being a trendsetter and a leader, he helped create the Fusion Movement in the 1960s.

MARTIN B. DUBERMAN is the author of *In White America*. His other works include *Paul Robeson: A Biography, About Time, Cures,* and *Stonewall*.

ADORA L. DUPREE came to the art of storytelling from a family tradition of the spoken word. An ordained minister and creative dramatist, she currently lives in Tennessee. She won the Liar's/Tall Telling Cup at the 1987 National Festival of Black Storytelling.

BABALOSA OBALORUM TEMUJIN EKUNFEA (TEMUJIN THE STORYTELLER) is a Babalosa priest in the Yoruba tradition. Based in Pittsburgh, Pennsylvania, he is an anthropologist, historian, musician, and instrument maker. He is always a favorite at the National Festival of Black Storytelling.

REX ELLIS is the director for the Office of Museum Programs in the Division of Arts and Humanities at the Smithsonian Institution. He formerly directed the Department of African-American Interpretation and Presentations at the Colonial Williamsburg Foundation in Williamsburg, Virginia. He is on the board of directors for the National Storytelling Association

RALPH ELLISON is the author of *Invisible Man,* which is considered one of the greatest novels in world literature. He won the National Book Award in 1952. His other works include *Shadow and Act* and *Going to the Territory*.

PAMELA MILLER FACEY was born in Manchester, Jamaica, and has been residing in Philadelphia, Pennsylvania, since 1990. She collects stories and riddles, many garnered from childhood trips to her grandparents' farm in the interior of Jamaica and from research in Jamaican creole at the University of the West Indies.

ROY FARRAR teaches English at Germantown Friends School in Philadelphia, Pennsylvania, where he also serves as coordinator of multicultural services, advisor, and coach. He has taught in prisons and studied with Sonia Sanchez. He is concerned with self-discovery, empowerment, community, and change.

WILLIAM J. FAULKNER was an ordained minister and author of the popular work *The Days When the Animals Talked: Black-American Folktales and How They Came to Be*. He was president of the Nashville, Tennessee, Branch of the NAACP and dean of the chapel at Fisk University from 1934 to 1953.

HAILE GERIMA, producer, writer, director, and editor, was born in Ethiopia. With the release and success of *Sankofa* and seven feature films, he has earned international acclaim. He is a torchbearer for the independent African and African-American film movement. In 1994 he was selected as one of seven filmmakers to direct a documentary for the BBC Fine Art Series.

GLORIA DAVIS GOODE is a demonstration vocal music teacher at the Masterman School in Philadelphia, Pennsylvania, and the 1993 Pennsylvania Secondary Teacher of the Year. She has published an article, "African-American Women in Nineteenth-Century Nantucket: Wives, Mothers, Modistes, and Visionaries," in *Historic Nantucket*.

ALEX HALEY is the celebrated author of *Roots* and coauthor of *The Autobiography of Malcolm X*. His other works include *Queenie*.

DOROTHY L. HEIGHT is president of the National Council of Negro Women, which sponsors the Black Family Reunion Celebration, a nationwide movement. She was inspired to enter a life of public service after meeting her mentor, Mary McLeod Bethune. For over sixty years she has been a defender of human rights and an advocate for women and their organizations around the world.

HUGH MORGAN HILL, known throughout the world as Brother Blue, is the father of contemporary storytelling in the U.S.A. During the 1960s he developed his free-flowing improvisational style of storytelling using blues, jazz, calypso, and rap rhythms. An ordained minister, he is the official storyteller of Cambridge, Massachusetts.

JARIBU AND NGOMA HILL: see **SERIOUS BIZNESS**.

CHARLENE WELCOME HOLLIS (G. Glenna) was born in Honduras and is a graduate of Queens College in New York, with a master's degree in bilingual education. After eighteen years of teaching she joined her husband Douglas as an owner and operator of a McDonald's restaurant.

DEBBIE WOOD HOLTON, a Southside Chicago native, is assistant professor at DePaul University. She is currently editing a volume of essays and creative work by women who have been influenced by Lorraine Hansberry, entitled *Shared Illuminations: Women's Visions of Lorraine Hansberry and Her Work*.

LANGSTON HUGHES is the poet laureate of African-American people. His first published poem, "The Negro Speaks of Rivers," is recited throughout the world. He was the author of more than thirty-five books, including *The Weary Blues, Dream Keeper, Selected Poems, Panther and the Lash, The Sweet Flypaper of Life, Simple Speaks His Mind, First Book of Africa, The First Book of Jazz, The Big Sea, I Wonder as I Wander,* and *The Book of Negro Folklore* with Arna Bontemps.

LUCY HURSTON is the niece of Zora Neale Hurston. She was born in Brooklyn, New York, and currently lives in Connecticut. As a writer and lecturer she travels throughout the country dispelling the myths about Zora Neale Hurston.

ZORA NEALE HURSTON, a major influence on African-American women writers, was a folklorist, novelist, anthropologist, and dramatist. Her works include *Mules and Men, Their Eyes Were Watching God: A Novel, Jonah's Gourd Vine: A Novel, Tell My Horse: Voodoo and Life in Haiti and Jamaica, Moses: Man of the Mountain, Dust Tracks on a Road,* and *Seraph on the Suwanee.* She collaborated with Langston Hughes on the controversial play *Mule Bone.*

HARRIETTE BIAS INSIGNARES is a professor of communications at Tennessee State University. She was the first African-American storyteller featured at the National Storytelling Festival and the first Black elected to its board of directors. She is the official state poet of Tennessee. A monument was erected in her honor in her hometown of Savannah, Georgia.

JOHN IROAGANACHI is the coauthor of the fable "How the Leopard Got Its Claws."

JAWARA: see **JANICE BISHOP.**

LEROI JONES: see **AMIRI BARAKA.**

LYNN JOSEPH was born and raised in Trinidad. She is the author of *Coconut Kind of Day: Island Poems, A Wave in Her Pocket, Jasmin's Parlor Day,* and *The Mermaid's Twin Sister: Stories from Trinidad.* She lives in New York City.

PAUL KEENS-DOUGLAS was born in Trinidad but spent his early childhood in Grenada. The characters he has created, such as Tanti Merle, Vibert, Slim, Sugar George, and many others, are as familiar to the man in the street as to their next-door neighbor. His works include *When Moon Shine, Tim Tim, Tell me Again, Is Town Say So, Lal Shop, Twice Upon a Time,* and *Tanti at de Oval.* He is popularly known as "Tim Tim."

BABA M. JAMAL KORAM (THE STORY MAN) is the founder of the African-American Storytelling Arts Institute. He was named the Best Storyteller of Baltimore for 1994 by *Baltimore Magazine.* He is an elder of The Griot's Circle and past president of the National Association of Black Storytellers. His works include *When Lions Could Fly* and *Aesop: Tales of Aethiop the African* (two volumes).

MAXINE A. LEGALL grew up in Houston, Texas, listening to the "spin doctors" of her childhood—grandmother, Annie Weber, and brothers Fitzherbert, Charles, and Kenneth —recount everyday events with animation and an endless cast of characters. She is an assistant professor of communications at the University of the District of Columbia (Washington, D.C.) and was co-director of the 1985 National Festival of Black Storytelling in Washington, D.C.

VICKEY LUSK is a storyteller, wife, and mother who uses storytelling as an educational tool in her work and at home. She is the host, creator, and director of "Vickey and Friends," a children's television program that encourages children to share their feelings through art.

ISAAC L. MAEFIELD, wood carver, drummer, poet, and storyteller, was born and currently lives in Philadelphia, Pennsylvania. He conducts workshops throughout the area. He is vice-president of Keepers of the Culture and is a panelist on the Artist-in-Education Committee for the Pennsylvania Council on the Arts.

MALCOLM X, popular name of **EL-HAJJ MALIK EL-SHABAZZ,** was one of the great leaders of African-American people and a cultural icon for young people. He was assassinated on February 21, 1965. A film based on his autobiography was directed by Spike Lee.

MUNAH MAYO lives in Philadelphia, Pennsylvania, where she is employed with Pepper, Hamilton & Scheetz, an international corporate law firm. Born in Liberia, she has lived in most major cities in the world and speaks five languages. What gives her the most fulfillment are her responsibilities as a women's division district leader in the SGI-USA.

ALICE McGILL, born and reared in Scotland Neck, North Carolina, is an international performer of stories, chants, and rhythms seeped in the African diaspora. Widely known for her portrayal of Sojourner Truth, she completed a performance and a gathering-of-stories tour in London and southern Africa, under the auspices of Arts America, in April 1994.

PATRICIA C. McKISSACK is the author of *The Dark-Thirty,* a Caldecott Honor Book, and *Mirandy and Brother Win,* also a Caldecott Honor Book. Her other works include *A Long Hard Journey: The Story of The Pullman Porter* (coauthored with her husband Frederick), *A Million Fish . . . More or Less!, Nettie Jo's Friends,* and *The Royal Kingdoms of Ghana, Mali, and Songhay: Life in Medieval Africa.*

TERRY McMILLAN is the author of the best-selling book *Waiting to Exhale,* soon to be a major motion picture. Her other works include *Mama, Disappearing Acts* and *Breaking Ice: An Anthology of Contemporary American Black Fiction.*

WILLIE LOUISE MARTIN McNEAR was born in McMinnville, Tennessee, and raised in Alcoa, Tennessee, where she is a noted speaker and community leader. She was a schoolteacher for nearly forty years in the Alcoa public schools. In 1982 she received a Distinguished Service Award from the governor of Tennessee. She is the mother of storyteller Linda Goss.

TONI MORRISON, world-acclaimed writer, is the first African-American woman to receive the Nobel Prize for Literature, in 1993. She is the author of *Beloved,* which won a Pulitzer Prize. Her other works include *The Bluest Eye, Sula, Song of Solomon, Tar Baby, Jazz, Playing in the Dark,* and *Race-ing Justice, En-gendering Power.*

SHANTA NURULLAH: see **SHANTA.**

GRACE OGOT was born in Kenya. She worked as a journalist and was a delegate from Kenya to the United Nations. Her works include *The Promise Land, Land Without Thunder, The Other Woman, The Land of Tears,* and *The Graduate.*

TEJUMOLA F. OLOGBONI was director of the 1993 National Festival of Black Storytelling in Milwaukee, Wisconsin. He was the winner of the "Kikombe Cha Acthiope" (Aesop's Cup) at the first Liars/Tall Tellers contest at the 1986 National Festival of Black Storytelling in Chicago, Illinois. He blends the African tradition of call and response with the

African-American rap beats, which makes his audiences jump up and sing along with him.

JOSE PENA is fourteen years old and a student at Central East Middle School in Philadelphia, Pennsylvania. He won second place in the adaptation category for his story "Uglyrella" at the second annual Zora Neale Hurston Storytelling Competition. His other stories include "The Guardian Angel" and "Mother Nature." He is interested in a career in computer programming.

MARGARET RAMSEY is a registered nurse, folk painter, storyteller, and weaver who didn't start painting until she was forty-six. Her paintings have been exhibited throughout her native state of Georgia and are in the permanent collection at the Morris Museum of Art in Augusta, Georgia.

BERNICE JOHNSON REAGON is the artistic director and founder of Sweet Honey in the Rock. She was a member of the Freedom Singers who chronicalized the civil rights movement in song. She is the author of *We'll Understand it Better By and By* and *We Who Believe in Freedom*. A recipient of a MacArthur Fellowship, she is a curator at the Museum of American History at the Smithsonian Institution.

CAROLIESE I. FRINK REED is a mother, librarian, and storyteller all at once, all the time. She grew up in the small town of Fernandina Beach, Florida, on Amelia Island. "My ninety-four-year-old father is a natural storyteller, and if I have any talent for storytelling, it is from him." She is currently the president of the National Association of Black Storytellers.

SONIA SANCHEZ holds the Laura Carnell Chair in English at Temple University in Philadelphia, Pennsylvania. Known for her powerful and dynamic poetry readings, she is the author of thirteen books, including *Homecoming, We a BaddDDD People, Love Poems, I've Been a Woman, A Sound Investment and Other Stories, Homegirls and Handgrenades,* and *Under a Soprano Sky*. She won an American Book Award in 1985.

SERIOUS BIZNESS is the husband and wife team of Jaribu and Ngoma Hill. They write and perform contemporary freedom music. Their music has been heard at labor conferences and rallies; on striking workers' picket lines; at community forums, church group meetings, and colleges. Their albums include *Serious Bizness: For Your Immediate Attention, Serious Bizness: How Many More,* and *Serious Bizness: Storm Warning*.

NTOZAKE SHANGE is a poet, playwright, and novelist. Her Obie Award–winning play *For Colored Girls Who Have Considered Suicide/When the Rainbow is Enuf* was acclaimed for its impact on feminist consciousness. Her other works include *Nappy Edges and Sassafras, A Photograph: A Still Life with Shadows/A Photograph: A Study in Cruelty,* Spell #7, *Betsey Brown, I Live in Music,* and *Lilliane*.

SHANTA is a storyteller, musician, and channel. She co-leads the women's band Samana. Her recordings include *The Adventures of Shedoobee: Searching for the Good Life* and *Light Worker*. She is the owner of Storywiz Records and is on the board of directors of the Women's Self Employment Project. She teaches storytelling at Columbia College in Chicago, Illinois.

ED SHOCKLEY has a master's of fine arts from Temple Univesity in Philadelphia, Pennsylvania. He is the author of three dozen plays. His best-known works are *A Nite in the Life of Bessie Smith, Bobos* (coauthored with James McBride), and the stage adaptation of Mildred Taylor's *Roll of Thunder Hear My Cry.* Awards include the Stephen Sondheim, the Lorraine Hansberry, the American Minority Playwrights' Festival, and the HBO New Writers Project.

VERTAMAE SMART-GROSVENOR, a culinary anthropologist, is the author of *Vibration Cooking or the Travel Notes of a Geechee Girl.* She is the host of two National Public Radio series, "Horizons" and "Seasonings," a food and culture show. She is also a commentator on NPR's "All Things Considered."

ANNA DEAVERE SMITH is an actress and playwright. She is an associate professor of drama at Stanford University. Her work, *Fires in the Mirror,* was awarded a Special Citation Obie and was a finalist for the Pulitzer Prize in Drama. Her other work, *Twilight,* was nominated for a Tony award.

MARY CARTER SMITH is the Official Griot for the state of Maryland and "Mother Griot" and cofounder of In The Tradition: National Festival of Black Storytelling. She is also cofounder and chairperson of the board for the National Association of Black Storytellers. Her likeness is included in the Great Blacks in Wax museum in Baltimore, Maryland. She is the author of *Heart to Heart* and *Town Child,* and coauthor of *The Griot's Cookbook.*

WOLE SOYINKA, winner of the 1986 Nobel Prize in Literature, is one of Africa's most prolific and influential writers. His works include *The Road, The Lion and the Jewel, Kongi's Harvest, Madmen and Specialists, The Trials of Brother Jero, The Strong Breed,* and *Death and the King's Horsemen.* His autobiography is entitled *Ake: The Years of Childhood.*

DARLENE STERLING is the grand prize winner of the first Zora Neale Hurston Storytelling Competition. She was fourteen years old when she wrote "Frozen in Time," the story that won the prize. Trained under Alice Ross at the John Wanamaker Middle School in Philadelphia, Pennsylvania, she is an honor student at the Bodine High School for International Affairs.

E. J. STEWART was born in Eastern, North Carolina, to sharecropping parents. She inherited the gifts of writing and oral expression from her mother and father. In 1990, while attending the Eighth National Festival of Black Storytelling in New Orleans, Louisiana, she decided to pursue her dream of tale weaving. She travels to small Carolina tobacco farm communities to share her stories.

GLORIA TUGGLE STILL is the official spokesperson and storyteller for the Still family. She was born in Baltimore, Maryland and studied with Yolanda Du Bois Williams, daughter of W. E. B. Du Bois. In February 1957 she met Kenneth Still; fourteen days later they were married. The Still family has been featured in *Ebony* magazine and *National Geographic.*

CANDECE TARPLEY is a mother, actress, storyteller, writer, dancer, and jewelry maker. She was featured in the film *It Could Happen to You.* Born in Washington, D.C., she currently lives in New York City.

TEJU THE STORYTELLER: see TEJUMOLA F. OLOGBONI.

TEMUJIN THE STORYTELLER: see BABALOSA OBALORUM TEMUJIN EKUNFEA.

JACKIE TORRENCE is one of the most popular storytellers in the world. Always a favorite teller at the National Storytelling Festival in Jonesborough, Tennessee, she has been featured on David Letterman's TV show. In 1988 she received the Annie Glenn Award, given to professionals who have overcome a speech or hearing defect. In 1991 she received the Zora Neale Hurston Award at the National Festival of Black Storytelling. She is the author of *The Importance of Pot Liquor* and is featured in *I Dream a World: Portraits of Black Women Who Changed America.*

QUINCY TROUPE is a poet, journalist, and teacher. He won the 1980 American Book Award for Poetry. His works include *Embryo, Snake-back Solos, Skulls Along the River,* and *Weather Report.* He coauthored *Miles: The Autobiography of Miles Davis* and edited *James Baldwin: The Legacy.*

AMOS TUTUOLA was born in Abeokuta, Nigeria, the son of a farmer whose death put an end to Amos's education. He worked as a blacksmith and civil servant. A modern-day Aesop, his book *The Palm-Wine Drinkard,* published in 1952, gave him an international reputation. His other works include *My Life in the Bush of Ghosts, The Brave African Huntress, The Witch-Herbalist of the Remote Town, Pauper, Brawler and Slanderer,* and *The Village Witch Doctor and Other Stories.*

DEREK WALCOTT, poet and playwright, is the winner of the 1992 Nobel Prize for Literature. He was born in Trinidad, and his works include *Omeros, Collected Poems 1948–1984, The Arkansas Testament, Dream on Monkey Mountain and Other Plays,* and *Ti-Jean and His Brothers.*

ALICE WALKER is the winner of an American Book Award and a Pulitzer Prize for her novel *The Color Purple.* She reintroduced Zora Neale Hurston and her work to the American public. Her other works include *The Temple of My Familiar, Possessing the Secret of Joy, Warrior Marks, To Hell with Dying, Finding the Green Stone,* and *Revolutionary Petunias.*

JOHN EDGAR WIDEMAN, novelist and Rhodes scholar, grew up in the Homewood section of Pittsburgh, Pennsylvania, the setting for much of his fiction. His works include *Reuben, Philadelphia Fire, Fever, Damballah, Sent for You Yesterday, Hiding Place, The Lynchers, Hurry Home, A Glance Away, Brothers and Keepers,* and his current book *Father Along.*

For Further Reading

━━ ✑ ━━

General Works and Background Information

ABRAHAMS, ROGER D. *Singing the Master*. New York: Penguin, 1992.

BASCOM, WILLIAM. *African Folktales in the New World*. Bloomington, IN: Indiana University Press, 1992.

CALLAHAN, JOHN F. *In the African-American Grain: Call and Response in Twentieth-Century Black Fiction*. Middleton, CT: Wesleyan University Press, 1988.

CUNARD, NANCY, ED. *Negro*. New York: Ungar, 1971.

DU BOIS, W. E. B. *The Souls of Black Folks*. New York: Signet, 1969.

GEORGIA WRITERS' PROJECT/SAVANNAH UNIT. *Drums and Shadows*. Athens, GA: The University of Georgia Press, 1940.

GOSS, LINDA, AND MARIAN BARNES. *Talk That Talk: An Anthology of African-American Storytelling*. New York: Simon & Schuster, 1989.

HARRIS, TRUDIER. *Fiction and Folklore: The Novels of Toni Morrison*. Knoxville, TN: University of Tennessee Press, 1991.

HARRISON, PAUL CARTER. *The Drama of Nommo*. New York: Grove Press, 1972.

HERSKOVITZ, MELVILLE J. *The Myth of the Negro Past*. Boston: Beacon Press, 1958.

HOLLOWAY, JOSEPH F. *Africanisms in American Culture*. Bloomington, IN: Indiana University Press, 1991.

JAHN, JANHEINZ. *Muntu: African Culture and the Western World*. New York: Grove Weidenfield, 1989.

JONES, GAYL. *Liberating Voices: Oral Tradition in African-American Literature*. New York: Penguin, 1991.

JOYNER, CHARLES. *Down by the Riverside*. Urbana, IL: University of Illinois Press, 1984.

MAYOR, CLARENCE. *Juba to Jive: A Dictionary of African-American Slang*. New York: Penguin, 1994.

MBITI, JOHN S. *African Religions and Philosophy*. New York: Anchor, 1970.

NASTA, SUSHEILA. *Motherlands*. New Brunswick, NJ: Rutgers University Press, 1992.

PELTON, ROBERT D. *The Trickster in West Africa*. Berkeley, CA: University of California Press, 1980.

SOYINKA, WOLE. *Myth, Literature and the African World*. New York: Cambridge University Press, 1976.

STUCKEY, STERLING. *Slave Culture*. New York: Oxford University Press, 1987.

SZWED, JOHN, AND ROGER ABRAHAMS. *Afro-American Folk Culture: An Annotated Bibliography of Materials from North, Central, South America and the West Indies*. Philadelphia, PA: Institute for the Study of Human Issues, 1978.

THOMPSON, ROBERT FARRIS, *Flash of the Spirit:* African and Afro-American Art and Philosophy. New York: Vintage, 1984.

TURNER, PATRICIA A. *I Heard It Through the Grapevine*. Berkeley, CA: University of California Press, 1993.

WATKINS, MEL. *On the Real Side: Laughing, Lying, and Signifying—the Underground Tradition of African-American Humor that Transformed American Culture, from Slavery to Richard Pryor.* New York: Simon & Schuster, 1994.

WEBBER, THOMAS L. *Deep Like the Rivers: Education in the Slave Quarter Community 1831–1865.* New York: Norton, 1978.

Personal and Family Narrative

BEALS, MELBA PATTILLO. *Warriors Don't Cry.* New York: Pocket Books, 1994.

BELL-SCOTT PATRICIA. *Lifenotes.* New York: Norton, 1994.

BOLTON, RUTHIE. *Gal: A True Life.* New York: Harcourt, Brace, 1994.

BROWN, CLAUDE. *Manchild in the Promised Land.* New York: Macmillan, 1969.

COMER, JAMES P. *Maggie's American Dream.* New York: Plume, 1989.

DELANY, SARAH AND A. ELIZABETH WITH AMY HILL HEARTH. *Having Our Say.* New York: Kodansha International, 1993.

GATES, HENRY LOUIS, JR. *Colored People.* New York: Random House, 1994.

HAIZLIP, SHIRLEE TAYLOR. *The Sweeter the Juice.* New York: Simon & Schuster, 1994.

LAWRENCE-LIGHTFOOT, SARA. *I've Known Rivers: Lives of Loss and Liberation.* New York: Merloyd Lawrence/Addison-Wesley, 1994.

MATHABANE, MARK. *African Women.* New York: HarperCollins, 1994.

McCALL, NATHAN. *Makes Me Wanna Holler.* New York: Random House, 1994.

MOODY, ANNE. *Coming of Age in Mississippi.* New York: Dell, 1968.

MURRAY, ALBERT. *Train Whistle Guitar.* Boston: Northeastern University Press, 1974.

SOME, MALIDOMA PATRICE. *Of Water and the Spirit.* New York: Tarcher/Putnam, 1994.

STERLING, DOROTHY. *The Trouble They Seen: The Story of Reconstruction in the Words of African-Americans.* New York: Da Capo, 1994.

——. *We Are Your Sisters: Black Women in the Nineteenth Century.* New York: Norton, 1984.

TEISH, LUISAH. *Jambalaya: The Natural Woman's Book of Personal Charms and Practical Rituals.* San Francisco: Harper & Row, 1985.

WASHINGTON, MARY HELEN. *Invented Lives: Narratives of Black Women 1860–1960.* New York: Anchor, 1987.

WRIGHT, RICHARD. *Black Boy.* New York: Harper & Row, 1966.

YOUNG, AL. *Snakes.* New York: Dell, 1970.

Caribbean Folktale Collections and Contemporary Writing

BERRY, JAMES. *Spiderman Anancy.* New York: Holt, 1988.

——. *A Thief in the Village.* New York: Puffin, 1990.

BROWN, STEWART. *Caribbean New Wave.* Portsmouth, NH: Heinemann, 1990.

COURLANDER, HAROLD. *The Drum and the Hoe: The Life and Lore of Haitian People.* Berkeley, CA: University of California Press, 1960.

HAUSMAN, GERALD. *Duppy Talk.* New York: Simon & Schuster, 1994.

JOSEPH, LYNN. *The Mermaid's Twin Sister,* New York: Clarion, 1994.

——. *A Wave in her Pocket.* New York: Clarion, 1991.

KINCAID, JAMAICA. *At the Bottom of the River*. New York: Plume, 1992.
LESSAC, FRANE. *Caribbean Canvas*. New York: Lippincott, 1987.
——. *My Little Island*. New York: HarperCollins, 1987.
SHERLOCK, PHILIP. *West Indian Folk-Tales*. Oxford, England: Oxford University Press, 1988.
TORENNE DES PRES, FRANÇOIS. *Children of Yayoute: Folktales of Haiti*. New York: Universe Publishers, 1994.

African and African-American Folktale Collections and Contemporary Writing

ACHEBE, CHINUA AND C. L. INNES, EDS. *African Short Stories*. Oxford, England: Heinemann, 1987.
BELL-SCOTT, PATRICIA ET AL., EDS. *Doublestitch: Black Women Write About Mothers and Daughters*. Boston: Beacon Press, 1991.
BERRY, JACK. *West African Folktales*. Evanston, IL: Northwestern University Press, 1991.
BROWN, STERLING A., ARTHUR P. DAVIS, AND ULYSSES LEE, EDS., *The Negro Caravan*. Salem, NH: Ayer Press, 1969.
BUSBY, MARGARET, ED. *Daughters of Africa*. New York: Ballantine, 1992.
CHAPMAN, ABRAHAM, ED. *Black Voices*. New York: Mentor, 1968.
——. *New Black Voices*. New York: Mentor, 1972.
CLARKE, JOHN HENRIK, ED. *Harlem U.S.A.* Camden, ME: Seven Seas, 1964.
DADIE, BERNARD. *The Black Cloth*. Amherst, MA: University of Massachusetts Press, 1987.
GEORGE, NELSON. *Buppies, B-Boys, Bop & Bobos*. New York: HarperCollins, 1994.
GLEASON, JUDITH, ED. *Leaf and Bone: African Praise-Poems*. New York: Penguin, 1994.
HARPER, MICHAEL AND ANTHONY WALTON, EDS. *Every Shut Eye Ain't Asleep*. New York: Back Bay/HarperCollins, 1994.
JONES, LEROI AND LARRY NEAL, EDS. *Black Fire*. New York: Morrow, 1969.
JONES, LISA. *Bulletproof Diva: Tales of Race, Sex and Hair*. New York: Doubleday, 1994.
MAJOR, CLARENCE. *Calling the Wind*. New York: HarperPerennial, 1993.
OBRADOVIC, NADEZA, ED. *African Rhapsody*. New York: Anchor, 1994.
——. *Looking for a Rain God*. New York: Fireside, 1991.
PEPLOW, MICHAEL W. AND ARTHUR P. DAVIS, EDS. *The New Negro Renaissance*. New York: Holt, Rinehart and Winston, 1975.
POWELL, KEVIN AND RAS BARAKA, EDS. *In the Tradition: An Anthology of Young Black Writers*. New York: Harlem River Press/ Writers & Readers, 1992.
RADIN, PAUL, ED. *African Folktales*. New York: Schocken, 1981.
TATE, GREG. *Flyboy in the Buttermilk*. New York: Fireside, 1992.
WASHINGTON, MARY HELEN. *Black-Eyed Susans*. New York: Anchor, 1990.
——. *Memory of Kin*. New York: Anchor, 1991.
WOOD, PAULA L. AND FELIX H. LIDDELL, EDS. *I Hear a Symphony*. New York: Anchor, 1994.
ZENANI, NONGENILE MASITHATHU. *The World and the Word: Tales and Observations from the Xhosa Oral Tradition*. Edited by Harold Scheub. Madison, WI: University of Wisconsin Press, 1992.

Young Readers (Kindergarten to Fifth Grade)

AARDEMA VERNA. *Misoso*. New York: Random House, 1994.

———. *Sebgugugu the Glutton: A Bantu Tale from Rwanda*. Trenton, NJ: Africa World Press, 1993.

ECHEWA, T. OBINKARAM. *The Ancestor Tree*. New York: Dutton, 1994.

EVERETT, GWEN. *Li'l Sis and Uncle Willie*. New York: National Museum of American Art Smithsonian Institution/Rizzoli, 1991.

GOSS, LINDA. *The Frog Who Wanted to Be a Singer*. New York: Orchard Books (to be published in 1996).

GOSS, LINDA AND CLAY GOSS *It's Kwanzaa Time*. New York: Putnam, 1995.

HOPKINSON, DEBORAH. *Sweet Clara and the Freedom Quilt*. New York: Knopf, 1993.

HUMPHREY, MARGO. *The River That Gave Gifts*. San Francisco, CA: Children's Book Press, 1987.

JOHNSON, ANGELA. *When I Am Old with You*. New York: Orchard Books, 1990.

KIM, HOLLY C. *The Iroko-Man*. New York: Orchard Books, 1994.

KIMMEL, ERIC. *Anansi and the Moss-Covered Rock*. New York: Holiday House, 1988.

———. *Anansi and the Talking Melon*. New York: Holiday House, 1994.

———. *Anansi Goes Fishing*. New York: Holiday House, 1992.

KNUTSON, BARBARA. *Sungura and Leopard: A Swahili Trickster Tale*. Boston, MA: Little, Brown, 1993.

LAWRENCE, JACOB. *The Great Migration*. New York: HarperCollins, 1993.

———. *Harriet and the Promised Land*. New York: Simon & Schuster, 1993.

LESTER, JULIUS. *John Henry*. New York: Viking/Penguin, 1994.

MITCHELL, MARGARET KING. *Uncle Jed's Barbershop*. New York: Simon & Schuster, 1993.

MYERS, WALTER DEAN. *Brown Angels*. New York: HarperCollins, 1993.

RINGGOLD, FAITH. *Tar Beach*. New York: Crown Publishers, 1991.

SAN SOUCI, ROBERT D. *The Boy and the Ghost*. New York: Simon & Schuster, 1989.

———. *The Talking Eggs*. New York: Dial Books, 1989.

STEPTOE, JOHN. *Mufaro's Beautiful Daughters*. New York: Lothrop, Lee & Shepard, 1987.

WISNIEWSKI, DAVID. *Sundiata, Lion King of Mali*. New York: Clarion Books, 1992.

WRIGHT, COURTNI C. *Jumping the Broom*. New York: Holiday House, 1994.

Young Readers (Fifth Grade and Up)

APPIAH, PEGGY. *Tales of an Ashanti Father*. Boston: Beacon, 1967.

ARNOTT, KATHLEEN. *African Myths and Legends*. Oxford, England: Oxford University Press, 1962.

BERRY, JACK. *West African Folktales*. Evanston, IL: Northwestern University Press, 1991.

BOLDEN, TONYA. *Rites of Passage: Stories About Growing Up by Black Writers from Around the World*. New York: Hyperion, 1994.

FAIRMAN, TONY. *Bury My Bones but Keep My Words*. New York: Henry Holt, 1991.

GREAVES, NICK. *When Hippo Was Hairy*. New York: Barrons, 1990.

———. *When Lion Could Fly*. New York: Barrons, 1993.

HAMILTON, VIRGINIA. *Many Thousand Gone*. New York: Knopf, 1993.

JAFFE, NINA. *Patakin: World Tales of Drums and Drummers*. New York: Henry Holt, 1994.

JOHNSON, CHARLES. *The Sorcerer's Apprentice*. New York: Penguin: 1987.

LESTER, JULIUS. *Further Tales of Uncle Remus*. New York: Dial 1988.

——. *The Last Tales of Uncle Remus*. New York: Dial, 1994.

——. *Long Journey Home*. New York: Scholastic, 1988.

——. *More Tales of Uncle Remus*. New York: Dial, 1990.

LEVINE, ELLEN. *Freedom's Children: Young Civil Rights Activists Tell Their Own Stories*. New York: Putnam, 1993.

LYONS, MARY E., ED. *Raw Head, Bloody Bones: African-American Tales of the Supernatural*. New York: Scribners, 1991.

SMITH, ALEXANDER MCCALL. *Children of the Wax: African Folktales*. New York: Interlink Books, 1989.

TATE, ELEANORA E. *Front Porch Stories at the One-Room School*. New York: Bantam, 1992.

YOUNG, JUDY DOCKREY AND RICHARD. *African-American Folktales*. Little Rock, AR: August House Publishers, 1994.

Index of Selected Stories for Children

Index of Authors and Titles

About the Editors and Ossie Davis

LINDA GOSS and CLAY GOSS are a wife and husband team who live in Philadelphia, Pennsylvania. Linda, born in Alcoa, Tennessee, near the Great Smoky Mountains, is a well-loved award-winning storyteller who is the Official Storyteller of Philadelphia. She is cofounder of the National Festival of Black Storytelling and was the first president of the National Association of Black Storytellers. She is the coauthor of *Talk That Talk* and the author of *The Frog Who Wanted to be a Singer*. Clay Goss was born in Philadelphia and is a playwright and director with an M.F.A. from Temple University. He is the author of *Homecookin'* and *Bill Pickett: Black Bulldogger*. His work is featured in *The Drama of Nommo, Kuntu Drama*, and *The New Lafayette Theater Presents*. Together, Linda and Clay are the authors of *The Baby Leopard, It's Kwanzaa Time*, and *Jump Up and Say!*

The Gosses met on the campus of Howard University where their poems were first published in *We Speak as Liberators*. They have three children.

OSSIE DAVIS has had a distinguished career in theater, film (in *The Hill, Do the Right Thing, Jungle Fever*, and *Malcolm X*, for example) and television ("Evening Shade"). He was born in Georgia and attended Howard University. He is the author of five plays: *Purlie Victorious; Curtain Call; Mr. Aldridge, Sir; Langston;* and *Escape to Freedom*, and a novel, *Just Like Martin*. He directed the film *Cotton Comes to Harlem*.

Ossie Davis is married to award-winning actress Ruby Dee. They have three children.